PENGUIN B
THE BEST OF SA'

Satyajit Ray was born on 2 Ma, .. _
generally regarded as India's greatest filmmaker ever, with
films like *Pather Panchali* (1955), *Charulata* (1964), *Shatranj
Ke Khilari* (1977) and *Ghare Baire* (1984) to his credit. Both
the British Federation of Film Societies and the Moscow Film
Festival Committee named him one of the greatest directors of
the second half of the twentieth century. In 1992, he was
awarded the Oscar for Lifetime Achievement by the Academy
of Motion Picture Arts and Science and, in the same year, was
also honoured with the Bharat Ratna.

Apart from being a filmmaker, Satyajit Ray was a writer of
repute. In 1961, he revived the Bengali children's magazine,
Sandesh, to which he contributed numerous poems, stories
and essays over the years. He has to his credit a series of
bestsellers featuring the characters Feluda, Professor Shonku
and Uncle Tarini, as well as several collections of short
stories. In 1978, Oxford University awarded him its D.Litt
degree.

Satyajit Ray died in Calcutta in April 1992.

*

Gopa Majumdar was born and brought up in Delhi. Growing
up amidst people from various parts of the country, she learnt
to communicate with those who did not speak her language,
and whose language she could not understand. It taught her
the basic principles of translation quite early in life.

Namaste magazine was the first to publish her translation of
Bengali short stories. Subsequently, nine volumes of her
translations of Satyajit Ray have been published by Penguin
Books. Among her other notable works are her translations of
Ashapurna Debi's *Subarnalata*, Bibhutibhushan
Bandyopadhyay's *Aparajito* and Taslima Nasrin's *My
Girlhood*. In 1995, she was given the Katha award for
translation. She lives in Britain at present, and is actively
involved in promoting Indian literature abroad.

The Best of
Satyajit Ray

Translated from the Bengali by the
author and Gopa Majumdar

PENGUIN BOOKS

Penguin Books India (P) Ltd., 11 Community Centre, Panchsheel Park, New Delhi 110017, India
Penguin Books Ltd., 80 Strand, London WC2R 0RL, UK
Penguin Putnam Inc., 375 Hudson Street, New York, New York 10014, USA
Penguin Books Australia Ltd., 250 Camberwell Road, Camberwell, Victoria 3124, Australia
Penguin Books Canada Ltd., 10 Alcorn Avenue, Suite 300, Toronto, Ontario M4V 3B2, Canada
Penguin Books (NZ) Ltd., Cnr Rosedale & Airborne Roads, Albany, Auckland, New Zealand

First published by Penguin Books India 2001
Copyright © The Estate of Satyajit Ray 2001
This translation copyright © Penguin Books India 2001

The stories in this selection were first published in Bengali in book form by Ananda Publishers Pvt. Ltd. in the following books: *Ek Dojon Goppo* (1970), *Aaro Ek Dojon* (1976), *Aaro Baaro* (1981), *Ebaro Baaro* (1984) and *Pikoor Diary O Onanyo* (1992).

Versions of 'Ratan Babu and that Man', 'Ashamanja Babu's Dog', 'Patol Babu, Film Star', 'Indigo', 'Big Bill' and 'Khagam' first appeared in *Stories* by Satyajit Ray published by Secker and Warburg 1987.

Versions of 'Bipin Chowdhury's Lapse of Memory' and 'The Small World of Sadananda' first appeared in *Target* in 1984 and 1988 respectively.

Gopa Majumdar's translation of 'The Two Magicians' first appeared in *Namaste* in 1989.

10 9 8 7 6 5 4 3 2 1

Typeset in Optima by Mantra Virtual Services, New Delhi
Printed at Saurabh Print-O-Pack, NOIDA

CONTENTS

INTRODUCTION

In 1950, Satyajit Ray stood behind a camera and began shooting his first film, *Pather Panchali* (*Song of the Little Road*). No one knew it then, but he was soon to be established as one of the world's great filmmakers.

In 1961, he did something else that was to have wide-ranging repercussions. He decided to revive *Sandesh*, the children's magazine that was once produced by his father and grandfather. The camera was put aside for a while. Ray picked up a pen instead, to write for *Sandesh* and to embellish its pages with unforgettable illustrations. That simple act was to turn him into the most successful writer in modern Bengal. Nearly ten years have passed after his death, but his position as Bengal's foremost author remains unchallenged even today.

Between 1961 and 1992, Ray wrote more than seventy-five short stories on a variety of themes, in addition to thirty-five detective stories featuring the sleuth, Feluda, and nearly forty science-fiction stories describing the adventures of Professor Shonku. Feluda and Shonku acquired a large number of admirers, so much so that eventually they were 'hijacked' by other magazines. What appeared almost exclusively in *Sandesh* were the short stories.

It has always been my belief that even if Ray had not written a single Feluda or Shonku story—remarkable though each one is—his success as a writer would not have been affected in any way. His short stories in themselves are memorable enough to guarantee him captivated readers through several generations of posterity. The reason for this, however, is not easy to pin down. Why do his stories make such an impact on his readers? Is it his language? His style? The wide range of his interests? The very sensitive treatment of his characters? His humour? Or the plots, which can rival those of the best storytellers in the business?

The truth is that there is no one specific reason; it is simply a combination of all these factors that produce the final, magical effect. Before compiling the list of stories for this collection, I asked several readers which they thought might qualify as 'the best' of Ray's stories, which stood out in their memory better and sharper than all the others. The response was quick and unanimous. The stories with a supernatural element got the highest votes. Why? It is a genre that has always been popular with writers; scores of ghost stories and other spooky tales had been written long before Ray produced his first. In fact, he admitted freely to having a 'special fascination' for 'tales of the fantastic and the supernatural'. It is not surprising that he chose to write about friendly aliens (years before ET or anything of that ilk entered our lives), or a carnivorous plant with a terrifying appetite, or the spine-chilling curse of a sadhu that could transform a man into a snake. The question is, what made these stories different from the others? What was so special about them?

One reader put it rather aptly, 'Ray doesn't go into lengthy descriptions. Yet, you can see—even *feel*—it all happening. That's enough to bring out the goose pimples!' Clearly, here the filmmaker in Ray gave him an edge over other writers. His words were brief, simple, lucid. But the impression that emerged was extraordinarily rich in detail.

The same applied to all his other stories, whatever their

theme. However, the apparent simplicity in these stories was often deceptive. Behind it lay complex emotions and a tangled web of events. That was the reason why they appealed to young and old alike. The young were happy with a simple tale. It was left to the adults to pick up the subtleties.

The best example of this is the story 'Pikoo's Diary', which appears here for the first time in translation. It is unquestionably one of the most powerful stories that Ray ever wrote; certainly, it was the most difficult to translate. It is, in fact, one of those rare stories that Ray wrote specifically for adults. In 1981, he made a telefilm (*Pikoo*) based on this story. Those who have seen the film will recognize most of the details in the story. But the telling of the story itself remains unique, captured as it is through the eyes of a child. Having seen his grandfather write a diary, Pikoo decides to follow suit. His language is childish, his spellings appalling, his knowledge of punctuation virtually non-existent. Yet, one vivid image chases another, like images in a kaleidoscope.

When the story was written—in 1970—the Naxalite movement in Bengal was at its height. Anyone who lived in Calcutta at the time would recall the frequent explosions in the streets and the ensuing fear and anxiety. It was not unusual then for a young man to get involved in politics, and disappear from home. In this particular case, the home itself is torn apart by strife between Pikoo's parents and an adulterous affair—and little Pikoo faithfully records every detail in his notebook, without even realizing the implication of what he is writing. In order to preserve the flavour of the original, this story has been set in a child's handwriting font.

There are three other stories that I have translated especially for this collection: 'The Hungry Septopus', 'Bonku Babu's Friend' and 'Mr Eccentric'. Translations of 'The Two Magicians',

'Bipin Chowdhury's Lapse of Memory' and 'The Small World of Sadananda' are made available here in volume form over a decade after their first publication. The other stories have appeared previously in *Stranger* and *Indigo*, the two collections of Ray's stories published by Penguin India. In all there are twenty-one stories that I have chosen as the 'best', of which no less than eight were translated by Ray himself. The dates of original composition (in Bengali) have been provided at the end of each story for the interested reader.

Although a number of readers were consulted before a decision was made on what might comprise 'the best', some may well feel that their own favourite story has been left out. I must offer my apologies to these readers. But I hope that they will, nonetheless, share my joy in seeing this compilation published in time to mark the eightieth anniversary of the birth of the author.

This very special book is dedicated to a very special person—Souradeep Ray, who celebrates his eleventh birthday in 2001. This book is for you, Souradeep, because your grandfather would certainly have wanted you to have the best.

London   Gopa Majumdar
October 2001

THE HUNGRY SEPTOPUS

There it was again—the sound of someone rattling the knocker on my front door. I gave an involuntary exclamation of annoyance. This was the fourth interruption this evening. How was a man expected to work? There was no sign of Kartik, either. He had left for the market a long time ago.

I was forced to leave my desk and open the door myself. It took me a while to recognize the man who was standing outside. When I did, I felt profoundly startled. Why, it was Kanti Babu!

'What a surprise! Do come in,' I said.

'So you have recognized me?'

'Yes, but it wasn't easy.'

I showed him into the living room and offered him a seat. I had not seen him in ten years. His appearance had undergone a remarkable change in that time. In 1950, I had seen the same man in a forest in Assam, jumping around with a magnifying glass in his hand. He was nearly fifty then, but all his hair was still black. He bubbled all the time with energy and endless enthusiasm. Such vitality would be hard to find even among the young.

'Are you still interested in orchids?' Kanti Babu asked.

There was an orchid in a pot resting on my window-sill. It was, in fact, a gift from Kanti Babu himself. I wasn't really interested in plants any more. It was Kanti Babu who had once aroused my curiosity about them. But after he went abroad, I had lost my interest gradually. There were other hobbies and interests, too, but I had given them up as well. Now my only passion was writing.

Things had changed over the years. Now it was possible to make money just by writing. To tell the truth, my last three books had brought me an income that was almost wholly sufficient to meet my household expenses. Not that I had a big house to run—there was only my widowed mother to take care of, and my servant, Kartik. I still had a job, but was hoping to give it up if my writing continued to bring me success. I would write full-time, and when I could take a break, I would travel. That was my plan.

Suddenly, Kanti Babu shivered. 'Are you feeling cold? Shall I close the window? The winter in Calcutta this year . . .' I began.

'No, no. You saw me shiver? It happens sometimes. I am getting old, you see. So my nerves are no longer . . .'

I wanted to ask a lot of questions. Kartik had returned. I asked him to bring us tea.

'I won't take up a lot of your time,' said Kanti Babu. 'I came across one of your novels recently. So I got in touch with your publisher, took your address, and well, here I am. There is a special reason why I had to see you.'

'Yes? Tell me all about it. But before you do, there's so much I want to know. When did you return? Where were you all these years? Where are you now?'

'I returned two years ago. Before that I was in America. Now I live in Barasat.'

'Barasat?'

'I bought a house there.'

'Does it have a garden?'

'Yes.'

'And a greenhouse?'

In the house that I had visited before, Kanti Babu had a
lovely greenhouse, in which he tended, with great care, several
of his rare plants. I had seen such a large number of strange and
weird plants there! Of orchids alone he had more than sixty
varieties. One could easily pass a whole day just looking at and
enjoying their different colours and other characteristics.

Kanti Babu paused for a second before saying, 'Yes, there is
a greenhouse.'

'So you're still as mad about plants as you were ten years
ago?'

'Yes.'

Kanti Babu was staring at the opposite wall. Automatically, I
followed his gaze. The wall was covered by the skin of a Royal
Bengal tiger, including the head.

'Does it seem familiar to you?' I asked.

'Is it that same tiger?'

'Yes. See that hole close to its left ear? That's where the
bullet passed through.'

'You were a remarkable shot. Can you still shoot with such
perfect accuracy?'

'I don't know. I haven't used my gun for a long time. I gave
up shikar more than five years ago.'

'Why?'

'I had had enough. I mean, I had killed enough animals.
After all, I'm not getting any younger. It was time to stop
destroying wild life.'

'Really? So have you stopped eating meat? Are you now a
vegetarian?'

'No. No, I am not.'

'Why not? Killing a wild animal is just plain killing. Say you
destroy a tiger, or a crocodile, or a bison, and then you hang its
head, or just its horns on your wall. What happens? Your room

acquires a special air, some of your visitors are horrified, others are impressed, and you can relive the moments of your youthful adventures. That's all. But think of the chicken, goats and fish you are not just killing, but also eating every day. It's more than mere destruction, isn't it? Why, it's the *digestion* of a living creature!'

There was really nothing I could say in reply. So I remained silent.

Kartik brought us tea.

Kanti Babu remained lost in thought for a few moments, then suddenly shivered again and picked up his cup. 'It isn't unusual for one particular animal to eat another. Nature made things that way. See that gecko lying in wait over there?' he asked.

Over a calendar on the wall sprawled a gecko, staring unblinkingly at an insect, just a couple of inches away from its mouth. Then it moved slowly, ever so slowly, before springing forward in one leap and swallowing its prey.

'There!' exclaimed Kanti Babu. 'That takes care of his dinner. Eating is all most creatures are concerned with. Just think about it. A tiger would eat a man, a man would eat a goat, and a goat would eat anything! Doesn't it all seem terribly wild, primitive and violent? Yet, that is how nature wills it. Stop this cycle, and the whole natural order would be thrown out of gear.'

'Perhaps being a vegetarian is more . . . er . . . civilized?'

'Who told you that? You think leaves and vegetables and plants are lifeless? Do they not live?'

'Yes, of course they do. Thanks to Jagadish Bose and you, I can never forget about the life of plants. But it's different, isn't it? I mean, animals and plants are not the same, surely?'

'Oh? You think there are a lot of differences between the two?'

'Aren't there? A tree cannot move, walk, make a noise,

express thoughts or feelings—in fact, there's no way to find out if a tree has a mind at all. Isn't that true?'

Kanti Babu opened his mouth to speak, then shut it without saying a word. Silently, he finished his tea and sat with his head bowed. Eventually, when he looked up and met my eyes, I suddenly felt afraid to see the look of tragic uncertainty in his. Truly, the change in the man was extraordinary.

When he spoke, his voice was quiet. 'Parimal,' he said, 'I live twenty-one miles away. And I am fifty-eight years old. But despite my age and the long distance I had to travel, I took the trouble to get your address and visit you here. Surely I don't need to tell you now that there is a very important reason behind my visit? You can see that, can't you? Or have you lost all your intelligence in trying to produce popular fiction? Are you looking at me right now and thinking: here's a new type—I can use him in a story?'

I had to look away, flushing with embarrassment. Kanti Babu was right. The thought of using him as a character had indeed occurred to me.

'Remember this,' he went on. 'If you lose touch with the realities of life, whatever you write will simply be lies, empty and hollow. Besides, no matter how lively your imagination is, what emerges from it can never match the surprises real life can come up with. Anyway, I didn't come here to give you a lecture. I came, to tell you the truth, to ask a favour.'

Kanti Babu glanced at the tiger again. What favour was he talking about?

'Do you still have your gun, or did you get rid of it?'

I gave a slight start, and glanced quickly at him. Why did he mention my gun?

'No, I have still got it. But it may well be rusted. Why do you ask?'

'Can you come to my house tomorrow, with your gun?'

I scanned his face. No, there was not even the slightest sign to imply that he might be joking.

'Of course,' he added, 'you'll need bullets, too. The gun alone won't be good enough.'

I could not immediately think of anything to say in reply to Kanti Babu's request. It even occurred to me once that perhaps he had gone mad, although one could not be sure. He was certainly given to crazy whims. Or else why should he have risked his life in a jungle to look for rare plants?

'I can quite easily take my gun, there's no problem,' I said finally. 'But I am dying to know the reason why it might be needed. Is there an animal bothering the residents in your area? Or perhaps there are burglars and thieves?'

'I will explain everything once you get there. Who knows, we might not even have to use the gun. But even if we do, I can assure you that you will not be arrested!'

Kanti Babu rose to his feet. Then he came closer and laid a hand on my shoulder. 'I came to you because when I last saw you, you had struck me as a man who would welcome a new experience, very much like myself. Besides, I don't know many other people. The number of people I actually visited was always small, and now I see virtually no one. The handful of people I could think of contacting are all very different, you see. None of them has the special qualities that you have.'

Just for a minute, I could feel, in the sudden tightening of my muscles, the same thrill that the mere mention of an adventure used to bring, all those years ago.

'When would you like me to get there? How would I find your house?' I asked.

'I'll tell you. Just go straight down Jessore Road until you get to the railway station in Barasat. Then you need to find a lake called Madhumurali Deeghi. It's another four miles from the station. Anyone there will tell you where it is. Next to the lake is an old and abandoned indigo factory. My house is right behind it. Do you have a car?'

'No, but a friend of mine has.'

'Who is this friend?'

'His name is Abhijit. He and I were in college together.'

'What kind of a man is he? Do I know him?'

'No, I don't think so. But he's a good man. I mean, if you're wondering whether he's reliable, I can tell you that he is. Totally.'

'Very well. You may bring him with you. But please make sure that you reach my house before evening. It's important, needless to say.'

Kanti Babu left. Since I did not have a telephone at home, I went to our local chemist just across the road to ring Abhijit. 'Come to my house at once,' I said to him, 'I've got something urgent to discuss.'

'Urgent? You mean you've got a new story you'd like to read out to me? I'll go to sleep again, let me tell you!'

'No, no. It's not about a story. Something quite different.'

'What is it? Why are you speaking so softly?'

'I've come to know about a pup. Mastiff. The man selling it is sitting in my house, right now.'

I knew Abhijit would not stir out of his house unless I could lure him out by talking of dogs. He had eleven dogs. Each one of them belonged to a different species. Three of those dogs had won prizes. Even five years ago, things were different. But now, Abhijit thought and dreamt of nothing but dogs.

Apart from his love of dogs, there was something else that made him very special. Abhijit had unflinching faith in my talent and judgement. When my first novel was turned down by publishers, it was Abhijit who provided the money to publish it privately. 'Mind you,' he told me, 'I know nothing of books and literature. But if you have written this book, it cannot possibly be absolute garbage. These publishers are complete idiots!' As it happened, things turned out quite well. The book was well received and sold a large number of copies. As a result, Abhijit's faith in me grew stronger.

He turned up soon enough, and gave me a painful punch when he discovered that I had lied about the pup. However, seeing his enthusiasm regarding the real reason for calling him out, I soon forgot the pain.

'We haven't had an outing for long time, have we?' Abhijit said eagerly. 'The last time was when we went snipe-shooting in Shonarpur. But who is this man? What's it all about? Why don't you come clean, my friend?'

'How can I, when he told me nothing? Besides, a little mystery is a good thing. I like it. It should give us the chance to use our imagination.'

'All right, but who is this man? What does he do?'

'His name is Kanticharan Chatterjee. Does that mean anything to you? He was once a professor of botany. Used to teach in Scottish Church College. Then he gave up his job and began looking for rare plants in jungles and forests. Sometimes he wrote about them. He had a wonderful collection of plants, particularly of orchids.'

'How did you get to meet him?'

'I met him in a forest bungalow in Assam. I was there to hunt down a tiger. He was hunting everywhere for a nepenthes.'

'Hunting for what?'

'Nepenthes. It's the botanical name for what is commonly called a pitcher-plant. You can get it in the forests of Assam. It eats insects. I did not see it myself, but Kanti Babu told me about it.'

'Eats insects? A plant? It . . . chomps on insects?'

'You did not ever study botany, did you?'

'No.'

'I have seen pictures of this plant. There is no reason to sound so sceptical. It exists.'

'OK. What happened next?'

'Very little. I finished my shikar and came away. Kanti Babu stayed on. I have no idea whether he found that plant or not. What I was afraid of was that he might be killed by a wild animal, or bitten by a snake. When he set off to look for a plant, he thought of nothing else, not even of the dangers in a forest. After coming back to Calcutta, I met him only a couple of times. But I thought of him often, because for a time I developed quite a passion for orchids. Kanti Babu offered to bring me some good quality orchids from America.'

'America? This man went to America?'

'Yes. One of his articles was published in an English botanical journal. It made him quite well known in those circles. Then he was invited to a conference of botanists in America. That was in 1951, or was it '52? That's when I last saw him.'

'Was he there all this while? What was he doing?'

'No idea. Hopefully, he'll tell us tomorrow.'

'He's not . . . ? I mean, is he perhaps a little eccentric?'

'Not any more than you. I can tell you that much. You fill your life with dogs. He fills his with plants.'

We were now going down Jessore Road in the direction of Barasat, travelling in Abhijit's Standard.

There was a third passenger in the car. It was Abhijit's dog, Badshah. It was my own fault, really. I should have known that, unless otherwise instructed, Abhijit was bound to bring one of his eleven dogs.

Badshah was a Rampur hound, a ferocious animal. He had spread himself out on the back seat and was sitting very comfortably as its sole occupant, looking out of the window at the wide, open rice fields. Each time a stray dog from a local village came into view, Badshah gave a mild, contemptuous growl.

When I saw Abhijit arrive with Badshah, I tried to put up a faint protest. At this, Abhijit said, 'I don't have a great deal of faith in your skill, you see. That's why I brought him along. You haven't handled your gun for years. Should there be trouble, Badshah would probably be of far more use than you. He has an extraordinary sense of smell and is quite, quite fearless.'

Kanti Babu's house was not difficult to find. By the time we got there, it was half past two. A driveway led to the house, which was built in the style of a bungalow. Behind the house was an open space. A huge old shirish tree stood where this space ended. By its side was a structure with a tin roof. It looked like a small factory. In front of the house was a garden, at the end of which a long area was covered by another tin roof. A number of shining glass cases stood there in a row.

Kanti Babu came out to greet us, then frowned slightly as he saw Badshah. 'Is he a trained dog?' he asked.

'He'll listen to everything I say,' Abhijit told him. 'But if there's an untrained dog in the vicinity, and Badshah sees him, well, I couldn't tell you what he might do then. Is there such a dog?'

'No. But for the moment, please tie your dog to one of the bars on that window.'

Abhijit gave me a sidelong glance, winked and did as he was told, like an obedient child. Badshah protested a couple of times, but did not seem to mind too much.

We sat on cane chairs on the front veranda. 'My servant Prayag injured his right hand. So I made tea for you and put it in a flask. Let me know when you'd like some.'

It was a very quiet and peaceful place. I could hear nothing but a few chirping birds. How could there be serious danger lurking somewhere in a place like this? I felt a little foolish, sitting with the gun in my hands. So I propped it up against a wall.

Abhijit could never sit still. He was very much a 'city' man; the beauties of nature offered by the countryside, the leaves on a peepal tree, trembling in a slight breeze, or the call of an unknown bird, did nothing to move him. He looked around, shifted restlessly, and suddenly blurted out, 'Parimal told me that you once went to a forest in Assam looking for some weird plant, and nearly got gobbled up by a tiger. Is that true?'

This was something else Abhijit was wont to do. He could not speak without exaggerating everything. I felt afraid Kanti Babu might be offended. But he just laughed and said, 'Do you always think of a tiger whenever you think of danger? But that's not surprising, many people would do that. No, I never came across a tiger. Leeches in the forest caused me some discomfort, but that was nothing serious, either.'

'Did you find that plant?'

The same question had occurred to me, too.

'Which plant?'

'Oh, that . . . pot? . . . No, pitcher-plant or something?'

'Yes. Nepenthes. Yes, I did find it and, in fact, have still got it. I'll show it to you. I am no longer interested in ordinary plants; now I restrict myself only to carnivorous ones. I've got rid of most of my orchids, too.'

Kanti Babu rose and went indoors. Abhijit and I exchanged glances. Carnivorous plants? Plants that ate meat? A few pages and pictures I had studied fifteen years ago in a book on botany dimly wafted before my eyes.

When Kanti Babu re-emerged, there was a bottle in his hand. It contained house-crickets and a few other insects, still alive. The stopper on the bottle, I noticed, had tiny holes, like those on a pepper-shaker.

'Feeding time!' said Kanti Babu with a smile. 'Come with me.'

We followed Kanti Babu out to the long strip of ground at

the back of his garden which contained the glass cases.

Each of the cases held a different plant. I had seen none of them before.

'Except for nepenthes,' Kanti Babu told us, 'not a single one is from our country. One of them is from Nepal, another from Africa. The rest are virtually all from Central America.'

'If that is so,' Abhijit asked, 'how do they survive here? I mean, does the soil here have . . .?'

'No. These plants have nothing to do with the soil.'

'No?'

'No. They do not derive sustenance from the soil. Just as human beings can survive anywhere in the world as long as they are fed properly, so can these plants. Adequate and appropriate food is all they need, no matter where they are kept.'

Kanti Babu stopped before a glass case. In it was an extraordinary plant. Its leaves were about two inches long, their edges were white and were serrated, as if they had teeth.

The front of the case had a kind of door, though it was big enough only for the mouth of the bottle to go through. It was bolted from outside. Kanti Babu unbolted it. Then he removed the stopper from the bottle and quickly slipped the bottle through the 'door'. A house-cricket leapt out into the case. Kanti Babu removed the bottle and replaced the stopper. Then he pushed the bolt back into place.

The house-cricket moved restlessly for a few seconds. Then it went and sat on a leaf. At once, the leaf folded itself and caught the insect. To my complete amazement, I saw that the two sets of teeth had closed in and clamped on each other so tightly that the poor house-cricket had no chance of escaping. I had no idea nature could set such a strange, horrific trap. Certainly, I had never seen anything like it before.

Abhijit was the first to speak. 'Is there any guarantee,' he asked hoarsely, 'that the insect would sit on a leaf?'

'Of course. You see, the plant exudes a smell that attracts insects. This plant is called the Venus fly trap. I brought it from Central America. If you go through books on botany, you may find pictures of this plant.'

I was still staring in speechless amazement at the house-cricket. At first, it was struggling to get out, but now it was just lying in its trap, quite lifeless. The pressure from the leaf's 'teeth' appeared to be getting stronger. This plant was every bit as violent as a gecko.

Abhijit laughed dryly. 'If I could keep such a plant in my house, I'd be safe from insects. At least, I wouldn't have to use DDT to kill cockroaches!'

'No, this particular plant couldn't eat—and digest—a cockroach. Its leaves are too small. There's a different plant to deal with cockroaches. Come this way,' invited Kanti Babu.

The next glass case had a plant whose long, large leaves looked like those of a lily. Each leaf had a strange object hanging from its tip. It looked like a pitcher-shaped bag, complete with a lid. I had already seen its picture. It was not difficult to recognize it.

'This,' Kanti Babu declared, 'is nepenthes, or a pitcher-plant. It requires bigger creatures to survive. When I first found it, there were the crushed remains of a small bird in one of those pitchers.'

'Oh my God!' Abhijit exclaimed. The faint contempt his tone had held earlier was quickly disappearing. 'What does it eat now?'

'Cockroaches, caterpillars, even butterflies. Once I found a rat in my rat-trap. I fed it to that plant, it didn't seem to mind. But sometimes these plants eat more than they can digest, and then they die. They're a greedy lot. There are times when they just can't figure out how much strain their own digestive system can bear!'

We moved on to look at other plants, our astonishment

mounting higher. There were butterwort, sundew, bladderwort, arozia—plants whose pictures I had seen. But the others were totally new, completely astounding, perfectly incredible. Kanti Babu had collected at least twenty different species of carnivorous plants, some of which, he said, were not included in any other collection in the world.

The prettiest amongst these was the sundew. It had fine strands of hair around its leaves. A droplet glistened on the tip of each hair. Kanti Babu tied a tiny piece of meat—no bigger than a peppercorn—to a thread and took it close to a leaf. We could see, even from a distance, all the hair rise at once, grasping at the piece of meat greedily. But Kanti Babu removed his hand before the meat could be taken.

'If it did get that piece of meat, it would have crushed it, just like the fly trap. Then it would have absorbed whatever nourishment it could get, and rejected the chewed pulp. Not really that different from the way you and I eat meat, is it?'

We left the shed and came out to the garden. The shirish tree was casting a long shadow. I looked at my watch. It was half past four.

'You will find mention of most of these plants in your books,' said Kanti Babu. 'But no one knows about the one I am now going to show you. It will never get written about, unless I write about it myself. In fact, I called you over here really to show you this plant. Come, Parimal. Come with me, Abhijit Babu.'

This time, Kanti Babu led the way to what looked like a factory behind the shirish tree. The door, made of tin, was locked. There was a window on either side. Kanti Babu pushed one of these open, peered in, then withdrew. 'Have a look!' he said.

Abhijit and I placed ourselves at the window. The room was only partially lit by the sunlight that came in through two skylights set high on the opposite wall.

The object the room contained hardly looked like a plant, or a tree. As a matter of fact, it was more like a weird animal—one with large, thick tentacles. A closer look, however, did reveal a trunk. It rose from the ground by several feet to end at what might be described as a head. About eighteen inches below this head, surrounding it, were tentacles. I counted them. There were seven.

The bark of the tree was pale, but it had round brown marks all over.

The tentacles were hanging limply, resting on the ground. The whole object appeared lifeless. Yet, I could feel my flesh creep.

I noticed something else, as my eyes got used to the dark. The floor around the plant was littered with the feathers of some bird.

Neither Abhijit nor I could speak. How long the silence continued, I cannot tell. It was Kanti Babu's voice that broke it. 'The plant is asleep at this moment. It's almost time for it to wake up.'

'Is it really a plant?' Abhijit asked incredulously.

'Well, it has grown out of the ground. What else would you call it? It doesn't, however, behave like a plant. No botanical reference book, or encyclopaedia, could give you a suitable name for it.'

'What do you call it?'

'Septopus. Because it has seven tentacles.'

We began walking back to the house.

'Where did you find it?' I asked.

'There is a dense forest near Lake Nicaragua in Central America. That's where I found it.'

'You must have had to search the area pretty thoroughly?'

'Yes, but I knew that the plant was available there. You

haven't heard of Professor Dunston, have you? He was a botanist and an explorer. He died in Central America, looking for rare plants. But his death was quite mysterious. No one ever found his body, no one knows exactly how he died. This particular plant was mentioned in his diary, towards the very end.

'So I went to Nicaragua at the first opportunity. When I got to Guatemala, I heard people talking about this plant. They called it the Satan's Tree. Eventually, I saw a number of these plants. I saw them eat monkeys, armadillos, and other animals. Then, after many days of careful searching, I found a small sapling and brought it with me. You can see how big it has grown in two years.'

'What does it eat here?'

'Whatever I give it. Sometimes I catch rats in my trap to feed it. Prayag has been told to get hold of dogs and cats that get run over. It has eaten those, too. Sometimes I give it the same things that you and I would eat—chicken or goat. Recently, its appetite seems to have grown quite a lot. I can't keep up with it. When it wakes up in the evening, it gets really restless. Yesterday, something happened . . . it was just terrible. Prayag had gone to feed it a chicken. It has to be fed in much the same way as an elephant. The head of this plant has a kind of lid. First of all, it opens its lid. Then it grabs the food with one of its tentacles, as an elephant picks up its food with its trunk, and places it into the opening in the head. After that, it remains quiet for a while. When it starts swinging its tentacles, that means it wants to eat some more.

'So far, a couple of chickens or a lamb was proving to be quite sufficient for a day's meal. Things have changed since yesterday. Prayag fed it the second chicken, shut the door and came away. When the plant gets restless, it strikes its tentacles against the floor, which creates a noise. Prayag heard this noise even after the second chicken had disappeared. So he went back to investigate.

'I was in my room at the time, making entries in my diary. A sudden scream made me come running here to see what was going on. What I saw was horrible. The plant had grabbed Prayag's right hand with a tentacle. Prayag was trying desperately to free his hand, but another tentacle was raised and making its way to him.

'I had to pick up my stick and strike at that tentacle with all my might, and then put both my arms round Prayag to pull him back. Yes, I rescued him all right, but what I saw the plant do next left me feeling positively alarmed. It had managed to tear off a piece of flesh from Prayag's hand. I saw it remove the lid on its head and put it in. I saw it with my own eyes!'

We had reached the front veranda once again. Kanti Babu sat down on a chair. Then he took out a handkerchief and wiped his forehead. 'I had no idea that the Septopus would wish to attack a human being. But now . . . since there has been such an indication . . . I don't have any option. I have got to kill it. I decided to do so immediately after I saw Prayag being attacked, and I put poison in its food. But that plant has such amazing intelligence, it picked the food up with a tentacle, but threw it away instantly. Now the only thing I can do is shoot it. Parimal, now do you understand why I called you here?'

I remained quiet for a few moments. Then I said, 'Do you know for sure that it will die if it's shot?'

'No, I cannot be sure. But I do believe that it has a brain. Besides, I have proof that it can think and judge. I have gone near it so many times, it has never attacked me. It seems to know me well, just as a dog knows its master. It dislikes Prayag because sometimes Prayag has, in the past, teased it and played tricks on it. He has tempted it with food, then refused to feed it. I have seen Prayag take its food close to its tentacles, then withdraw it before the plant could grasp it. Yes, it most definitely has a brain, and that is where it should be, in its head. You must aim and fire at the spot from which those tentacles have grown.'

This time, Abhijit spoke. 'That's not a problem!' he said casually. 'It will only take a minute. Parimal, get your gun.'

Kanti Babu raised a hand to stop Abhijit. 'If the prey is asleep, is it right to kill it? What does your hunting code say, Parimal?'

'It is quite unethical to kill a sleeping animal. In this case, the prey is incapable of running away. There is no question of killing it until it wakes up.'

Kanti Babu rose and poured tea out of a flask. The Septopus woke within fifteen minutes of our finishing the tea.

Badshah, in the living room, had grown increasingly restive while we were talking. The sound of his keening and scratching noises made both Abhijit and me jump up and go inside. We found Badshah straining at his leash and trying to bite his collar. Abhijit began to calm him down, but at that moment, we heard a swishing noise coming from the factory. It was accompanied by a sharp, pungent smell. It is difficult to describe it. When I was a child, I had had my tonsils removed. Before the operation, I had smelt chloroform. It was somewhat similar.

Kanti Babu swept into the living room. 'Come on, it's time!' he said.

'What is that smell?' I asked.

'It's coming from the Septopus. That's the smell it spreads to attract ani . . .'

Kanti Babu could not finish. Badshah broke free with a mighty pull at the leash, knocked Abhijit out of the way, and leapt in the direction of the factory, to look for the source of the smell.

'Oh God, no!' cried Abhijit, picking himself up and running after his dog.

I picked up my loaded gun and followed him quickly. When

I got there only a few seconds later, Badshah was springing up to the open window, ignoring Abhijit's futile attempts to stop him. Then he jumped into the room.

Kanti Babu ran to unlock the door. We heard the agonized screams of the Rampur hound even as Kanti Babu turned the key in the lock.

We tumbled into the room, to witness a horrible sight. One tentacle was not enough this time. The Septopus was wrapping a second, and then a third tentacle around Badshah, in a deadly embrace.

Kanti Babu shouted, 'Don't get any closer, either of you. Parimal, fire!'

I raised my gun, but another voice yelled: 'Stop!'

Now I realized how precious his dog was to Abhijit. He paid no attention to Kanti Babu's warning. I saw him run to the plant, and clutch with both hands one of the three tentacles that were wrapped around Badshah.

What followed froze my blood.

All three tentacles left Badshah immediately and attacked Abhijit. And the remaining four, perhaps aroused by the prospect of tasting human blood, rose from the ground, swaying greedily.

Kanti Babu spoke again. 'Come on, shoot. Look, there's the head!'

A lid from the top of the head was being slowly removed, revealing a dark cavern. The tentacles, lifting and carrying Abhijit with them, were moving towards that yawning gap.

Abhijit's face looked deathly pale, his eyes were bursting out of their sockets.

At any moment of crisis, I had noticed before, my nerves would become perfectly steady and calm, as if by magic.

I raised my gun, took aim and fired at the head of the Septopus, between two brown circular marks in the centre. My hands did not tremble, and my bullet found its mark.

In the next instant, I remember, thick red blood began spurting out of the wounded plant, gushing forth like a fountain. And the tentacles released Abhijit, hanging low, dropping down to the ground, still and lifeless. The last thing I remember is the smell, which suddenly grew ten times stronger, overwhelming my senses, blocking out consciousness, numbing my thoughts . . .

Four months had passed since that day. I had only recently resumed writing. My novel was still incomplete.

It had proved impossible to save Badshah. But Abhijit had already found a mastiff and a Tibetan pup. He was looking for another Rampur hound, I had learnt. Two of his ribs were fractured as a result of his encounter with the Septopus. It took him two months to recover.

Kanti Babu visited me yesterday. He was thinking of getting rid of all his plants that ate insects, he said.

'It might be a good idea to experiment with vegetables, don't you think? I mean, I could grow courgettes, gourds, marrows, things like that. If you like, I can give you some of my old plants. You did so much for me, I am very grateful to you. Say I give you a nepenthes? It can at least take care of the insects in your house . . .?'

'No, no!' I interrupted him. 'If you wish to get rid of those plants, do. Just throw them out. I don't need a plant to catch my insects.'

This last remark received wholehearted support from the gecko sprawled over the calendar.

'Tik, tik, tik!' it said.

(1962)   *Translated by Gopa Majumdar*

RATAN BABU AND THAT MAN

Stepping out of the train onto the platform, Ratan Babu heaved a sigh of relief. The place seemed quite inviting. A shirish tree reared its head from behind the station house. There was a spot of red in its green leaves where a kite was caught in a branch. There was no sign of busyness in the few people around and a pleasant earthy smell was floating in the air. All in all, he found the surroundings most agreeable.

As he had only a small holdall and a leather suitcase, he didn't need a coolie. He lifted his luggage with both hands and made for the exit.

He had no trouble finding a cycle-rickshaw outside.

'Where to, sir?' asked the young driver in striped shorts.

'You know the New Mahamaya hotel?' asked Ratan Babu.

The driver nodded. 'Hop in, sir.'

Travelling was almost an obsession with Ratan Babu. He went out of Calcutta whenever the opportunity came, though that was not very often. Ratan Babu had a regular job. For twenty-four years he had been a clerk in the Calcutta office of the Geological Survey. He could get away only once a year, when he clubbed his yearly leave with the month-long Puja holidays and set off all by himself. He never took anyone with him, nor would it have occurred to him to do so. There was a time when he had felt the need for companionship; in fact, he had once talked about it to Keshab Babu who occupied the adjacent desk in his office. It was a few days before the holidays; and Ratan Babu was still planning his getaway. 'You're pretty much on your own, like me,' he had said. 'Why don't we go off together somewhere this time?'

Keshab Babu had stuck his pen behind his ear, put his palms together and said with a wry smile, 'I don't think you and I have the same tastes, you know. You go to places no one has heard of, places where there's nothing much to see, nor any decent places to stay or eat at. No sir, I'd sooner go to Harinabhi and visit my brother-in-law.'

In time, Ratan Babu had come to realize that there was virtually no one who saw eye to eye with him. His likes and dislikes were quite different from the average person's, so it was best to give up hopes of finding a suitable companion.

There was no doubt that Ratan Babu possessed traits which were quite unusual. Keshab Babu had been quite right. Ratan Babu was never attracted to places where people normally went for vacations. 'All right,' he would say, 'so there is the sea in Puri and the temple of Jagannath; you can see the Kanchenjunga from Darjeeling, and there are hills and forests in Hazaribagh and the Hudroo falls in Ranchi. So what? You've heard them described so many times that you almost feel you've seen them yourself.'

What Ratan Babu looked for was a little town somewhere with a railway station not too far away. Every year before the holidays he would open the timetable, pick such a town and make his way there. No one bothered to ask where he was going and he never told anyone. In fact, there had been occasions when he had gone to places he had never even heard of, and wherever he had gone he had discovered things which had delighted him. To others, such things might appear trivial, like the old fig tree in Rajabhatkhaoa which had coiled itself around a kul and coconut tree; or the ruins of the indigo factory in Maheshgunj; or the delicious dal barfi sold in a sweet shop in Moina . . .

This time Ratan Babu had decided on a town called Shini—fifteen miles from Tatanagar. Shini was not picked from the timetable; his colleague Anukul Mitra had mentioned it to him. The New Mahamaya hotel, too, was recommended by him.

To Ratan Babu, the hotel seemed quite adequate. His room wasn't large, but that didn't matter. There were windows to the east and the south with pleasant views of the countryside. The servant Pancha seemed an amiable sort. Ratan Babu was in the habit of bathing twice a day in tepid water throughout the year, and Pancha had assured him that there would be no trouble about that. The cooking was passable, which was all right with Ratan Babu since he was not fussy about food. There was only one thing he insisted on: he needed to have rice with fish curry and chapatis with dal and vegetables. He had informed Pancha about this as soon as he had arrived, and Pancha had passed on the information to the manager.

Ratan Babu was also in the habit of going for a walk in the afternoon when he arrived in a new place. The first day at Shini was no exception. He finished the cup of tea brought by Pancha and set out by four.

After a few minutes' walk he found himself in the open country. The terrain was uneven and criss-crossed with paths. Ratan Babu chose one at random and after half an hour's walk, discovered a charming spot. It was a pond with water lilies growing in it with a large variety of birds flying around. Of these there were some like cranes, snipes, kingfishers and magpies which Ratan Babu recognized; the others were unfamiliar.

Ratan Babu could well have spent all his afternoons sitting beside this pond, but on the second day he took a different path

in the hope of discovering something new. Having walked a
mile or so, he had to stop for a herd of goats to cross his path. As
the road cleared, he went on for another five minutes until a
wooden bridge came into view. As he approached it, he
realized that a railway line passed below it. He went and stood
on the bridge. To the east he could see the railway station; to the
west the parallel lines stretched as far as the eye could see. What
if a train were suddenly to appear and go thundering
underneath? The very thought thrilled him.

Perhaps because he had his eyes on the tracks, he failed to
notice another man who had come and stood beside him. Ratan
Babu looked around and gave a start.

The stranger was clad in a dhoti and shirt, a snuff-coloured
shawl on his shoulder. He wore bifocals and his feet were clad
in brown canvas shoes. Ratan Babu had an odd feeling. Where
had he seen this person before? Wasn't there something familiar
about him? Medium height, medium complexion, a pensive
look in his eyes . . . How old could he be? Surely not over fifty.

The stranger smiled and folded his hands in greeting. Ratan
Babu was about to return the greeting when he realized in a
flash why he had that odd feeling. No wonder the stranger's face
seemed familiar. He had seen that face many, many times—in
his own mirror. The resemblance was uncanny. The squarish
jaw with the cleft chin, the way the hair was parted, the carefully
trimmed moustache, the shape of the ear lobes—they were all
strikingly like his own. Only, the stranger seemed a shade fairer
than him, his eyebrows a little bushier and the hair at the back a
trifle longer.

The stranger spoke, and Ratan Babu got another shock.
Sushanto, a boy from his neighbourhood, had once recorded his
voice in a tape recorder and played it back to him. There was no
difference between that voice and the one that spoke now.

'My name is Manilal Majumdar. I believe you're staying at

the New Mahamaya?'

Ratanlal—Manilal . . . the names were similar too. Ratan Babu managed to shake off his bewilderment and introduced himself.

The stranger said, 'I don't suppose you'd know, but I have seen you once before.'

'Where?'

'Weren't you in Dhulian last year?'

Ratan Babu's eyebrows shot up. 'Don't tell me you were there too!'

'Yes, sir. I go off on trips every Puja. I'm on my own. No friends to speak of. It's fun to be in a new place all by myself. A colleague of mine recommended Shini to me. Nice place, isn't it?'

Ratan Babu swallowed, and then nodded in assent. He felt a strange mixture of disbelief and uneasiness in his mind.

'Have you seen the pond on the other side where a lot of birds gather in the evening?' asked Manilal Babu.

Ratan Babu said yes, he had.

'Some of the birds I could recognize,' said Manilal Babu, 'others I have never seen before in Bengal. What do you think?'

Ratan Babu had recovered somewhat in the meantime. He said, 'I had the same feeling; I didn't recognize some birds either.'

Just then they heard a booming sound. It was a train. Ratan Babu saw a point of light growing bigger as the train approached from the east. Both the men moved closer to the railing of the bridge. The train hurtled up and passed below them, making the bridge shake. Both of them crossed to the other side and kept looking until the train disappeared from view. Ratan Babu felt the same thrill as he did as a small boy. 'How strange!' said Manilal Babu, 'even at this age watching trains never fails to excite me.'

On the way back Ratan Babu learnt that Manilal Babu had arrived in Shini three days ago. He was staying at the Kalika hotel. His home was in Calcutta where he had a job in a trading company. One doesn't ask another person about his salary, but an indomitable urge made Ratan Babu throw discretion to the wind and put the question. The answer made him gasp in astonishment. How was such a thing possible? Both Ratan Babu and Manilal Babu drew exactly the same salary—437 rupees a month—and both had received exactly the same Puja bonus.

Ratan Babu found it difficult to believe that the other man had somehow found out all about him beforehand and was playing some mysterious game. No one had ever bothered about him before; he kept very much to himself. Outside his office he spoke only to his servant and never made calls on anyone. Even if it was possible for an outsider to find out about his salary, such details as when he went to bed, his tastes in food, what newspapers he read, what plays and films he had seen lately—these were known only to himself. And yet everything tallied exactly with what this man was saying.

He couldn't say this to Manilal Babu. All he did was listen to what the man had to say and marvel at the extraordinary similarity. He revealed nothing about his own habits.

They came to Ratan Babu's hotel first, and stopped in front of it. 'What's the food here like?' asked Manilal Babu.

'They make a good fish curry,' replied Ratan Babu. 'The rest is just adequate.'

'I'm afraid the cooking in my hotel is rather indifferent,' said Manilal Babu. 'I've heard they make very good luchis and chholar dal at the Jagannath Restaurant. What about having a meal there tonight?'

'I don't mind,' said Ratan Babu, 'shall we meet around eight then?'

'Right. I'll wait for you, then we'll walk down together.'

After Manilal Babu left, Ratan Babu roamed about in the street for a while. Darkness had fallen. It was a clear night. So clear that the Milky Way could be seen stretching from one end of the star-filled sky to the other. What a strange thing to happen! All these years Ratan Babu had regretted that he couldn't find anyone to share his tastes and become friends with him. Now at last in Shini he had run into someone who might well be an exact replica of himself. There was a slight difference in their looks perhaps, but in every other respect such similarity was rare even amongst twins.

Did it mean that he had found a friend at last?

Ratan Babu couldn't find a ready answer to the question. Perhaps he would find it when he got to know the man a little better. One thing was clear—he no longer had the feeling of being isolated from his fellow men. All these years there had been another person exactly like him, and he had come to know him quite by chance.

In Jagannath Restaurant, sitting face to face across the table, Ratan Babu observed that, like him, Manilal Babu ate with a fastidious relish; like him, he didn't drink any water during the meal; and like him, he squeezed lemon into the dal. Ratan Babu always had sweet curd to round off his meals, and so did Manilal Babu.

While eating, Ratan Babu had the uncomfortable feeling that diners at other tables were watching them. Did they notice how alike they were? Was the likeness so obvious to onlookers?

After dinner, the two of them walked for a while in the moonlight. There was something which Ratan Babu wanted to ask, and he did so now. 'Have you turned fifty yet?'

Manilal Babu smiled. 'I'll be doing so soon,' he said, 'I'll be fifty on the twenty-ninth of December.'

Ratan Babu's head swam. They were both born on the same day: the twenty-ninth of December, 1916. Half an hour later, as they were taking leave, Manilal Babu said, 'It has been a great pleasure knowing you. I don't seem to get on very well with people, but you're an exception. I can now look forward to an enjoyable vacation.'

Usually, Ratan Babu was in bed by ten. He would glance through a magazine, and gradually feel a drowsiness stealing over him. He would then put down the magazine, turn off the bedlamp and within a few minutes would start snoring softly. But tonight he found that sleep wouldn't come. Nor did he feel like reading. He picked up the magazine and put it down again.

Manilal Majumdar . . .

Ratan Babu had read somewhere that of the billions of people who inhabited the earth, no two looked exactly alike. And yet every one had the same number of features—eyes, ears, nose, lips and so on. But even if no two persons looked alike, was it possible for them to have the same tastes, feelings, attitudes—as it was with him and his new friend? Age, profession, voice, gait, even the power of their glasses—were identical. One would think such a thing impossible, and yet here was proof that it was not, and Ratan Babu had learnt it again and again in the last four hours.

At about midnight, he got out of bed, poured some water from the carafe and splashed it on his head. Sleep was impossible in his feverish state. He passed a towel lightly over his head and went back to bed. At least the wet pillow would keep his head cool for a while.

Silence had descended over the neighbourhood. An owl went screeching overhead. Moonlight streamed in through the window and onto the bed. Slowly, Ratan Babu's mind regained its calm and his eyes closed of their own accord.

It was almost eight when Ratan Babu woke up the next morning. Manilal Babu was supposed to come at nine. It was Tuesday—the day when the weekly market or haat was held at a spot a mile or so away. The night before, the two had almost simultaneously expressed a wish to visit the haat, more to look around than to buy anything.

It was almost nine when Ratan Babu finished breakfast. He helped himself to a pinch of mouth-freshners from the saucer on the table, came out of the hotel and saw Manilal Babu approaching.

'I couldn't sleep for a long time last night,' were Manilal Babu's first words. 'I lay in bed thinking how alike you and I were. It was five to eight when I woke this morning. I am usually up by six.'

Ratan Babu refrained from comment. The two set off towards the haat. They had to pass some youngsters standing in a cluster by the roadside. 'Hey, look at Tweedledum and Tweedledee!' one of them cried out. Ratan Babu tried his best to ignore the remark and went on ahead. It took them about twenty minutes to reach the haat.

The market was a bustling affair. There were shops for fruits and vegetables, utensils, clothes, and even livestock. The two men wove their way through the milling crowd casting glances at the goods on display.

Who was that? Wasn't it Pancha? For some reason, Ratan Babu couldn't bring himself to face the hotel servant. That remark about Tweedledum and Tweedledee had made him realize it would be prudent not to be seen alongside Manilal Babu.

As they jostled through the crowd a thought suddenly occurred to Ratan Babu. He realized he was better off as he was—alone, without a friend. He didn't need a friend. Or, at any rate, not someone like Manilal Babu. Whenever he spoke to Manilal Babu, it seemed as if he was carrying on a conversation with himself. He knew all the answers before he asked the questions. There was no room for argument, no possibility of misunderstanding. Were these signs of friendship? Two of his colleagues, Kartik Ray and Mukunda Chakravarty, were bosom friends. Did that mean they had no arguments? Of course they did. But they were still friends—close friends.

The thought kept buzzing around his head and he couldn't rid himself of the feeling that it would have been better if Manilal Babu hadn't come into his life. Even if two identical men existed, it was wrong that they should meet. The very thought that they might continue to meet even after returning to Calcutta made Ratan Babu shudder.

One of the shops was selling cane walking sticks. Ratan Babu had always wanted to possess one, but seeing Manilal Babu haggling with the shopkeeper, he checked himself. Manilal Babu bought two sticks and gave one to Ratan Babu saying, 'I hope you won't mind accepting this as a token of our friendship.'

On the way back to the hotel, Manilal Babu spoke a lot about himself—his childhood, his parents, his school and college days. Ratan Babu felt that his own life story was being recounted.

The plan came to Ratan Babu in the afternoon as the two were on their way to the railway bridge. He didn't have to talk much, so he could think. He had been thinking, since midday, of getting rid of this man, but he couldn't decide on a method. Ratan Babu had just turned his eyes to the clouds gathering in the west when a plan suddenly occurred to him with blazing clarity. The vision he saw was of the two of them standing by the railing of the bridge. In the distance a train was approaching. As the engine got within twenty yards, Ratan Babu gathered his strength and gave a hefty push—He closed his eyes involuntarily. Then he opened them again and shot a glance at his companion. Manilal Babu seemed quite unconcerned. But if the two had so much in common, perhaps he too was thinking of a way to get rid of him?

But the man's looks didn't betray any such thoughts. As a matter of fact, he was humming a Hindi film tune which Ratan Babu himself was in the habit of humming from time to time.

The dark clouds had just covered the sun which would in any case set in a few minutes. Ratan Babu looked around and saw they were quite alone. Thank God for that. Had there been anyone else, his plan wouldn't have worked.

It was strange that even though his mind was bent on murder, Ratan Babu couldn't think of himself as a culprit. Had Manilal Babu possessed any traits which endowed him with a personality different from his own, Ratan Babu could never have thought of killing him. But now he felt that there was no sense in both of them being alive at the same time. It was enough that he alone should continue to exist.

The two arrived at the bridge.

'Bit stuffy today,' commented Manilal Babu. 'It may rain tonight, and that could be the start of a cold spell.'

Ratan Babu stole a glance at his wristwatch. Twelve minutes to six. The train was supposed to be very punctual. There wasn't much time left. Ratan Babu contrived a yawn to ease his tension. 'Even if it does rain,' he said, 'it is not likely to happen for another four or five hours.'

'Care for a betel nut?'

Manilal Babu had produced a small round tin box from his pocket. Ratan Babu too was carrying a metal box with betel nuts in it, but didn't mention the fact to Manilal Babu. He helped himself to a nut and tossed it into his mouth.

Just then they heard the sound of the train.

Manilal Babu advanced towards the railing, glanced at his watch and said, 'Seven minutes before time.'

The thick cloud in the sky had made the evening a little darker than usual. The headlight seemed brighter in contrast.

The train was still far away but the light was growing brighter every second.

Krrrring . . . krrring.

A cyclist was approaching from the road towards the bridge. Good God! Was he going to stop?

No. Ratan Babu's apprehension proved baseless. The cyclist rode swiftly past them and disappeared into the gathering darkness down the other side of the road.

The train was hurtling up at great speed. It was impossible to gauge the distance in the blinding glare of the headlight. In a few seconds the bridge would start shaking.

Now the sound of the train was deafening.

Manilal Babu was looking down with his hands on the railing. A flash of lightning in the sky and Ratan Babu gathered all his strength, flattened his palms against the back of Manilal Babu, and heaved. Manilal Babu's body vaulted over the four-foot-high railing and plummeted down towards the thundering engine. That very moment the bridge began to shake.

Ratan Babu wound his shawl tightly around his neck and started on his way back.

Towards the end of his walk he had to break into a run in a vain effort to avoid being pelted by the first big drops of rain. Panting with the effort, he rushed into the hotel.

As soon as he entered he felt there was something wrong.

Where had he come? The lobby of the New Mahamaya was not like this at all—the tables, the chairs, the pictures on the wall . . . Looking around, his eyes suddenly caught a signboard on the wall. What a stupid mistake! He had come into the Kalika hotel instead. Wasn't this where Manilal Babu was staying?

'So you couldn't avoid getting wet?'

Somebody was talking to him. Ratan Babu turned round and saw a man with curly hair and a green shawl—probably a resident of the hotel—looking at him with a cup of tea in his hand. 'Sorry,' said the man, seeing Ratan Babu's face, 'for a moment I thought you were Manilal Babu.'

It was this mistake which raised the first doubts in Ratan Babu's mind. Had he been careful enough about the crime he had committed? Many must have seen the two of them going out together, but had they really noticed? Would they remember what they had seen? And if they did, would the suspicion then fall on him? He was sure no one had seen them after they had reached the outskirts of the town. And after reaching that bridge—oh yes, the cyclist. He must have seen them. But by that time it had turned quite dark and the cyclist passed by at a high speed. Was it likely that he would remember their faces? Certainly not.

The more Ratan Babu pondered, the more reassured he felt. There was no doubt that Manilal Babu's dead body would be discovered. But he just could not believe that it would lead to him being suspected of the crime, and that he would be tried, found guilty, and brought to the gallows.

Since it was still raining, Ratan Babu stayed for a cup of tea. Around seven-thirty the rain stopped and he went directly to the New Mahamaya. He found it almost funny the way he had blundered into the wrong hotel.

At dinner, he ate well and with relish; then he slipped into bed with a magazine, read an article on the aborigines of Australia, turned off the bedlamp and closed his eyes with not a worry in his mind. Once again he was on his own; and unique. He didn't have a friend, and didn't need one. He would spend the rest of his days in exactly the same way he had done so far. What could be better?

It had started to rain again. There were flashes of lightning and claps of thunder. But none of it mattered. Ratan Babu had already started to snore.

'Did you buy that stick from the haat, sir?' asked Pancha when he brought Ratan Babu his morning tea.

'Yes,' said Ratan Babu.

'How much did you pay for it?'

Ratan Babu mentioned the price. Then he asked casually, 'Were you at the haat too?'

Pancha broke into a broad smile. 'Yes, sir,' he said, 'and I saw you. Didn't you see me?'

'Why, no.'

That ended the conversation.

After his tea, Ratan Babu made his way to the Kalika hotel. The curly-haired man was talking to a group of people outside the hotel. He heard Manilal Babu's name and the word 'suicide' mentioned several times. He edged closer to hear better. Not only that, he was bold enough to put a question.

'Who has died?'

The curly-haired man said, 'It was the same man I had mistaken you for yesterday.'

'Suicide, was it?'

'It looks like that. The dead body was found by the railway tracks below the bridge. It seems he threw himself from it. An odd character, he was. Hardly spoke to anyone. We used to talk about him.'

'I suppose the dead body . . .?'

'In police custody. He came here for a change of air from Calcutta. Didn't know anyone here. Nothing more has been found out.'

Ratan Babu shook his head, made a few clucking noises and went off.

Suicide! So nobody had thought of murder at all. Luck was on his side. How simple it was, this business of murder! He wondered what made people quail at the thought.

Ratan Babu felt quite light-hearted. After two days he would now be able to walk alone again. The very thought filled him with pleasure.

It was probably while he pushed Manilal Babu yesterday that a button from his shirt had got ripped and come off. He found a tailor's shop and had the button replaced. Then he went into a store and bought a tube of Neem toothpaste.

As he walked a few steps from the store, he heard the sound of keertan coming from a house. He stood for a while listening to the song, then made for the open terrain outside the town. He walked a mile or so along a new path, came back to the hotel at about eleven, had his bath and lunch, and took his afternoon nap.

As usual he woke up around three, and realized almost immediately that he had to pay another visit to the bridge that evening. For obvious reasons he had not been able to enjoy the sight of the train yesterday. The sky was still cloudy but it didn't seem that it would rain. Today he would be able to watch the train from the moment it appeared till it vanished into the horizon.

He had his afternoon tea at five and went down to the lobby. The manager Shambhu Babu sat at his desk by the front door. He saw Ratan Babu and said, 'Did you know the man who was killed yesterday?'

Ratan Babu looked at Shambhu Babu, feigning surprise. Then he said, 'Why do you ask?'

'Well, it's only that Pancha mentioned he had seen you two together in the haat.'

Ratan Babu smiled. 'I haven't really got to know anyone here,' he said calmly. 'I did speak to a few people in the haat, but the fact is, I don't even know which person was killed.'

'I see,' said Shambhu Babu, laughing. He was jovial by nature and prone to laughter. 'He too had come for a change,' he added. 'He had put up at the Kalika.'

'I see.'

Ratan Babu went out. It was a two-mile walk to the bridge. If he didn't hurry he might miss the train.

Nobody cast suspicious glances at him in the street. Yesterday's youngsters were not in their usual place. That remark about Tweedledum and Tweedledee had nettled him. He wondered where the boys were. The sound of drums could be heard from somewhere close by. There was a puja on in the neighbourhood. That's where the boys must have gone. Good.

At last he was all by himself on the path in the open field. Until he met Manilal Babu, he had been well content with his lot; but today he felt more relaxed than ever before.

There it was—the babla tree. The bridge was only a short distance away. The sky was still overcast, but not with thick black clouds like yesterday. These were grey clouds, and there was no breeze; the sky stood ashen and still.

Ratan Babu's heart leaped with joy at the sight of the bridge. He quickened his pace. Who knows, the train might turn up even earlier than yesterday. A flock of cranes passed overhead. Migratory cranes? He couldn't tell.

As he stood on the bridge, Ratan Babu became aware of the stillness of the evening. Straining his ears, he could hear faint drumbeats from the direction of the town. Otherwise all was quiet.

He moved over to the railing. He could see the signal, and beyond that, the station. What was that now? Lower down the railing, in a crack in the wood was lodged a shiny object. Ratan Babu bent down and prised it out. A small round tin box with betel nuts in it. Ratan Babu smiled and tossed it over the railing. There was a metallic clink as it hit the ground. Who knows how long it would lie there?

What was that light?

Ah, the train. No sound yet, just an advancing point of light.

Ratan Babu stood and stared fascinated at the headlight. A sudden gust of wind whipped the shawl off his shoulder. He wrapped it properly around him once more.

Now he could hear the sound. It was like the low rumble of an approaching storm.

Ratan Babu suddenly had the feeling that somebody was standing behind him. It was difficult to take his eyes off the train, but even so he cast a quick glance around. Not a soul anywhere. It was not as dark as the day before, hence the visibility was much better. No, except for himself and that approaching train, there was no one for miles around.

The train was now within a hundred yards.

Ratan Babu edged further towards the railing. Had the train been an old-fashioned one with a steam engine, he couldn't have gone so close to the edge as the smoke would have got into his eyes. This was a smokeless diesel engine. There was only a deep, earthshaking rumble and the blinding glare of the headlight.

Now the train was about to go under the bridge.

Ratan Babu placed his elbows on the railing and leaned forward to watch.

At that very moment a pair of hands came up from behind and gave him a savage push. Ratan Babu went clean over the four-foot-high railing.

As usual, the train made the bridge shudder as it passed under it and sped towards the west where the sky had just begun to turn purple.

Ratan Babu no longer stands on the bridge, but as a token of his presence a small shining object is stuck in a crack in the wooden railing.

It is an aluminium box with betel nuts in it.

(1970)   *Translated by Satyajit Ray*

BONKU BABU'S FRIEND

No one had ever seen Bonku Babu get cross. To tell the truth, it was difficult to imagine what he might say or do, if one day he did get angry.

It was not as if there was never any reason for him to lose his temper. For the last twenty-two years, Bonku Babu had taught geography and Bengali at the Kankurgachhi Primary School. Every year, a new batch of students replaced the old one, but old or new, the tradition of teasing poor Bonku Babu continued among all the students. Some drew his picture on the blackboard; others put glue on his chair; or, on the night of Kali Puja, they lit a 'chasing-rocket' and set it off to chase him.

Bonku Babu did not get upset by any of this. Only sometimes, he cleared his throat and said, 'Shame on you, boys!'

One of the reasons for maintaining his calm was simply that he could not afford to do otherwise. If he did lose his temper and left his job in a fit of pique, he knew how difficult it would then be to find another, at his age. Another reason was that in every class, there were always a few good students, even if the rest of the class was full of pranksters. Teaching this handful of good boys was so rewarding that, to Bonku Babu, that alone made life as a teacher worth living. At times, he invited those boys to his house, offered them snacks and told them tales of foreign lands and exciting adventures. He told them about life in Africa, the discovery of the North Pole, the fish in Brazil that ate human flesh, and about Atlantis, the continent submerged under the sea. He was a good storyteller, he had his audience enthralled.

During the weekend, Bonku Babu went to the lawyer, Sripati Majumdar's house, to spend the evenings with other regulars. On a number of occasions, he had come back thinking, 'Enough, never again!' The reason was simply that he could put up with the pranks played by the boys in his school, but when grown, even middle-aged men started making fun of him, it became too much to bear. At these meetings that Sripati Babu hosted in the evenings, nearly everyone poked fun at Bonku Babu, sometimes bringing his endurance to breaking point.

Only the other day—less than two months ago—they were talking about ghosts. Usually, Bonku Babu kept his mouth shut. That day, for some unknown reason, he opened it and declared that he was not afraid of ghosts. That was all. But it was enough to offer a golden opportunity to the others. On his way back later that night, Bonku Babu was attacked by a 'spook'. As he was passing a tamarind tree, a tall, thin figure leapt down and landed on his back. As it happened, this apparition had smeared black ink all over itself, possibly at the suggestion of someone at the meeting.

Bonku Babu did not feel frightened. But he was injured. For three days, his neck ached. Worst of all—his new kurta was torn and it had black stains all over. What kind of a joke was this?

Other 'jokes', less serious in nature, were often played on him. His umbrella or his shoes were hidden sometimes; at others, a paan would be filled with dust instead of masala, and handed to him; or he would be forced to sing.

Even so, Bonku Babu had to come to these meetings. If he didn't, what would Sripati Babu think? Not only was he a very

important man in the village, but he couldn't do without Bonku
Babu. According to Sripati Majumdar, it was essential to have a
butt of ridicule, who could provide amusement to all. Or what
was the point in having a meeting? So Bonku Babu was fetched,
even if he tried to keep away.

On one particular day, the topic of conversation was
high-flying—in other words, they were talking of satellites. Soon
after sunset, a moving point of light had been seen in the
northern sky. A similar light was seen three months ago, which
had led to much speculation. In the end, it turned out to be a
Russian satellite, called Khotka—or was it Phoshka? Anyway,
this satellite was supposed to be going round the earth at a
height of 400 miles, and providing a lot of valuable information
to scientists.

That evening, Bonku Babu was the first to spot that strange
light. Then he called Nidhu Babu and showed it to him.
However, he arrived at the meeting to find that Nidhu Babu had
coolly claimed full credit for being the first to see it, and was
boasting a great deal. Bonku Babu said nothing.

No one knew much about satellites, but there was nothing
to stop them from offering their views. Said Chandi Babu, 'You
can say what you like, but I don't think we should waste our time
worrying about satellites. Somebody sees a point of light in some
obscure corner of the sky, and the press gets all excited about it.
Then we read a report, say how clever it all is, have a chat about
it in our living rooms, perhaps while we casually chew a paan,
and behave as if we have achieved something. Humbug!'

Ramkanai countered this remark. He was still young. 'No, it
may not be any of us here, but it is human achievement, surely?
And a great achievement, at that.'

'Oh, come off it! Of course it's a human achievement . . .

who'd build a satellite except men? You wouldn't expect a bunch of monkeys to do that, would you?'

'All right,' said Nidhu Babu, 'let's not talk of satellites. After all, it's just a machine, going round the earth, they say. No different from a spinning top. A top would start spinning if you got it going; or a fan would start to rotate if you pressed a switch. A satellite's the same. But think of a rocket. That can't be dismissed so easily, can it?'

Chandi Babu wrinkled his nose. 'A rocket? Why, what good is a rocket? All right, if one was made here in our country, took off from the maidan in Calcutta, and we could all go and buy tickets to watch the show . . . well then, that would be nice. But . . .'

'You're right,' Ramkanai agreed. 'A rocket has no meaning for us here.'

Bhairav Chakravarty spoke next. 'Suppose some creature from a different planet arrived on earth . . . ?'

'So what? Even if it did, you and I would never be able to see it.'

'Yes, that's true enough.'

Everyone turned their attention to their cups of tea. There did not seem to be anything left to be said. After a few moments of silence, Bonku Babu cleared his throat and said gently, 'Suppose . . . suppose they came here?'

Nidhu Babu feigned total amazement. 'Hey, Bunkum wants to say something! What did you say, Bunkum? Who's going to come here? Where from?'

Bonku Babu repeated his words, his tone still gentle: 'Suppose someone from a different planet came here?'

As was his wont, Bhairav Chakravarty slapped Bonku Babu's back loudly and rudely, grinned and said, 'Bravo! What a thing to say! Where is a creature from another planet going to land? Not Moscow, not London, not New York, not even

Calcutta, but here? In Kankurgachhi? You do think big, don't you?'

Bonku Babu fell silent. But several questions rose in his mind. Was it really impossible? If an alien had to visit the earth, would it really matter where it arrived first? It might not aim to go straight to any other part of the world. All right, it was highly unlikely that such a thing would happen in Kankurgachhi, but who was to say for sure that it could not happen at all?

Sripati Babu was silent so far. Now, as he shifted in his seat, everyone looked at him. He put his cup down and spoke knowledgeably: 'Look, if someone from a different planet does come to earth, I can assure you that he will not come to this God-forsaken place. Those people are no fools. It is my belief that they are sahibs, and they will land in some western country, where all the sahibs live. Understand?'

Everyone agreed, with the sole exception of Bonku Babu.

Chandi Babu decided to take things a bit further. He nudged Nidhu Babu silently, pointed at Bonku Babu and spoke innocently: 'Why, I think Bonku is quite right. Isn't it natural that aliens should want to come to a place where there's a man like our Bonkubihari? If they wanted to take away a specimen, could they find anything better?'

'No, I don't think so!' Nidhu Babu joined in. 'Consider his looks, not to mention his brains . . . yes, Bunkum is the ideal specimen!'

'Right. Suitable for keeping in a museum. Or a zoo,' Ramkanai chipped in.

Bonku Babu did not reply, but wondered silently: if anyone were to look for a specimen, weren't the others just as suitable? Look at Sripati Babu. His chin was so much like a camel's. And that Bhairav Chakravarty, his eyes were like the eyes of a tortoise. Nidhu Babu looked like a mole, Ramkanai like a goat, and Chandi Babu like a flittermouse. If a zoo really had to be filled up . . .

Tears sprang to his eyes. Bonku Babu had come to the meeting hoping, for once, to enjoy himself. That was clearly not to be. He could not stay here any longer. He rose to his feet.

'Why, what's the matter? Are you leaving already?' Sripati Babu asked, sounding concerned.

'Yes, it's getting late.'

'Late? Pooh, it's not late at all. Anyway, tomorrow is a holiday. Sit down, have some more tea.'

'No, thank you. I must go. I have some papers to mark. Namaskar.'

'Take care, Bonkuda,' warned Ramkanai, 'it's a moonless night, remember. And it's a Saturday. Very auspicious for ghosts and spooks!'

Bonku Babu saw the light when he was about halfway through the bamboo grove. Poncha Ghosh owned that entire area. Bonku Babu was not carrying a torch or a lantern. There was no need for it. It was too cold for snakes to be out and about, and he knew his way very well. Normally, not many people took this route, but it meant a short-cut for him.

In the last few minutes he had become aware of something unusual. At first, he could not put his finger on it. Somehow, things were different tonight. What was wrong? What was missing? Suddenly, he realized that the crickets were silent. Not one was chirping. Usually, the crickets sounded louder as he delved deeper into the bamboo grove. Today, there was only an eerie silence. What had happened to the crickets? Were they all asleep?

Puzzled, Bonku Babu walked another twenty yards, and then saw the light. At first, he thought a fire had broken out. Bang in the middle of the bamboo grove, in the clearing near a small pond, quite a large area was glowing pink. A dull light shone on every branch and every leaf. Down below, the ground behind the pond was lit by a much stronger pink light. But it was not a fire, for it was still.

Bonku Babu kept moving.

Soon, his ears began ringing. He felt as if someone was humming loudly—a long, steady noise—there was no way he could stop it. Bonku Babu broke into goosepimples, but an irrepressible curiosity drove him further forward.

As he went past a cluster of bamboo stems, an object came into view. It looked like a giant glass bowl, turned upside-down, covering the pond completely. It was through its translucent shade that a strong, yet gentle pink light was shining out, to turn the whole area radiant.

Not even in a dream had Bonku Babu witnessed such a strange scene.

After staring at it for a few stunned minutes, he noticed that although the object was still, it did not appear to be lifeless. There was the odd flicker; and the glass mound was rising and falling, exactly as one's chest heaves while breathing.

He took a few steps to get a better look, but felt suddenly as if an electric current had passed through his body. In the next instant, he was rendered completely immobile. His hands and feet were tied with an invisible rope. There was no strength left in his body. He could move neither forward, nor backward.

A few moments later, Bonku Babu—still standing stiffly on the same spot—saw that the object gradually stopped 'breathing'. At once, his ears ceased ringing and the humming stopped. A second later, a voice spoke, shattering the silence of the night. It sounded human, but was extraordinarily thin.

'Milipi-ping kruk! Milipi-ping kruk!' it said loudly.

Bonku Babu gave a start. What did it mean? What language

was this? And where was the speaker?

The next words the voice spoke made his heart jump again.

'Who are you? Who are you?'

Why, these were English words! Was the question addressed to him? Bonku Babu swallowed. 'I am Bonkubihari Datta, sir. Bonkubihari Datta,' he replied.

'Are you English? Are you English?' the voice went on.

'No, sir!' Bonku Babu shouted back. 'Bengali, sir. A Bengali kayastha.'

This was followed by a short pause. Then the voice came back, speaking clearly: 'Namaskar!'

Bonku Babu heaved a sigh of relief and returned the greeting. 'Namaskar!' he said, suddenly realizing that the invisible bonds that were holding him tightly had disappeared. He was free to run away, but he did not. Now his astounded eyes could see that a portion of the glass mound was sliding to one side, opening out like a door.

Through that door emerged a head—like a plain, smooth ball—and then the body of a weird creature.

Its arms and legs were amazingly thin. With the exception of its head, its whole body was covered by a shiny, pink outfit. Instead of ears, it had a tiny hole on each side of its head. On its face were two holes where it should have had a nose, and another gaping hole instead of a mouth. There was no sign of hair anywhere. Its eyes were round and bright yellow. They appeared to be glowing in the dark.

The creature walked slowly towards Bonku Babu, and stopped only a few feet away. Then it gave him a steady, unblinking stare. Automatically, Bonku Babu found himself folding his hands. Having stared at him for nearly a minute, it spoke in the same voice that sounded more like a flute than anything else: 'Are you human?'

'Yes.'

'Is this Earth?'

'Yes.'

'Ah, I thought as much. My instruments are not working properly. I was supposed to go to Pluto. I wasn't sure where I had landed, so I spoke to you first in the language they use on Pluto. When you didn't reply, I could tell I had landed on Earth. A complete waste of time and effort. It happened once before. Instead of going to Mars, I veered off and went to Jupiter. Delayed me by a whole day, it did. Heh heh heh!'

Bonku Babu did not know what to say. He was feeling quite uncomfortable, for the creature had started to press his arms and legs with its long, slim fingers. When it finished, it introduced itself. 'I am Ang, from the planet Craneus. A far superior being than man.'

What! This creature, barely four feet tall, with such thin limbs and weird face, was superior to man? Bonku Babu nearly burst out laughing. Ang read his mind immediately. 'There's no need to be so sceptical. I can prove it. How many languages do you know?'

Bonku Babu scratched his head. 'Bengali, English and . . . er . . . Hindi . . . a little Hindi . . . I mean . . .'

'You mean two and a half?'

'Yes.'

'I know 14,000. There isn't a single language in your solar system that I do not know. I also know thirty-one languages spoken on planets outside your system. I have been to twenty-five of them. How old are you?'

'I am fifty.'

'I am 833. Do you eat animals?'

Bonku Babu had had meat curry only recently, on the day of Kali Puja. How could he deny it?

'We stopped eating meat several centuries ago,' Ang informed him. 'Before that, we used to eat the flesh of most creatures. I might have eaten you.'

Bonku Babu swallowed hard.

'Take a look at this!' Ang offered him a small object. It looked like a pebble. Bonku Babu touched it for an instant, and felt the same electric current pass through his body. He withdrew his hand at once.

Ang smiled. 'A little while ago, you could not move an inch. Do you know why? It was only because I had this little thing in my hand. It would stop anyone from getting closer. Nothing can be more effective than this in making an enemy perfectly powerless, without actually hurting him physically.'

Now Bonku Babu felt genuinely taken aback. His mind was feeling far less stunned.

Ang said, 'Is there any place that you have wished to visit, or a scene that you have longed to see, but never could?'

Bonku Babu thought: why, the whole world remained to be seen! He taught geography, but what had he seen except a few villages and towns in Bengal? There was so much in Bengal itself that he had never had the chance to see. The snow-capped Himalayas, the sea in Digha, the forests in the Sunderbans, or even that famous banyan tree in Shibpur.

However, he mentioned none of these thoughts to Ang. 'There is so much I would like to see,' he finally admitted, 'but most of all . . . I think I would like to visit the North Pole. I come from a warm country, you see, so . . .'

Ang took out a small tube, one end of which was covered by a piece of glass. 'Take a look through this!' Ang invited. Bonku Babu peered through the glass, and felt all his hair rise. Could this be true? Could he really believe his eyes? Before him stretched an endless expanse of snow, dotted with large mounds, also covered with ice and snow. Above him, against a deep blue sky, all the colours of a rainbow were forming different patterns, changing every second. The Aurora Borealis!

What was that? An igloo. There was a group of polar bears. Wait, there was another animal. A strange, peculiar creature . . . Yes! It was a walrus. There were two of them, in fact. And they were fighting. Their tusks were bared—large as radishes—and they were attacking each other. Streams of bright red blood were running on the soft white snow . . .

It was December, and Bonku Babu was looking at an area hidden under layers of snow. Still, he broke into a sweat.

'What about Brazil? Don't you wish to go there?' asked Ang.

Bonku Babu remembered instantly—piranhas, those deadly carnivorous fish! Amazing. How did this Ang know what he would like to see?

Bonku Babu peered through the tube again. He could see a dense forest. Only a little scattered sunlight had crept in through the almost impenetrable foliage. There was a huge tree, and hanging from a branch . . . what was that? Oh God, he could never even have imagined the size of that snake. Anaconda! The name flashed through his mind. Yes, he had read somewhere about it. It was said to be much, much larger than a python.

But where was the fish? Oh, here was a canal. Crocodiles lined its banks, sleeping in the sun. One of them moved. It was going to go into the water. Splash! Bonku Babu could almost hear the noise. But . . . what was that? The crocodile had jumped out of the water very quickly. Was . . . could it be the same one that went in only a few seconds ago? With his eyes nearly popping out, Bonku Babu noted that there was virtually no flesh left on the belly of the crocodile, bones were showing through clearly. Attached to the remaining flesh were five fish with amazingly sharp teeth and a monstrous appetite. Pirahnas!

Bonku Babu could not bear to watch any more. His limbs were trembling, his head reeled painfully.

'Now do you believe that we are superior?' Ang wanted to know.

Bonku Babu ran his tongue over his parched lips. 'Yes. Oh yes. Certainly. Of course!' he croaked.

'Very well. Look, I have been watching you. And I have examined your arms and legs. You belong to a much inferior species. There is no doubt about that. However, as human beings go, you are not too bad. I mean, you are a good man. But you have a major fault. You are much too meek and mild. That is why you have made so little progress in life. You must always speak up against injustice, and protest if anyone hurts or insults you without any provocation. To take it quietly is wrong, not just for man, but for any creature anywhere. Anyway, it was nice to have met you, although I wasn't really supposed to be here at this time. There's no point in wasting more time on your Earth. I had better go.'

'Goodbye, Mr Ang. I am very glad to have made your . . .'

Bonku Babu could not complete his sentence. In less than a second, almost before he could grasp what was happening, Ang had leapt into his spaceship and risen over Poncha Ghosh's bamboo grove. Then he vanished completely. Bonku Babu realized that the crickets had started chirping again. It was really quite late.

Bonku Babu resumed walking towards his house, his mind still in a wondrous haze. Slowly, the full implications of the recent events began to sink in. A man—no, it was not a man, it was Ang—came here from some unknown planet, who knew if anyone had ever heard its name, and spoken to him. How extraordinary! How completely incredible! There were billions and billions of people in the world. But who got the chance to have this wonderful experience? Bonkubihari Datta, teacher of geography and Bengali in the Kankurgachhi Primary School. No one else. From today, at least in this particular matter, he was unique, in the whole wide world.

Bonku Babu realized that he was no longer walking. With a spring in every step, he was actually dancing.

The next day was a Sunday. Everyone had turned up for their usual meeting at Sripati Babu's house. There was a report in the local paper about a strange light, but it was only a small report. This light had been seen by a handful of people in only two places in Bengal. It was therefore being put in the same category as sightings of flying saucers.

Tonight, Poncha Ghosh was also present at the meeting. He was talking about his bamboo grove. All the bamboo around the pond in the middle of the wood had shed all their leaves. It was not unusual for leaves to drop in winter, but for so many plants to become totally bare overnight was certainly a remarkable occurrence. Everyone was talking about it, when suddenly Bhairav Chakravarty said, 'Why is Bonku so late today?'

Everyone stopped talking. So far, no one had noticed Bonku Babu's absence.

'I don't think Bunkum will show his face here today. Didn't he get an earful yesterday when he tried to open his mouth?' said Nidhu Babu.

'No, no,' Sripati Babu sounded concerned, 'we must have Bonku. Ramkanai, go and see if you can get hold of him.'

'OK, I'll go as soon as I've had my tea,' replied Ramkanai and was about to take a sip, when Bonku Babu entered the room. No, to say 'entered' would be wrong. It was as if a small hurricane swept in, in the guise of a short, dark man, throwing everyone into stunned silence.

Then it swung into action. Bonku Babu burst into a guffaw, and laughed uproariously for a whole minute, the like of which no one had heard before, not even Bonku Babu himself.

When he could finally stop, he cleared his throat and began speaking:

'Friends! I have great pleasure in telling you that this is the last time you will see me at your meeting. The only reason I am here today is simply that I would like to tell you a few things before I go. Number one—this is for all of you—you speak a great deal of rubbish. Only fools talk of things they don't know anything about. Number two—this is for Chandi Babu—at your age, hiding other people's shoes and umbrellas is not just childish, but totally wrong. Kindly bring my umbrella and brown canvas shoes to my house tomorrow. Nidhu Babu, if you call me Bunkum, I will call you Nitwit, and you must learn to live with that. And Sripati Babu, you are an important man, of course you must have hangers-on. But let me tell you, from today you can count me out. If you like, I can send my cat, it's quite good at licking feet. And . . . oh, you are here as well, Poncha Babu! Let me inform you and everyone else, that last night, an Ang arrived from the planet Craneus and landed on the pond in your bamboo grove. We had a long chat. The man . . . sorry, the Ang . . . was most amiable.'

Bonku Babu finished his speech and slapped Bhairav Chakravarty's back so hard that he choked. Then he made his exit, walking swiftly, his head held high.

In the same instant, the cup fell from Ramkanai's hand, shattering to pieces, and splattering hot tea on most of the others.

(1962)   *Translated by Gopa Majumdar*

THE TWO MAGICIANS

'Five, six, seven, eight, nine, ten, eleven.' Surapati finished counting the trunks and turned towards his assistant, Anil. 'All right,' he said, 'Have these loaded into the brake van. Just twenty-five minutes left.'

'I have checked your reservation, sir,' said Anil. 'It's a coupé. Both berths are reserved in your name. It'll be all right.' Then he smiled a little and added, 'The guard is a fan of yours. He's seen your show at the New Empire. Here, sir, come this way!'

The guard, Biren Bakshi, came forward with an outstretched hand and a broad smile. 'Do allow me,' he said, 'to shake the famous hand that has performed all those tricks that gave me so much joy. It is an honour indeed!'

One only had to look at any of Surapati Mondol's eleven trunks to realize who he was. Each bore the legend 'Mondol's Miracles' in large letters both on its sides and its lid. He needed no further introduction. It was barely two months since his last show at the New Empire Theatre in Calcutta, where a large audience, enchanted by his magic show, had expressed genuine appreciation through thunderous applause again and again. The newspapers, too, had carried rave reviews. The week-long show had to be extended to four, on popular demand. Eventually, Surapati had to promise the authorities another show over

Christmas break.

'If you need any help, do let me know,' said the guard as he ushered Surapati into his coupé. Surapati looked around and heaved a sigh of relief. He liked the little compartment.

'All right then, sir. May I take your leave?'

'Many thanks.'

The guard left. Surapati settled down by the window and fished out a packet of cigarettes. He felt this was only the beginning of his success. Uttar Pradesh: Delhi, Agra, Allahabad, Varanasi, Lucknow. There were so many other states to visit, so many, many places to go to. A whole new world waited for him. He would travel abroad; and he would show them how a young man from Bengal could be successful anywhere in the world—even in America, the land that had produced the famous Houdini. Oh yes, he would show them all. This was just the beginning.

Anil came panting. 'Everything's fine,' he said.

'Did you check the locks?'

'Yes, sir.'

'Good.'

'I'm in the third bogey from yours.'

'Have they given the "line-clear" signal?'

'They're about to. I'll go now, sir. Would you like a cup of tea at Burdwan?'

'Yes, that would be nice.'

'I'll get it then.'

Anil left. Surapati lit his cigarette and looked out of the window absentmindedly. The sight of the jostling crowds, the porters running about and the sound of the hawker's cry soon melted away. His mind went back to his childhood. He was thirty-three now; on that particular day he could not have been more than eight. By the side of the road in the small village where he lived sat an old woman with a gunny bag in front of her, surrounded by a large crowd. How old could she have been? Sixty? Ninety? It might have been anything. Her age did not matter. What mattered was what she did with her hands. She'd take any object—a coin, a marble, a top, a betel nut, even a guava—and it would vanish before their eyes. The old woman kept up an endless patter until the lost object reappeared out of nowhere. She took a rupee from Kalu Kaka and it disappeared. Much upset, Kalu Kaka began to lose his temper. The old woman giggled and—hey presto—the rupee was there for all to see. Kalu Kaka's eyes nearly popped out.

Surapati could not concentrate on anything much after that day. He never saw that old woman again. Nor did he see such a startling performance anywhere else.

He was sixteen when he came to Calcutta for further studies. The first thing he did upon arrival was to buy as many books on magic as he possibly could and to begin practising the tricks they taught. It meant standing before a mirror for hours with several packs of cards, going through the instructions step by step. But soon, he had mastered them all. Then he began performing at small get-togethers and parties given by friends.

When he was in his second year in college, one of his friends, Gautam, invited Surapati to his sister's wedding. It later proved to be the most memorable evening in the history of Surapati's training as a magician, for that day he met Tripura Babu for the first time.

A huge shamiana stood behind a house in Swinhoe Street. Tripuracharan Mallik sat under it, surrounded by a group of other wedding guests. At the first glance, he seemed quite ordinary. About forty-eight years old, curly hair parted at one side, a smile on his lips, the corners of his mouth streaked with the juice of paan. A man no different from the millions one saw every day. But a closer look at what was happening on the mattress in front of him was enough for one's judgement to undergo a quick change. Surapati, at first, could not believe his own eyes. A silver coin went rolling towards a golden ring kept about a yard away. It stopped beside the ring and then both came rolling back to Tripura Babu. Even before Surapati could recover from the shock, Gautam's uncle accidentally dropped a matchbox on the ground. All the sticks spilled out. 'Don't bother to pick them up,' said Tripura Babu, 'I'll pick them up for you.' With one sweeping movement of his hand, he placed the matchsticks in a heap on the mattress. Then, taking the empty matchbox in his left hand, he began calling, 'Come to me, my dear. Come, come, come . . .' The sticks rose in the air one by one and slipped back into the box as though they were all his pet animals used to obeying their master's command.

Surapati went to him straight after dinner. Tripura Babu seemed very surprised at his interest. 'I have never seen anyone interested in learning magic. Most seem happy simply to see a performance,' he said.

Surapati went to his house a couple of days later. It was, actually, much less than a house. Tripura Babu lived in a small room in an old and dilapidated boarding-house. Poverty stared out of every corner. Tripura Babu told him how he tried to make a living out of his magic shows. He charged fifty rupees per show, but did not get too many invitations. The main reason for this, Surapati soon discovered, was Tripura Babu's own lack of enthusiasm. Surapati could not imagine how anyone so talented could be so totally devoid of ambition. When he mentioned this, Tripura Babu said with a sigh, 'What would be the use of trying to do more shows? How many people would be interested? How many people appreciate the talent of a true artist? Didn't you see for yourself how everyone rushed off at that wedding the minute dinner was announced? Did anyone, with the sole exception of yourself, come back to me?'

Surapati spoke to his friends after this and arranged a few

shows. Tripura Babu agreed to teach him his art, possibly partly out of gratitude and partly out of a genuine affection for the boy. 'I do not want any payment,' he said firmly. 'I am only glad that there will be someone to take things forward after I've gone. But remember—you must be patient. Nothing can be learnt in a hurry. If you learn something well, you will know what joy there is in creation. Do not expect a lot of success or fame to come to you immediately. But I know you will do much better in life than I have done, for you have got what I haven't: ambition.'

Slightly nervous, Surapati asked, 'Will you teach me all that you know? Even the one with the coin and the ring?' Tripura Babu laughed. 'You must learn to walk step by step. Patience and diligence are the key words in this form of art. It evolved in ancient times when man's will-power and concentration were far more intense. It is not easy for modern man to get there. You don't know what an effort I had to make!'

Surapati began to go to Tripura Babu regularly. But about six months later, something happened that changed his life completely.

One day on his way to college, Surapati noticed a lot of colourful posters on the walls of Chowringhee: 'Shefallo the Great', they said. A closer look revealed that Shefallo was an Italian magician. He was coming to Calcutta, accompanied by his assistant, Madame Palarmo.

They performed at the New Empire. Surapati sat in a one-rupee seat and watched each item, absolutely entranced. He had only read about these in books. Men disappeared into a cloud of smoke before his eyes, and then reappeared from the same spiralling smoke like the djinn of Alladin. A girl was placed inside a wooden box. Shefallo sawed the box into two halves, but the girl came out smiling from another box, quite unharmed. Surapati's palms hurt from clapping that night.

He watched Shefallo carefully. He seemed as good an actor

as a magician. He wore a shining black suit. In his hand was a magic wand and on his head a top hat. An endless stream of objects kept pouring out of the hat. He put his hand in it once and pulled out a rabbit by its ear. Even before the poor creature had stopped flicking its long ears, out came one pigeon after another—one, two, three, four. They began to flutter around the stage. In the meantime, Shefallo had brought out a lot of chocolates from the hat which he began to throw at the audience.

Surapati noticed one more thing. Shefallo did not stop talking for an instant while he performed. He learnt later that this was what was known as magician's patter. While the audience stayed captivated by his constant flow of words, the magician quietly performed his tricks: the sleight of hand, the little deceptions.

But Madame Palarmo was different. She did not utter a word. How, then, could she deceive everyone? Surapati later learnt the answer to this one. It was possible to show certain items on the stage where the magician's own hands had very little to do. Everything could be controlled by highly mechanized equipment, operated by men from behind a black curtain. To show a man vanish into smoke or to saw a girl in two halves were both such tricks, dependent entirely on the use of equipment. Anyone who had enough money could buy the equipment and perform on stage. But, of course, one had to know the art of presentation, too. One had to have the right flair, the right touch of glamour in the total presentation of the act. Not everyone could do that. Not everyone . . .

Surapati came out of his reverie with a start. The train had just begun to pull out of the station rather jerkily when a man opened the door of his carriage from outside and clambered in. Surapati was about to protest, saying the seats were reserved, but one look at the man's face made him stop short in amazement.

Good God—it was Tripura Babu!

Tripuracharan Mallik!

There had been instances in the past when Surapati had had a similar experience. To see an acquaintance in person soon after thinking about him was something that had happened to Surapati before. But finding Tripura Babu in his carriage like this made every other incident of the past pale into insignificance.

Surapati remained speechless. Tripura Babu wiped his forehead with the edge of his dhoti, placed the bundle he was carrying on the bench opposite and sat down. Then he looked at Surapati and smiled: 'Surprised, aren't you?'

Surapati swallowed hard. 'I . . . yes, I'm surprised. In fact, I wasn't sure that you were still alive!'

'Really?'

'Yes. I went to your boarding-house soon after I finished college. I found your room locked. The manager told me you had been run over by a car . . .'

Tripura Babu laughed. 'That would have been rather nice. At least I might have escaped from all my worries and anxieties.'

'Besides,' said Surapati, 'I was thinking of you a little while ago.'

'Oh yes?' a shadow passed over Tripura Babu's face. 'Were you indeed thinking of me? You mean you still do? That's amazing!'

Surapati bit his lip in embarrassment. 'Don't say that, Tripura Babu! How could I forget you? Were you not my first teacher? I was thinking of our days together. This is the first time I am going out of Bengal to perform. I am now a professional magician—did you know that?'

Tripura Babu nodded. 'Yes. I know all about you. That is why I have come to see you today. You see, I have followed your career very closely for the last twelve years. When you had your show at the New Empire, I went there the very first day and sat in the last row. I saw how everyone applauded. Yes, I did feel proud of you. But . . .'

He stopped. Surapati could not find anything to say. There was very little to be said anyway. One could not blame Tripura Babu if he had ended up feeling hurt and left out. After all, if he had not helped Surapati in the very beginning, Surapati could not be where he was today. But what had he done for Tripura Babu in return? Nothing. On the contrary, the memory of Tripura Babu and his early days had grown quite faint in his mind. So had the feeling of gratitude.

Tripura Babu began speaking again. 'Yes, I felt proud of you that day, seeing how successful you were. But I also felt slightly sorry. Do you know why? It was because the path you have chosen is not the right path for a true magician. You may be able to provide entertainment to your audience and even impress them a good deal by using all those gadgets. None of the success would be your own. Do you remember my kind of magic?'

Surapati had not forgotten. He could also remember how Tripura Babu seemed to hesitate when it came to teaching him his best tricks. 'You need a little more time,' he would say. But the right time never came. Shefallo arrived soon afterwards and, two months later, Tripura Babu himself disappeared.

Surapati had felt both surprised and disappointed not to have found Tripura Babu where he lived. But these feelings did not last for very long. His mind was too full of Shefallo and dreams of his own future—to travel everywhere, to have shows in every place, to be a name everyone recognized, to hear only applause and praise wherever he went.

Tripura Babu was staring out of the window, preoccupied. Surapati looked at him a little more closely. He did seem to have hit upon hard times. Practically all his hair had turned grey, his skin sagged, his eyes had sunk very deep into their sockets. But had the look in them dimmed even a little? No! The look in his eyes was startlingly piercing.

He sighed, 'I know of course why you chose this path. I know you believe—and perhaps I am partly responsible for this—that simplicity itself is not often rewarded. A stage performance needs a touch of glamour and sophistication, does it not?'

Surapati did not disagree. Shefallo's performance had convinced him. Surely a bit of glamour did not do any harm? Things were different today. How much could one achieve by holding simple shows at weddings? How could one claim to be successful if one had to starve? Surapati had every respect for magic in its pure form without any trimmings. But that kind of magic had no future. Surapati knew it and had, therefore, decided to walk a different path.

He said as much to Tripura Babu, who suddenly became agitated. Sitting cross-legged on the bench, he leant forward excitedly. 'Listen, Surapati,' he said, 'if you knew what real magic was, you wouldn't chase what is fake. Magic is not just a sleight of hand, although even that requires years of careful practice. There is so much more to it! Hypnotism! Just think of it—you can control a person completely simply by looking at him. Then there is clairvoyance, telepathy and thought-reading. You can step into someone else's thoughts if you so wish. You can tell what a person is thinking just by feeling his pulse. If you can master this art, you need not even touch a person. All you need to do is just stare at him for a minute and you can read his thoughts. This is the greatest magic of all. Equipment and gadgets have no place in this. What is required is dedication, diligence and intense concentration.'

Tripura Babu stopped for breath. Then he slid closer to Surapati and went on, 'I wanted to teach you all this. But you couldn't wait. A fraud from abroad turned your head. You left the right path and went astray, only to make a fast buck in a world of pomp and show.'

Surapati remained silent. He could not deny any of this.

Tripura Babu seemed to relent a little. He laid a hand on Surapati's shoulder and continued in a milder tone, 'I have come today only to make a request. You may have guessed by now that my financial condition is not a sound one. I know a lot of tricks, but I haven't yet learnt the trick of making money. I know the only reason for this is my lack of ambition. Today I am almost desperate, Surapati. I do not have the strength any more to try to make my own living. All I am sure of is that you will help me, even if it means making a sacrifice. Do this for me, Surapati, and I promise not to bother you any more.'

Surapati was puzzled. What kind of help did the man want?

Tripura Babu went on, 'What I am going to tell you now may strike you as impertinent. But there is no other way. You see, it is not just money that I want. I have got a strange desire in my old age. I want to perform on a stage before a large audience. I want to show them the best trick I know. This may be the first and the last time, but I cannot put the thought out of my mind.'

A cold hand clutched at Surapati's heart. Tripura Babu finally came to the point. 'You are going to perform in Lucknow, aren't you? Suppose you fell ill at the last moment? You cannot, obviously, disappoint your audience. Suppose someone else took your place . . .?'

Surapati felt completely taken aback. What on earth was he saying? He really must be desperate, or he wouldn't come up with such a bizarre proposal.

His eyes fixed on Surapati, Tripura Babu said, 'All you need to do is tell people you cannot perform due to an unavoidable reason, but that your place would be taken by your guru. Would people be very sorry and heartbroken? I don't think so. I do believe they'd enjoy my show. But even so, I propose you take half of the proceeds of the first evening. I would be quite happy with the rest. After that you can go your own way. I will never disturb you again. But you must give me this opportunity, Surapati—just this once!'

'Impossible!' Surapati grew angry. 'What you're suggesting is quite impossible. You don't know what you're saying. This is the first time I'm going to perform outside Bengal. Can't you see how much this show in Lucknow means to me? Do you really expect me to begin my new career with a lie? How could you even think of it?'

Tripura Babu gave him a cool, level look. Then his voice cut across the railway carriage, rising clearly above all the noise: 'Are you still interested in that old trick with the coin and ring?'

Surapati started. But the look in Tripura Babu's eyes did not change.

'Why?' Surapati asked.

Tripura Babu smiled faintly, 'If you accept my proposal, I will teach you the trick. If you don't . . .'

His voice was drowned at this moment in the loud whistle of a Howrah-bound train that passed theirs. Its flashing lights caught the strange brilliance in his eyes.

'And if I don't?' Surapati asked softly once the noise had died down.

'You will regret it. There is something you ought to know. If I happen to be present among the audience, I do have the power to cause a magician—any magician—a lot of embarrassment. I can even make him completely helpless.'

Tripura Babu took out a pack of cards from his pocket. 'Let's see how good you are. Can you take this knave from the back and bring it forward to rest on this three of clubs, in just one movement of your hand?'

This was one of the first things Surapati had learnt. At the age of sixteen it had taken him only seven days to master this one.

And today?

Surapati took the pack of cards and realized that his fingers were beginning to feel numb. Then the numbness spread to his wrist, his elbow and, finally, the whole arm became paralysed. In a daze, Surapati looked at Tripura Babu. His mouth was twisted in a queer smile and his eyes stared straight into Surapati's. The look in them was almost inhuman. Little beads of perspiration broke out on Surapati's forehead. His whole body began to tremble.

'Do you now believe in my power?'

The pack of cards fell from Surapati's hand. Tripura Babu picked it up neatly and said, 'Would you now agree to my proposal?'

Surapati began to feel a little better. The numbness was passing. 'Will you really teach me that old trick?' he asked wearily.

Tripura Babu raised a finger, 'Your guru, Mr Tripuracharan Mallik, shall perform in your place in Lucknow because of your sudden illness. Is that right?'

'Yes.'

'You will give me half of your earnings that evening. Right?'

'Right.'

'Well, then . . .

Surapati fished out a fifty-paise coin from his pocket and took off his coral ring. Wordlessly, he handed them over to Tripura Babu.

When the train stopped at Burdwan, Anil appeared with a cup of tea and found his boss fast asleep.

'Sir!' said Anil after a few seconds of hesitation. Surapati woke instantly.

'Who . . . what is it?'

'Your tea, sir. Sorry I disturbed you.'

'But . . .?' Surapati looked around wildly.

'What's the matter?'

'Tripura Babu? Where is he?'

'Tripura Babu?' Anil sounded perplexed.

'Oh, no, no. He was run over, wasn't he? Way back in '51. But where is my ring?'

'Which one, sir? The one with the coral is on your finger!'

'Yes, yes, of course. And . . .'

Surapati put his hand in his pocket and took out a coin. Anil noticed that his employer's hands were trembling visibly. 'Anil,' Surapati called, 'come in quickly. Shut the windows. OK. Now watch this.'

Surapati placed the ring at one end of the bench and the coin at the other. 'Help me God!' he prayed silently and turned a deep hypnotic stare fully on the coin, just as he had been taught a few minutes ago. The coin began rolling towards the ring and then both coin and ring rolled back to Surapati like a couple of obedient children.

Anil would have dropped the cup on the floor he was carrying if Surapati had not stretched out a hand miraculously at the last moment and caught it in mid-air.

Surapati began his show in Lucknow by paying tribute to Tripuracharan Mallik, his guru, who was no more.

The last item he presented that evening was introduced as true Indian magic. The trick of the coin and the ring.

(1963)   *Translated by Gopa Majumdar*

ASHAMANJA BABU'S DOG

On a visit to a friend in Hashimara, Ashamanja Babu was able to fulfil one of his long-cherished desires.

Ashamanja Babu lived in a small flat on Mohini Mohan Road in Bhowanipore. A clerk in the registry department of Lajpat Rai Post Office, Ashamanja Babu was fortunate as he could walk to his office in seven minutes flat without having to fight his way into the buses and trains of Calcutta. He lived a rather carefree life as he was not the kind of person to sit and brood about what might have been had Fate been kinder to him. On the whole, he was quite content with his lot. Two Hindi films and a dozen packets of cigarettes a month, and fish twice a week—these were enough to keep him happy. The only thing that perturbed him at times was his lack of companionship. A bachelor with few friends and relatives, he often wished he had a dog to keep him company. It need not be a huge Alsatian like the one owned by the Talukdars, who lived two houses down the lane, it could be any ordinary little dog which would follow him around morning and evening, wag its tail when he came home from work and obey his orders with alacrity. Ashamanja Babu's secret desires were that he would speak to his dog in English. 'Stand up', 'Sit down', 'Shake hands'—how nice it would be if his dog obeyed such commands! Ashamanja Babu liked to believe that dogs belonged to the English race. Yes, an

English dog, and he would be its master. That would make him really happy.

On a cloudy day marked by a steady drizzle, Ashamanja Babu went to the market in Hashimara to buy some oranges. At one end of the market, beside a stunted kul tree, sat a Bhutanese holding a cigarette between his thumb and forefinger. As their eyes met, the man smiled. Was he a beggar? His clothes made him look like one. Ashamanja Babu noticed at least five sewn-on patches on his trousers and jacket. But the man didn't have a begging bowl. Instead, by his side was a shoe-box with a little pup sticking its head out of it.

'Good morning!' said the man in English, his eyes reduced to slits as he smiled. Ashamanja Babu was obliged to return the greeting.

'Buy dog? Dog buy? Very good dog.' The man had taken the pup out of the box and had put it down on the ground. 'Very cheap. Very good. Happy dog.'

The pup shook the raindrops off its coat, looked at Ashamanja Babu and wagged its minuscule two-inch tail. Ashamanja Babu moved closer to the pup, crouched on the ground and stretched out his hand. The pup gave his ring finger a lick with its pink tongue. Nice, friendly dog.

'How much? What price?'

'Ten rupees.'

A little haggling, and the price came down to seven-fifty. Ashamanja Babu paid the money, put the pup back in the shoe-box, closed the lid to save it from the drizzle, and turned homewards, forgetting all about the oranges.

Biren Babu, who worked in the Hashimara State Bank, had no idea about his friend's wish to own a dog. He was naturally surprised and a bit alarmed to see what the shoe-box contained. But when he heard the price, he heaved a sigh of relief. He said in a tone of mild reprimand, 'Why come all the way to

Hashimara to buy a mongrel? You could easily have bought one in Bhowanipore.'

That was not true; Ashamanja Babu knew it. He had often seen mongrel pups in the streets in his neighbourhood. None of them had ever wagged its tail at him or licked his fingers. Whatever Biren might say, this dog was something special. But the fact that the pup was a mongrel was something of a disappointment to Ashamanja Babu too, and he said so. Biren Babu's retort came sharp and quick. 'But do you know what it means to keep a pedigree dog as a pet? The vet's fees alone would cost you half a month's salary. With this dog you have no worries. You don't even need to give it a special diet. He'll eat what you eat. But don't give him fish. Fish is for cats; dogs have trouble with fish-bones.'

Back in Calcutta, it occurred to Ashamanja Babu that he had to think of a name for the pup. He wanted to give it an English name, but the only one he could think of was Tom. Then, looking at the pup one day, it struck him that since it was brown in colour, Brownie would be a good name for it. A cousin of his had a camera of an English make called Brownie, so the name must be an English one. The moment he decided on the name and tried it on the pup, it jumped off a wicker stool and padded up to him wagging its tail. Ashamanja Babu said, 'Sit down,' and immediately the dog sat on its haunches and opened its mouth in a tiny yawn. Ashamanja Babu had a fleeting vision of Brownie winning the first prize for cleverness in a dog show.

It was lucky that his servant Bipin had also taken a fancy to the dog. While Ashamanja Babu was away at work, Bipin gladly took it upon himself to look after Brownie. Ashamanja Babu had warned Bipin against feeding the dog rubbish. 'And see that he doesn't go out into the street. Car drivers these days seem to wear blinkers.' But however much he might instruct his servant, his worry would linger until he returned from work, and

Brownie greeted him ecstatically, his tail wagging fast.

The incident took place three months after returning from Hashimara. It was a Saturday, and the date was November the twenty-third. Ashamanja Babu had just got back from work and sat down on the old wooden chair—the only piece of furniture in the room apart from the bed and the wicker stool—when it suddenly collapsed under him and sent him sprawling on the floor. Naturally, he was hurt and, in fact, was wondering if, like the rickety leg of the chair, his right elbow was also out of commission, when an unexpected sound made him forget all about his pain.

It had come from the bed. It was the sound of laughter or, more accurately, a giggle, the source of which was undoubtedly Brownie, who sat on the bed, his lips still curled up.

If Ashamanja Babu's general knowledge had been wider, he would surely have known that dogs never laughed. And if he had any modicum of imagination, the incident would have robbed him of his sleep. In the absence of either, what Ashamanja Babu did was to sit down with the book *All About Dogs* which he had bought for two rupees from a second-hand book shop in Free School Street. He searched for an hour but found no mention in the book of laughing dogs.

And yet there wasn't the slightest doubt that Brownie had laughed. Not only that, he had laughed because there had been cause for laughter. Ashamanja Babu could clearly recall a similar incident from his own childhood. A doctor had come on a visit to their house in Chandernagore and had sat on a chair which had collapsed under him. Ashamanja Babu had burst out in a fit of laughter, and as a result had his ears twisted by his father.

He shut the book and looked at Brownie. As their eyes met, Brownie put his front paws on the pillow and wagged his tail, which had grown an inch and a half longer in three months.

There was no trace of a smile on his face now. Why should there be? To laugh without reason was a sign of madness. Ashamanja Babu felt relieved that Brownie was not a mad dog.

On two more occasions within a week of this incident, Brownie had reason to laugh. The first took place at night, at around nine-thirty. Ashamanja Babu had just spread a white sheet on the floor for Brownie to sleep on when a cockroach came fluttering into the room and settled on the wall. Ashamanja Babu picked up a slipper and flung it at the insect. The slipper missed its target, landed on the mirror hanging on the wall, and sent it crashing to the floor. This time Brownie's laughter more than compensated for the loss of his mirror.

The second time it was not laughter, but a brief snicker. Ashamanja Babu was puzzled, nothing had happened. So why the snicker? His servant Bipin provided the answer when he came into the room. He glanced at his master and said, smiling, 'There's shaving soap right by your ears, sir.' With his mirror broken, Ashamanja Babu had to use one of the window panes for shaving. He now felt with his fingers and found that Bipin was right.

That Brownie should laugh even when the reason was so trifling surprised Ashamanja Babu a great deal. Sitting at his desk in the post office, he found his thoughts turning again and again to the smile on Brownie's face and the sound of the snicker. *All About Dogs* may say nothing about a dog's laughter, but if he could get hold of something like an encyclopaedia of dogs, there was sure to be a mention of laughter in it.

When four book shops in Bhowanipore—and all the ones in New Market—failed to produce such an encyclopaedia, Ashamanja Babu wondered whether he should call on Mr Rajani Chatterji. The retired professor lived not far from his house on the same street. Ashamanja Babu didn't know what subject Rajani Babu had taught, but he had seen through the

window of his house many fat books in a bookcase in what
appeared to be the professor's study.

So, on a Sunday morning, Ashamanja Babu offered up a
silent prayer to goddess Durga for help in this adventure, and
made his way to Professor Chatterji's house. He had seen him
several times from a distance, and had no idea he had such thick
eyebrows and a voice so grating. But since the professor didn't
turn him away from the door, Ashamanja Babu took courage
and sat himself down on a sofa opposite the professor. Then he
gave a short cough and waited. Professor Chatterji put aside the
newspaper he was reading and turned his attention to the visitor.

'Your face seems familiar.'

'I live close by.'

'I see. Well?'

'I have seen a dog in your house; that is why . . .'

'So what? We have two dogs, not one.'

'I see, I have one too.'

'Are you employed to count the number of dogs in the city?'

Ashamanja Babu missed the sarcasm in the question. He
said, 'I have come to ask if you have something I've been
looking for.'

'What is it?'

'I wonder if you have a dog encyclopaedia.'

'No, I don't. Why do you need one?'

'You see, my dog laughs. So I wanted to find out if it was
natural for dogs to laugh. Do your dogs laugh?'

Throughout the time it took the wall clock in the room took
to strike eight, Professor Chatterji looked steadily at Ashamanja
Babu. Then he asked, 'Does your dog laugh at night?'

'Well, yes—even at night.'

'And what are your preferences in drugs? Only ganja can't
produce such symptoms. Perhaps you take charas and hashish
as well?'

Ashamanja Babu meekly answered that his only vice was smoking—and even that he had had to reduce from three packets a week to two ever since the arrival of his dog.

'And yet you say your dog laughs?'

'I have seen and heard him laugh, with my own eyes and ears.'

'Listen.' Professor Chatterji took off his spectacles, cleaned them with his handkerchief, put them on again and fixed Ashamanja Babu with a hard stare. Then he declaimed in the tones of a classroom lecture:

'I am amazed at your ignorance concerning a fundamental fact of nature. Of all the creatures created by God, only the human species is capable of laughter. This is one of the prime differences between Homo sapiens and other creatures. Don't ask me why it should be so, because I do not know. I have heard that a marine species called the dolphin has a sense of humour. Dolphins may be the single exception. Apart from them there are none. It is not clearly understood why human beings should laugh. Great philosophers have racked their brains to find out why; but have not succeeded. Do you understand?'

Ashamanja Babu understood; he also understood that it was time for him to take his leave because the professor had once again picked up his newspaper and disappeared behind it.

Doctor Sukhomoy Bhowmick—some called him Doctor Bow-wow-mick—was a well-known vet. Hoping that a vet might listen to him even if other people didn't, Ashamanja Babu made an appointment on the phone and took Brownie to the vet's residence on Gokhale Road. Brownie had laughed seventeen times in the last four months. One thing Ashamanja Babu had noticed was that Brownie didn't laugh at funny remarks; only at funny incidents. Ashamanja Babu had recited the nonsense-rhyme *King of Bombardia* to Brownie, and it had produced no effect on him. And yet when a potato from a curry slipped from Ashamanja Babu's fingers and landed in a plate of curd, Brownie had almost choked with laughter. Professor Chatterji had lectured him about God's creatures but here was living proof that the learned gentleman was wrong.

So Ashamanja Babu went to the vet, though he knew that he would be charged twenty rupees for the visit. But even before the vet heard of the dog's unique trait, his eyebrows had shot up at the dog's appearance. 'I've seen mongrels, but never one like this.'

He lifted the dog and placed him on the table. Brownie sniffed at the brass paperweight at his feet.

'What do you feed him?'

'He eats what I eat, sir. He has no pedigree, you see . . .'

Doctor Bhowmick frowned. He was observing the dog with great interest. 'We can tell a pedigree dog when we see one. But sometimes we are not so sure. This one, for instance. I would hesitate to call him a mongrel. I suggest that you stop feeding him rice and daal. I'll make a diet chart for him.'

Ashamanja Babu now made an attempt to come out with the real reason for his visit. 'I—er, my dog has a speciality—which is why I have brought him to you.'

'Speciality?'

'The dog laughs.'

'Laughs—?'

'Yes, laughs, like you and me.'

'You don't say! Well, can you make him laugh now, so I can see?'

Now Ashamanja Babu was stumped. By nature a shy person, he was quite unable to make faces at Brownie to make him laugh, nor was it likely that something funny should happen here at this very moment. So he had to tell the doctor that Brownie didn't laugh when asked to, but only when he saw something funny happening.

After this Doctor Bhowmick didn't have much time left for Ashamanja Babu. He said, 'Your dog looks distinctive enough; don't try to make him more so by claiming that he laughs. I can tell you from my twenty-two years' experience that dogs cry, dogs feel afraid, dogs show anger, hatred, distrust and jealousy. Dogs even dream, but dogs don't laugh.'

After this encounter, Ashamanja Babu decided that he would never tell anyone about Brownie's laughter again. Why court embarrassment when he could not prove his story? What did it matter if others never knew? He himself knew. Brownie was his dog, his own property. Why drag outsiders into their private world?

But things don't always go according to plans. One day, Brownie's laughter was revealed to an outsider.

For some time, Ashamanja Babu had developed the habit of taking Brownie for a walk in the afternoon near the Victoria Memorial. One April day, in the middle of their walk, a big storm came up suddenly. Ashamanja Babu glanced at the sky and decided that it wasn't safe to try to get back home as the rain would start pelting down any minute. So he ran with Brownie and took shelter below the marble arch with the black equestrian statue on it.

Meanwhile, huge drops of rain had started to fall and people were looking for shelter. A stout man in a white bush shirt and trousers, twenty paces away from the arch, opened his umbrella and held it over his head when a sudden strong gust of wind turned the umbrella inside out with a loud snap.

To tell the truth, Ashamanja Babu himself was about to burst out laughing, but Brownie beat him to it with a loud canine guffaw the sound of which rose above the cacophony of the storm and reached the ear of the hapless gentleman. The man stopped trying to bring the umbrella back to its original shape and stared at Brownie in utter amazement. Brownie was now quite helpless with laughter. Ashamanja Babu had tried frantically to suppress it by clapping his hand over the dog's mouth, but had given up.

The dumbfounded gentleman walked over to Ashamanja Babu as if he had seen a ghost. Brownie's paroxysm was now subsiding, but it was still enough to make the gentleman's eyes pop out of his head.

'A laughing dog!'

'Yes, a laughing dog,' said Ashamanja Babu.

'But how extraordinary!'

Ashamanja Babu could make out that the man was not a Bengali. Perhaps he was a Gujrati or a Parsi. Ashamanja Babu braced himself to answer in English the questions he knew he would soon be bombarded with.

The rain had turned into a heavy shower. The gentleman took shelter alongside Ashamanja Babu, and in ten minutes had found out all there was to know about Brownie. He also took down Ashamanja Babu's address. He said his name was Piloo Pochkanwalla, that he knew a lot about dogs and wrote about them occasionally, and that his experience today had surpassed anything that had ever happened to him, or was likely to happen in the future. He felt something had to be done about it, since Ashamanja Babu himself was obviously unaware of what a priceless treasure he owned.

It wouldn't be wrong to say that Brownie was responsible for Mr Pochkanwalla being knocked down by a minibus while crossing Chowringhee Road soon after the rain had stopped—it was the thought of the laughing dog running through his head which made him a little unmindful of the traffic. After spending two and half months in hospital, Pochkanwalla went off to Nainital to recuperate. He came back to Calcutta after a month in the hills, and the same evening, he made his way to the Bengal Club and described the incident of the laughing dog to his friends Mr Balaporia and Mr Biswas. Within half an hour, the story had reached the ears of twenty-seven other members and three bearers of the club. By next morning, the incident was known to at least a thousand citizens of Calcutta.

Brownie hadn't laughed once during these three and a half months. One good reason was that he had seen no funny incidents. Ashamanja Babu didn't see it as cause for alarm; it had never crossed his mind to cash in on Brownie's unique gift. He was happy with the way Brownie had filled a yawning gap in his life, and felt more drawn to him than he had to any human being.

Among those who got the news of the laughing dog was an executive in the office of the *Statesman*. He sent for reporter Rajat Chowdhury and suggested that he should interview the owner of this laughing dog.

Ashamanja Babu was greatly surprised that a reporter should think of calling on him. It was when Rajat Chowdhury mentioned Pochkanwalla that the reason for the visit became clear. He asked the reporter into his bedroom. The wooden chair had been fitted with a new leg, and Ashamanja Babu offered it to the reporter while he himself sat on the bed. Brownie had been observing a line of ants crawling up the wall; he now jumped up on the bed and sat beside Ashamanja Babu.

Rajat Chowdhury was about to press the recording switch on his tape recorder when it suddenly occurred to Ashamanja Babu that a word of warning was needed. 'By the way, sir, my dog used to laugh quite frequently, but in the last few months he hasn't laughed at all. So you may be disappointed if you are expecting to see him laugh.'

Like many a young energetic reporter, Rajat Chowdhury exuded a cheerful confidence in the presence of a good story. Although he was slightly disappointed, he was careful not to show it. He said, 'That's all right. I just want to get some details from you. To start with, his name. What do you call your dog?'

Ashamanja Babu bent down to speak closer to the mike. 'Brownie.'

'Brownie . . .'

The watchful eye of the reporter had noted that the dog had wagged his tail at the mention of his name. 'How old is he?'

'Thirteen months.'

'Where did you f-f-find the dog?'

This had happened before. Rajat Chowdhury's greatest handicap often showed itself in the middle of interviews, causing him no end of embarrassment. Here, too, the same thing might have happened had it not, unexpectedly, helped in drawing out Brownie's special characteristic. Thus Rajat Chowdhury was the second outsider after Pochkanwalla to see with his own eyes a dog laughing like a human being.

The morning of the following Sunday, sitting in his air-conditioned room in the Grand Hotel, Mr William P. Moody of Cincinnati, USA, read in the papers about the laughing dog and at once asked the hotel operator to put him through to Mr Nandy of the Indian Tourist Bureau. That Mr Nandy knew his way about the city had been made abundantly clear in the last couple of days when Mr Moody had occasion to use his services. The *Statesman* had printed the name and address of the owner of the laughing dog and Mr Moody was very anxious to meet this character.

Ashamanja Babu didn't read the *Statesman*. Besides, Rajat Chowdhury hadn't told him when the interview would appear in print, or he might have bought a copy. It was in the fish market that his neighbour Kalikrishna Dutt told him about it.

'You're a fine man,' said Mr Dutt. 'You've been guarding such a treasure in your house for over a year, and you haven't breathed a word to anybody about it? I must drop in at your place some time this evening and say hello to your dog.'

Ashamanja Babu's heart sank. He could see there was trouble ahead. There were many more like Mr Dutt in and around his neighbourhood who read the *Statesman* and who would want to 'drop in and say hello' to his dog. It was a most unnerving prospect.

Ashamanja Babu quickly made up his mind. He would spend the day away from home. So, with Brownie under his arm, for the first time in his life, he called a taxi and headed to the Ballygunge station where he boarded a train to Port Canning. Halfway there, the train pulled up at a station called Palsit. Ashamanja Babu liked the look of the place and got off. He spent the whole day roaming in the quiet bamboo groves and mango orchards and felt greatly refreshed. Brownie, too, seemed to enjoy himself. The gentle smile that played around his lips was something Ashamanja Babu had never noticed before. This was a benign smile, a smile of peace and contentment, a smile of inner happiness. He had read somewhere that a year in the life of a dog equalled seven years in the life of a human being. And yet he could scarcely imagine such tranquil behaviour in such surroundings from a seven-year-old human child.

It was past seven in the evening when Ashamanja Babu got back home. He asked Bipin if anyone had called. So when Bipin said he had to open the door to callers at least forty times, Ashamanja Babu obviously could not help congratulating himself on his foresight. He had just taken off his shoes and asked Bipin for a cup of tea when there was another knock on the front door. 'Oh, hell!' swore Ashamanja Babu. He went to the door and opened it, and found himself staring at a foreigner. 'Wrong number,' he was at the point of saying, when he caught sight of a young Bengali man standing behind the foreigner. 'Whom do you want?'

'You,' said Shyamol Nandy of the Indian Tourist Bureau.

'That is to say, if the dog standing behind you is yours. He certainly looks like the one described in the papers today. May we come in?'

Ashamanja Babu was obliged to ask them into his bedroom. The foreigner sat on the chair, Mr Nandy on the wicker stool, and Ashamanja Babu on his bed. Brownie, who seemed a bit ill at ease, chose to stay outside the threshold; probably because he had never seen two strangers in the room before.

'Brownie! Brownie! Brownie!' The foreigner leaned towards the dog and called him repeatedly. Brownie, with his eyes fixed on the stranger, was unmoved.

Who were these people, Ashamanja Babu was wondering to himself, when Mr Nandy provided the answer. The foreigner was a wealthy and distinguished citizen of the United States whose main purpose in coming to India was to look for old Rolls-Royce cars.

The American had now got off the chair and, sitting on his haunches, was making faces at the dog.

After three minutes of abortive clowning, the man gave up, turned to Ashamanja Babu and asked, 'Is he sick?'

Ashamanja Babu shook his head.

'Does he really laugh?' asked the American.

In case Ashamanja Babu was unable to follow the American's speech, Mr Nandy translated it for him.

'Brownie laughs,' said Ashamanja Babu, 'but only when he feels amused.'

A tinge of red spread over the American's face when Nandy translated Ashamanja Babu's answer to him. In no uncertain terms he let it be known that he wasn't willing to squander any money on the dog unless he had proof that it really laughed. He refused to be saddled with something which might later prove useless. He further let it be known that in his house he had precious objects from China to Peru, and that he had a parrot which spoke only Latin. 'I have brought my cheque book with me to pay for the laughing dog, but only if I have proof that it actually does so.'

He then proceeded to pull out a blue cheque book from his pocket to prove his statement. Ashamanja Babu glanced at it out of the corner of his eyes. Citibank of New York, it said on the cover.

'You would be walking on air,' said Mr Nandy temptingly. 'If you know a way to make the dog laugh, then out with it. This gentleman is ready to pay up to 20,000 dollars. That's two lakhs of rupees.'

The Bible says that God created the universe in six days. A human being, with his imagination, can do the same thing in six seconds. An image floated into Ashamanja Babu's mind at Mr Nandy's words. It was of himself in a spacious air-conditioned office, sitting in a swivel chair with his legs up on the table, the heady smell of hasu-no-hana wafting in through the window. But the image vanished like a pricked balloon at a sudden sound.

Brownie was laughing.

He had never laughed like this before.

'But he is laughing!'

Mr Moody was down on his knees, tense with excitement, watching the extraordinary spectacle. The cheque book came out again and, along with that, his gold Parker pen.

Brownie was still laughing. Ashamanja Babu was puzzled because he couldn't make out the reason for the laughter. Nobody had stammered, nobody had stumbled, nobody's umbrella had turned inside out, and no mirror on the wall had been hit with a slipper. Why then was Brownie laughing?

'You're very lucky,' commented Mr Nandy. 'I think I ought to get a percentage of the sale—wouldn't you say so?'

Mr Moody rose from the floor and sat down on the chair. He

said, 'Ask him how he spells his name.'

Although Mr Nandy relayed the question in Bengali, Ashamanja Babu didn't answer, because he had just seen the light, and the light filled his heart with a great sense of wonder. Instead of spelling his name, he said, 'Please tell the foreign gentleman that if he only knew why the dog was laughing, he wouldn't have opened his cheque book.'

'Why don't you tell me?' Mr Nandy snapped in a dry voice. He certainly didn't like the way events were shaping up. If the mission failed, he knew the American's wrath would fall on him.

Brownie had at last stopped laughing. Ashamanja Babu lifted him up on his lap, wiped his tears and said, 'My dog's laughing because the gentleman thinks money can buy everything.'

'I see,' said Mr Nandy. 'So your dog's a philosopher, is he?'

'Yes, sir.'

'That means you won't sell him?'

'No, sir.'

To Mr Moody, Shyamol Nandy only said that the owner had no intention of selling the dog. Mr Moody put the cheque book back in his pocket, slapped the dust off his knees and, on his way out of the room, said with a shake of his head, 'The guy must be crazy!'

When the sound of the American's car had faded away, Ashamanja Babu looked into Brownie's eyes and said, 'I was right about why you laughed, wasn't I?'

Brownie chuckled in assent.

(1978)   *Translated by Satyajit Ray*

PATOL BABU, FILM STAR

Patol Babu had just hung his shopping-bag on his shoulder when Nishikanto Babu called from outside the main door. 'Patol, are you in?'

'Oh, yes,' said Patol Babu. 'Just a minute.'

Nishikanto Ghosh lived three houses away from Patol Babu in Nepal Bhattacharji Lane. He was a genial person.

Patol Babu came out with the bag. 'What brings you here so early in the morning?'

'Listen, what time will you be back?'

'In an hour or so. Why?'

'I hope you'll stay in after that. I met my youngest brother-in-law in Netaji Pharmacy yesterday. He is in the film business, in the production department. He said he was looking for an actor for a scene in a film they're now shooting. The way he described the character—fiftyish, short, bald-headed—it reminded me of you. So I gave him your address and asked him to get in touch with you directly. I hope you won't turn him away. They'll pay you, of course.'

Patol Babu hadn't expected such news early in the morning. That an offer to act in a film could come to a fifty-two-year-old non-entity like him was beyond his wildest dreams.

'Well, yes or no?' asked Nishikanto Babu. 'I believe you did some acting on the stage at one time?'

'That's true,' said Patol Babu. 'I really don't see why I should say no. But let's talk to your brother-in-law first and find out some details. What's his name?'

'Naresh. Naresh Dutt. He's about thirty. A strapping young fellow. He said he would be here around ten-thirty.'

In the market, Patol Babu mixed up his wife's orders and bought red chillies instead of onion seeds. And he quite forgot about the aubergines. This was not surprising. At one time Patol Babu had a real passion for the stage; in fact, it verged on obsession. In jatras, in amateur theatricals, in plays put up by the club in his neighbourhood, Patol Babu was always in demand. His name had appeared in handbills on countless occasions. Once it appeared in bold type near the top: 'Sitalakanto Ray (Patol Babu) in the role of Parasar'. Indeed, there was a time when people bought tickets especially to see him.

That was when he used to live in Kanchrapara. He had a job in the railway factory there. In 1934, he was offered higher pay in a clerical post with Hudson and Kimberley in Calcutta, and was also lucky to find a flat in Nepal Bhattacharji Lane. He gave up his factory job and came to Calcutta with his wife. The sailing was smooth for some years, and Patol Babu was in his boss's good books. In 1943, when he was just toying with the idea of starting a club in his neighbourhood, sudden retrenchment in his office due to the war cost him his nine-year-old job.

Ever since then Patol Babu had struggled to make a living. At first he opened a variety store which he had to wind up after five years. Then he had a job in a Bengali firm which he gave up in disgust when his boss began to treat him in too high-handed a fashion. Then, for ten long years, starting as an insurance salesman, Patol Babu tried every means of earning a livelihood without ever succeeding in improving his lot. Of late he had been paying regular visits to a small establishment dealing in scrap iron where a cousin of his had promised him a job.

And acting? That had become a thing of the remote past; something which he recalled at times with a sigh. Endowed with a wonderful memory, Patol Babu would still reel off lines from some of the best parts he had played. 'Listen, O listen to the thunderous twang of the mighty bow Gandiva engaged in gory conflict, and to the angry roar of the mountainous club whizzing through the air in the hands of the great Brikodara!' It sent a shiver down his spine just to think of such lines.

Naresh Dutt turned up at half past twelve. Patol Babu had given up hope and was about to go for his bath when there was a knock on the front door.

'Come in, come in, sir!' Patol Babu almost dragged the young man in and pushed the broken-armed chair towards him. 'Do sit down.'

'No, thanks. I—er—I expect Nishikanto Babu told you about me?'

'Oh yes. I must say I was quite taken aback. After so many years . . .'

'I hope you have no objection?'

'You think I'll be all right for the part?' Patol Babu asked with great diffidence.

Naresh Dutt cast an appraising look at Patol Babu and gave a nod. 'Oh yes,' he said. 'There is no doubt about that. By the way, the shooting takes place tomorrow morning.'

'Tomorrow? Sunday?'

'Yes, and not in the studio. I'll tell you where you have to go. You know Faraday House near the crossing of Bentinck Street and Mission Row? It's a seven-storey office building. The shooting takes place outside the office in front of the entrance. We'll expect you there at eight-thirty sharp. You'll be through by midday.'

Naresh Dutt prepared to leave. 'But you haven't told me about the part,' said Patol Babu anxiously.

'Oh yes, sorry. The part is that of a—pedestrian. An absent-minded, short-tempered pedestrian. By the way, do you have a jacket which buttons up to the neck?'

'I think I do. You mean the old-fashioned kind?'

'Yes. That's what you'll wear. What colour is it?'

'Sort of nut-brown. But woollen.'

'That's all right. The story is supposed to take place in winter, so that would be just right. Tomorrow at 8.30 a.m. sharp. Faraday House.'

Patol Babu suddenly thought of a crucial question.

'I hope the part calls for some dialogue?'

'Certainly. It's a speaking part. You have acted before, haven't you?'

'Well, as a matter of fact, yes . . .'

'Fine. I wouldn't have come to you for just a walk-on part. For that we pick people from the street. Of course there's dialogue and you'll be given your lines as soon as you show up tomorrow.'

After Naresh Dutt left, Patol Babu broke the news to his wife.

'As far as I can see, the part isn't a big one. I'll be paid, of course, but that's not the main thing. The thing is—remember how I started on the stage? Remember my first part? I played a dead soldier! All I had to do was lie still on the stage with my arms and legs spread. And remember where I went from there? Remember Mr Watts shaking me by the hand? And the silver medal which the chairman of our municipality gave me? Remember? This is only the first step on the ladder, my dear! Yes—the first step that would—God willing—mark the rise to fame and fortune of your beloved husband!'

Suddenly, the fifty-two-year-old Patol Babu did a little skip. 'What are you doing?' his wife asked, aghast.

'Don't worry. Do you remember how Sisir Bhaduri used to

leap about on the stage at the age of seventy? I feel as if I've been born again!'

'Counting your chickens again before they're hatched, are you? No wonder you could never make a go of it.'

'But it's the real thing this time! Go and make me a cup of tea, will you? And remind me to take some ginger juice tonight. It's very good for the throat.'

The clock in the Metropolitan building showed seven minutes past eight when Patol Babu reached Esplanade. It took him another ten minutes to walk to Faraday House.

There was a big crowd outside the building. Three or four cars stood on the road. There was also a bus loaded with equipment on its roof. On the edge of the pavement there was an instrument on three legs around which a bunch of people were walking about looking busy. Near the entrance stood—also on three legs—a pole which had a long arm extending from its top with what looked like a small oblong beehive suspended at the end. Surrounding these instruments was a crowd of people among which Patol Babu noticed some non-Bengalis. What they were supposed to do he couldn't tell.

But where was Naresh Dutt? He was the only one who knew him.

With a slight tremor in his heart, Patol Babu advanced towards the entrance. It was the middle of summer, and the warm jacket buttoned up to his neck felt heavy. Patol Babu could feel beads of perspiration forming around the high collar.

'This way, Atul Babu!'

Atul Babu? Patol Babu spotted Naresh Dutt standing at the entrance and gesturing towards him. He had got his name wrong. No wonder, since they had only had a brief meeting. Patol Babu walked up, put his palms together in a namaskar and said, 'I suppose you haven't yet noted down my name. Sitalakanto Ray—although people know me better by my nickname Patol. I used it on the stage too.'

'Good, good. I must say you're quite punctual.'

Patol Babu rose to his full height.

'I was with Hudson and Kimberley for nine years and wasn't late for a single day.'

'Is that so? Well, I suggest you go and wait in the shade there. We have a few things to attend to before we get going.'

'Naresh!'

Somebody standing by the three-legged instrument called out.

'Sir?'

'Is he one of our men?'

'Yes, sir. He is—er—in that shot where they bump into each other.'

'Okay. Now, clear the entrance, will you? We're about to start.'

Patol Babu withdrew and stood in the shade of a paan shop.

He had never watched a film shooting before. How hard these people worked! A youngster of twenty or so was carrying that three-legged instrument on his shoulder. Must weigh at least sixty pounds.

But what about his dialogue? There wasn't much time left, and he still didn't know what he was supposed to do or say.

Patol Babu suddenly felt a little nervous. Should he ask somebody? There was Naresh Dutt there; should he go and remind him? It didn't matter if the part was small, but, if he had to make the most of it, he had to learn his lines beforehand. How small he would feel if he muffed in the presence of so many people! The last time he acted on stage was twenty years ago.

Patol Babu was about to step forward when he was pulled up short by a voice shouting 'Silence!'

This was followed by Naresh Dutt loudly announcing with hands cupped over his mouth: 'We're about to start shooting. Everybody please stop talking. Don't move from your positions and don't crowd round the camera, please!'

Once again the voice was heard shouting 'Silence! Taking!' Now Patol Babu could see the owner of the voice. He was a stout man of medium height, and he stood by the camera. Around his neck hung something which looked like a small telescope. Was he the director? How strange!—He hadn't even bothered to find out the name of the director!

Now a series of shouts followed in quick succession—'Start sound!' 'Running!' 'Camera!' 'Rolling!' 'Action!'

Patol Babu noticed that as soon as the word 'Action' was uttered, a car came up from the crossing and pulled up in front of the office entrance. Then a young man in a grey suit and pink make-up shot out of the back of the car, took a few hurried steps towards the entrance and stopped abruptly. The next moment Patol Babu heard the shout 'Cut!' and immediately the hubbub from the crowd resumed.

A man standing next to Patol Babu now turned to him. 'Did you recognize the young fellow?' he asked.

'What, no,' said Patol Babu.

'Chanchal Kumar,' said the man. 'He's coming up fast. Playing the lead in four films at the moment.'

Patol Babu saw very few films, but he seemed to have heard the name Chanchal Kumar. It was probably the same boy Koti Babu was praising the other day. Nice make-up the fellow had on. If he had been wearing a Bengali dhoti and kurta instead of a suit, and given a peacock to ride on, he would make a perfect Kartik, the god considered to be the epitome of good looks. Monotosh of Kanchrapara—who was better known by his nickname Chinu—had the same kind of looks. He used to be very good at playing female parts, recalled Patol Babu.

Patol Babu now turned to his neighbour and asked in a whisper, 'Who is the director?'

The man raised his eyebrows and said, 'Why, don't you know? He's Baren Mullick. He's had three smash hits in a row.'

Well, at least he had gathered some useful information. It wouldn't have done for him to say he didn't know if his wife had asked whose film he had acted in and with which actor.

Naresh Dutt now came up to him with tea in a small clay cup.

'Here you are, sir—the hot tea will help your throat. Your turn will come shortly.'

Patol Babu now had to come out with it.

'If you let me have my lines now . . .'

'Your lines? Come with me.'

Naresh Dutt went towards the three-legged instrument with Patol Babu at his heels.

'I say, Shoshanko.'

A young fellow in short-sleeved shirt turned towards Naresh Dutt. 'This gentleman wants his lines. Why don't you write them down on a piece of paper and give it to him? He's the one who . . .'

'I know, I know.'

Shoshanko now turned to Patol Babu.

'Come along, Dadu. I say, Jyoti, can I borrow your pen for a sec? Grandpa wants his lines written down.'

The youngster Jyoti produced a red ballpoint pen from his pocket and gave it to Shoshanko. Shoshanko tore off a page from the notebook he was carrying, scribbled something on it and handed it to Patol Babu.

Patol Babu glanced at the paper and found that a single word had been scrawled on it—'Oh!'

Patol Babu felt a sudden throbbing in his head. He wished he could take off his jacket. The heat was unbearable.

Shoshanko said, 'What's the matter, Dadu? You don't seem too pleased.'

Were these people pulling his leg? Was the whole thing a gigantic hoax? A meek, harmless man like him, and they had to drag him into the middle of the city to make a laughing stock out of him. How could anyone be so cruel?

Patol Babu said in a voice hardly audible, 'I find it rather strange.'

'Why, Dadu?'

'Just "Oh"? Is that all I have to say?'

Shoshanko's eyebrows shot up.

'What are you saying, Dadu? You think that's nothing? Why, this is a regular speaking part! A speaking part in a Baren Mullick film—do you realize what that means? Why, you're the luckiest of actors. Do you know that till now more than a hundred persons have appeared in this film who have had nothing to say? They just walked past the camera. Some didn't even walk; they just stood in one spot. There were others whose faces didn't register at all. Even today—look at all those people standing by the lamp-post; they all appear in today's scene but have nothing to say. Even our hero Chanchal Kumar has no lines to speak today. You are the only one who has—see?'

Now the young man called Jyoti came up, put his hand on Patol Babu's shoulder and said, 'Listen, Dadu. I'll tell you what you have to do. Chanchal Kumar is a rising young executive. He is informed that an embezzlement has taken place in his office, and he comes to find out what has happened. He gets out of his car and charges across the pavement towards the entrance. Just then he collides with an absent-minded pedestrian. That's you. You're hurt in the head and say "Oh!", but Chanchal Kumar pays no attention to you and goes into the office. The fact that he ignores you reflects his extreme preoccupation—see? Just think how crucial the shot is.'

'I hope everything is clear now,' said Shoshanko. 'Now, if you just move over to where you were standing . . . the fewer people crowding around here the better. There's one more shot left before your turn comes.'

Patol Babu slowly went back to the paan shop. Standing in the shade, he glanced down at the paper in his hand, cast a quick look around to see if anyone was watching, crumpled the paper into a ball and threw it into the roadside drain.

Oh . . . A sigh came out of the depths of his heart.

Just one word—no, not even a word; a sound—'Oh!'

The heat was stifling. The jacket seemed to weigh a ton. Patol Babu couldn't keep standing in one spot any more; his legs felt heavy.

He moved up to the office beyond the paan shop and sat down on the steps. It was nearly half-past nine. Every Sunday morning, devotional songs were sung in Karali Babu's house. Patol Babu went there every week and enjoyed it. What if he were to go there now? What harm would there be? Why waste a Sunday morning in the company of these useless people, and be made to look foolish on top of that?

'Silence!'

Stuff and nonsense! To hell with your 'silence'! They had to put up this pompous show for something so trivial. Things were much better on the stage.

The stage . . . the stage . . . A faint memory was stirring in Patol Babu's mind. Words of advice, given in a deep, mellow voice: 'Remember one thing, Patol; however small a part you're offered, never consider it beneath your dignity to accept it. As an artist your aim should be to make the most of your opportunity, and squeeze the last drop of meaning out of your lines. A play involves the work of many and it is the combined effort of many that makes a success of the play.'

It was Mr Pakrashi who gave the advice. Gogon Pakrashi, Patol Babu's mentor. A wonderful actor, without a trace of vanity in him; a saintly person, and an actor in a million.

There was something else which Mr Pakrashi used to say. 'Each word spoken in a play is like a fruit in a tree. Not everyone in the audience can reach it. But you, the actor, must know how to pluck it, get at its essence, and serve it up to the audience for their edification.'

The memory of his guru made Patol Babu bow his head in obeisance.

Was it really true that there was nothing in the part he had been given today? He had only one word to say—'Oh!', but was that word so devoid of meaning as to be dismissed summarily?

Oh, oh, oh, oh, oh—Patol Babu uttered the word over and over again, giving it a different inflection each time. After doing this for a number of times he made an astonishing discovery. The same exclamation, when spoken in different ways, carried different shades of meaning. A man when hurt said 'Oh' in one way. Despair brought forth a difficult kind of 'Oh', while sorrow provoked yet another kind. In fact, there were so many kinds of Ohs—the short Oh, the long-drawn Oh, Oh shouted and Oh whispered, the high-pitched Oh, the low-pitched Oh, the Oh starting low and ending high, and the Oh starting high and ending low . . . Strange! Patol Babu suddenly felt that he could write a whole thesis on that one monosyllabic exclamation. Why had he felt so disheartened when this single word contained a gold mine of meaning? The true actor could make a mark with this one single syllable.

'Silence!'

The director had raised his voice again. Patol Babu spotted young Jyoti clearing the crowd. There was something he had to ask him. He quickly went over to him.

'How long will it be before my turn comes, bhai?'

'Why are you so impatient, Dadu? You have to learn to be patient in this line of business. It'll be another half an hour before you're called.'

'That's all right. I'll certainly wait. I'll be in that side street across the road.'

'Okay—so long as you don't sneak off.'

'Start sound!'

Patol Babu crossed the road on tiptoe and went into the quiet little side street. It was good that he had a little time on his hands. While these people didn't seem to believe in rehearsals, he himself would rehearse his own bit. There was no one about. These were office buildings, so very few people lived here. Those who did—the shopkeepers—had all gone to watch the shooting.

Patol Babu cleared his throat and began to practise speaking this one-syllable dialogue in various ways. Along with that he tried working out how he would react to the actual collision—how his features would be twisted in pain, how he would fling out his arms, how his body would double up in pain and surprise—all these postures he performed in front of a large glass window.

Patol Babu was called in exactly after half an hour. Now he had got over his apathy completely. All he felt was keen anticipation and suppressed excitement. It was the feeling he used to have twenty years ago just before he stepped on to the stage.

The director, Baren Mullick, called Patol Babu to him. 'I hope you know what you're supposed to do?' he asked.

'Yes, sir.'

'Very good. I'll first say "Start sound". The recordists will reply by saying "Running". That's the signal for the camera to start. Then I will say "Action". That will be your cue to start walking from that pillar, and for the hero to come out of the car and make a dash for the office. You work out your steps so that the collision takes place at this spot, here. The hero ignores you and strides into the office, while you register pain by saying

"Oh!", stop for a couple of seconds, then resume walking—okay?'

Patol Babu suggested a rehearsal, but Baren Mullick shook his head impatiently. 'There's a large patch of cloud approaching the sun,' he said. 'This scene must be shot in sunlight.'

'One question please.'

'Yes?'

An idea had occurred to Patol Babu while rehearsing; he now came out with it.

'Er—I was thinking—if I had a newspaper open in my hand, and if the collision took place while I had my eyes on the paper, then perhaps—'

Baren Mullick cut him short by addressing a bystander who was carrying a Bengali newspaper. 'Do you mind handing your paper to this gentleman, just for this one shot? Thanks . . . Now you take your position beside the pillar. Chanchal, are you ready?'

'Yes, sir.'

'Good. Silence!'

Baren Mullick raised his hand, then brought it down again, saying, 'Just a minute. Kesto, I think if we gave the pedestrian a moustache, it would be more interesting.'

'What kind, sir? Walrus, Ronald Colman or butterfly? I have them all ready.'

'Butterfly, butterfly—and make it snappy!'

The elderly make-up man went up to Patol Babu, took out a small grey moustache from a box, and stuck it on with spirit-gum below Patol Babu's nose.

Patol Babu said, 'I hope it won't come off at the time of the collision?'

The make-up man smiled. 'Collision?' he said. 'Even if you wrestle with Dara Singh the moustache will stay in place.'

Patol Babu took a quick glance in the mirror the man was holding. True enough, the moustache suited him very well. Patol Babu silently commended the director's judgement.

'Silence! Silence!'

The business with the moustache had provoked a wave of comments from the spectators which Baren Mullick's shout now silenced.

Patol Babu noticed that most of the bystanders' eyes were turned towards him.'Start sound!'

Patol Babu cleared his throat. One, two, three, four, five—five steps would take him to the spot where the collision was to take place. And Chanchal Kumar would have to walk four steps. So if both were to start together, Patol Babu would have to walk a little faster than the hero, or else—

'Running!'

Patol Babu held the newspaper open in his hand. He had worked out that when he said 'Oh!' he had to mix sixty parts of irritation with forty parts of surprise.

'Action!'

Clop, clop, clop, clop, clop—Wham!

Patol Babu saw stars before his eyes. The hero's head had banged against his forehead, and an excruciating pain robbed him of his senses for a second.

But the next moment, by a supreme effort of will, Patol Babu pulled himself together, and mixing fifty parts of anguish with twenty-five of surprise and twenty-five of irritation, cried 'Oh!' Then after a brief pause, he resumed his walk.

'Cut!'

'Was that all right?' asked Patol Babu anxiously, stepping towards Baren Mullick.

'Jolly good! Why, you're quite an actor! Shoshanko, just take a look at the sky through the dark glass, will you.'

Jyoti now came up to Patol Babu and said, 'I hope Dadu

wasn't hurt too badly?'

'My God!' said Chanchal Kumar, massaging his head. 'You timed it so well that I nearly passed out!'

Naresh Dutt elbowed his way through the crowd, came up to Patol Babu and said, 'Please go back to where you were standing. I'll come to you in a short while and do the needful.'

Patol Babu took his place once again by the paan shop. The cloud had just covered the sun and there was a slight chill in the air. Nevertheless, Patol Babu took off his woollen jacket and heaved a sigh of relief. A feeling of complete satisfaction swept over him.

He had done his job well. All those years of struggle hadn't blunted his sensibility. Gogon Pakrashi would have been pleased with his performance. But all the labour and imagination he had put into this one shot—did these people appreciate that? He doubted it. They probably got people off the streets, made them go through a set of motions, paid them for their labours and forgot all about it. Paid them, yes, but how much? Ten, fifteen, twenty rupees? It was true that he needed money very badly, but what was twenty rupees when measured against the intense satisfaction of a small job done with perfection and dedication?

Ten minutes later Naresh Dutt went looking for Patol Babu near the paan shop and found no one there. 'That's odd—the man hadn't been paid yet. What a strange fellow!'

'The sun has come out,' Baren Mullick was heard shouting. 'Silence! Silence!—Naresh, hurry up and get these people out of the way!'

(1963)   *Translated by Satyajit Ray*

INDIGO

My name is Aniruddha Bose. I am twenty-nine years old and a bachelor. For the last eight years I've been working in an advertising agency in Calcutta. With the salary I get I live in reasonable comfort in a flat in Sardar Shankar Road. The flat has two south-facing rooms and is on the ground floor. Two years ago I bought an Ambassador car which I drive myself. I do a bit of writing in my spare time. Three of my stories have been published in magazines and have been well-appreciated by my acquaintances, but I know I cannot make a living by writing alone.

For the last few months I haven't been writing at all. Instead, I have read a lot about indigo plantations in Bengal and Bihar in the nineteenth century. I am something of an authority on the subject now: how the British exploited the poor peasants; how the peasants rose in revolt; and how, finally, with the invention of synthetic indigo in Germany, the cultivation of indigo was wiped out from our country—all this I know by heart. It is to describe the terrible experience which instilled in me this interest in indigo that I have taken up my pen today.

At this point I must tell you something about my past.

My father was a well-known physician in Monghyr, a town in Bihar. That is where I was born and that is where I did my schooling in a missionary school. I have a brother five years older than me. He studied medicine in England and is now attached to a hospital in a suburb of London called Golders Green. He has no plans to return to India.

My father died when I was sixteen. Soon after his death, my mother and I left Monghyr and came to Calcutta where we stayed with my maternal uncle. I went to St. Xavier's College and took my bachelor's degree. Soon after that I got my job with the advertising agency. My uncle's influence helped, but I wasn't an unworthy candidate myself. I had been a good student, I spoke English fluently, and most of all, I had the ability to carry myself well in an interview.

My early years in Monghyr had instilled certain habits in me which I have not been able to give up. One of these was an overpowering desire to go far away from the hectic life of Calcutta from time to time. I had done so several times ever since I bought my car. On weekends I made trips to Diamond Harbour, Port Canning, and Hassanabad along the Dum Dum Road. Each time I had gone alone because, to be quite honest, I didn't really have a close friend in Calcutta. That is why Promode's letter made me so happy. Promode had been my classmate in Monghyr. After I came away to Calcutta, we continued to keep in touch for three or four years. Then, perhaps it was I who stopped writing. Suddenly the other day when I came back from work, I found a letter from Promode waiting for me on my desk. He had written from Dumka—'I have a job in the Forest Department here. I have my own quarters. Why don't you take a week's leave and come over . . .?'

Some leave was due to me, so I spoke to my boss, and on the twenty-seventh of April—I shall remember the date as long as I live—I packed my bags and set off for Dumka.

Promode hadn't suggested that I go by car; it was my idea. Dumka was 200 miles away, so it would take about five or six hours at the most. I decided to have a big breakfast, set off by ten and reach there before dusk.

At least that was the plan, but there was a snag right at the start. I had my meal and was about to put a paan into my mouth, when my father's old friend Uncle Mohit suddenly turned up. He is a grave old man whom I was meeting after ten years. So there was no question of giving him short shrift. I had to offer him tea and listen to him chat for over an hour.

I saw Uncle Mohit off and shoved my suitcase and bedding into the back seat of my car. Just then, my ground-floor neighbour Bhola Babu walked up with his four-year-old son Pintu in tow.

'Where are you off to all by yourself?' Bhola Babu asked.

When I told him, he said with some concern, 'But that's a long way. Shouldn't you have arranged for a driver?'

I said I was a very cautious driver myself, and that I had taken such care of my car that it was still as good as new—'So there's nothing to worry about.'

Bhola Babu wished me luck and went into the house. I glanced at my wristwatch before turning the ignition key. It was ten minutes past eleven.

Although I avoided Howrah and took the Bally Bridge road, it took me an hour and a half to reach Chandernagore. Driving through dingy towns, these first thirty miles were so dreary that the fun of a car journey was quite lost. But from there on, as the car emerged into open country, the effect was magical. Where in the city did one get to see such a clear blue sky free from chimney smoke, and breathe air so pure and so redolent of the smell of earth?

At about half-past twelve, as I was nearing Burdwan, I began to feel the consequence of having eaten so early. Hungry, I pulled up by the station which fell on the way, went into a restaurant and had a light meal of toast, omelette and coffee. Then I resumed my journey. I still had a 135 miles to go.

Twenty miles from Burdwan, there was a small town called Panagarh. There I had to leave the Grand Trunk Road and take the road to Ilambazar. From Ilambazar the road went via Suri and Massanjore to Dumka.

The military camp at Panagarh had just come into view when there was a bang from the rear of my car. I had a flat tyre.

I got down. I had a spare tyre and could easily fit it. The thought that other cars would go whizzing by, their occupants laughing at my predicament, was not a pleasant one. Nevertheless I brought out the jack from the boot and set to work.

By the time I finished putting the new tyre on, I was dripping with sweat. My watch showed half past two. It had turned muggy in the meantime. The cool breeze which was blowing even an hour ago, and was making the bamboo trees sway, had stopped. Now everything was still. As I got back into the car I noticed a blue-black patch in the west above the treetops. Clouds. Was a storm brewing up? A norwester? It was useless to speculate. I must drive faster. I helped myself to some hot tea from the flask and resumed my journey.

But before I could cross Ilambazar, I was caught in the storm. I had enjoyed such norwesters in the past, sitting in my room, and had even recited Tagore poems to myself to blend with the mood. I had no idea that driving through open country, such a norwester could strike terror into the heart. Claps of thunder always make me uncomfortable. They seem to show a nasty side of nature; a vicious assault on helpless humanity. It seemed as if the shafts of lightning were all aimed at my poor Ambassador, and one of them was sure to find its mark sooner or later.

In this precarious state I passed Suri and was well on my way to Massanjore when there was yet another bang which no one could mistake for a thunderclap. I realized that another of my tyres had decided to call it a day.

I gave up hope. It was now pouring with rain. My watch said half past five. For the last twenty miles I had had to keep the speedometer down to fifteen, or I would have been well past Massanjore by now. Where was I? Up ahead nothing was visible through the rainswept windscreen. The wiper was on but its efforts were more frolicsome than effective. It being April, the sun should still be up, but it seemed more like late evening.

I opened the door on my right slightly and looked out. What I saw didn't suggest the presence of a town, though I could make out a couple of buildings through the trees. There was no question of getting out of the car and exploring, but one thing was clear enough: there were no shops along the road as far as the eye could see.

And I had no more spare tyres.

After waiting in the car for a quarter of an hour, it struck me that no other vehicle had passed by in all this time. Was I on the right road? There had been no mistake up to Suri, but suppose I had taken a wrong turning after that? It was not impossible in the blinding rain.

But even if I had made a mistake, it was not as if I had strayed into the jungles of Africa or South America. Wherever I was, there was no doubt that I was still in the district of Birbhum, within fifty miles of Santiniketan, and as soon as the rain stopped my troubles would be over—I might even find a repair shop within a mile or so.

I pulled out a packet of Wills from my pocket and lit a cigarette. I recalled Bhola Babu's warning. He must have gone through the same trying experience, or how could he have given me such sound advice? In future—Honk! Honk! Honk!

I turned round and saw a truck standing behind. Why was it blowing its horn? Was I standing right in the middle of the road?

The rain had let up a little. I opened the door, got out and found that it was no fault of the truck. When my tyre burst the car had swerved at an angle and was now blocking most of the road. There was no room for the truck to pass.

'Take the car to one side, sir.'

The Sikh driver had by now come out of the truck.

'What's the matter?' he asked. 'A puncture?'

I shrugged to convey my state of helplessness. 'If you could lend a hand,' I said, 'we could move the car to one side and let you pass.'

The Sikh driver's helper came out too. The three of us pushed the car to one side of the road. Then I found out from the two men that I was indeed on the wrong road for Dumka. I had taken a wrong turning and would have to drive back three miles to get back on the right track. I also learnt that there were no repair shops nearby.

The truck went on its way. As its noise faded away, the truth struck me like a hammer blow.

I had reached a dead end.

There was no way I could reach Dumka that night, and I had no idea how and where I would spend the night.

The roadside puddles were alive with the chorus of frogs. The rain had now been reduced to a light drizzle.

I got back into the car and was about to light a second cigarette when I spotted a light through the window on my side. I opened the door again. Through the branches of a tree I saw a rectangle of orange light. A window. Just as smoke meant the presence of fire, a kerosene lamp meant the presence of a human being. There was a house nearby and there were occupants in it.

I got out of the car with my torch. The window wasn't too far away. I had to go and investigate. There was a narrow footpath branching off from the main road which seemed to go in the direction of the house with the window.

I locked the car and set off.

I made my way avoiding puddles as far as possible. As I passed a tamarind tree, the house came into view. Well, hardly a house. It was a small cottage with a corrugated tin roof. Through an open door I could see a hurricane lantern and the leg of a bed.

'Is anybody there?' I called out.

A stocky, middle-aged man with a thick moustache came out of the room and squinted at my torch. I turned the spot away from his face.

'Where are you from, sir?' the man asked.

In a few words I described my predicament. 'Is there a place here where I can spend the night?' I asked. 'I shall pay for it, of course.'

'In the dak bungalow, you mean?'

Dak bungalow? I didn't see any dak bungalow.

But immediately, I realized my mistake. I had followed the light of the lantern, and had therefore failed to look around. Now I turned the torch to my left and immediately a large bungalow came into view. 'You mean that one?' I asked.

'Yes sir, but there is no bedding. And you can't have meals there.'

'I'm carrying my own bedding,' I said. 'I hope there's a bed there?'

'Yes sir. A charpoy.'

'And I see there's a stove lit in your room. You must be cooking your own meal?'

The man broke into a smile and asked if I would care for coarse chapatis prepared by him and urad-ka-dal cooked by his wife. I said it would do very nicely. I liked all kinds of chapatis, and urad was my favourite dal.

I don't know what the bungalow must have been like in its heyday, but now it was hardly what one understood by a dak bungalow. Constructed during the time of the Raj, the bedroom was large and the ceiling was high. The furniture consisted of a charpoy, a table set against the wall on one side, and a chair with a broken arm.

The chowkidar, or the caretaker, had in the meantime lit a lantern for me. He now put it on the table. 'What is your name?' I asked.

'Sukhanram, sir.'

'Has anybody ever lived in this bungalow or am I the first one?'

'Oh, no sir, others have come too. There was a gentleman who stayed here for two nights last winter.'

'I hope there are no ghosts here,' I said in a jocular tone.

'God forbid!' he said. 'No one has ever complained of ghosts.'

I must say I found his words reassuring. If a place is spooky, and old dak bungalows have a reputation for being so, it will be so at all times. 'When was this bungalow built?' I asked.

Sukhan began to unroll my bedding and said, 'This used to be a sahib's bungalow, sir.'

'A sahib?'

'Yes sir. An indigo planter. There used to be an indigo factory close by. Now only the chimney is standing.'

I knew indigo was cultivated in these parts at one time. I had seen ruins of indigo factories in Monghyr too in my childhood.

It was ten-thirty when I went to bed after dining on Sukhan's coarse chapatis and urad-ka-dal. I had sent a telegram to Promode from Calcutta saying that I would arrive this afternoon. He would naturally wonder what had happened. But it was useless to think of that now. All I could do now was congratulate myself on having found a shelter, and that too without much trouble. In future I would do as Bhola Babu had advised. I had learnt a lesson, and lessons learnt the hard way are not forgotten easily.

I put the lantern in the adjoining bathroom. The little light that seeped through the door which I had kept slightly ajar was enough. Usually I find it difficult to sleep with a light on, and yet I did not extinguish the light even though what I badly needed now was sleep. I was worried about my car which I had left standing on the road, but it was certainly safer to do so in a village than in the city.

The sound of drizzle had stopped. The air was now filled with the croaking of frogs and the shrill chirping of crickets. From my bed in that ancient bungalow in this remote village, the city seemed to belong to another planet. Indigo . . . I thought of the play by Dinabandhu Mitra, *Nildarpan* (The Mirror of Indigo). As a college student I had watched a performance of it in a theatre on Cornwallis Street.

I didn't know how long I had slept, when a sound suddenly awakened me. Something was scratching at the door. The door was bolted. Must be a dog or a jackal, I thought, and in a minute or so the noise stopped.

I shut my eyes in an effort to sleep, but the barking of a dog put an end to my efforts. This was not the bark of a stray village dog, but the unmistakable bay of a hound. I was familiar with it. Two houses away from us in Monghyr lived Mr Martin. He had a hound which bayed just like this. Who on earth kept a pet hound here? I thought of opening the door to find out as the sound seemed quite near. But then I thought, why bother? It was better to get some more sleep. What time was it now?

A faint moonlight came in through the window. I raised my left hand to glance at the wristwatch, and gave a start. My wristwatch was gone.

And yet, because it was an automatic watch, I always wore it to bed. Where did it disappear? And how? Were there thieves around? What would happen to my car then?

I felt beside my pillow for my torch and found it gone too.

I jumped out of bed, knelt on the floor and looked underneath it. My suitcase too had disappeared.

My head started spinning. Something had to be done about it. I called out: 'Chowkidar!'

There was no answer.

I went to the door and found that it was still bolted. The window had bars. So how did the thief enter?

As I was about to unfasten the bolt, I glanced at my hand and experienced an odd feeling.

Had whitewash from the wall got on to my hand? Or was it white powder? Why did it look so pale?

I had gone to bed wearing a vest; why then was I now wearing a long-sleeved silk shirt? I felt a throbbing in my head. I opened the door and went out into the veranda.

'Chowkidar!'

The word that came out was spoken with the unmistakable accent of an Englishman. And where was the chowkidar, and where was his little cottage? There was now a wide open field in front of the bungalow. In the distance was a building with a high chimney. The surroundings were unusually quiet.

They had changed.

And so had I.

I came back into the bedroom in a sweat. My eyes had got used to the darkness. I could now clearly make out the details.

The bed was there, but it was covered with a mosquito net. I hadn't been using one. The pillow too was unlike the one I had brought with me. This one had a border with frills; mine didn't. The table and the chair stood where they did, but they had lost their aged look. The varnished wood shone even in the soft light. On the table stood not a lantern but a kerosene lamp with an ornate shade.

There were other objects in the room which gradually came into view: a pair of steel trunks in a corner, a folding bracket on the wall from which hung a coat, an unfamiliar type of headgear and a hunting crop. Below the bracket, standing against the wall, was a pair of galoshes.

I turned away from the objects and took another look at myself. Till now I had only noticed the silk shirt; now I saw the narrow trousers and the socks. I didn't have shoes on, but saw a pair of black boots on the floor by the bed.

I passed my right hand over my face and realized that not only my complexion but my features too had changed. I didn't possess such a sharp nose, nor such thin lips or narrow chin. I felt the hair on my head and found that it was wavy and that there were sideburns which reached below my ears.

In spite of my surprise and terror, I suddenly felt a great urge to find out what I looked like. But where to find a mirror?

I strode towards the bathroom, opened the door with a sharp push and went in.

There had been nothing there but a bucket. Now I saw a metal bath tub and a mug kept on a stool beside it. The thing I was looking for was right in front of me: an oval mirror fixed to a dressing-table. I looked into it, but the person reflected in it was not me. By some devilish trick I had turned into a nineteenth-century Englishman with a sallow complexion, blond hair and light eyes from which shone a strange mixture of hardness and suffering. How old would the Englishman be? Not more than thirty, but it looked as if either illness or hard work, or both, had aged him prematurely.

I went closer and had a good look at 'my' face. As I looked, a deep sigh rose from the depths of my heart.

The voice was not mine. The sigh, too, expressed not my feelings but those of the Englishman.

What followed made it clear that all my limbs were acting of their own volition. And yet it was surprising that I—Aniruddha Bose—was perfectly aware of the change in identity. But I didn't know if the change was permanent, or if there was any way to regain my lost self.

I came back to the bedroom.

Now I glanced at the table. Below the lamp was a notebook bound in leather. It was open at a blank page. Beside it was an inkwell with a quill pen dipped in it.

I walked over to the table. Some unseen force made me sit in the chair and pick up the pen with my right hand. The hand now moved towards the left-hand page of the notebook, and the silent room was filled with the noise of a quill scratching the blank page. This is what I wrote:

27 April 1868
Those fiendish mosquitoes are singing in my ears again. So that's how the son of a mighty empire has to meet his end—at the hands of a tiny insect. What strange will of God is this? Eric has made his escape. Percy and Tony too left earlier. Perhaps I was greedier than them. So in spite of repeated attacks of malaria I couldn't resist the lure of indigo. No, not only that. One mustn't lie in one's diary. My countrymen know me only too well. I didn't lead a blameless life at home either; and they surely have not forgotten that. So I do not dare go back home. I know I will have to stay here and lay down my life on this alien soil. My place will be beside the graves of my wife Mary and my dear little son Toby. I have treated the natives here so badly that there is no one to shed a tear at my passing away. Perhaps Mirjan would miss me—my faithful trusted bearer Mirjan.

And Rex? My real worry is about Rex. Alas, faithful Rex! When I die, these people will not spare you. They will either stone you or club you to death. If only I could do something about you!

I could write no more. The hands were shaking. Not mine, the diarist's.

I put down the pen.

Then my right hand dropped and moved to the right and made for the handle of the drawer.

I opened it.

Inside there was a pin cushion, a brass paperweight, a pipe and some papers.

The drawer opened a little more. A metal object glinted in the half-light.

It was a pistol, its butt inlaid with ivory.

The hand pulled out the pistol. It had stopped shaking.

A group of jackals cried out. It was as if in answer to the jackals' cry that the hound bayed again.

I left the chair and advanced towards the door. I went out into the veranda.

The field in front was bathed in moonlight.

About ten yards from the veranda stood a large greyhound. He wagged his tail as he saw me.

'Rex!'

It was the same deep English voice. The echo of the call came floating back from the faraway factory and bamboo grove—Rex! Rex!

Rex came up towards the veranda.

As he stepped from the grass onto the cement, my right hand rose to my waist, the pistol pointing towards the hound. Rex stopped in his tracks, his eye on the pistol. He gave a low growl.

My right forefinger pressed the trigger.

As the gun throbbed with a blinding flash, smoke and the smell of gunpowder filled the air.

Rex's lifeless, blood-spattered body lay partly on the veranda and partly on the grass.

The sound of the pistol had wakened the crows in the

nearby trees. A hubbub now rose from the direction of the factory.

I came back into the bedroom, bolted the door and sat on the bed. The shouting drew near.

I placed the still hot muzzle of the pistol by my right ear.

That is all I remember.

I woke up at the sound of knocking.

'I've brought your tea, sir.'

Daylight flooded in through the window. Out of sheer habit my eyes strayed to my left wrist.

Thirteen minutes past six. I brought the watch closer to my eyes to read the date, April the twenty-eighth.

I now opened the door and let Sukhanram in.

'There's a car repair shop half an hour down the road, sir,' he said. 'It'll open at seven.'

'Very good,' I said, and proceeded to drink my tea.

Would anyone believe me when they heard of my experience on the night of the hundredth anniversary of the death of an English indigo planter in Birbhum?

(1968)   *Translated by Satyajit Ray*

BIPIN CHOWDHURY'S LAPSE OF MEMORY

Every Monday, on his way back from work, Bipin Chowdhury would drop in at Kalicharan's in New Market to buy books. Crime stories, ghost stories and thrillers. He had to buy at least five at a time to last him through the week. He lived alone, was not a good mixer, had few friends, and didn't like spending time in idle chat. Those who called in the evening got through their business quickly and left. Those who didn't show signs of leaving would be told around eight o'clock by Bipin Babu that he was under doctor's orders to have dinner at eight-thirty. After dinner he would rest for half an hour and then turn in with a book. This was a routine which had persisted unbroken for years.

Today, at Kalicharan's, Bipin Babu had the feeling that someone was observing him from close quarters. He turned round and found himself looking at a round-faced, meek-looking man who now broke into a smile.

'I don't suppose you recognize me.'

Bipin Babu felt ill at ease. It didn't seem that he had ever encountered this man before. The face seemed quite unfamiliar.

'But you're a busy man. You must meet all kinds of people all the time.'

'Have we met before?' asked Bipin Babu.

The man looked greatly surprised. 'We met every day for a whole week. I arranged for a car to take you to the Hudroo falls. In 1958. In Ranchi. My name is Parimal Ghose.'

'Ranchi?'

Now Bipin Babu realized that it was not he but this man who was making a mistake. Bipin Babu had never been to Ranchi. He had been at the point of going several times, but had never made it. He smiled and said, 'Do you know who I am?'

The man raised his eyebrows, bit his tongue and said, 'Do I know you? Who doesn't know Bipin Chowdhury?'

Bipin Babu now turned towards the bookshelves and said, 'Still you're making a mistake. One often does. I've never been to Ranchi.'

The man now laughed aloud.

'What are you saying, Mr Chowdhury? You had a fall in Hudroo and cut your right knee. I brought you iodine. I had fixed up a car for you to go to Netarhat the next day, but you couldn't because of the pain in the knee. Can't you recall anything? Someone else you know was also in Ranchi at that time. Mr Dinesh Mukerjee. You stayed in a bungalow. You said you didn't like hotel food and would prefer to have your meals cooked by a bawarchi. Mr Mukerjee stayed with his sister. You had a big argument about the moon landing, remember? I'll tell you more: you always carried a bag with your books in it on your sightseeing trips. Am I right or not?'

Bipin Babu spoke quietly, his eyes still on the books.

'Which month in fifty-eight are you talking about?'

The man said, 'Just before the pujas. October.'

'No, sir,' said Bipin Babu. 'I spent puja in fifty-eight with a friend in Kanpur. You're making a mistake. Good day.'

But the man didn't go, nor did he stop talking.

'Very strange. One evening I had tea with you on the

veranda of your bungalow. You spoke about your family. You said you had no children, and that you had lost your wife ten years ago. Your only brother had died insane, which is why you didn't want to visit the mental hospital in Ranchi . . .'

When Bipin Babu had paid for the books and was leaving the shop, the man was still looking at him in utter disbelief.

Bipin Babu's car was safely parked in Bertram Street by the Lighthouse cinema. He told the driver as he got into the car, 'Just drive by the Ganga, will you, Sitaram.' Driving up the Strand Road, Bipin Babu regretted having paid so much attention to the intruder. He had never been to Ranchi—no question about it. It was inconceivable that he should forget such an incident which took place only six or seven years ago. He had an excellent memory. Unless—Bipin Babu's head reeled.

Unless he was losing his mind.

But how could that be? He was working daily in his office. It was a big firm, and he had a responsible job. He wasn't aware of anything ever going seriously wrong. Only today he had spoken for half an hour at an important meeting. And yet . . .

And yet that man knew a great deal about him. How? He even seemed to know some intimate details. The bag of books, wife's death, brother's insanity . . . The only mistake was about his having gone to Ranchi. Not a mistake; a deliberate lie. In 1958, during the pujas, he was in Kanpur at his friend Haridas Bagchi's place. All Bipin Babu had to do was write to—no, there was no way of writing to Haridas. Bipin Babu suddenly remembered that Haridas had not left his address.

But where was the need for proof? If it so happened that the police were trying to pin a crime on him which had taken place in Ranchi in 1958, he might have needed to prove he hadn't been there. He himself was fully aware that he hadn't been to Ranchi—and that was that.

The river breeze was bracing, and yet a slight discomfort

lingered in Bipin Babu's mind.

Around Hastings, Bipin Babu had the sudden notion of rolling up his trousers and taking a look at his right knee.

There was the mark of an old inch-long cut. It was impossible to tell when the injury had occurred. Had he never had a fall as a boy and cut his knee? He tried to recall such an incident, but couldn't.

Then Bipin Babu suddenly thought of Dinesh Mukerjee. That man had said that Dinesh was in Ranchi at the same time. The best thing surely would be to ask him. He lived quite near—in Beninandan Street. What about going right now? But then, if he had really never been to Ranchi, what would Dinesh think if Bipin Babu asked for a confirmation? He would probably conclude Bipin Babu was going nuts. No—it would be ridiculous to ask him. And he knew how ruthless Dinesh's sarcasm could be.

Sipping a cold drink in his air-conditioned living room, Bipin Babu felt at ease again. Such a nuisance the man was! He probably had nothing else to do, so he went about getting into other people's hair.

After dinner, snuggling into bed with one of the new thrillers, Bipin Babu forgot all about the man in New Market.

Next day, in the office, Bipin Babu noticed that with every passing hour, the previous day's encounter was occupying more and more of his mind. That look of round-eyed surprise on that round face, the disbelieving snigger . . . If the man knew so much about the details of Bipin Babu's life, how could he be so wrong about the Ranchi trip?

Just before lunch—at five minutes to one—Bipin Babu couldn't check himself any more. He opened the phone book. He had to ring up Dinesh Mukerjee. It was better to settle the question over the phone; at least the embarrassment on his face wouldn't show.

Two-three-five-six-one-six.

Bipin Babu dialled the number.

'Hello.'

'Is that Dinesh? This is Bipin here.'

'Well, well—what's the news?'

'I just wanted to find out if you recalled an incident which took place in fifty-eight.'

'Fifty-eight? What incident?'

'Were you in Calcutta right through that year? That's the first thing I've got to know.'

'Wait just a minute . . . fifty-eight . . . just let me check in my diary.'

For a minute there was silence. Bipin Babu could feel that his heartbeat had gone up. He was sweating a little.

'Hello.'

'Yes.'

'I've got it. I had been out twice.'

'Where?'

'Once in February—nearby—to Krishnanagar to a nephew's wedding. And then . . . but you'd know about this one. The trip to Ranchi. You were there too. That's all. But what's all this sleuthing about?'

'No, I just wanted to—anyway, thanks.'

Bipin Babu slammed the receiver down and gripped his head with his hands. He felt his head swimming. A chill seemed to spread over his body. There were sandwiches in his tiffin box, but he didn't feel like eating them. He had lost his appetite. Completely.

After lunchtime, Bipin Babu realized that he couldn't possibly carry on sitting at his desk and working. This was the first time something like this had happened in his twenty-five years with the firm. He had a reputation for being a tireless, conscientious worker. The men who worked under him all held him in awe. In the worst moments of crisis, even when faced with the most acute problems, Bipin Babu had always kept his cool and weathered the storm. But today his head was in a whirl.

Back home at two-thirty, Bipin Babu shut himself up in his bedroom, lay down in bed and tried to gather his wits together. He knew that it was possible to lose one's memory through an injury to the head, but he didn't know of a single instance of someone remembering everything except one particular incident—and a fairly recent and significant one at that. He had always wanted to go to Ranchi; to have gone there, done things, and not to remember was something utterly impossible.

At seven, Bipin Babu's servant came and announced that Seth Girdhariprasad had come. A rich businessman—and a VIP—this Girdhariprasad. And he had come by appointment. But Bipin Babu was feeling so low that he had to tell his servant that it was not possible for him to leave his bed. To hell with VIPs.

At seven-thirty, the servant came again. Bipin Babu had just dozed off and was in the middle of an unpleasant dream when the servant's knock woke him up. Who was it this time? 'Chuni Babu, sir. Says it's very urgent.'

Bipin Babu knew what the urgency was. Chunilal was a childhood friend of his. He had fallen on bad times recently, and had been pestering Bipin Babu for a job. Bipin Babu had kept fobbing him off, but Chuni kept coming back. What a persistent bore.

Bipin Babu sent word that not only was it not possible for him to see Chuni now, but not in several weeks as well.

But as soon as the servant stepped out of the room, it struck Bipin Babu that Chuni might remember something about the '58 trip. There was no harm in asking him.

He sped downstairs. Chuni had got up to leave. Seeing Bipin Babu, he turned around with a flicker of hope in his eyes.

Bipin Babu didn't beat about the bush.

'Listen, Chuni—I want to ask you something. You have a good memory, and you've been seeing me off and on for a long time. Just throw your mind back and tell me—did I go to Ranchi in fifty-eight?'

Chuni said, 'Fifty-eight? It must have been fifty-eight. Or was it fifty-nine?'

'You're sure that I did go to Ranchi?'

Chuni's look of amazement was not unmixed with worry.

'D'you mean you have doubts about having gone at all?'

'Did I go? Do you remember clearly?'

Chuni was standing up; he now sat down on the sofa, fixed Bipin Babu with a long, hard stare and said, 'Bipin, have you taken to drugs or something? As far as I know, you had a clean record where such things were concerned. I know that old friendships don't mean much to you, but at least you had a good memory. You can't really mean that you've forgotten about the Ranchi trip?'

Bipin Babu had to turn away from Chuni's incredulous stare.

'D'you remember what my last job was?' asked Chunilal.

'Of course. You worked in a travel agency.'

'You remember that and you don't remember that it was I who fixed up your booking for Ranchi? I went to the station to see you off; one of the fans in your compartment was not working—I got an electrician to fix it. Have you forgotten everything? Whatever is the matter with you? You don't look too well, you know.'

Bipin Babu sighed and shook his head.

'I've been working too hard,' he said at last. 'That must be the reason. Must see about consulting a specialist.'

Doubtless it was Bipin Babu's condition which made Chunilal leave without mentioning anything about a job.

Paresh Chanda was a young physician with a pair of bright eyes and a sharp nose. He became thoughtful when he heard about Bipin Babu's symptoms. 'Look, Dr Chanda,' said Bipin Babu desperately, 'you must cure me of this horrible illness. I can't tell you how it's affecting my work. There are so many kinds of drugs these days; isn't there something specific for such a complaint? I can have it sent from abroad if it's not to be had here. But I must be rid of these symptoms.'

Dr Chanda shook his head.

'You know what, Mr Chowdhury,' he said, 'I've never had to deal with a case such as yours. Frankly, this is quite outside my field of experience. But I have one suggestion. I don't know if it'll work, but it's worth a try. It can do no harm.'

Bipin Babu leaned forward anxiously.

'As far as I can make out,' said Dr Chanda, 'and I think you're of the same opinion—you have been to Ranchi, but due to some unknown reason, the entire episode has slipped out of your mind. What I suggest is that you go to Ranchi once again. The sight of the place may remind you of your trip. This is not impossible. More than that I cannot do at the moment. I'm prescribing a nerve tonic and a tranquilizer. Sleep is essential, or the symptoms will get more pronounced.'

It may have been the sleeping pill, and the advice which the doctor gave, which made Bipin Babu feel somewhat better the next morning.

After breakfast, he rang up his office, gave some instructions, and then procured a first-class ticket to Ranchi for the same evening.

Getting off the train at Ranchi next morning, he realized at once that he had never been there before.

He came out of the station, hired a taxi and drove around the town for a while. It was clear that the streets, the buildings, the hotels, the bazaars, the Morabadi Hill were all unfamiliar—

with none of these had he the slightest acquaintance. Would a trip to the Hudroo Falls help? He didn't believe so, but, at the same time, he didn't wish to leave with the feeling that he hadn't tried hard enough. So he arranged for a car and left for Hudroo in the afternoon.

At five o'clock the same afternoon in Hudroo, two Gujarati gentlemen from a group of picnickers discovered Bipin Babu lying unconscious beside a boulder. When the ministrations of the two gentlemen brought him around, the first thing Bipin Babu said was, 'I'm finished. There's no hope left.'

Next morning, Bipin Babu was back in Calcutta. He realized that there was truly no hope for him. Soon he would lose everything: his will to work, his confidence, his ability, his balance of mind. Was he going to end up in the asylum at Ranchi . . . ? Bipin Babu couldn't think any more.

Back home, he rang up Dr Chanda and asked him to come over. Then, after a shower, he got into bed with an icebag clamped to his head. Just then the servant brought him a letter which someone had left in the letter box. A greenish envelope with his name in red ink on it. Above the name it said 'Urgent and Confidential'. In spite of his condition, Bipin Babu had a feeling that he ought to go through the letter. He tore open the envelope and took out the letter. This is what he read—

Dear Bipin,
I had no idea that affluence would bring about the kind of change in you that it has done. Was it so difficult for you to help out an old friend down on his luck? I have no money, so my resources are limited. What I have is imagination, a part of which is used in retribution of your unfeeling behaviour.
The man in New Market is a neighbour and acquaintance of mine and a capable actor who played

the part I wrote for him. Dinesh Mukerjee has never been particularly well-disposed towards you: so he was quite willing to help. As for the mark on your knee, you will surely recall that you tripped on a rope in Chandpal Ghat back in 1939.

Well, you'll be all right again now. A novel I've written is being considered by a publisher. If he likes it enough, it'll see me through the next few months.

Yours,
Chunilal

When Dr Chanda came, Bipin Babu said, 'I'm fine. It all came back as soon as I got off the train at Ranchi.'

'A unique case,' said Dr Chanda. 'I shall certainly write about it in a medical journal.'

'The reason why I sent for you,' said Bipin Babu, 'is that I have a pain in the hip from a fall I had in Ranchi. If you could prescribe a pain killer . . .'

(1963)   *Translated by Satyajit Ray*

FRITZ

After having stared at Jayanto for a whole minute, I could not help asking him, 'Are you well? You seem to be in low spirits today.'

Jayanto quickly lost his slightly preoccupied air, gave me a boyish smile and said, 'No. On the contrary, I am feeling a lot better. This place is truly wonderful.'

'You've been here before. Didn't you know how good it was?'

'I had nearly forgotten,' Jayanto sighed. 'Now some of my memories are coming back slowly. The bungalow certainly appears unchanged. I can even recognize some of the old furniture, such as these cane chairs and tables.'

The bearer came in with tea and biscuits on a tray. I poured.

'When did you come here last?'

'Thirty-one years ago. I was six then.'

We were sitting in the garden of the circuit house in Bundi. We had arrived only that morning. Jayanto and I were old friends. We had gone to the same school and college. He now worked in the editorial division of a newspaper and I taught in a school. Although we had different kinds of jobs, it had not made any difference to our friendship. We had been planning a trip to Rajasthan for quite some time. The main difficulty lay in both of us being able to get away together. That had, at last, been made possible.

Most people go to Jaipur, Udaipur or Chittor when they go to Rajasthan; but Jayanto kept talking about going to Bundi. I had no objection for, having read Tagore's poem 'The Fort of Bundi', I was certainly familiar with the name of the place and felt a pleasurable excitement at the prospect of actually seeing the fort. Not many people came to Bundi. But that did not mean that there was not much to see there. It could be that, from the point of view of a historian, Udaipur, Jodhpur and Chittor had a lot more to offer; but simply as a beautiful place, Bundi was perfect.

However, Jayanto's insistence on Bundi did puzzle me somewhat. I learnt the reason on the train when we were coming down. Jayanto's father, Animesh Das Gupta, had worked in the Archaeological Department. His work sometimes took him to historical places, and Jayanto had as a child come to Bundi. He had always wanted to return after growing up, just to see how much the modern Bundi compared to the image he had in his mind.

The circuit house was really rather splendid. Built during the time of the British, it must have been at least a hundred years old. It was a single-storeyed building with a sloping tiled roof. The rooms had high ceilings and the skylights had long, dangling ropes which could be pulled to open and shut them. The veranda faced the east. Right opposite it was a huge garden with a large number of roses in full bloom. Behind these were a lot of trees which obviously housed a vast section of local birds. Parrots could be seen everywhere; and peacocks could be heard, but only outside the compound.

We had already been on a sightseeing tour of the town. The famous fort of Bundi was placed amidst the hills. We had seen it from a distance that day but decided to go back to take a closer look. The only reminders of modern times were the electric poles. Otherwise it seemed as though we were back in old Rajputana. The streets were cobbled, the houses had balconies jutting out from the first floor. The carvings done on these and the wooden doors bore evidence of the work of master craftsmen. It was difficult to believe we were living in the age of machines.

I noticed Jayanto had turned rather quiet after arriving in Bundi. Perhaps some of his memories had returned. It is easy enough to feel a little depressed when visiting a place one may have seen as a child. Besides, Jayanto was certainly more emotional than most people. Everyone knew that.

He put his cup down on the table and said, 'You know, Shankar, it is really quite strange. The first time I came here I used to sit cross-legged on these chairs. It seemed as though I was sitting on a throne. Now the chairs seem both small in size and very ordinary. The drawing-room here used to seem absolutely enormous. If I hadn't returned, those memories would have remained stuck in my mind for ever.'

I said, 'Yes, that's perfectly natural. As a child, one is small in size, so everything else seems large. One grows bigger with age, but the size of all the other things remains the same, doesn't it?'

We went for a stroll in the garden after tea. Jayanto suddenly stopped walking and said, 'Deodar.'

I stared at him.

'A deodar tree. It ought to be here somewhere,' he said and began striding towards the far end of the compound. Why did he suddenly think of a deodar tree?

A few seconds later I heard his voice exclaiming jubilantly, 'Yes, it's here! Exactly where it was before!'

'Of course it's where it was before,' I said. 'Would a tree go roaming about?'

Jayanto shook his head impatiently. 'No, that is not what I meant. All I meant was that the tree is where I thought it might be.'

'But why did you suddenly think of a tree?'

Jayanto stared at the trunk of the tree, frowning. Then he shook his head slowly and said, 'I can't remember that now. Something had brought me near the tree. I had done something here. A European . . .'

'European?'

'No, I can't recall anything at all. Memory is a strange business . . .'

They had a good cook in the circuit house. Later in the evening, while we sat at the oval dining table having dinner, Jayanto said, 'The cook they had in those days was called Dilawar. He had a scar on his left cheek and his eyes were always red. But he was an excellent cook.'

Jayanto's memories began returning one by one soon after dinner when we went back to the drawing-room. He could recall where his father used to sit and smoke a cheroot, where his mother used to knit, and what magazines lay on the table.

And, slowly, in bits and pieces, he recalled the whole business about his doll.

It was not the usual kind of doll little girls play with. One of Jayanto's uncles had brought for him from Switzerland a twelve-inch-long figure of an old man, dressed in traditional Swiss style. Apparently, it was very lifelike. Although it was not mechanized it was possible to bend and twist its limbs. Its face had a smile on it and, on its head, it wore a Swiss cap with a little yellow feather sticking out from it. Its clothes, especially in their little details, were perfect—belt, buttons, pockets, collars, socks. There were even little buckles on the shoes.

His uncle had returned from Europe shortly before Jayanto left for Bundi with his parents. The little old man had been bought in a village in Switzerland. The man who sold him had jokingly said to Jayanto's uncle, 'He's called Fritz. You must call him by this name. He won't respond to any other.'

Jayanto said, 'I had a lot of toys when I was small. My parents gave me practically everything I wanted, perhaps because I was their only child. But once I had Fritz, I forgot all my other toys. I played only with him. A time came when I began to spend hours just talking to him. Our conversation had to be one-sided, of course, but Fritz had such a funny smile on his lips and such a look in his eyes, that it seemed to me as though he could understand every word. Sometimes I wondered if he would actually converse with me if I could speak to him in German. Now it seems like a childish fantasy, but at that time the whole thing was very real to me. My parents did warn me not to overdo things, but I listened to no one. I had not yet been put in a school, so I had all the time in the world for Fritz.'

Jayanto fell silent. I looked at my watch and realized it was 9.30 p.m. It was very quiet outside. We were sitting in the drawing-room of the circuit house. An oil lamp burnt in the room.

I asked, 'What happened to the doll?'

Jayanto was still deep in thought. His answer to my question came so late that, by that time, I had started to think that he had not heard me at all.

'I had brought it to Bundi. It was destroyed here.'

'Destroyed? How?'

Jayanto sighed.

'We were sitting out on the lawn having tea. I had kept the doll by my side on the grass. I was not really old enough to have tea, but I insisted and, in the process, the cup tilted and some of the hot tea fell on my pants. I ran inside to change and came back to find that Fritz had disappeared. I looked around and found quite soon that a couple of stray dogs were having a nice tug-of-war with Fritz. Although he didn't actually come apart, his face was battered beyond recognition and his clothes were torn. In other words, Fritz did not exist for me any more. He was dead.'

'And then?' Jayanto's story intrigued me.

'What could possibly happen after that? I arranged his funeral, that's all.'

'Meaning?'

'I buried him under that deodar tree. I had wanted to make a coffin. Fritz was, after all, a European. But I could find nothing, not even a little box. So, in the end, I buried him just like that.'

At last, the mystery of the deodar tree was solved.

We went to bed at around ten. Our room was a large one and our beds had been neatly made. Not being used to doing a lot of walking, I was feeling rather tired after the day's activities. Besides, the bed was very comfortable. I fell asleep barely ten minutes after hitting the pillow.

A slight noise woke me a little later. I turned on my side and found Jayanto sitting up on his bed. The table lamp by his bed was switched on and, in its light, it was easy to see the look of anxiety on his face.

I asked, 'What is it? Are you not feeling well?'

Instead of answering my question, Jayanto asked me one himself.

'Do you think this circuit house has got small animals? I mean, things like cats or mice?'

'I shouldn't be surprised if it does. Why?'

'Something walked over my chest. That's what woke me.'

'Rats and mice usually come in through drains. But I've

never known them to climb on the bed.'

'This is the second time I've woken up, actually. The first time I had heard a shuffling noise near the window.'

'Oh, if it was near the window, it is more likely to be a cat.'

'Yes, but . . .'

Jayanto still sounded doubtful. I said, 'Didn't you see anything after you switched the light on?'

'Nothing. But then, I didn't switch it on immediately after opening my eyes. To tell you the truth, I felt rather scared at first. But when I did switch it on, there was nothing to be seen.'

'That means whatever came in must still be in the room.'

'Well . . . since both the doors are bolted from inside . . .'

I rose quickly and searched under the bed, behind our suitcases and everywhere else in the room. I could not find anything. The door to the bathroom was closed. I opened it and was about to start another search when Jayanto called out to me softly, 'Shankar!'

I came back to the room. Jayanto was staring hard at the cover of his quilt. Upon seeing me, he pulled a portion of it near the lamp and said, 'Look at this!'

I bent over the cloth and saw tiny, brown circular marks on it. I said, 'Well, these could have been made by a cat.'

Jayanto did not say anything. It was obvious that something had deeply disturbed him. But it was two-thirty in the morning. I simply had to get a little more sleep, or I knew I would just keep feeling tired. And we had plans of doing a lot of sightseeing the following day.

So, after murmuring a few soothing words—such as, don't worry, I am here with you and who knows, those marks may have been on your quilt already when you went to bed—I switched off the light once more and lay down. I had no doubt that Jayanto had only had a bad dream. All those memories of his childhood had upset him, obviously, and that was what had led to his dreaming of a cat walking on his chest.

I slept soundly for the rest of the night. If there were further disturbances, Jayanto did not tell me about them. But I could see in the morning that he had not slept well.

'Tonight I must give him one of the tranquillizers I brought with me,' I thought.

We finished our breakfast by nine, as we had planned, and left for the fort. A car had already been arranged. It was almost nine-thirty by the time we reached.

Some of Jayanto's old forgotten memories began coming back again, though—fortunately—they had nothing to do with his doll. In fact, his youthful exuberance made me think he had forgotten all about it.

'There—there's that elephant on top of the gate!' he exclaimed. 'And the turrets! And here is the bed made of silver and the throne. Look at that picture on the wall—I saw it the last time!'

But within an hour, his enthusiasm began to wane. I was so engrossed myself that I did not notice it at first. But, while walking through a hall and looking at the chandeliers hanging from the ceiling, I suddenly realized Jayanto was no longer walking by my side. Where was he?

We had a guide with us. 'Babu has gone out on the terrace,' he told me.

I came out of the hall and found Jayanto standing absent-mindedly near a wall on the other side of the terrace. He did not seem to notice my presence even when I went and stood beside him. He started when I called him by his name.

'What on earth is the matter with you?' I asked. 'Why are you standing here looking morose even in a beautiful place like this? I can't stand it.'

Jayanto simply said, 'Have you finished seeing everything? If so, let's . . .'

Had I been alone, I would definitely have spent a little more time at the fort. But one look at Jayanto made me decide in favour of returning to the circuit house.

A road through the hills took us back to town. Jayanto and I were both sitting in the back of the car. I offered him a cigarette, but he refused. I noticed a veiled excitement in the movement of his hands. One moment he placed them near the window, then on his lap and, immediately afterwards, began biting his nails. Jayanto was quiet by nature. This odd restlessness in him worried me.

After about ten minutes, I could not take it any more.

'It might help if you told me about your problem,' I said. Jayanto shook his head.

'It's no use telling you, for you're not going to believe me.'

'OK, even if I don't believe you, I can at least discuss the matter with you, can't I?'

'Fritz came into our room last night. Those little marks on my quilt were his footprints.'

There was very little I could do at this except catch hold of him by the shoulders and shake him. How could I talk sensibly to someone whose mind was obsessed with such an absurd idea?

'You didn't see anything, did you?' I said finally.

'No. But I could distinctly feel that whatever was walking on my chest had two feet, not four.'

As we got out of the car at the circuit house, I decided that Jayanto must be given a nerve tonic or some such thing. A tranquillizer might not be good enough. I could not allow a thirty-seven-year-old man to be so upset by a simple memory from his childhood.

I said to Jayanto upon reaching our room, 'It's nearly twelve o'clock. Should we not be thinking of having a bath?'

'You go first,' said Jayanto and flung himself on the bed.

An idea came to my mind in the bath. Perhaps this was the only way to bring Jayanto back to normalcy.

If a doll had been buried somewhere thirty years ago and if one knew the exact spot, it might be possible to dig the ground there. No doubt most of it would have been destroyed, but it was likely that we'd find just a few things, especially if they were made of metal, such as the buckle of a belt or brass buttons on a jacket. If Jayanto could actually be shown that that was all that was left of his precious doll, he might be able to rid himself of his weird notions; otherwise, he would have strange dreams every night and talk of Fritz walking on his chest. If this kind of thing was allowed to continue he might go totally mad.

Jayanto seemed to like my idea at first. But, after a little while, he said, 'Who will do the digging? Where will you find a spade?'

I laughed, 'Since there is a garden, there is bound to be a gardener. And that would mean there's a spade. If we offered him a little tip, I have no doubt that he would have no objection to digging up a bit of the ground near the trunk of a tree at the far end of the lawn.'

Jayanto did not accept the idea immediately, nor did I say anything further. He went and had his bath after a little bit of persuasion. At lunch, he ate nothing except a couple of chapatis with meat curry, although I knew he was quite fond of his food.

After lunch we went and sat in the cane chairs on the veranda that overlooked the garden. There appeared to be no one else in the circuit house. There was something eerie about the silence that afternoon. All we could hear was the noise made by a few monkeys sitting on the gulmohar tree across the cobbled path.

Around 3 p.m., we saw a man come into the garden, carrying a watering can. He was an old man. His hair, moustaches and sideburns all were white.

'Will you ask him or should I?'

At this question from Jayanto, I raised a reassuring hand and went straight to the gardener. After I had spoken to him, he looked at me rather suspiciously. Clearly, no one had ever made such a request. 'Why, babu?' he asked. I laid a friendly hand on his shoulder and said, 'Don't worry about the reason. I'll give you five rupees. Please do as you're told.'

He relented, going so far as to give me a salute accompanied by a broad grin.

I beckoned to Jayanto, who was still sitting on the veranda. He rose and began walking towards me. As he came closer, I saw the pallor on his face.

I did hope we would find at least some part of the doll.

The gardener, in the meantime, had fetched a spade. The three of us made our way to the deodar tree.

Jayanto pointed at the ground about a yard from the trunk of the tree and said, 'Here.'

'Are you sure?' I asked him.

Jayanto nodded silently.

'How much did you dig?'

'At least eight inches.'

The gardener started digging. The man had a sense of humour. As he lifted his spade, he asked if there was hidden treasure under the ground and, if so, whether we would be prepared to share it with him. I had to laugh at this, but Jayanto's face did not register even the slightest trace of amusement. It was the month of October and not at all warm in Bundi. Yet the collar of his shirt was soaked in sweat. He was staring at the ground unblinkingly. The gardener continued to dig. Why was there no sign of the doll?

The raucous cry of a peacock made me turn my head for a moment and, in that instant, Jayanto made a strange sound. I quickly looked at him. His eyes were bulging. He raised his right

hand and pointed at the hole in the ground with a finger that was
visibly trembling.

Then he asked in a voice turned hoarse with fear, 'What . . .
what is that?'

The spade slipped from the gardener's hand. I, too, gaped at
the ground, open-mouthed in horror, amazement and disbelief.

There lay at our feet, covered in dust, lying flat on its back, a
twelve-inch-long, pure white, perfect little human skeleton.

(1970)   *Translated by Gopa Majumdar*

BARIN BHOWMICK'S AILMENT

Mr Barin Bhowmick got into compartment D as instructed by the conductor and placed his suitcase under his seat. He would not need to open it during his journey. But he must keep the other smaller bag somewhere within easy reach. It contained such essentials as a comb, a hair brush, a toothbrush, his shaving kit, a book by James Hadley Chase to read on the way and several other knick-knacks, including throat pills. If the long train journey in a cold, air-conditioned compartment resulted in a sore throat, he would not be able to sing tomorrow. He quickly popped a pill into his mouth and put his bag on the small table in front of the window.

It was a Delhi-bound vestibule train. There were only about seven minutes left before its departure, and yet there was no sign of the other passengers. Would he be able to travel all the way to Delhi alone? Could he be so lucky? That would indeed be the height of luxury. The very idea brought a song to his lips.

He looked out of the window at the crowd on the platform. Two young men were glancing at him occasionally. Clearly, he had been recognized. This was not a new experience. People often recognized him for they were now familiar not just with his voice but also with his appearance. He had to give live performances at least half-a-dozen times every month. Listen to Barin Bhowmick tonight—he will sing songs written by Nazrul as well as modern hits. Money and fame—both had come to Barin Bhowmick in full measure.

However, this had happened only over the last five years. Before that he had struggled a lot. It was not enough to be a talented singer. He needed a suitable break and proper backing. This came in 1963 when Bhola-da—Bhola Banerjee—invited him to sing in the puja pandal in Unish Palli. Barin Bhowmick had not looked back since then.

In fact, he was now going to Delhi at the invitation of the Bengal Association to sing at their jubilee celebrations. They were paying for his travel by first class and had promised to make all arrangements for his stay in Delhi. He intended spending a couple of days in Delhi. Then he would go to Agra and Fatehpur Sikri and return to Calcutta a week later. After that it would be time for the pujas again and life would become madly hectic.

'Your order for lunch, sir . . .?'

The conductor-guard appeared in the doorway.

'What is available?'

'You are a non-vegetarian, aren't you? You could choose between Indian and western food. If you want Indian, we've got . . .'

Barin Babu placed his order for lunch and had just lit a Three Castles cigarette when another passenger came into his compartment; at the same instant, the train began pulling out of the station.

Barin Babu looked at the newcomer. Didn't he seem vaguely familiar? Barin Babu tried to smile, but his smile vanished quickly as there was no response from the other. Had he made a mistake? Oh, God—how embarrassing! Why did he have to smile like an idiot? A similar thing had happened to him once before. He had thumped a man very hard on the back with a boisterous, 'Hel-lo, Tridib-da! How are you?' only to discover he was not Tridib-da at all. The memory of this incident had caused him much discomfort for days afterwards. God laid so many traps to embarrass one!

Barin Bhowmick looked at the other man once more. He had kicked off his sandals and was sitting with his legs outstretched, leafing through the pages of the latest *Illustrated Weekly*. Again, Barin Babu got the feeling that he had seen him somewhere, and not just for a few minutes. He had spent a long time in this man's company. But when was it? And where? The man had bushy eyebrows, a thin moustache, shiny hair and a little mole in the middle of his forehead. Yes, this face was certainly familiar. Could he have seen this man when he used to work for Central Telegraph? But surely the whole thing could not have been one-sided? His companion was definitely not showing any sign of recognition.

'Your order for lunch, sir?'

The conductor-guard had reappeared. He was a portly, rather amiable gentleman.

'Well,' said the newcomer, 'we'll worry about lunch later. Could I have a cup of tea first?'

'Of course.'

'All I need is a cup and the beverage. I prefer drinking black tea.'

That did it. Barin Bhowmick suddenly began to feel rather unwell. There was a sinking feeling at the pit of his stomach. Then it seemed as though his heart had grown wings and flown straight into his throat. It was not just the man's voice but also the words he uttered with a special emphasis: black tea. That was enough to remove the uncertainties from Barin Babu's mind. Every memory came flooding back.

Barin Babu had indeed seen this man before and that too— strangely enough—in a similar air-conditioned compartment of a train going to Delhi. He himself was going to Patna to attend the wedding of his cousin, Shipra. Three days before he left, he had won a little more than 7,000 rupees at the races. He could, therefore, afford the luxury of travelling first class. This happened nine years ago, in 1964, long before he had become a well-known singer. He could vaguely recall the other man's surname. It began with a 'C'. Chowdhury? Chakravarty? Chatterjee?

The conductor-guard left. Barin Babu realized he could no longer sit facing the other man. He went and stood in the corridor outside, well away from his fellow passenger. Yes, coincidences did occur in life. But this one was unbelievable.

But had 'C' recognized him? If he had not, there might be two reasons for it. Perhaps he had a weak memory. Or perhaps Barin Babu's appearance had undergone significant changes in these nine years. He stared out of the window and tried to recall what these changes might possibly be.

He had gained a lot of weight, so presumably his face now looked fuller than it did before. He did not wear glasses in those days. Now he did. And his moustaches had gone. When did he shave them off? Ah yes. Not very long ago. He had gone to a salon on Hazra Road. The barber was both young and inexperienced. He failed to get the symmetry right while trimming the moustaches. Barin Babu himself did not notice it at first but when everyone in his office from the chatty old liftman, Sukdeo, to the sixty-two-year-old cashier, Keshav Babu, began commenting on it, he shaved his precious moustaches off totally. This had happened about four years ago.

So he had lost his moustaches, but gained a bit of flesh on his cheeks and acquired a pair of glasses. Feeling a little reassured, he returned to his carriage.

A bearer came in with a pot of tea and placed it in front of 'C'. Barin Babu, too, felt the need for a drink, but did not dare speak to the bearer. What if 'C' recognized his voice?

Barin Babu did not even want to think about what 'C' might do to him if he did get recognized. But, of course, everything depended on the kind of man 'C' was. If he was anything like Animesh-da, Barin Babu had nothing to fear. Once, in a bus, Animesh-da realized someone was trying to pick his pocket. But he was too shy to raise a hue-and-cry, so he practically gave away his wallet to the pickpocket, together with four crisp ten-rupee notes. He told his family afterwards, 'A big scene in a crowded bus with me playing a prominent role in it—no, I could not allow that to happen.'

Was this man a bit like that? Probably not. People like Animesh-da were hard to come by. Besides, his looks were not very reassuring. Everything about him—those bushy eyebrows, the blunt nose and that chin that jutted out—seemed to suggest that he would not hesitate at all to plant his hairy hands on Barin Babu's throat and say, 'Are you not the same man who stole my clock in 1964? Scoundrel! I have spent these nine years looking for you! Today, I shall . . .'

Barin Babu dared not think any more. Even in this air-conditioned compartment there were beads of perspiration on his forehead. He stretched himself out on his berth and covered his eyes with his left arm. It was one's eyes that gave one away. In fact, 'C' had seemed familiar only because Barin Babu had recognized the look in his eyes.

He could now recall the incidents vividly. It was not just the matter of stealing 'C''s clock. He could remember every little thing he had stolen in his life since his boyhood. Some were totally insignificant things like a ballpoint pen (Mukul Mama's), or a cheap magnifying glass (his classmate Akshay's), or a pair of bone cuff links that belonged to Chheni-da which he did not need at all. He never wore them even once. The only reason he stole these—and, for that matter, all those other things—was that they were near at hand and they belonged to someone else.

Between the ages of twelve and twenty-five, Barin Bhowmick had removed at least fifty different things from various people and made a collection in his house. What could one call it but stealing? The only difference between him and a regular thief was that a thief stole to survive in life; Barin Babu did it out of habit. Nobody ever suspected him. He had, therefore, never been caught. Barin Babu knew that this habit, this strange compulsion to steal things, was a kind of illness. Once he had even learnt the medical term for it from one of his friends who was a doctor, but now he could not remember what it was.

But 'C''s clock was the last thing he had stolen. In the last nine years, he had never experienced that sudden, strong urge. He knew he had got over his illness and was now totally cured.

The difference between stealing 'C''s clock and all the other petty thefts he had indulged in was that he had really wanted that clock. It was a beautiful travelling clock, made in Switzerland. It lay in a blue square box and stood upright the moment the lid was lifted. It was an alarm clock and the sound of the alarm was so sweet that it was a pleasure to wake up to it.

Barin Babu had used that clock consistently over these nine years. He took it with him wherever he went. Even today, the clock was resting within the depths of the bag kept on the table before the window.

'How far are you going?'

Barin Babu gave a violent start. The other man was actually speaking to him!

'Delhi.'

'Pardon?'

'Delhi.'

The first time, in an effort to disguise his voice, Barin Babu had spoken so softly that the man had clearly not heard him.

'Do you find it a bit too cold in here? Is that what's affecting your voice?'

'N-n-no.'

'It can happen, of course. Actually, I would have preferred going by ordinary first class if it wasn't for the dust.'

Barin Babu did not utter a word. He did not want to look at 'C', but his own curiosity forced him to cast frequent glances in 'C''s direction. Was 'C' showing signs of recognition? No. He appeared quite relaxed. Could he be pretending? There was no way of being sure. After all, Barin Babu did not know him well. All he had learnt the last time about his fellow passenger was that he liked having black tea and that he was wont to get down at every station to buy snacks. Thanks to this habit, Barin Babu had had the chance to eat a lot of tasty stuff.

Apart from this, Barin Babu had seen one other side to 'C''s character, just as they were about to reach Patna. This was directly related to the incident involving the clock.

They had been travelling by the Amritsar Mail. It was supposed to reach Patna at 5 a.m. The conductor came and woke Barin Babu at 4.30. 'C', too, was half awake, although he was going all the way to Delhi.

Just about three minutes before the train was to reach Patna, it suddenly screeched to a halt. What could be the reason? There were a few people with torches running about on the tracks. Was it anything serious? Eventually, the guard turned up and said that an old man had been run over by the train while crossing the track. The train would start as soon as his body was removed.

'C' got very excited at this news and clambered down quickly in the dark, still clad in his sleeping suit. Then he went out to see for himself what had happened.

It was during this brief absence that Barin Babu had removed the clock from 'C''s bag. He had seen 'C' wind it the night before, and had felt tempted immediately. But since the likelihood of finding a suitable opportunity was dim, he had told himself to forget the whole thing. However, when an opportunity presented itself so unexpectedly, Barin Babu simply could not stop himself. He had slipped his hand into 'C''s bag and had taken the clock out, then he had dropped it into his own case. It took him fifteen to twenty seconds to do this. 'C' had returned about five minutes later.

'A horrible business! A beggar, you see. The head's been totally severed from the body. I fail to see how an engine can possibly hit somebody despite a cow-catcher being there. Isn't it supposed to push aside all obstacles on the track?'

Barin Babu got off safely at Patna and was met by his uncle. The faint uneasiness at the pit of his stomach vanished the instant he got into his uncle's car and drove off. His heart told him that it was the end of the story. No one could catch him now. The chances of running into 'C' were one in a million, or perhaps even less than that.

But who knew that one day, years later, by such an incredible coincidence, they would meet again? 'A thing like this is enough to make one turn superstitious,' thought Barin Babu to himself.

'Do you live in Delhi? Or Calcutta?' asked 'C'.

He had asked him a lot of questions the last time as well, Barin Babu recalled. He hated people who tried to act friendly.

'Calcutta,' said Barin Babu. Oh no! He had spoken in his normal voice. He really must be more careful.

Good God—why was the man staring so hard at him? What could be the reason for such interest? Barin Babu's pulse began racing again.

'Did your photograph come out in the papers recently?'

Barin Babu realized it would be foolish not to tell the truth. There were other Bengali passengers on the train who might recognize him. There was no harm in telling this man who he was. In fact, if he could be informed that Barin Babu was a famous singer, he might find it difficult to relate him to the thief who had once stolen his clock.

'Where did you see this photograph?' Barin Babu threw a counter question.

'Do you sing?' came another one!

'Yes, a little.'

'Your name . . .?'

'Barindranath Bhowmick.'

'Ah, I see. Barin Bhowmick. That's why you seemed familiar. You sing on the radio, don't you?'

'Yes.'

'My wife is an admirer of yours. Are you going to Delhi to sing at some function?'

'Yes.'

Barin Babu was not going to tell him much. If a simple 'yes' or 'no' could suffice, there was no need to say anything more.

'I know a Bhowmick in Delhi. He's in the finance ministry. Nitish Bhowmick. Is he a relative or something?'

Indeed. Nitish was Barin Babu's first cousin. A man well known for his rigid discipline. A close relative, but not someone who was close to Barin Babu personally.

'No, I'm afraid I don't know him.'

Barin Babu decided to tell this one lie. He wished the man would stop talking. Why did he want to know so many things?

Oh good. Lunch had arrived. Hopefully, the volley of questions would cease, at least for a little while.

And so it did. 'C' obviously enjoyed eating. He began to concentrate on his food and fell silent. Barin Babu no longer felt all that nervous, but still he could not relax completely. They would have to spend at least another twenty hours in each other's company. Memory was such a strange phenomenon. Who could tell what little thing—a gesture, a look, a word—might make some old and forgotten memory come to life?

Black tea, for instance. Barin Babu believed that if those two words had not been uttered, he would never have recognized 'C'. What if something he said or something he did caused 'C' to recognize him?

The best thing, of course, would be not to say or do anything at all. Barin Babu lay down on his berth, hiding his face behind his paperback. When he finished the first chapter, he turned his head cautiously and stole a glance at 'C'. He seemed to be asleep. The *Illustrated Weekly* had dropped from his hand on to the floor. An arm was flung across his eyes, but from the way his chest rose and fell it seemed as though he had fallen into a deep sleep. Barin Babu looked out of the window. Open fields, trees, little huts—the barren landscape of Bihar flashed past. The noise of the wheels came very faintly through the double glass of the windows, sounding like distant drums being beaten in the same steady rhythm: dha-dhinak, na-dhinak, dha-dhinak, na-dhinak . . .

Another sound inside the compartment was soon added to this: the sound of 'C''s snoring.

Barin Babu felt a lot more reassured. He began humming a Nazrul song. His voice did not sound too bad. He cleared his throat once and began to sing a bit more loudly. But he had to stop almost immediately.

Something else was making a noise in the compartment. It shocked Barin Bhowmick into silence.

It was the sound of an alarm clock. The alarm on the Swiss clock kept in his bag had somehow been set off. And it continued to ring, non-stop.

Barin Babu discovered he could not move his limbs. They were paralysed with fear. His eyes fixed themselves on 'C'.

'C' moved his arm. Barin Babu stiffened.

'C' was now awake. He removed his arm from his eyes.

'Is it that glass? Could you please remove it? It's vibrating against the wall.'

The noise stopped the instant Barin Babu took the glass out of the iron ring attached to the wall. Before placing it on the table, he drank the water that was in it. This helped his throat, but he was still in no mood to start singing again.

Tea was served a little before they reached Hazaribagh Road. Two cups of hot tea and the absence of any further curious questions from 'C' helped Barin Babu relax more. He looked out once again and began humming softly. Soon, he was able to totally forget the danger he was in.

At Gaya, not unexpectedly, 'C' got down onto the platform and returned with two packets of peanuts. He gave one to Barin Babu. Barin Babu consumed the whole packet with considerable relish.

The sun had set by the time the train left the station. 'C' switched the lights on and said, 'Are we running late? What's the time on your watch?'

Barin Babu realized for the first time that 'C' was not wearing a watch. This surprised him and he could not help but show it. Then he remembered that 'C''s question had not been answered. He glanced at his wristwatch. 'It's 7.35,' he said.

'Then we're running more or less on time.'

'Yes.'

'My watch broke this morning. It was an HMT. . . gave excellent time . . . but this morning someone pulled my bedsheet so hard that the watch fell on the ground and . . .'

Barin Babu did not comment. Any mention of watches and clocks was reprehensible.

'What make is your watch?' asked 'C'.

'HMT.'

'Does it keep good time?'

'Yes.'

'Actually, I have always been unlucky in the matter of clocks.' Barin Babu tried to yawn, simply to assume an unconcerned air, but failed in his attempt. Even the muscles in his jaw appeared to be paralysed. He could not open his mouth. But his ears continued to function. He was forced to hear all that 'C' had to say.

'I had this Swiss travelling clock, you see. Made of gold. A friend of mine had brought it from Geneva. I had used it for barely a month when I was travelling to Delhi by train—in an air-conditioned compartment like this one. The clock was with me. There were only two of us—another Bengali chap. Do you know what he did? Just think of his audacity! In my absence—while I may have gone to the bathroom or something—he nicked that clock from me! He looked such a complete gentleman. But I suppose I'm lucky he didn't murder me in my sleep. I stopped travelling by train after that. This time, too, I would have gone by air, but the pilots' strike upset my plans . . .'

Barin Bhowmick's throat was dry, his hands felt numb. But he knew if he said absolutely nothing after a tale like that, it would seem odd. In fact, it would seem distinctly suspicious. With a tremendous effort, he forced himself to speak.

'Did . . . did you not look for it?'

'Ha! Can any stolen object be found simply by looking for it? But, for a long time, I could not forget what the man looked like. Even now I have a vague recollection. He was neither fair nor dark, had a moustache and must have been about the same height as you, but slimmer. If I could meet him again, I would teach him a lesson he'd remember all his life. I was a boxer once, you know. A light heavyweight champion. That man is lucky our paths never crossed again . . .'

Barin Babu could now remember the full name of his

companion. Chakravarty. Pulak Chakravarty. Strange! The minute he mentioned boxing, his name flashed in Barin Babu's mind like a title on a television screen. Pulak Chakravarty had talked a lot about boxing the last time.

But even if his name had come back to him, what good did that do? After all, it was Barin Babu who was the culprit. And now it had become impossible to carry his load of guilt. What if he went and confessed everything? And then returned the clock? There it was in that bag . . . so near at hand . . .!

No! Was he going mad? How could he entertain such thoughts? He was a famous vocalist. How could he admit to having stooped so low? Would his reputation not suffer? Would anyone ever invite him to sing at their function? What would his fans think? Where was the guarantee that this other man was not a journalist or someone connected with the media? No, there was no question of making a confession.

Perhaps there was no need for it, either. Perhaps he would be recognized, anyway. Pulak Chakravarty was giving him rather odd looks. Delhi was still sixteen hours away. There was every chance of being caught. In Barin Babu's mind flashed a sudden image—his moustaches had grown back, the flesh on his face had worn away, his glasses had vanished. Pulak Chakravarty was staring hard at the face he had seen nine years ago. The look of amazement in his slightly hazel eyes was slowly turning into a look filled with anger. His lips were parting in a slow, cruel smile. 'Ah ha!' he seemed to be saying, 'You are the same man, are you not? Good. I have waited all these years to lay my hands on you. Now I shall have my little revenge . . .'

By 10 p.m., Barin Babu had run up a fairly high temperature, accompanied by intense shivering. He called the guard and asked for an extra blanket. Then he covered himself from head to foot with both blankets and lay flat on his back. Pulak Chakravarty closed the door of their compartment and bolted it. Before switching off the lights, he turned towards Barin Babu and said, 'You appear unwell. I have some very effective pills with me—here, take these two. You're not used to travelling in an air-conditioned coach, are you?'

Barin Babu swallowed the tablets. Well, given his present condition, Pulak Chakravarty might spare him a ruthless punishment. But Barin Babu had made up his mind about one thing. He must transfer that clock to the suitcase of its rightful owner. He must try to get this done tonight, if possible. But he could not move until his temperature went down. His body was still shivering occasionally.

Pulak Chakravarty had switched on the reading lamp over his head. He had a paperback open in his hand. But was he reading it, or was he only staring at a page and thinking of something else? Why did he not turn the page? How long could it take to read a couple of pages?

Suddenly Barin Babu noticed Pulak's eyes were no longer fixed on the book. He had turned his head slightly and was looking at him. Barin Babu closed his eyes. After a long time, he opened one of them cautiously and glanced at Pulak Chakravarty. Yes, he was still staring hard at him. Barin Babu promptly shut his eye again. His heart was jumping like a frog, matching the rhythm of the wheels—lub dup, lub dup, lub dup.

A faint click told Barin Babu that the reading light had been switched off. Slightly reassured, he opened both his eyes this time. The light in the corridor outside was coming in through a crack in the door. Barin Babu saw Pulak Chakravarty put his book down on the table beside Barin Babu's bag. Then he pulled his blanket up to his chin, turned on his side, facing Barin Babu, and yawned noisily.

Barin Babu's heartbeats gradually returned to normal. Tomorrow—yes, tomorrow morning he must return the clock. He had noticed Pulak Chakravarty's suitcase was unlocked. He had gone and changed into a sleeping suit a little while ago.

Barin Babu had stopped shivering. Perhaps those tablets had started to work. What were they? He had swallowed them simply so that he would recover in time to be able to sing at that function in Delhi. Applause from an audience was something he had no wish to miss. But had he done a wise thing? What if those pills . . .?

No, he must not think about such things. The incident of the glass vibrating against the wall was bad enough. Obviously, all these strange ideas were simply a result of a sick and guilt-ridden mind. Tomorrow, he must find a remedy for this. Without a clear conscience, he could not have a clear voice and his performance would be a total failure. Bengal Association . . .

The tinkle of tea cups woke Barin Bhowmick in the morning. A waiter had come in with his breakfast: bread, butter, an omelette and tea. Should he be eating all this? Did he still have a slight fever? No, he did not. In fact, he felt just fine. What wonderful tablets those were! He began to feel quite grateful towards Pulak Chakravarty.

But where was he? In the bathroom, perhaps. Or was he in the corridor? Barin Babu went out to take a look as soon as the waiter had gone. There was no one in the corridor outside. How long ago had Pulak Chakravarty left? Should he take a chance?

Barin Babu took a chance, but did not quite succeed in his effort. He had taken the clock out of his own bag and had just bent down to pull out Pulak Chakravarty's suitcase from under his berth, when his fellow passenger walked in with a towel and a shaving kit in his hands. Barin Babu's right hand closed around the clock. He straightened himself.

'How are you? All right?'

'Yes, thank you. Er . . . can you recognize this?'

Barin Babu opened his palm. The clock lay on it. A strange determination had risen in his mind. He had got over the old compulsive urge to steal a long time ago. But this business of playing hide-and-seek, was this not a form of deception? All that tension, those uncertainties, the anxiety over should-I-do-it-or-shouldn't-I, this funny, empty feeling in his stomach, the parched throat, the jumping heart—all these were signs of a malady, were they not? This, too, had to be overcome. There could never be any peace of mind otherwise.

Pulak Chakravarty had only just started to rub his ears with his towel. The sight of the clock turned him into a statue. His hand holding the towel remained stuck to his ear.

Barin Babu said, 'Yes, I am that same man. I've put on a bit of weight, shaved my moustaches and have started wearing glasses. I was then going to Patna and you to Delhi. In 1964. Remember that man who got run over by our train? And you went out to investigate? Well, I took the clock in your absence.'

Pulak Chakravarty's eyes were now looking straight into Barin Babu's. Barin Babu saw him frowning deeply; the whites of his eyes had become rather prominent, his lips had parted as though he wanted to say something but could not find speech.

Barin Babu continued, 'Actually, it was an illness I used to suffer from. I mean, I am not really a thief. There is a medical term for it which escapes me at the moment. Anyway, I am cured now and am quite normal. I used your clock all these years and was taking it with me to Delhi. Since I happened to meet you—it's really a miracle, isn't it?—I thought I'd return it to you. I hope you will not hold any . . . er . . . against me.'

Pulak Chakravarty could do no more than say 'thanks' very faintly. He was still staring at the clock, now transferred to his own hand, totally dumbfounded.

Barin Babu collected his toothbrush, toothpaste, and shaving kit. Then he took the towel off its rack and went into the bathroom. He broke into a song as soon as he had closed the door, and was pleased to note that the old, natural melody in his voice was fully restored.

It took him about three minutes to get N.C. Bhowmick in the finance ministry in Delhi. Then, a deep, familiar voice boomed into his ear.

'Hello.'

'Nitish-da? This is Barin Babu.'

'Oh, so you've arrived, have you? I'm coming this evening to hear you sing. Even you have turned into a celebrity, haven't you? My, my, who would have thought it possible? But anyway, what made you call me?'

'Well—do you happen to know someone called Pulak Chakravarty? He is supposed to have been your batch-mate in college. He was a boxer.'

'Who? Old Pincho?'

'Pincho?'

'Yes, he used to pinch practically everything he saw. Fountain pens, books from the library, tennis racquets from our common room—it was he who stole my first Ronson. It was funny, because it wasn't as though he lacked anything in life. His father was a rich man. It was actually a kind of ailment.'

'Ailment?'

'Yes, haven't you ever heard of it? It's called kleptomania. K-l-e-p . . .'

Barin Babu put the receiver down and stared at his open suitcase. He had only just checked into his hotel and started to unpack. No, there was no mistake. A few items were certainly missing from it. A whole carton of Three Castles cigarettes, a pair of Japanese binoculars and a wallet containing five hundred-rupee notes.

Kleptomania. Barin Babu had forgotten the word. Now it would stay etched in his mind—forever.

(1973)   *Translated by Gopa Majumdar*

THE MATHS TEACHER, MR PINK
AND TIPU

Tipu closed his geography book and glanced at the clock. He had studied non-stop for exactly forty-seven minutes. It was now thirteen minutes past three. There was no harm in going out for a little while, was there? That strange creature had appeared the other day at around this time. Didn't he say that he would come back again if ever Tipu had reason to feel sad? There was a reason now. A very good reason. Should he go out for a minute?

Oh no. Mother had come out to the veranda. He just heard her shoo a crow away. Then the cane chair creaked. That meant she had sat down to sun herself. Tipu would have to wait for a while.

He could remember the creature so well. He had never seen anyone like him—so short, no beard or moustache—yet he was not a child. No child had such a deep voice. But then, the creature was not old either. At least, Tipu had been unable to figure out if he was. His skin was smooth, his complexion the colour of sandalwood tinged with pink. In fact, Tipu thought of him as Mr Pink. He did not know what he was actually called. He did ask, but the creature replied, 'It's no use telling you my name. It would twist your tongue to pronounce it.'

Tipu felt affronted by this. 'Why should I start stuttering? I can say things like gobbledygook and flabbergasted. I can even manage floccinaucinihilipilification. So why should your name be a tongue-twister?'

'You couldn't possibly manage with just one tongue.

'You mean you have more than one?'

'You need only one to talk in your language.'

The man was standing under the tall, bare shimul tree just behind the house. Not many people came here. There was a large open space behind the tree, followed by rice fields. And behind these, in the distance, stood the hills. Tipu had seen a mongoose disappear behind a bush only a few days ago. Today, he had brought a few pieces of bread with the intention of scattering them on the ground. The mongoose might be tempted to reappear.

His eyes suddenly fell on the man standing under the tree.

'Hello!' said the man, smiling.

Was he a westerner? Tipu knew he could not converse for very long if the man spoke only in English. So he just stared at him. The man walked across to him and said, 'Do you have reason to be sad?'

'Sad?'

'Yes.'

Tipu was taken aback. No one had ever asked him such a question. He said, 'Why, no, I don't think so.'

'Are you sure?'

'Of course.'

'But you're supposed to be sad. That's what the calculations showed.'

'What kind of sadness? I thought I might see the mongoose. But I didn't. Is that what you mean?'

'No, no. The kind of sadness I meant would make the back of your ears go blue. Your palms would feel dry.'

'You mean a very deep sadness.'

'Yes.'

'No, I am not feeling that sad.'

Now the man began to look rather sad himself. He shook his head and said, 'That means I cannot be released yet.'

'Released?'

'Yes, released. I cannot be free.'

'I know what release means,' said Tipu. 'Would you be set free if I felt unhappy?'

The man looked straight at Tipu. 'Are you ten-and-a-half years old?'

'Yes.'

'And your name is Master Tarpan Chowdhury?'

'Yes.'

'Then there is no mistake.'

Tipu could not figure out how the man knew such a lot about him. He asked, 'Does it have to be me? If someone else felt sad, wouldn't that do?'

'No. And it's not enough to feel sad. The cause of sadness must be removed.'

'But so many people are unhappy. A beggar called Nikunja comes to our house so often. He says he has no one in the world. He must be very unhappy indeed.'

'No, that won't do,' the man shook his head again. 'Tarpan Chowdhury, ten years old—is there someone else who has the same name and is of the·same age?'

'No, I don't think so.'

'Then it must be you.'

Tipu could not resist the next question.

'What release are you talking about? You appear to be walking about quite freely!'

'This is not my land. I have been exiled here.'

'Why?'

'You ask too many questions.'

'I'm interested, that's all. Look, I've met you for the first time. So naturally I'd like to know who you are, what you do, where you live, who else knows you—things like that. What's wrong with being interested?'

'You'll get jinjiria if you try to learn so much.'

The man did not actually say 'jinjiria'. What he did say sounded so completely unpronounceable that Tipu decided to settle for jinjiria. God knew what kind of an ailment it was.

But who did the man remind him of? Rumpelstiltskin? Or was he one of Snow White's seven dwarfs?

Tipu was passionately fond of fairy tales. His grandfather brought him three or four books of fairy tales every year from Calcutta. Tipu read them all avidly, his flights of fancy taking him far beyond the seven seas, thirteen rivers and thirty-six hills. In his mind, he became a prince, a pearl-studded turban on his head, a sword slung from his waist, flashing diamonds. Some days he would set forth to look for priceless jewels and to fight a dragon.

'Goodbye!' said the man.

Was he leaving already?

'You didn't tell me where you live!'

The man paid no attention. All he said was, 'We shall meet again when you feel sad.'

'But how will you know?'

There was no answer for by then, the man had jumped over a mulberry tree and vanished from sight—having broken all possible world records in high jump.

This had happened about six weeks ago. Tipu did not see the man again. But he needed him now for he was desperately unhappy.

The reason for his sorrow was the new maths teacher in his school, Narahari Babu.

Tipu had not liked him from the very beginning. When he

had come to class for the first time he had spent the first two minutes just staring at the boys. How hard he had stared! As though he wanted to kill everyone with that look before he began teaching. Tipu had never seen anyone with such a huge moustache. And his voice! What a deep, loud voice it was! Why did he have to speak so loudly? No one in the class was deaf, after all.

The disaster occurred two days later. It was a Thursday. The sky was overcast and it was cold outside. Tipu did not feel like going out in the lunch break. So he sat in his class reading the story of Dalimkumar. Who was to know the maths teacher would walk past his classroom and come in upon him?

'What book is that, Tarpan?'

One had to admit that the new teacher had a remarkable memory, for he had already learnt the name of each boy.

Tipu felt slightly nervous but took courage from the thought that no one could object to his reading a story-book in the lunch break. '*Tales from Grandma*, sir!' he said.

'Let's have a look.'

Tipu handed the book to his teacher. The latter thumbed its pages for a minute. Then he exploded, 'Kings, queens, princes and demons—birds of pearls on a tree of diamonds, abracadabra—what on earth are you reading? What a pack of nonsense! How do you suppose you'll ever learn mathematics if you keep reading this idiotic stuff?'

'But these are only stories, sir!' Tipu stammered.

'Stories? Shouldn't all stories make sense? Or is it enough simply to write what comes into one's head?'

Tipu was not going to give in so easily.

'Why, sir,' he said, 'even the *Ramayana* talks of Hanuman and Jambuvan. The *Mahabharata*, too, is full of tales of demons and monsters.'

'Don't argue,' snarled Narahari Babu. 'Those tales were

written by sages more than two thousand years ago. Ganesh
with the head of an elephant and the body of a man, and the
goddess Durga with ten arms are not the same as the kind of
nonsense you're reading. You should read about great men,
about explorers, scientific inventions, the evolution of man—
things to do with the real world. You belong to the twentieth
century, don't you? Foolish, ignorant people in villages might
once have enjoyed such absurd stories. Why should you? If you
do, you ought to go back to a village school and try learning
maths with the help of rhymed couplets. Can you do that?'

Tipu fell silent. He had not realized a small remark from him
would trigger off such a tirade.

'Who else in your class reads such books?' his teacher
asked.

To tell the truth, no one did. Sheetal had once borrowed *Folk
Tales of Hindustan* from Tipu and returned it the very next day,
saying, 'Rubbish! Phantom comics are a lot better than this!'

'No one, sir,' Tipu replied.

'Hmm . . . what's your father's name?'

'Taranath Chowdhury.'

'Where do you live?'

'Station Road. At number five.'

'Hmm.' His teacher dropped the book back on Tipu's desk
with a thud and left.

Tipu did not go back to his house straight after school. He
wandered off beyond the mango grove near the school and
found himself in front of Bishnuram Das's house. A white horse
was tethered outside it. Tipu leant against a jamrool tree and
stared at the horse absent-mindedly. Bishnuram Babu owned a
beedi factory. He rode to his factory every day. He was still fit
enough to do so, although he had crossed fifty.

Tipu came here often to look at the horse; but today his
mind was elsewhere. Deep down in his heart he knew the new

maths teacher would try to put a stop to his reading story-books. How would he survive without his books? He read them every day and he enjoyed reading most the ones his teacher had described as stuff and nonsense. His reading such stories had never stopped him from doing well in maths, had it? He had got forty-four out of fifty in the last test. His previous maths teacher Bhudeb Babu had never ticked him off for reading story-books!

The days being short in winter, Tipu knew he had to return home soon, and was about to leave when he saw something that made him hide quickly behind the tree.

His maths teacher, Narahari Babu, was coming towards him, a book and an umbrella under his arm.

Did that mean he lived somewhere close by? There were five other houses next to the one where Bishnuram Babu lived. Beyond these houses was a large, open space known as Hamlatuni's Field. A long time ago, there was a silk factory on the eastern side of the field. Its manager, Mr Hamilton, was reputed to be a hard taskmaster. He worked as manager for thirty-two years and then died in his bungalow, not far from the factory. His name got somewhat distorted and thus the whole area came to be known as Hamlatuni's Field.

In the gathering dusk of the winter evening, Tipu watched Narahari Babu from behind the jamrool tree. He was surprised at his behaviour. Narahari Babu was standing beside the horse, gently patting its back and making a strange chirrupping noise through his lips.

At that very moment, the front door of the house opened and, holding a cheroot in his hand, Bishnuram Babu himself came out.

'Namaskar.'

Narahari Babu took his hand off the horse's back and turned. Bishnuram Babu returned his greeting and asked, 'How about a game?'

'That's precisely why I've come!' said Tipu's teacher. This meant he played chess, because Tipu knew Bishnuram Babu did.

'Nice horse,' said Narahari Babu. 'Where did you get it?'

'Calcutta. I bought it from Dwarik Mitter of Shobhabazar. It used to be a race horse called Pegasus.'

Pegasus? The name seemed vaguely familiar but Tipu could not recall where he had heard it.

'Pegasus,' said the maths teacher. 'What a strange name!'

'Yes, race horses usually have funny names. Happy Birthday, Subhan Allah, Forget-Me-Not . . .'

'Do you ride this horse?'

'Of course. A very sturdy beast. Hasn't given me a day's trouble.'

Narahari Babu kept staring at the horse.

'I used to ride once.'

'Really?'

'We lived in Sherpur in those days. My father was a doctor. He used a horse for making house calls. I was in school then. I used to ride whenever I could. Oh, that was a long time ago!'

'Would you like to ride this one?'

'May I?'

'Go ahead!'

Tipu stared in amazement as his teacher dropped his book and his umbrella on the veranda and untied the horse. Then he climbed onto its back in one swift movement and pressed its flanks with his heels. The horse began to trot.

'Don't go far,' said Bishnuram Babu.

'Get the chessmen out,' said Narahari Babu. 'I'll be back in no time!'

Tipu did not wait any longer. What a day it had been!

But there was more in store.

It was around seven in the evening. Tipu had just finished

his homework and was contemplating reading a few stories when his father called him from downstairs.

Tipu walked into their living-room to find Narahari Babu sitting there with his father. His blood froze.

'Your teacher would like to see the books your grandfather has given you,' said Father. 'Go bring them.'

There were twenty-seven books. Tipu had to make three trips to get them all together.

His maths teacher took ten minutes to go through the lot, shaking his head occasionally and saying, 'Pooh!' Finally, he pushed the books aside and said, 'Look, Mr Chowdhury, what I am going to tell you is based on years of thinking and research. Fairy tales or folklore, call it what you will, can mean only one thing—sowing the seed of superstition in a young mind. A child will accept whatever it's told. Do you realize what an enormous responsibility we adults have? Should we be telling our children that the life of a man lies inside a fish and things like that, when the truth is that one's life beats in one's own heart? It cannot possibly exist anywhere else!'

Tipu could not figure out if Father agreed with all that the teacher said, but he did know that he believed in obeying a teacher's instructions.

'A child must learn to obey, Tipu,' he had told him so many times, 'especially what his elders tell him. You can do whatever you like after a certain age, when you have finished your studies and are standing on your own feet. You would then have the right to voice your own opinion. But not now.'

'Do you not have any other books for children?' asked Narahari Babu.

'Oh yes,' said Father, 'they're all here on my bookshelf. I won them as prizes in school. Haven't you seen them, Tipu?'

'I have read them all, Father,' said Tipu.

'Each one?'

'Each one. The biographies of Vidyasagar and Suresh Biswas, Captain Scott's expedition to the South Pole, Mungo Park's adventures in Africa, the story of steel and spaceships . . . you didn't win that many prizes, Father.'

'All right,' said Father, 'I'll buy you some more.'

'If you tell the Tirthankar Book Stall here, they can get you some books from Calcutta,' said Narahari Babu. 'You will read only those from now, Tarpan. Not these.'

Not these! Two little words—but they were enough to make Tipu's world come to an end. Not these!

Father took the books from Narahari Babu and locked them away in his cupboard.

Now they were quite out of reach.

Mother, however, appeared to be on Tipu's side. He could hear her grumble and, while they were having dinner, she went to the extent of saying, 'A man who can say such a thing does not deserve to be a teacher at all!'

Father disagreed, 'Can't you see what he has suggested is for Tipu's good?'

'Nonsense,' said Mother. Then she ruffled Tipu's hair affectionately and said, 'Don't worry. I will tell you stories. Your grandmother used to tell me lots of stories. I haven't forgotten them all.'

Tipu did not say anything. He had already heard a number of stories from his mother and did not think she knew any more. Even if she did, hearing a story from someone was not the same as reading it. With an open book in front of him, he could lose himself in a totally different world. But how could he make his mother see that?

Two days later, Tipu realized he was really feeling sad. It was decidedly the kind of sadness Mr Pink had mentioned. Now he was Tipu's only hope.

Today was Sunday. Father was taking a nap. Mother had left

the veranda and was now at her sewing machine. It was three-thirty. Should he try to slip out of the back door? If only the man had told him where he lived! Tipu would have gone to him straightaway.

Tipu tiptoed down the stairs and went out through the backdoor.

Despite bright sunlight, there was quite a nip in the air. In the distance, the rice fields stretching right up to the hills looked golden. A dove was cooing somewhere and the occasional rustle that came from the shirish tree meant that there was a squirrel hidden in the leaves.

'Hello!'

Oh, what a surprise! When did he arrive? Tipu had not seen him come.

'The back of your ears are blue, your palms seem dry. I can tell you have reason to feel sad.'

'You can say that again,' said Tipu.

The man came walking towards him. He was wearing the same clothes.

The wind blew his hair in tufts.

'I need to know what has happened, or else I'm gobbledygasted.'

Tipu wanted to laugh, but made no attempt to correct what the man had said. Instead, he briefly related his tale of woe. Tears pricked his eyes as he spoke, but Tipu managed to control himself.

'Hmm,' said the man and started nodding. His head went up and down sixteen times. Tipu began to feel a little nervous. Would he never stop? Or was it that he could find no solution to the problem? He felt like crying once more, but the man gave a final nod, stopped and said 'Hmm' again. Tipu went limp with relief.

'Do you think you can do something?' he asked timidly.

'I shall have to think carefully. Must exercise the intestines.'

'Intestines? You mean you wouldn't exercise your brain?'

The man did not reply. He said instead, 'Didn't I see Narahari Babu ride a horse yesterday in that field?'

'Which field? Oh, you mean Hamlatuni's Field?'

'The one that has a broken building in it.'

'Yes, yes. Is that where you stay?'

'My tridingipidi is lying just behind that building.'

Tipu could not have heard him right. But even if he had, he would probably have been totally unable to pronounce the word.

The man had started nodding again. This time he stopped after the thirty-first nod and said, 'There will be a full moon tonight. If you wish to see what happens then come to that field just as the moon reaches the top of the palm tree. But make sure no one sees you.'

Suddenly a rather alarming thought occurred to Tipu.

'You will not try to kill my maths teacher, will you?'

For the first time he saw the man throw back his head and laugh.

He also saw that there were two tongues in his mouth and no teeth.

'Kill him?' The man stopped laughing. 'No, no. We don't believe in killing. In fact, I was banished from my land because I had thought of pinching someone. The first set of calculations gave us the name "Earth" where I had to be sent. Then we got the name of this place and then came your own name. I will be set free as soon as I can wipe out the cause of your sadness.'

'All right then. See you . . .'

But the man had already taken another giant leap over the mulberry tree and disappeared.

The faint tingle that had set in Tipu's body stayed all evening. By an amazing stroke of luck his parents were going out to dinner that night. Tipu, too, had been invited, but his mother felt he should stay at home and study. His exams were just round the corner.

They left at 7.30. Tipu waited for about five minutes after they had gone. Then he set off. The eastern sky had started to turn yellow.

It took him almost ten minutes to reach Bishnuram Babu's house through the short cut behind his school. The horse was no longer there. It must be in its stable behind the house, Tipu thought. Light streamed through the open window of the living-room. The room was full of smoke from cheroots.

'Check.'

It was the voice of his maths teacher. He was obviously playing chess with Bishnuram Babu. Was he not going to ride the horse tonight? There was no way one could tell. But that man had asked Tipu to go to Hamlatuni's Field. He must go there, come what may.

It was a full moon night. The moon looked golden now, but would turn silver later. It would take another ten minutes to reach the top of the palm tree. The moonlight was not yet very bright, but things were fairly easily visible. There were plenty of plants and bushes. The derelict old factory stood at a distance. The man was supposed to be staying behind it. But where?

Tipu hid behind a bush, and prepared to wait. In his pocket was some jaggery wrapped in a piece of newspaper. He bit off a small portion of it and began chewing. He could hear jackals calling from the jungle far away. The black object that flew past must be an owl.

Tipu was wearing a brown shawl over his coat. It helped him merge into the darkness and kept him warm as well.

A clock struck eight somewhere, probably in Bishnuram Babu's house.

And, soon afterwards, Tipu heard another noise: clip-clop, clip-clop, clip-clop.

Was it the horse?

Tipu peeped from behind the bush and stared at the lane.

Yes, it was indeed the same horse with Narahari Babu on its back.

Disaster struck at this precise moment. A mosquito had been buzzing around Tipu's ears. He tried to wave it away, but it suddenly went straight into one nostril!

Tipu knew it was possible to stop a sneeze by pressing the nose hard. But if he did that now, the mosquito might never come out. So he allowed himself to sneeze, shattering the stillness of the night. The horse stopped.

Someone flashed a powerful torch on Tipu.

'Tarpan?'

Tipu began to go numb with fear. Why, why, why did this have to happen? He had gone and ruined whatever plans that man must have made. What on earth would he think of Tipu?

The horse began to trot up to him with his maths teacher on its back. But suddenly it raised its forelegs high in the air, neighed loudly, and veered off from the lane. Then it jumped into the field.

What followed took Tipu's breath away. The horse took off from the ground, flapping two large wings which had grown from its sides! Tipu's teacher flung his arms around the horse's neck and hung on as best as he could. The torch had fallen from his hand.

The moon had reached the top of the palm tree. In the bright moonlight, Tipu saw the horse rise higher and higher in the sky until it disappeared among the stars.

Pegasus!

It came back to Tipu in a flash. It was a Greek tale. Medusa was an ogress—every strand of whose hair was a venomous snake, the very sight of whom made men turn into stone. The valiant Perseus chopped off her head with his sword and from her blood was born Pegasus, the winged horse.

'Go home, Tarpan!'

That strange man was standing beside Tipu, his golden hair gleaming in the moonlight.

'Everything is all right.'

Narahari Babu had to go to a hospital. He stayed there three days, although there was no sign of any physical injury. He talked to no one. Upon being asked what the matter was, he only shivered and looked away.

On the fourth day he was discharged. He came straight to Tipu's house. What transpired between him and Father, Tipu could not make out. But, as soon as he had gone, Father called Tipu and said, 'Er . . . you may take your books from my cupboard. Narahari Babu said he didn't mind your reading fairy tales any more.'

Tipu never saw the strange man again. He went looking for him behind the old factory and passed Bishnuram Babu's house on the way. The horse was still tethered to the same post. But there was absolutely nothing behind the factory, except a chameleon—pink from head to tail.

(1982)   *Translated by Gopa Majumdar*

BIG BILL

By Tulsi Babu's desk in his office on the ninth floor of a building in Old Court House Street, there was a window which opened onto a vast expanse of the western sky. Tulsi Babu's neighbour Jaganmoy Dutt had just gone to spit betel juice out of the window one morning in the rainy season when he noticed a double rainbow in the sky. He uttered an exclamation of surprise and turned to Tulsi Babu. 'Come here, sir. You won't see the like of it every day.'

Tulsi Babu left his desk, went to the window, and looked out.

'What do you want me to see?' he asked.

'Why, the double rainbow!' said Jaganmoy Dutt. 'Are you colour-blind?'

Tulsi Babu went back to his desk. 'I can't see what is so special about a double rainbow. Even if there were twenty rainbows in the sky, there would be nothing surprising about that. Why, in that case one can just as well go and stare at the double-spired church on Lower Circular Road!'

Not everyone is endowed with the same sense of wonder, but there was good reason to doubt whether Tulsi Babu possessed any at all. There was only one thing that never ceased to surprise him, and that was the excellence of the mutton kebab at Mansur's. The only person who was aware of this was Tulsi

Babu's friend and colleague, Prodyot Chanda.

Therefore, being endowed with this sceptical temperament, when Tulsi Babu found an unusually large egg while looking for medicinal plants in the forests of Dandakaranya, he was not particularly surprised.

Tulsi Babu had been dabbling in ayurvedic medicine for the last fifteen years. His father was a well-known herbalist. Though Tulsi Babu's main source of income was as an upper division clerk in Arbuthnot & Co., he had not been able to discard the family profession altogether. Of late he had started devoting a little more time to it because two fairly distinguished citizens of Calcutta had benefited from his prescriptions, thus giving a boost to his reputation as a part-time herbalist.

The search for these herbs had brought him to Dandakaranya. He had heard that thirty miles to the north of Jagdalpur, there lived a holy man in a mountain cave who knew of some medicinal plants including one for high blood pressure. This plant was supposedly even more efficacious than the more common Rawolfia serpentina. Tulsi Babu suffered from hypertension; serpentina hadn't worked too well in his case, and he had no faith in homoeopathy or allopathy.

Tulsi Babu took his friend Prodyot Babu with him on a trip to Jagdalpur. Prodyot Babu had often been bothered by his friend's unflappable nature. One day he had been forced to comment, 'All one needs to feel a sense of wonder is a little imagination. You are so devoid of it that even if a full-fledged ghost were to appear before you, you wouldn't be surprised.' Tulsi Babu had replied calmly, 'To feign surprise when one doesn't actually feel it is an affectation. I do not approve of it.'

But this didn't get in the way of their friendship.

The two checked into a hotel in Jagdalpur during the autumn vacation. On the way, in the Madras Mail, two foreign youngsters had got into their compartment. They had turned out to be Swedes. One of them was so tall that his head nearly touched the roof of the compartment. Prodyot Babu had asked him how tall he was and the young man had replied, 'Two metres and seven centimetres.' That was nearly seven feet. Prodyot Babu couldn't take his eyes off this young giant during the rest of the journey; but Tulsi Babu did not register even a flicker of amazement. He said such extraordinary height was simply the result of the diet of the Swedish people, and therefore nothing to wonder about.

They reached the cave of the holy man Dhumai Baba after walking through the forest for a mile or so and then climbing up about 500 feet. The cave was a large one, but since no sunlight penetrated inside, they only had to take ten steps to be engulfed in a darkness thickened by the ever-present smoke from the Baba's brazier. Prodyot Babu was absorbed in watching, by the light of his torch, the profusion of stalactites and stalagmites while Tulsi Babu enquired after his herbal medicine. The tree that Dhumai Baba referred to was known as chakraparna, meaning 'round leaves' in Sanskrit. Tulsi Babu had never heard of it, nor was it mentioned in any of the half-dozen books he had read on herbal medicine. It was not a tree but a shrub, and was found only in one part of the forest of Dandakaranya, and nowhere else. Dhumai Baba gave adequate directions which Tulsi Babu noted down carefully.

Once out of the cave, Tulsi Babu lost no time in setting off in quest of the herb. Prodyot Babu was happy to keep his friend company; he had hunted big game at one time—conservation had put an end to that, but the lure of the jungle persisted.

The holy man's directions proved accurate. Half an hour's walk brought them to a ravine which they crossed and in three minutes they found the shrub seven steps to the south of a neem tree scorched by lightning. It was a waist-high plant with round green leaves, each with a pink dot in the centre.

'What kind of a place is this?' asked Prodyot Babu, looking around.

'Why, what's wrong with it?'

'But for the neem, there isn't a single tree here that I can recognize. And see how damp it is. Quite unlike the places we've passed through.'

It was moist underfoot, but Tulsi Babu saw nothing strange in that. Why, in Calcutta itself, the temperature varied between one neighbourhood and another. Tollygunge in the south was much cooler than Shyambazar in the north. What was so strange about one part of a forest being different from another? It was nothing but a quirk of nature.

Tulsi Babu had just put the bag down on the ground and stooped towards the shrub when a sharp query from Prodyot Babu interrupted him. 'What on earth is that?'

Tulsi Babu had seen the thing too, but had not been bothered by it. 'Must be some sort of an egg,' he said.

Prodyot Babu thought it was a piece of egg-shaped rock, but on getting closer he realized that it was a genuine egg: yellow, with brown stripes flecked with blue. What creature could such a large egg belong to? A python?

Meanwhile, Tulsi Babu had already plucked some leafy branches off the shrub and put them in his bag. He wanted to take some more but was forced to stop. The egg chose that very moment to hatch. Prodyot Babu jumped back at the sound of the cracking shell, but then gathered courage and took a few steps towards it. The head was already out of the shell. It was not a snake, nor a crocodile or a turtle, but a bird. Soon the whole body was out. The bird stood on its spindly legs and looked around. It was quite large; about the size of a hen. Prodyot Babu was very fond of birds and kept a mynah and a bulbul as pets; but he had never seen a chick as large as this. It had a big beak and long legs. Its purple plumes were unique, as was its alert behaviour so soon after birth.

Tulsi Babu, however, was not in the least interested in the chick. He had been intent on stuffing his bag with as many leaves from the plant as he could fit in.

Prodyot Babu looked around and commented, 'Very surprising; there seems to be no sign of its parents, at least not in the vicinity.'

'I think that's enough surprises for a day,' said Tulsi Babu, hoisting his bag on his shoulder. 'It's almost four. We must be out of the forest before it gets dark.'

Somewhat reluctantly, Prodyot Babu turned away from the chick and started walking with his friend. It would take at least half an hour to reach the waiting taxi.

A patter of feet made Prodyot Babu stop and turn round. The chick was looking straight at him.

Then it padded across and stopped in front of Tulsi Babu and, opening its unusually large beak, gripped the edge of Tulsi Babu's dhoti.

Prodyot Babu was so surprised that he didn't know what to say, until he saw Tulsi Babu pick up the chick and shove it into his bag. 'What do you think you're doing?' he cried in consternation. 'You put that unknown bird in your bag?'

'I've always wanted to keep a pet,' said Tulsi Babu, resuming his walk. 'Even mongrels are kept as pets. What's wrong with a nameless chick?'

Prodyot Babu saw the bird sticking its neck out of the swinging bag and glancing around with wide eyes.

Tulsi Babu lived in a flat on the second floor of a building in Masjidbari Street. He was a bachelor and besides him, there was only his servant Natabar and his cook Joykesto. There was another flat on the same floor, occupied by Tarit Sanyal, who was the proprietor of the Nabarun Press. Mr Sanyal was a short-tempered man made even more so by repeated power failures in the city which seriously affected the working of his press.

Two months had passed since Tulsi Babu's return from Dandakaranya. He had put the chick in a cage which he had specially ordered immediately upon his return. The cage was kept in a corner of the inner veranda. He had found a name for the chick: Big Bill; soon the Big was dropped and now it was just Bill.

The very first day he had acquired the chick in Jagdalpur, Tulsi Babu had tried to feed it grain but the chick had refused. Tulsi Babu had guessed, and rightly, that it was probably a non-vegetarian, and ever since he had been feeding it moths, cockroaches and whatever other insects he could find. Of late the bird's appetite seemed to have grown. It had started dragging its beak across the bars of the cage showing its immense dissatisfaction. Hence Tulsi Babu had been obliged to feed it meat. Natabar bought meat regularly from the market for its meals, which explained the bird's rapid growth in size.

Tulsi Babu had been far-sighted enough to buy a cage which was several sizes too large for the bird. His instinct had told him that the bird belonged to a large species. The roof of the cage was two and a half feet from the ground. But soon he noticed that when Bill stood straight his head nearly touched the roof, even though he was only two months old; he would soon need a larger cage.

The cry of the bird was a terrible sound. It had made Mr Sanyal choke on his tea one morning while he stood on the veranda. Normally the two neighbours hardly spoke to each other; but that day, after he had got over his fit of coughing, Mr Sanyal demanded to know what kind of an animal Tulsi Babu kept in his cage that yelled like that. It was true that the cry was more beast-like than bird-like.

Tulsi Babu was getting dressed to go to work. He appeared at the bedroom door and said, 'Not an animal, a bird. And whatever its cry, it certainly doesn't keep one awake at night the way your cat does.'

Tulsi Babu's retort put an end to the argument, but Mr Sanyal kept grumbling. It was a good thing the cage couldn't be seen from his flat; one sight of the bird would have led to even more serious consequences.

Although its looks didn't bother Tulsi Babu, they certainly worried Prodyot Babu. The two met rarely outside office hours, except once a week for a meal of kebabs and parathas at Mansur's. Prodyot Babu had a large family and many responsibilities. But since the visit to Dandakaranya, Tulsi Babu's pet was often on his mind. As a result he had started to drop in at Tulsi Babu's from time to time in the evenings. The bird's astonishing rate of growth and the change in its appearance were a constant source of amazement to Prodyot Babu. He was at a loss to see why Tulsi Babu should show no concern about it. Prodyot Babu had never imagined that the look in a bird's eye could be so malevolent. The black pupils in the amber irises would fix him with such an unwavering look that he would feel most uneasy. The bird's beak naturally grew in proportion with its body; shiny black in colour, it resembled an eagle's beak but was much larger in relation to the rest of the body. It was clear, from its rudimentary wings and its long sturdy legs and sharp talons, that the bird couldn't fly. Prodyot Babu had described the bird to many acquaintances, but no one had been able to identify it.

One Sunday Prodyot Babu came to Tulsi Babu with a camera borrowed from a nephew. There wasn't enough light in the cage, so he had come armed with a flash gun. Photography had been a hobby with him once, and he was able to summon up enough courage to point the camera at the bird in the cage and press the shutter. The scream of protest from the bird as the flash went off sent Prodyot Babu reeling back a full yard, and it struck him that the bird's cry should be recorded. Showing the photograph and playing back the cry might help in identifying the species. Something rankled in Prodyot Babu's mind; he hadn't yet mentioned it to his friend, but somewhere in a book or a magazine he had once seen a picture of a bird which greatly resembled this pet of Tulsi Babu's. If he came across the picture again, he would compare it with the photograph.

Later, when the two friends were having tea, Tulsi Babu came out with a new piece of information. Ever since Bill had arrived, crows and sparrows had stopped coming to the flat. This was a blessing because the sparrows would build nests in the most unlikely places, while the crows would make off with food from the kitchen. All that had stopped.

'Is that so?' asked Prodyot Babu, surprised as usual.

'Well, you've been here all this time; have you seen any other birds?'

Prodyot Babu realized that he hadn't. 'But what about your two servants? Have they got used to Bill?'

'The cook never goes near the cage, but Natabar feeds it meat with pincers. Even if he does have any objection, he hasn't come out with it. And when the bird turns nasty, one sight of me calms it down. By the way, what was the idea behind taking the photograph?'

Prodyot Babu didn't mention the real reason. He said, 'When it's no more, it'll remind you of it.'

Prodyot Babu had the photograph developed and printed the following day. He also had two enlargements made. One he gave to Tulsi Babu and the other he took to the ornithologist Ranajoy Shome. Only the other day an article by Mr Shome on the birds of Sikkim had appeared in the weekly magazine *Desh*.

But Mr Shome failed to identify the bird from the photograph. He asked where the bird could be seen, and Prodyot Babu answered with a barefaced lie. 'A friend of mine had sent this photograph from Osaka. He wanted me to identify the bird for him.'

Tulsi Babu noted the date in his diary: February the fourteenth, 1980. Big Bill, who had been transferred from a three-and-a-half-foot cage to a four-and-a-half-foot one only last month, had been guilty of a misdeed the previous night.

Tulsi Babu had been awakened by a suspicious sound in the middle of the night—a series of hard, metallic twangs. But the sound had soon stopped and had been followed by total silence.

Still, the suspicion that something was up lingered in Tulsi Babu's mind. He came out of the mosquito net. Moonlight fell on the floor through the grilled window. Tulsi Babu put on his slippers, took the electric torch from the table, and came out onto the veranda.

In the beam of the torch light he saw that the meshing on the cage had been ripped apart and a hole large enough for the bird to escape had been made. The cage was now empty.

Tulsi Babu's torch revealed nothing on this side. At the opposite end, the veranda turned right towards Mr Sanyal's flat.

Tulsi Babu reached the corner in a flash and swung his torch to the right.

It was just as he had feared.

Mr Sanyal's cat was now a helpless captive in Bill's beak. The shiny spots on the floor were obviously drops of blood. But the cat was still alive and thrashing its legs about.

Tulsi Babu cried out 'Bill' and the bird promptly dropped the cat from its beak.

Then it advanced with long strides, turned the corner, and went quietly back to its cage.

Even in this moment of crisis, Tulsi Babu couldn't help heaving a sigh of relief.

A padlock hung on the door of Mr Sanyal's room; he had left three days ago for a holiday, after the busy months of December and January when school books were printed in his press.

The best thing to do with the cat would be to toss it out of the window on to the street. Stray cats and dogs were run over every day on the streets of Calcutta; this would be just one more of them.

The rest of the night Tulsi Babu couldn't sleep.

The next day he had to absent himself from work for an hour or so while he went to the railway booking office; he happened to know one of the booking clerks which made his task easier. Prodyot Babu had asked after the bird and Tulsi Babu had replied that it was fine. Then he had added after a brief reflection—'I'm thinking of framing the photo you took of it.'

On the twenty-fourth of February, Tulsi Babu arrived in Jagdalpur for the second time. A packing case with Bill in it arrived in the luggage van on the same train. The case was provided with a hole for ventilation.

From Jagdalpur, Tulsi Babu set off with two coolies and the case in a car for the precise spot in the forest where he had found the bird.

At a certain milepost on the main road, Tulsi Babu got off the vehicle and, with the coolies carrying the packing case, set off for the scorched neem tree. It took him nearly an hour to reach the spot. The coolies put the case down. They had already been generously tipped and told that they would have to open the packing case. This was done, and Tulsi Babu was relieved to see that Bill was in fine fettle. The coolies, of course, bolted screaming at the sight of the bird, but that didn't worry Tulsi Babu. His purpose had been served. Bill was looking at him with a fixed stare. Its head already touched the four-and-a-half-foot high roof of the cage.

'Goodbye, Bill.'

The sooner the parting took place the better.

Tulsi Babu started on his journey back.

He hadn't told anybody in the office about his trip, not even Prodyot Babu, who naturally asked where he had been when he appeared at his desk on Monday. Tulsi Babu replied briefly that he had been to a niece's wedding in Naihati.

About a fortnight later, on a visit to Tulsi Babu's place, Prodyot Babu was surprised to see the cage empty. He asked about the bird. 'It's gone,' said Tulsi Babu.

Prodyot Babu naturally assumed that the bird was dead. He felt a twinge of remorse. He hadn't meant it seriously when he had said that the photo would remind Tulsi Babu of his pet when it was no more; he had no idea the bird would die so soon. The photograph he had taken had been framed and was hanging on the wall of the bedroom. Tulsi Babu seemed out of sorts; altogether the atmosphere was gloomy. To relieve the gloom, Prodyot Babu made a suggestion. 'We haven't been to Mansur's in a long while. What about going tonight for a meal of kebabs and parathas?'

'I'm afraid I have quite lost my taste for them.'

Prodyot Babu couldn't believe his ears. 'Lost your taste for kebabs? What's the matter? Aren't you well? Have you tried the herb the holy man prescribed?'

Tulsi Babu said that his blood pressure had come down to normal since he started having the juice of the chakraparna. What he didn't bother to mention was that he had forgotten all about herbal medicines as long as Bill had been with him, and that he had gone back to them only a week ago.

'By the way,' remarked Prodyot Babu, 'the mention of the herb reminds me—did you read in the papers today about the forest of Dandakaranya?'

'What did the papers say?'

Tulsi Babu bought a daily newspaper all right, but rarely got beyond the first page. The paper was near at hand. Prodyot Babu pointed out the news to him. The headline said: 'THE TERROR OF DANDAKARANYA'.

The news described a sudden and unexpected threat to the domestic animals and poultry in the village around the forests of Dandakaranya. Some unknown species of animal had started to devour them. No tigers were known to exist in that area, and proof had been found that something other than a feline species had been causing the havoc. Tigers usually drag their prey to their lairs; this particular beast didn't. The shikaris engaged by the Madhya Pradesh government had searched for a week but failed to locate any beast capable of such carnage. As a result, panic had spread amongst the villagers. One particular villager claimed that he had seen a two-legged creature running away from his cowshed. He had gone to investigate, and found his buffalo lying dead with a sizeable portion of its lower abdomen eaten away.

Tulsi Babu read the news, folded the paper, and put it back on the table.

'Don't tell me you don't find anything exceptional in the story?' said Prodyot Babu.

Tulsi Babu shook his head. In other words, he didn't.

Three days later, a strange thing happened to Prodyot Babu.

His wife had just opened a tin of digestive biscuits at breakfast and was about to serve them to him with his tea when Prodyot Babu abruptly left the dining table and rushed out of the house.

By the time he reached his friend Animesh's flat in Ekdalia Road, he was trembling with excitement.

He snatched the newspaper away from his friend's hands, threw it aside and said panting: 'Where do you keep your copies of *Reader's Digest*? Quick—it's most important!'

Animesh shared with million of others a taste for *Reader's Digest*. He was greatly surprised by his friend's behaviour but scarcely had the opportunity to show it. He went to a bookcase and dragged out some dozen issues of the magazine from the bottom shelf.

'Which number are you looking for?'

Prodyot Babu took the whole bunch, flipped through the pages of a number of issues, and finally found what he was looking for.

'Yes—this is the bird. No doubt about it.'

His fingers rested on a picture of a conjectural model of a bird kept in the Chicago Museum of Natural History. It showed an attendant cleaning the model with a brush.

'Andalgalornis,' said Prodyot Babu, reading out the name. The name meant terror-bird. The article with the picture described it as a huge prehistoric species, carnivorous, faster than a horse, and extremely ferocious.

The doubt which had crept into Prodyot Babu's mind was proved right when in the office next morning Tulsi Babu came to him and said that he had to go to Dandakaranya once again, and that he would be delighted if Prodyot Babu would join him and bring his gun with him. There was too little time to obtain sleeping accommodation in the train, but that couldn't be helped as the matter was very urgent.

Prodyot Babu agreed at once.

In the excitement of the pursuit, the two friends didn't mind the discomfort of the journey. Prodyot Babu said nothing about the bird in the *Reader's Digest*. He could do so later; there was plenty of time for that. Tulsi Babu had in the meantime told him everything. He had also mentioned that he didn't really believe the gun would be needed; he had suggested taking it only as a precaution. Prodyot Babu, on the other hand, couldn't share his friend's optimism. He believed the gun was essential, and he was fully prepared for any eventuality. The morning paper had mentioned that the Madhya Pradesh government had announced a reward of 5,000 rupees to anyone who succeeded in killing or capturing the creature, which had been declared a man-eater ever since a woodcutter's son had fallen victim to it.

In Jagdalpur, permission to shoot the creature was obtained from the conservator of forests, Mr Tirumalai. But he warned that Tulsi Babu and Prodyot Babu would have to go on their own as nobody could be persuaded to go into the forest any more.

Prodyot Babu asked if any information had been received from the shikaris who had preceded them. Tirumalai turned grave. 'So far four shikaris have attempted to kill the beast. Three of them had no success. The fourth never returned.'

'Never returned?'

'No. Ever since then shikaris have been refusing to go. So you had better think twice before undertaking the trip.'

Prodyot Babu was shaken, but his friend's nonchalance brought back his courage. 'I think we will go,' he said.

This time they had to walk a little further because the taxi refused to take the dirt road which went part of the way into the forest. Tulsi Babu was confident that the job would be over in two hours, and the taxi driver agreed to wait that long upon being given a tip of fifty rupees. The two friends set off on their quest.

It was spring now, and the forest wore a different look from the previous trips. Nature was following its course, and yet there was an unnatural silence. There were no bird calls; not even the cries of cuckoos.

As usual, Tulsi Babu was carrying his shoulder bag. Prodyot Babu knew there was a packet in it, but he didn't know what it contained. Prodyot Babu himself was carrying his rifle and bullets.

As the undergrowth became thinner, they could see farther into the forest. That was why the two friends were able to see from a distance the body of a man lying spreadeagled on the ground behind a jackfruit tree. Tulsi Babu hadn't noticed it at first, and stopped only when Prodyot Babu pointed it out to him.

Prodyot Babu took a firm grip on the gun and walked towards the body. Tulsi Babu went halfway, and then turned back.

'You look as if you've seen a ghost,' said Tulsi Babu when his friend rejoined him. 'Isn't that the missing shikari?'

'It must be,' said Prodyot Babu hoarsely. 'But it won't be easy to identify the corpse. The head's missing.'

The rest of the way they didn't speak at all.

It took one hour to reach the neem tree, which meant they must have walked at least three miles. Prodyot Babu noticed that the medicinal shrub had grown fresh leaves and was back to its old shape.

'Bill! Billie!'

There was something faintly comic about the call, and Prodyot Babu couldn't help smiling. But the next moment he realized that for Tulsi Babu the call was quite natural. He had succeeded in taming the monster bird, which Prodyot Babu had seen with his own eyes.

Tulsi Babu's call resounded in the forest.

'Bill! Bill! Billie!'

Now Prodyot Babu saw something stirring in the depths of the forest. It was coming towards them, and at such a speed that it seemed to grow bigger and bigger every second.

It was the bird.

The gun in Prodyot Babu's hand suddenly felt very heavy. He wondered if he would be able to use it at all.

The bird slowed down and approached them stealthily through the vegetation.

Andalgalornis. Prodyot Babu would never forget the name. A bird as tall as a man. Ostriches too were tall; but that was largely because of their neck. This bird's back itself was as high as an average man. In other words, the bird had grown a foot and a half in just about a month. The colour of its plumes had changed too. There were blotches of black on the purple now.

And the malevolent look in its amber eyes which Prodyot Babu found he could confront when the bird was in captivity, was now for him unbearably terrifying. The look was directed at its ex-master.

There was no knowing what the bird would do. Thinking its stillness to be a prelude to an attack, Prodyot Babu made an attempt to raise the gun with his shaking hands. But the moment he did so, the bird turned its gaze at him, its feathers puffing out to give it an even more terrifying appearance.

'Lower the gun,' hissed Tulsi Babu in a tone of admonition.

Prodyot Babu obeyed. The bird lowered its feathers too and transferred its gaze to its master.

'I don't know if you are still hungry,' said Tulsi Babu, 'but I hope you will eat this because I am giving it to you.'

Tulsi Babu had already brought out the packet from the bag. He now unwrapped it and tossed the contents towards the bird. It was a large chunk of meat.

'You've been the cause of my shame. I hope you will behave yourself from now on.'

Amazed, Prodyot Babu watched as the bird picked up the chunk with its huge beak, and put it inside its mouth.

'This time it really is goodbye.'

Tulsi Babu turned. Prodyot Babu was afraid to turn his back on the bird, and for a while walked backwards with his eyes on the bird. When he found that the bird was making no attempt to follow him or attack him, he too turned round and joined his friend.

A week later the news came out in the papers of the end of the terror in Dandakaranya. Prodyot Babu had not mentioned anything to Tulsi Babu about Andalgalornis, and the fact that the bird had been extinct for three million years. But the news in the papers obliged him to come to his friend. 'I'm at a loss to know how it happened,' he said. 'Perhaps you can throw some light on it.'

'There's no mystery at all,' said Tulsi Babu. 'I only mixed some of my medicine with the meat I gave him.'

'Medicine?'

'An extract of chakraparna. It turns one into a vegetarian. Just as it has done with me.'

(1980)   *Translated by Satyajit Ray*

KHAGAM

We were having dinner by the light of a petromax lamp. I had just helped myself to some curried egg when Lachhman, the cook and caretaker of the rest house, said, 'Aren't you going to pay a visit to Imli Baba?'

I had to tell him that since we were not familiar with the name of Imli Baba, the question of paying him a visit hadn't arisen. Lachhman said that the driver of the forest department jeep, which had been engaged for our sightseeing, would take us to the Baba if we told him. Baba's hut was in the forest and the surroundings were picturesque. As a holy man he was apparently held in very high regard; important people from all over India came to him to pay their respects and seek his blessings. What really aroused my curiosity was the information that the Baba kept a king cobra as a pet which lived in a hole near his hut and came to him every evening to drink goat's milk.

Dhurjati Babu's comment on this was that the country was being overrun by fake holy men. The more scientific knowledge was spreading in the West, he said, the more our people were heading towards superstition. 'It's a hopeless situation. It puts my back up just to think of it.'

As he finished talking, he picked up the fly swatter and brought it down with unerring aim on a mosquito which had settled on the dining table. Dhurjati Babu was a short, pale-looking man in his late forties, with sharp features and grey eyes. We had met in the rest house in Bharatpur; I was there on my way to Agra from where I was going to my elder brother in Jaipur, with whom I had planned to spend a fortnight's holiday. Both the tourist bungalow and the circuit house being full, I had to fall back on the forest rest house. Not that I regretted it; living in the heart of the forest offers a special kind of thrill along with quiet comfort.

Dhurjati Babu had preceded me by a day. We had shared the forest department jeep for our sightseeing. The previous day we had been to Deeg, twenty-two miles to the east from here, to see the fortress and the palace. That morning we saw the fortress in Bharatpur, and in the afternoon we saw the bird sanctuary at Keoladeo which was something very special. It was a seven-mile stretch of marshland dotted with tiny islands where strange birds from far corners of the globe came and made their homes. I was absorbed in watching the birds, but Dhurjati Babu grumbled and made vain efforts to wave away the tiny insects buzzing around us. These unkis have a tendency to settle on your face, but they are so small that most people can ignore them. Not Dhurjati Babu.

By half-past eight we had finished dinner and were sitting on cane chairs on the terrace and admiring the beauty of the forest in moonlight. 'The holy man the servant mentioned,' I remarked, 'what about going and taking a look at him?'

Flicking his cigarette towards a eucalyptus tree, Dhurjati Babu said, 'King cobras can never be tamed. I know a lot about snakes. I spent my boyhood in Jalpaiguri, and killed many snakes with my own hands. The king cobra is the deadliest, most vicious snake there is. The story of the holy man feeding it goat's milk should be taken with a pinch of salt.'

I said, 'We are going to see the fortress at Bayan tomorrow morning. In the afternoon we have nothing to do.'

'I take it you have a lot of faith in holy men?'

I could see the question was a barbed one. However, I answered calmly.

'The question of faith doesn't arise because I've never had anything to do with holy men. But I can't deny that I am a bit curious about this one.'

'I too was curious at one time, but after an experience I had with one . . .'

It turned out that Dhurjati Babu suffered from high blood pressure. An uncle of his had persuaded him to try a medicine prescribed by a holy man. Dhurjati Babu had done so, and as a result had suffered intense stomach pains. This had caused his blood pressure to shoot up even more. Ever since, he had looked upon Dindayalnety per cent of India's holy men as fakes.

I found this allergy quite amusing, and just to provoke him said, 'You said it wasn't possible to tame king cobras; I'm sure ordinary people like us couldn't do it, but I've heard of sadhus up in the Himalayas living in caves with tigers.'

'You may have heard about it, but have you seen it with your own eyes?'

I had to admit that I hadn't.

'You never will,' said Dhurjati Babu. 'This is the land of tall stories. You'll hear of strange happenings all the time, but never see one yourself. Look at our *Ramayana* and *Mahabharata*. It is said they're history, but actually they're no more than a bundle of nonsense. The ten-headed Ravana, the monkey-god Hanuman with a flame at the end of his tail setting fire to a whole city, Bhima's appetite, Ghatotkacha, Hidimba, the flying chariot Pushpak, Kumbhakarna—can you imagine anything more absurd than these? And the epics are full of fake holy men as well. That's where it all started. Yet everyone—even the educated—swallows these stories.'

Despite Dhurjati Babu's reservations, the following day we

lunched in the rest house after visiting the fortress at Bayan and, after a couple of hours' rest, reached the holy man's hermitage a little after four. Dhurjati Babu didn't object to the trip. Perhaps he too was a little curious about the Baba. The hermitage was in a clearing in the forest below a huge tamarind tree, which is why he was called Imli Baba by the local people, imli being the Hindi word for tamarind. His real name was not known.

In a hut made of date-palm leaves, the Baba sat on a bearskin with a young disciple by his side. It was impossible to guess the Baba's age. There was still an hour or so until sunset, but the dense covering of foliage made the place quite dark. A fire burnt before the Baba, who had a ganja pipe in his hand. We could see by the light of the fire a clothesline stretched across the wall of the hut from which hung a towel, a loincloth, and about a dozen sloughed-off snakeskins.

Dhurjati Babu whispered in my ear: 'Let's not beat about the bush; ask him about the snake's feeding time.'

'So you want to see Balkishen?' asked the Baba, reading our minds and smiling from behind his pipe. The driver of the jeep, Dindayal, had told us a little while ago that the snake was called Balkishen. We told Baba that we had heard of his pet snake and were most anxious to see it drink milk. Was there any likelihood of our wish being fulfilled?

Imli Baba shook his head sadly. He said that as a rule Balkishen came every day in the evening in answer to Baba's call, and had come even two days ago. But since the day before he had not been feeling well. 'Today is the day of the full moon,' said the Baba, 'so he will not come. But he will surely come again tomorrow evening.'

That snakes too could feel indisposed was news to me. And yet, why not? After all, it was a tame snake. Weren't there hospitals for dogs, horses and cows?

The Baba's disciple gave us another piece of news: red ants

had got into the snake's hole while it lay ill, and had been pestering it. Baba had exterminated them all with a curse. Dhurjati Babu threw a sidelong glance at me at this point. I turned my eyes towards Baba. With his saffron robe, his long, matted hair, his iron earrings, rudraksha necklaces and copper amulets, there was nothing to distinguish him from a host of other holy men. And yet in the dim light of dusk, I couldn't take my eyes away from the man.

Seeing us standing, the disciple produced a pair of reed mats and spread them on the floor in front of the Baba. But what was the point of sitting down when there was no hope of seeing the pet snake? A delay would mean driving through the forest in the dark, and we knew there were wild animals about; we had seen herds of deer while coming. So we decided to leave. We bowed to the Baba who responded by nodding without taking the pipe away from his mouth. Then we set off for the jeep parked about 200 yards away on the road. Only a little while ago, the place had been alive with the calls of birds coming home to roost. Now all was quiet.

We had gone a few steps when Dhurjati Babu suddenly said, 'We could at least have asked to see the hole where the snake lives.'

I said, 'For that we don't have to ask the Baba; our driver Dindayal said he had seen the hole.'

'That's right.'

We fetched Dindayal from the car and he showed us the way. Instead of going towards the hut, we took a narrow path by an almond tree and arrived at a bush. The stone rubble which surrounded the bush suggested that there had been some sort of an edifice here in the past. Dindayal said the hole was right behind the bush. It was barely visible in the failing light, so Dhurjati Babu produced a small electric torch from his pocket. As the light from it hit the bush we saw the hole. But what about the snake? Was it likely to crawl out just to show its face to a couple of curious visitors? To be quite honest, while I was ready to watch it being fed by the Baba, I had no wish to see it come out of the hole now. But my companion seemed consumed with curiosity. When the beam from the torch had no effect, he started to pelt the bush with clods of dirt.

I felt this was taking things too far, and said, 'What's the matter? You seem determined to drag the snake out, and you didn't even believe in its existence at first.'

Dhurjati Babu now picked up a large clod and said, 'I still don't. If this one doesn't drag him out, I'll know that a cock-and-bull story about the Baba has been spread. The more such false notions are destroyed the better.'

The clod landed with a thud on the bush and destroyed a part of the thorny cluster. Dhurjati Babu had his torch trained on the hole. For a few seconds there was silence but for a lone cricket which had just started to chirp. Now there was another sound added to it; a dry, soft whistle of indeterminate pitch. Then there was a rustle of leaves and the light of the torch revealed something black and shiny slowly slipping out of the hole.

The leaves of the bush stirred, and the next moment, through a parting in them, emerged the head of a snake. The light showed its glinting eyes and its forked tongue flicking in and out of its mouth. Dindayal had been pleading with us to go back to the jeep for some time; he now said, 'Let it be, sir. You have seen it, now let us go back.'

The snake's eyes were fixed on us, perhaps because of the light shining on it. I have seen many snakes, but never a king cobra at such close quarters. And I have never heard of a king cobra making no attempt to attack intruders.

Suddenly the light of the torch trembled and was whisked away from the snake. What happened next was something I was not prepared for at all. Dhurjati Babu swiftly picked up a stone and hurled it with all his strength at the snake. Then he followed it in quick succession with two more such missiles. I was suddenly gripped by a horrible premonition and cried out, 'Why on earth did you have to do that, Dhurjati Babu?'

The man shouted in triumph, panting, 'That's the end of at least one vicious reptile!'

Dindayal was staring open-mouthed at the bush. I took the torch from Dhurjati Babu's hand and flashed it on the hole. I could see a part of the lifeless form of the snake. The leaves around were splattered with blood.

I had no idea that Imli Baba and his disciple had arrived to take their place right behind us. Dhurjati Babu was the first to turn round, and then I too turned and saw the Baba standing with a staff in his hand, a dozen feet behind us. He had his eyes fixed on Dhurjati Babu. It is beyond me to describe the look in them. I can only say that I have never seen such a mixture of surprise, anger and hatred in anyone's eyes.

Then Baba lifted his right arm towards Dhurjati Babu. The index finger shot out towards him. I noticed for the first time that Baba's fingernails were over an inch long. Who did he remind me of? Yes, of a figure in a painting by Ravi Varma which I had seen as a child in a framed reproduction in my uncle's house. It was the sage Durbasha cursing the hapless Sakuntala. He too had his arm raised like that, and the same look in his eyes.

But Imli Baba said nothing about a curse. All he said in Hindi in his deep voice was: 'One Balkishen is gone; another will come to take his place. Balkishen is deathless . . .'

Dhurjati Babu wiped his hands with his handkerchief, turned to me and said, 'Let's go.' Baba's disciple lifted the lifeless snake from the ground and went off, probably to arrange for its cremation. The length of the snake made me gasp; I had no idea king cobras could be that long. Imli Baba slowly made his way towards the hut. The three of us went back to the jeep.

On the way back, Dhurjati Babu was gloomy and silent. I asked him why he had to kill the snake when it was doing him no harm. I thought he would burst out once more and fulminate against snakes and Babas. Instead he put a question which seemed to have no bearing on the incident.

'Do you know who Khagam was?'

Khagam? The name seemed to ring a bell, but I couldn't remember where I had heard it. Dhurjati Babu muttered the name two or three times, then lapsed into silence.

It was half-past six when we reached the guest house. My mind went back again and again to Imli Baba glowering at Dhurjati Babu with his finger pointing at him. I didn't know why my companion had behaved in such a fashion. However, I felt that we had seen the end of the incident, so there was no point in worrying about it. Baba himself had said Balkishen was deathless. There must be other king cobras in the jungles of Bharatpur. I was sure another one would be caught soon by the disciples of the Baba.

Lachhman had prepared chicken curry, daal and chapatis for dinner. A whole day's sightseeing can leave one famished and I found I ate twice as much here as I ate at home. Dhurjati Babu, although a small man, was a hearty eater; but today he seemed to have no appetite. I asked him if he felt unwell. He made no reply. I now enquired of him, 'Do you feel remorse for having killed the snake?'

Dhurjati Babu was staring at the petromax. What he said was not an answer to my question. 'The snake was whistling,' he said in a soft, thin voice. 'The snake was whistling . . .'

I said, smiling, 'Whistling, or hissing?'

Dhurjati Babu didn't turn away from the light. 'Yes, hissing,' he said. 'Snakes speak when snakes hiss . . . yes,

Snakes speak when snakes hiss
I know this, I know this . . .'

Dhurjati Babu stopped and made some hissing noises himself. Then he broke into rhyme again, his head swaying in rhythm.

'Snakes speak when snakes hiss
I know this, I know this.
Snakes kill when snakes kiss
I know this, I know this . . .

What is this? Goat's milk?'

The question was directed at the pudding in the plate before him.

Lachhman missed the 'goat' bit and answered, 'Yes, sir—there is milk and there is egg.'

Dhurjati Babu was by nature whimsical, but his behaviour today seemed excessive. Perhaps he himself realized it, because he seemed to make an effort to control himself. 'Been out in the sun too long these last few days,' he said. 'Must go easy from tomorrow.'

The night was noticeably chillier than usual; so instead of sitting out on the terrace, I went into the bedroom and started to pack my suitcase. I was going to catch the train next evening. I would have to change in the middle of the night at Sawai-Madhopur and arrive in Jaipur at five in the morning.

At least that was my plan, but it came to nothing. I had to send a wire to my elder brother saying that I would be arriving a day later. Why this was necessary will be clear from what I'm about to say now. I shall try to describe everything as clearly and accurately as possible. I don't expect everyone to believe me, but the proof is still lying on the ground fifty yards away from the

Baba's hut. I feel a cold shiver just thinking of it, so it is not surprising that I couldn't pick it up and bring it as proof of my story. Let me now set down what happened.

I had just finished packing my suitcase, turned down the wick of my lantern and got into my pyjamas when there was a knock on the door on the east side of the room. Dhurjati Babu's room was behind that door.

As soon as I opened the door the man said in a hoarse whisper: 'Do you have some Flit, or something to keep off mosquitoes?'

I asked: 'Where did you find mosquitoes? Aren't your windows covered with netting?'

'Yes, they are.'

'Well, then?'

'Even then something is biting me.'

'How do you know that?'

'There are marks on my skin.'

It was dark near the door, so I couldn't see his face clearly. I said, 'Come into my room. Let me see what kind of marks they are.'

Dhurjati Babu stepped into my room. I raised the lantern and could see the marks immediately. They were greyish, diamond-shaped blotches. I had never seen anything like them before, and I didn't like what I saw. 'You seem to have caught some strange disease,' I said. 'It may be an allergy, of course. We must get hold of a doctor first thing tomorrow morning. Try and go to sleep and don't worry about the marks. I don't think they're caused by insects. Are they painful?'

'No.'

'Then don't worry. Go back to bed.'

He went off. I shut the door, climbed into bed and slipped under the blanket. I'm used to reading in bed before going to sleep, but this was not possible by lantern-light. Not that I needed to read. I knew the day's exertions would put me to sleep within ten minutes of putting my head on the pillow.

But that was not to be tonight. I was about to drop off when there was the sound of a car arriving, followed soon by English voices and the bark of a dog. Foreign tourists obviously. The dog stopped barking at a sharp rebuke. Soon there was quiet again except for the crickets. No, not just the crickets; my neighbour was still awake and walking about. And yet through the crack under the door I had seen the lantern either being put out, or removed to the bathroom. Why was the man pacing about in the dark?

For the first time I had a suspicion that he was more than just whimsical. I had known him for just two days. I knew nothing beyond what he had told me about himself. And yet, to be quite honest, I had not seen any signs of what could be called madness in him until only a few hours ago. The comments that he had made while touring the forts at Bayan and Deeg suggested that he was quite well up on history. Not only that: he also knew quite a bit about art, and spoke knowledgeably about the work of Hindu and Muslim architects in the palaces of Rajasthan. No—the man was obviously ill. We must look for a doctor tomorrow.

The luminous dial on my watch showed a quarter to eleven. There was another rap on the east-side door. This time I shouted from the bed.

'What is it, Dhurjati Babu?'

'S-s-s-s-'

'What?'

'S-s-s-s-'

I could see that he was having difficulty with his speech. A fine mess I had got myself into. I shouted again: 'Tell me clearly what the matter is.'

'S-s-s-s-'

I had to leave the bed. When I opened the door, the man came out with such an absurd question that it really annoyed me.

'Is s-s-s-snake spelt with one "s"?'

I made no effort to hide my annoyance.

'You knocked on the door at this time of the night just to ask me that?'

'Only one "s"', he repeated.

'Yes, sir. No English word begins with two s's.'

'I s-s-see. And curs-s-s-e?'

'That's one "s" too.'

'Thank you. S-s-s-sleep well.'

I felt pity for the poor man. I said, 'Let me give you a sleeping pill. Would you like one?'

'Oh no. I s-s-s-sleep s-s-s-soundly enough. But when the s-s-sun was s-s-s-setting this evening—'

I interrupted him. 'Are you having trouble with your tongue? Why are you stammering? Give me your torch for a minute.'

I followed Dhurjati Babu into his room. The torch was on the dressing table. I flashed it on his face and he put out his tongue.

There was no doubt that something was wrong with it. A thin red line had appeared down the middle.

'Don't you feel any pain?'

'No. No pain.'

I was at a loss to know what the matter with him was.

Now my eyes fell on the man's bed. It was apparent that he hadn't got into it at all. I was quite stern about it. I said, 'I want to see you turn in before I go back. And I urge you please not to knock on my door again. I know I won't have any sleep in the train tomorrow, so I want to have a good night's rest now.'

But the man showed no signs of going to bed. The lantern being kept in the bathroom, the bedroom was in semi-darkness.

Outside there was a full moon. Moonlight flooded in through the
north window and fell on the floor. I could see Dhurjati Babu in
the soft reflected glow from it. He was standing in his
nightclothes, making occasional efforts to whistle through
parted lips. I had wrapped the blanket around me when I left my
bed, but Dhurjati Babu had nothing warm on him. If he caught a
chill then it would be difficult for me to leave him alone and go
away. After all, we were both away from home; if one was in
trouble, it wouldn't do for the other to leave him in the lurch and
push off.

I told him again to go to bed. When I found he wouldn't, I
realized I would have to use force. If he insisted on behaving like
a child, I had no choice but to act the stern elder.

But the moment I touched his hand I sprang back as if from
an electric shock.

Dhurjati Babu's body was as cold as ice. I couldn't imagine
that a living person's body could be so cold.

It was perhaps my reaction which brought a smile to his lips.
He now regarded me with his grey eyes wrinkled in amusement.
I asked him in a hoarse voice: 'What is the matter with you?'

Dhurjati Babu kept looking at me for a whole minute. I
noticed that he didn't blink once during the whole time. I also
noticed that he kept sticking out his tongue again and again.
Then he dropped his voice to a whisper and said, 'Baba is
calling me—"Balkishen!" . . . I can hear him call.' His knees now
buckled and he went down on the floor. Flattening himself on
his chest, he started dragging himself back on his elbows until he
disappeared into the darkness under the bed.

I was drenched in a cold sweat and shivering in every limb.
It was difficult for me to keep standing. I was no longer worried
about the man. All I felt was a mixture of horror and disbelief.

I came back to my room, shut the door and bolted it. Then I
got back into bed and covered myself from head to toe with the

blanket. In a while the shivering stopped and I could think a little more clearly. I tried to figure out where the matter stood, and the implication of what I had seen with my own eyes. Dhurjati Babu had killed Imli Baba's pet cobra by pelting it with stones. Immediately after that Imli Baba had pointed to Dhurjati Babu with his finger and said, 'One Balkishen is gone. Another will come to take his place.' The question was: was the second Balkishen a snake or a man?

Or a man turned into a snake?

What were those diamond-shaped blotches on Dhurjati Babu's skin?

What was the red mark on his tongue?

Did it mean that his tongue was about to be forked?

Why was he so cold to the touch?

Why did he crawl under the bed?

I suddenly recalled something in a flash. Dhurjati Babu had asked about Khagam. The name had sounded familiar, but I couldn't quite place it then. Now I remembered. It was a story I had read in the *Mahabharata* when I was a boy. Khagam was the name of a sage. His curse had turned his friend into a snake. Khagam—snake—curse—it all fitted. But the friend had turned into a harmless non-poisonous snake, while this man . . . Somebody was knocking on the door again. At the foot of the door this time. Once, twice, thrice . . . I didn't stir out of the bed. I was not going to open the door. Not again.

The knocking stopped. I held my breath and waited. There was a hissing sound now, moving away from the door.

Then there was silence, except for my pounding heartbeat.

What was that sound now? A squeak. No, something between a squeak and a screech. I knew there were rats in the bungalow. I had seen one in my bedroom the very first night. I had told Lachhman, and he had brought a rat-trap from the pantry to show me a rat in it. 'Not only rats, sir; there are moles too.'

The screeching had stopped. There was silence again. Minutes passed. I glanced at my watch. A quarter to one. Sleep had vanished. I could see the trees in the moonlight through my window. The moon was overhead now.

There was the sound of a door opening. It was the door of Dhurjati Babu's room which led to the veranda. The door was on the same side as my window. The line of trees was six or seven yards away from the edge of the veranda.

Dhurjati Babu was out on the veranda now. Where was he going? What was he up to? I stared fixedly at my window.

The hissing was growing louder. Now it was right outside my window. Thank God the window was covered with netting!

Something was climbing up the wall towards the window. A head appeared behind the netting. In the dim light of the lantern shone a pair of beady eyes staring fixedly at me.

They stayed staring for a minute; then there was the bark of a dog. The head turned towards the bark, and then dropped out of sight.

The dog was barking at the top of its voice. I heard its owner shouting at it. The barking turned into a moan, and then stopped. Once again there was silence. I kept my senses alert for another ten minutes or so. The lines of a verse I had heard earlier that night kept coming back to me—

Snakes speak when snakes hiss
I know this, I know this.
Snakes kill when snakes kiss
I know this, I know this . . .

Then the rhyme grew dim in my mind and I felt a drowsiness stealing over me.

I woke up to the sound of agitated English voices. My watch showed ten minutes to six. Something was happening. I got up quickly, dressed and came out on the veranda. A pet dog belonging to two English tourists had died during the night. The dog had slept in the bedroom with its owners who hadn't bothered to lock the door. It was surmised that a snake or something equally venomous had got into the room and bitten it.

Instead of wasting my time on the dog, I went to the door of Dhurjati Babu's room at the other end of the veranda. The door was ajar and the room empty. Lachhman gets up every morning at five to light the stove and put the tea-kettle on the boil. I asked him. He said he hadn't seen Dhurjati Babu.

All sorts of anxious thoughts ran in my head. I had to find Dhurjati Babu. He couldn't have gone far on foot. But a thorough search of the woods around proved abortive.

The jeep arrived at half-past ten. I couldn't leave Bharatpur without finding out what had happened to my companion. So I sent a cable to my brother from the post office, got my train ticket postponed by a day and came back to the rest house to learn that there was still no sign of Dhurjati Babu. The two Englishmen had in the meantime buried their dog and left.

I spent the whole afternoon exploring around the rest house. Following my instruction, the jeep arrived again in the afternoon. I was now working on a hunch and had a faint hope of success. I told the driver to drive straight to Imli Baba's hermitage.

I reached it about the same time as we did the day before. Baba was seated with the pipe in hand and the fire burning in front of him. There were two more disciples with him today.

Baba nodded briefly in answer to my greeting. The look in his eyes today held no hint of the blazing intensity that had appeared in them yesterday. I went straight to the point: did the Baba have any information on the gentleman who came with me yesterday? A gentle smile spread over Baba's face. He said,

'Indeed I have! Your friend has fulfilled my hope. He has brought back my Balkishen to me.'

I noticed for the first time the stone pot on Baba's right-hand side. The white liquid it contained was obviously milk. But I hadn't come all this way to see a snake and a bowl of milk. I had come in quest of Dhurjati Babu. He couldn't have simply vanished into thin air. If only I could see some sign of his existence!

I had noticed earlier that Imli Baba could read one's mind. He took a long pull at the pipe of ganja, passed it on to one of his disciples and said, 'I'm afraid you won't find your friend in the state you knew him, but he has left a memento behind. You will find that fifty steps to the south of Balkishen's home. Go carefully; there are thorny bushes around.'

I went to the hole where the king cobra lived. I was not the least concerned with whether another snake had taken the place of the first one. I took fifty steps south through grass, thorny shrubs and rubble, and reached a bel tree at the foot of which lay something the likes of which I had seen hanging from a line in the Baba's hut a few minutes ago.

It was a freshly sloughed-off skin marked all over with a pattern of diamonds.

But was it really a snakeskin? A snake was never that broad, and a snake didn't have arms and legs sticking out of its body.

It was actually the sloughed-off skin of a man. A man who had ceased to be a man. He was now lying coiled inside that hole. He was a king cobra with poison fangs.

There, I could hear him hissing. The sun had just gone down. The Baba was calling: 'Balkishen—Balkishen—Balkishen.'

(1973)   *Translated by Satyajit Ray*

ANATH BABU'S TERROR

I met Anath Babu on a train to Raghunathpur, where I was going on a holiday. I worked for one of the dailies in Calcutta. The pressure of work over the last few months had been killing. I definitely needed a break. Besides, writing being my hobby, I had ideas for a couple of short stories that needed further thought. And I needed peace and quiet to think. So I applied for ten days' leave and left with a packet of writing paper in my suitcase.

There was a reason for choosing Raghunathpur. An old college mate of mine, Biren Biswas, had his ancestral home there. We were chatting in the Coffee House one evening, talking of possible places where one might spend one's holiday. When he heard that I had applied for leave, Biren promptly offered me free accommodation in Raghunathpur. 'I would have gone with you,' he said, 'but you know how tied up I am at the moment. You won't have any problem, though. Bharadwaj will look after you. He's worked for our family for fifty years.'

Our coach was packed. Anathbandhu Mitra happened to be sitting right next to me. He was around fifty, not very tall, hair parted in the middle, a sharp look in his eyes and an amused smile playing on his lips. But his clothes! He appeared to have dressed for a role in a play set fifty years ago. Nobody these days wore a jacket like that, or such collars, glasses or boots.

We began to chat. It turned out that he, too, was going to Raghunathpur. 'Are you also going on a holiday?' I asked him. But he did not answer and seemed to grow a little pensive. Or it may be that he had failed to hear my question in the racket that the train was making.

The sight of Biren's house pleased me very much. It was a nice house, with a strip of land in front that had both vegetables and flowers growing in it. There were no other houses nearby, so the possibility of being disturbed by the neighbours was non-existent.

Despite protests from Bharadwaj, I chose the room in the attic for myself. It was an airy little room, very comfortable and totally private. I moved my things upstairs and began to unpack. It was then that I realized I had left my razor blades behind. 'Never mind,' said Bharadwaj, 'Kundu Babu's shop is only a five-minute walk from here. You'll get your bilades there.'

I left for the shop soon after tea, at around 4 p.m. It appeared that the place was used more or less like a club. About seven middle-aged men were seated inside on wooden benches, chatting away merrily. One of them was saying rather agitatedly, 'Well, it's not something I have only heard about. I saw the whole thing with my own eyes. All right, so it happened thirty years ago. But that kind of thing cannot get wiped out from one's memory, can it? I shall never forget what happened, especially since Haladhar Datta was a close friend of mine. In fact, even now I can't help feeling partly responsible for his death.'

I bought a packet of 7 O'Clock blades. Then I began to loiter, looking at things I didn't really need. The gentleman continued, 'Just imagine, my own friend laid a bet with me for just ten rupees and went to spend a night in that west room. I waited for a long time the next morning for him to turn up but when he didn't, I went with Jiten Bakshi, Haricharan Saha and a few others to look for him in the Haldar mansion. And we found him in the same room—lying dead on the floor, stone cold, eyes open and staring at the ceiling. The naked fear I saw in those eyes could only mean one thing, I tell you: ghosts. There was no injury on his person, no sign of snake-bite or anything like that. So what else could have killed him but a ghost? You tell me?'

Another five minutes in the shop gave me a rough idea of what they were talking about. There was, apparently, a two-hundred-year-old mansion in the southern corner of Raghunathpur, which had once been owned by the Haldars, the local zamindars. It had lain abandoned for years. A particular room in this mansion that faced the west was supposed to be haunted. Although in the last thirty years no one had dared to spend a night in it after the death of Haladhar Datta, the residents of Raghunathpur still felt a certain thrill thinking of the unhappy spirit that haunted the room. The reason behind this belief was both the mysterious death of Haladhar Datta, and the many instances of murders and suicides in the history of the Haldar family.

Intrigued by this conversation, I came out of the shop to find Anathbandhu Mitra, the gentleman I had met on the train, standing outside, a smile on his lips.

'Did you hear what they were saying?' he asked.

'Yes, I couldn't help it.'

'Do you believe in it?'

'In what? Ghosts?'

'Yes.'

'Well, you see, I have heard of haunted houses often enough. But never have I met anyone who has actually stayed in one and seen anything. So I don't quite . . .'

Anath Babu's smile deepened.

'Would you like to see it?' he said.

'What?'

'That house.'

'See? How do you mean?'

'Only from the outside. It's not very far from here. One mile, at the most. If you go straight down this road, past the twin temples and then turn right, it's only a quarter of a mile from there.'

The man seemed quite interesting. Besides, there was no need to return home quite so soon. So I went with him.

The Haldar mansion was not easily visible. Most of it was covered by a thick growth of wild plants and creepers. Only the top of the gate that towered above everything else was visible a good ten minutes before one reached the house. The gate was really huge. The nahabatkhana over it was a shambles. A long drive led to the front veranda. A couple of statues and the remains of a fountain told us that there used to be a garden in the space between the house and the gate. The house was strangely structured. There was absolutely nothing in it that could have met even the lowest of aesthetic standards. The whole thing seemed only a shapeless heap. The last rays of the setting sun fell across the mossy walls.

Anath Babu stared at it for a minute. Then he said, 'As far as I know, ghosts and spirits don't come out in daylight. Why don't we,' he added, winking, 'go and take a look at that room?'

'That west room? The one . . .?'

'Yes. The one in which Haladhar Datta died.'

The man's interest in the matter seemed a bit exaggerated. Anath Babu read my mind.

'I can see you're surprised. Well, I don't mind telling you the truth. The only reason behind my arrival in Raghunathpur is this house.'

'Really?'

'Yes. In Calcutta I had heard that the house was haunted. I

came all the way to see if I could catch a glimpse of the ghost. You asked me on the train why I was coming here. I didn't reply, which must have appeared rude. But I had decided to wait until I got to know you a little better before telling you.'

'But why did you have to come all the way from Calcutta to chase a ghost?'

'I'll explain that in a minute. I haven't yet told you about my profession, have I? The fact is that I am an authority on ghosts and all things supernatural. I have spent the last twenty-five years doing research in this area. I have read everything that's ever been published on life after death, spirits that haunt the earth, vampires, werewolves, black magic, voodoo—the lot. I had to learn seven different languages to do this. There is a Professor Norton in London who has a similar interest. I have been in correspondence with him over the last three years. My articles have been published in well-known magazines in Britain. I don't wish to sound boastful, but I think it would be fair to say that no one in this country has as much knowledge about these things as I do.'

He spoke very sincerely. The thought that he might be telling lies or exaggerating did not cross my mind at all. On the contrary, I found it quite easy to believe what he told me and even felt some respect for the man.

After a few moments of silence, he said, 'I have stayed in at least three hundred haunted houses all over the country.'

'Goodness!'

'Yes. In places like Jabalpur, Cherrapunji, Kanthi, Katoa, Jodhpur, Azimganj, Hazaribagh, Shiuri, Barasat . . . and so many others. I've stayed in fifty-six dak bungalows, and at least thirty indigo cottages. Besides these, there are about fifty haunted houses in Calcutta and its suburbs where I've spent my nights. But . . .'

Anath Babu stopped. Then he shook his head and said, 'The

ghosts have eluded me. Perhaps they like to visit only those who don't want to have anything to do with them. I have been disappointed time and again. Only once did I feel the presence of something strange in an old building in Tiruchirapalli near Madras. It used to be a club during British times. Do you know what happened? The room was dark and there was no breeze at all. Yet, each time I tried to light a candle, someone—or something—kept snuffing it out. I had to waste twelve matchsticks. However, with the thirteenth I did manage to light the candle but, as soon as it was lit, the spirit vanished. Once, in a house in Calcutta, too, I had a rather interesting experience. I was sitting in a dark room as usual, waiting for something to happen, when I suddenly felt a mosquito bite my scalp! Quite taken aback, I felt my head and discovered that every single strand of my hair had disappeared. I was totally bald! Was it really my own head? Or had I touched someone else's? But no, the mosquito bite was real enough. I switched on my torch quickly and peered into the mirror. All my hair was intact. There was no sign of baldness.

'These were the only two ghostly experiences I've had in all these years. I had given up all hope of finding anything anywhere. But, recently, I happened to read in an old magazine about this house in Raghunathpur. So I thought I'd come and try my luck for the last time.'

We had reached the front door. Anath Babu looked at his watch and said, 'The sun sets today at 5.31 p.m. It's now 5.15. Let's go and take a quick look before it gets dark.'

Perhaps his interest in the supernatural was contagious. I readily accepted his proposal. Like him, I felt eager to see the inside of the house and that room in particular.

We walked in through the front door. There was a huge courtyard and something that looked like a stage. It must have been used for pujas and other festivals. There was no sign now of the joy and laughter it must once have witnessed.

There were verandas around the courtyard. To our right lay a broken palanquin, and beyond it was a staircase going up.

It was so dark on the staircase that Anath Babu had to take a torch out of his pocket and switch it on. We had to demolish an invisible wall of cobwebs to make our way. When we finally reached the first floor, I thought to myself, 'It wouldn't be surprising at all if this house did turn out to be haunted.'

We stood in the passage and made some rough calculations. The room on our left must be the famous west room, we decided. Anath Babu said, 'Let's not waste any time. Come with me.'

There was only one thing in the passage—a grandfather clock. Its glass was broken, one of its hands was missing and the pendulum lay to one side.

The door to the west room was closed. Anath Babu pushed it gently with his forefinger. A nameless fear gave me goose-pimples. The door swung open.

But the room revealed nothing unusual. It may have been a living-room once. There was a big table in the middle with a missing top. Only the four legs stood upright. An easy chair stood near the window, although sitting in it now would not be very easy as it had lost one of its arms and a portion of its seat.

I glanced up and saw that bits and pieces of an old-fashioned, hand-pulled fan still hung from the ceiling. It didn't have a rope, the wooden bar was broken and its main body torn.

Apart from these objects, the room had a shelf that must once have held rifles, a pipeless hookah, and two ordinary chairs, also with broken arms.

Anath Babu appeared to be deep in thought. After a while, he said, 'Can you smell something?'

'Smell what?'

'Incense, oil and burning flesh . . . all mixed together . . .' I inhaled deeply, but could smell nothing beyond the usual musty smell that comes from a room that has been kept shut for a long time.

So I said, 'Why, no, I don't think I can . . .'

Anath Babu did not say anything. Then, suddenly, he struck his left hand with his right and exclaimed, 'God! I know this smell well! There is bound to be a spirit lurking about in this house, though whether or not he'll make an appearance remains to be seen. Let's go!'

Anath Babu decided to spend the following night in the Haldar mansion. On our way back, he said, 'I won't go tonight because tomorrow is a moonless night, the most appropriate time for ghosts and spirits to come out. Besides, I need a few things which I haven't got with me today. I'll bring those tomorrow. Today I had come only to make a survey.'

Before we parted company near Biren's house, he lowered his voice and said, 'Please don't tell anyone else about my plan. From what I heard today, people here are so superstitious and easily frightened that they might actually try to stop me from going in if they came to know of my plan. And,' he added, 'please don't mind that I didn't ask you to join me. One has to be alone, you see, for something like this . . .'

I sat down the next day to write, but could not concentrate. My mind kept going back to the west room in that mansion. God knew what kind of experience awaited Anath Babu. I could not help feeling a little restless and anxious.

I accompanied Anath Babu in the evening, right up to the gate of the Haldar mansion. He was wearing a black high-necked jacket today. From his shoulder hung a flask and in his hand he carried the same torch he had used the day before.

He took out a couple of small bottles from his pocket before going into the house. 'Look,' he said, 'this one has a special oil, made with my own formula. It is an excellent mosquito repellent. And this one here has carbolic acid in it. If I spread it in and around the room, I'll be safe from snakes.'

He put the bottles back in his pocket, raised the torch and touched his head with it. Then he waved me a final salute and walked in, his heavy boots clicking on the gravel.

I could not sleep well that night. As soon as dawn broke, I told Bharadwaj to fill a thermos flask with enough tea for two. When the flask arrived, I left once more for the Haldar mansion.

No one was about. Should I call out to Anath Babu, or should I go straight up to the west room? As I stood debating, a voice said, 'Here—this way!'

Anath Babu was coming out of the little jungle of wild plants from the eastern side of the house, a neem twig in his hand. He certainly did not look like a man who might have had an unnatural or horrific experience the night before.

He grinned broadly as he came closer.

'I had to search for about half an hour before I could find a neem tree. I prefer this to a toothbrush, you see.'

I felt hesitant to ask him about the previous night.

'I brought some tea,' I said instead. 'Would you like some here, or would you rather go home?'

'Oh, come along. Let's sit by that fountain.'

Anath Babu took a long sip of his tea and said, 'Aaah!' with great relish. Then he turned to me and said with a twinkle in his eye, 'You're dying to know what happened, aren't you?'

'Yes, I mean . . . yes, a little . . .'

'All right. I will tell you everything. But let me just say this one thing right away—the whole expedition was highly successful!'

He poured himself a second mug of tea and began his tale:

'It was 5 p.m. when you left me here. I looked around for a bit before going into the house. One has to be careful, you know. There are times when animals and other living beings can cause more harm than ghosts. But I didn't find anything dangerous. Then I went in and looked into the rooms in the ground floor that were open. None had any furniture left. All I could find was some old rubbish in one and a few bats hanging from the ceiling in another. They didn't budge as I went in, so I came out again without disturbing them.

'I went upstairs at around 6.30 p.m. and began making preparations for the night. I had taken a duster with me. The first thing I did was to dust that easy chair. Heaven knows how long it had lain there.

'The room felt stuffy, so I opened the window. The door to the passage was also left open, just in case Mr Ghost wished to make his entry through it. Then I placed the flask and the torch on the floor and lay down on the easy chair. It was quite uncomfortable but, having spent many a night before under far more weird circumstances, I did not mind.

'The sun had set at 5.30. It grew dark quite soon. And that smell grew stronger. I don't usually get worked up, but I must admit last night I felt a strange excitement.

'I couldn't tell you the exact time, but I guess it must have been around 9 p.m. when a firefly flew in through the window and buzzed around the room for a minute before flying out.

'Gradually, the jackals in the distance stopped their chorus, and the crickets fell silent. I cannot tell when I fell asleep.

'I was awoken by a noise. It was the noise of a clock striking midnight. A deep, yet melodious chime came from the passage. Now fully awake, I noticed two other things—first, I was lying quite comfortably in the easy chair. The torn portion wasn't torn any more, and someone had tucked a cushion behind my back. Secondly, a brand new fan hung over my head; a long rope from it went out to the passage and an unseen hand was pulling it gently.

'I was staring at these things and enjoying them thoroughly, when I realized that from somewhere in the moonless night a full moon had appeared. The room was flooded with bright moonlight. Then the aroma of something totally unexpected hit my nostrils. I turned and found a hookah by my side, the rich smell of the best quality tobacco filling the room.'

Anath Babu stopped. Then he smiled and said, 'Quite a pleasant situation, wouldn't you agree?'

I said, 'Yes, indeed. So you spent the rest of the night pretty comfortably, did you?'

At this, Anath Babu suddenly grew grave and sank into a deep silence. I waited for him to resume speaking, but when he didn't, I turned impatient. 'Do you mean to say,' I asked, 'that you really didn't have any reason to feel frightened? You didn't see a ghost, after all?'

Anath Babu looked at me. But there was not even the slightest trace of a smile on his lips. His voice sounded hoarse as he asked, 'When you went into the room the day before yesterday, did you happen to look carefully at the ceiling?'

'No, I don't think I did. Why?'

'There is something rather special about it. I cannot tell you the rest of my story without showing it to you. Come, let's go in.'

We began climbing the dark staircase again. On our way to the first floor, Anath Babu said only one thing: 'I will not have to chase ghosts again, Sitesh Babu. Never. I have finished with them.'

I looked at the grandfather clock in the passage. It stood just as it had done two days ago.

We stopped in front of the west room. 'Go in,' said Anath Babu.

The door was closed. I pushed it open and went in. Then my

eyes fell on the floor, and a wave of horror swept over me.

Who was lying on the floor, heavy boots on his feet? And whose laughter was that, loud and raucous, coming from the passage outside, echoing through every corner of the Haldar mansion? Drowning me in it, paralysing my senses, my mind . . .? Could it be . . .? I could think no more.

When I opened my eyes, I found Bharadwaj standing at the foot of my bed, and Bhabatosh Majumdar fanning me furiously. 'Oh, thank goodness you've come around!' he exclaimed. 'If Sidhucharan hadn't seen you go into that house, heaven knows what might have happened. Why on earth did you go there, anyway?'

I could only mutter faintly, 'Last night, Anath Babu . . .'

Bhabatosh Babu cut me short, 'Anath Babu! It's too late now to do anything about him. Obviously, he didn't believe a word of what I had said the other day. Thank God you didn't go with him to spend the night in that room. You saw what happened to him, didn't you? Exactly the same thing had happened to Haladhar Datta all those years ago. Lying on the floor, cold and stiff, the same look of horror in his open eyes, staring at the ceiling.'

I thought quietly to myself, 'No, he's not lying there cold and stiff. I know what's become of Anath Babu after his death. I might find him, even tomorrow morning, perhaps, if I bothered to go back. There he would be wearing a black jacket and heavy boots, coming out of the jungle in the Haldar mansion, a neem twig in his hand, grinning from ear to ear.'

(1962)   *Translated by Gopa Majumdar*

THE SMALL WORLD OF SADANANDA

I am feeling quite cheerful today, so this is a good time to tell you everything. I know you will believe me. You are not like my people; they only laugh at me. They think I am making it up. So I have stopped talking to them.

It is midday now, so there is no one in my room. They will come in the afternoon. Now there are only two here—myself and my friend Lal Bahadur. Lal Bahadur Singh! Oh, how worried I was for his sake yesterday! I couldn't believe he would ever come back to me. He is very clever, so he was able to escape unhurt. Anyone else would have been finished by now.

How silly of me!—I have told you my friend's name, but haven't told you my own.

My name is Sadananda Chakraborty. It sounds like the name of a bearded old man, doesn't it? Actually, I am only thirteen. I can't help it if my name is old fashioned. After all, I didn't choose it; my grandma did.

If only she knew how much trouble it would cause me, she would have surely called me something else. How could she have known that people could pester me by saying, 'Why are you so glum when your name means "ever-happy"?' Such fools!

As if laughing like a jackass was the only way to show that one was happy. There are so many ways of being happy even when one doesn't smile.

For instance, suppose there's a twig sticking out of the ground and you find a grasshopper landing on its tip again and again. It would certainly make you happy to see it, but if you burst out laughing at it, people would think you were out of your mind. Like that mad uncle of mine. I never saw him, but I was told that he laughed all the time. Even when they had to put him in chains, he found it so funny that he almost split his sides laughing. The truth is, I get fun out of things which most people don't even notice. Even when I am lying in bed I notice things which make me happy. Sometimes a cotton seed will come floating in through the window. Small wispy things which the slightest breath of air sends wafting hither and thither. What a happy sight it is! If it comes floating down towards you, you blow on it and send it shooting up into the air again.

And if a crow comes and settles on the window, watching it is like watching a circus clown. I always go absolutely still when a crow comes and sits nearby, and watch its antics out of the corner of my eyes.

But if you ask me what gives me the most fun, I would say—watching ants. Of course, it is no longer just funny; it is . . . but no, I mustn't tell everything now or the fun will be spoilt. It's better that I begin at the beginning.

Once, about a year ago, I had fever. It was nothing new, as I am often laid up with fever. I catch a chill rather easily. Mother says it's because I spend so much time out of doors sitting on the grass.

As always, the first couple of days in bed was fun. A nice, chilly feeling mixed with a feeling of laziness. Added to this was the fun of not having to go to school. I lay in bed watching a squirrel climbing up the madar tree outside the window when

Mother came and gave me a bitter mixture to drink. I drank it up like a good boy and then took the glass of water, drank some of it and blew the rest out of the window in a spray. I wrapped the blanket around me and was about to close my eyes for a doze when I noticed something.

A few drops of water had fallen on the window-sill, and in one of these drops a small black ant was trying desperately to save itself from drowning.

I found it so strange that I propped myself up on my elbows and leaned forward to bring my eyes up close to the ant.

As I watched intently, it suddenly seemed as if the ant was not an ant any more but a man. In fact, it reminded me of Jhontu's brother-in-law who had slipped down the bank into a pond while fishing and, not being able to swim, wildly thrashed his arms about to keep himself afloat. In the end he was saved by Jhontu's elder brother and their servant Narahari.

As soon as I recalled the incident, I had a wish to save the ant.

Although I had fever, I jumped out of bed, ran out of the room, rushed into my father's study and tore off a piece of blotting paper from his writing pad. Then I ran back into my room, jumped onto the bed and held the blotting paper such that its edge touched the drop of water. The water was sucked up in no time.

The suddenly rescued ant seemed not to know which way to go. It rushed about this way and that for a while, and then disappeared down the drainpipe on the far side of the sill.

No more ants appeared on the sill that day.

The next day the fever went up. Around midday Mother came and said, 'Why are you staring at the window? You should try and get some sleep.'

I shut my eyes to please Mother, but as soon as she left, I opened them again and looked at the drainpipe.

In the afternoon, when the sun was behind the madar tree, I saw an ant poking its head out of the mouth of the pipe.

Suddenly it came out and started to move about briskly on the sill.

Although all black ants look alike, I somehow had the feeling that this was the same ant which had nearly drowned yesterday. I had acted as its friend, so it had come to pay me a visit.

I had made my plans beforehand. I had brought some sugar from the pantry, wrapped it up in paper and put it beside my pillow. I now opened the wrapper, took out a large grain of sugar and put it on the sill.

The ant seemed startled and stopped in its tracks. Then it cautiously approached the sugar and prodded it with its head from all sides. Then it suddenly made for the drainpipe and disappeared into it.

I thought: that's odd. I gave it such a nice grain of sugar and it left it behind. Why did it have to come at all if not for food?

The doctor came in a short while. He felt my pulse, looked at my tongue and placed the stethoscope on my chest and back. Then he said that I must take some more of the bitter mixture and the fever would go in a couple of days. That didn't make me happy at all. No fever meant going to school, and going to school meant not watching the drainpipe in the afternoon when the ants came out. Anyway, as soon as the doctor left, I turned towards the window and was delighted to see a whole army of black ants coming out of the drainpipe onto the sill. The leader must be the ant I knew, and it must have informed the other ants of the grain of sugar and led them to it.

Watching for a while I was able to see for myself how clever the ants were. All the ants now banded together to push the grain towards the drainpipe. I can't describe how funny it was, I imagined that if they had been coolies pushing a heavy weight, they'd have shouted, 'All together, heave ho! A little further, heave ho! That's the spirit, heave ho!'

After my fever was gone, school was a bore for a few days. My thoughts would go back again and again to the window-sill. There must be ants coming there every afternoon. I would leave a few grains of sugar on the sill every morning before going to school, and when I returned in the afternoon I would find them gone.

In the class I used to sit at a desk towards the middle of the room. Beside me sat Sital. One day I was a little late and found Phani sitting in my place. So I had no choice but to sit at the back of the class, in front of the wall. In the last period before recess we read history. In his thin, piping voice Haradhan Babu the history teacher was describing how brave Hannibal was. Hannibal had led an army from Carthage and had crossed the Alps to invade Italy.

As I listened, I suddenly had the feeling that Hannibal's army was in the classroom and was on the march very close to me.

I looked around and my eyes travelled to the wall behind me. Down the wall ran a long line of ants—hundreds of small black ants, exactly like a mighty army on the way to battle.

I looked down and found a crack in the wall near the floor through which the ants were going out.

As soon as the bell rang for the recess, I ran out to the back of our classroom and spotted the crack. The ants were coming out of it and making their way through the grass towards a guava tree.

I followed the ants and found, at the foot of the guava tree, something which can only be described as a castle.

It was a mound of earth with a tiny opening at the base through which the ants entered.

I had a great urge to look inside that castle.

I had my pencil in my pocket, and with its tip I began to dig carefully into the mound. At first I found nothing inside, but on digging a little further, I had the surprise of my life. I found there were countless small chambers inside the mound, and a maze of passages leading from one chamber to another. How very strange! How could the ants build such a castle with their tiny arms and legs? How could they be so clever? Did they have schools where they were taught? Did they also learn from books, draw pictures, build things? Did that mean they were no different from human beings except in looks? How was it that they could build their own house while tigers, elephants, bears and horses couldn't? Even Bhulo, my pet dog, couldn't.

Of course, birds build nests. But how many birds can live in a single nest? Can the birds build a castle where thousands of them can live?

Because I had spoilt a part of the mound, there was a great flurry amongst the ants. I felt sorry for them. I thought: now that I have done them harm, I must make up by doing them a good turn, or they will look upon me as their enemy, which I am not. I was truly their friend.

So the next day I took half of a sweetmeat which Mother gave me to eat, wrapped it up in a sal leaf and carried it in my pocket to school. Just before the bell rang for the classes to begin, I put the sweetmeat by the anthill. The ants would have to travel to find food; today they'd find it right at their doorstep. Surely this was doing them a good turn.

In a few weeks the summer holidays began and my friendship with ants began to grow. I would tell the elders about my observations of how ants behaved, but they paid no attention to me. What really put my back up was that they laughed at me. So I decided not to tell anybody anything. Whatever I did, I would do on my own and keep what I learned to myself.

One day, in the afternoon, I sat by the compound wall of Pintu's house watching a hill made by red ants. People will say that you can't sit near red ants for long because they bite. I had been bitten by red ants myself, but of late I had noticed that they didn't bite me any more. So I was watching them without fear when I suddenly saw Chhiku striding up.

I haven't mentioned Chhiku yet. His real name is Srikumar. He is in the same class as me, but he must be older than me because there's a thin line of moustache above his lips. Chhiku is a bully, so nobody likes him. I usually don't meddle with him because he is stronger than me. Chhiku saw me and called out, 'You there, you silly ass, what are you doing squatting there on the ground?' I didn't pay any attention to him. He came up towards me. I kept my eyes on the ants.

Chhiku drew up and said, 'Well, what are you up to? I don't like the look of it.'

I made no attempt to hide what I was doing and told him the truth. Chhiku made a face and said, 'What do you mean—watching ants? What is there to watch? And aren't there ants in your own house that you have to come all the way here?'

I felt very angry. What was it to him what I did? Why did he have to poke his nose into other people's affairs?

I said, 'I'm watching them because I like doing so. You know nothing about ants. Why don't you mind your own business? Why come and bother me?'

Chhiku hissed like an angry cat and said, 'So you like watching ants, eh? Well–there! There!' Before I could do or say anything, Chhiku had levelled the anthill with three vicious jabs of his heel, thereby squashing at least 500 ants.

Chhiku gave a hollow laugh and was about to walk away when something suddenly happened to me. I jumped up on Chhiku's back, grabbed hold of his hair, and knocked his head four or five times against Pintu's compound wall. Then I let go of him. Chhiku burst into tears and went off.

When I got back home, I learnt that Chhiku had already been there to complain against me.

But I was surprised when at first Mother neither scolded nor beat me. Perhaps she hadn't believed Chhiku, because I had never hit anyone before. Besides, Mother knew that I was scared of Chhiku. But when Mother asked what had happened, I couldn't lie to her.

Mother was very surprised. 'You mean you really bashed his head against the wall?'

I said, 'Yes, I did. And why only Chhiku? I would do the same to anyone who trampled on anthills.' This made Mother so angry that she slapped me.

It was a Saturday. Father came back from the office early. When he heard from Mother what had happened he locked me up in my room.

Although my cheeks smarted from the slaps, I wasn't really sorry for myself. I was very sorry for the ants. Once in Sahibgunge where cousin Parimal lives, there was a collision between two trains which killed 300 people. Today it took Chhiku only a few seconds to kill so many ants!

It seemed so wrong, so very, very wrong.

As I lay in bed thinking of all that had happened, I suddenly felt a little chilly and had to draw the blanket over myself.

And then I went off to sleep. I was awakened by a strange noise.

A thin, high-pitched sound, very beautiful, going up and down in a regular beat, like a song.

My ears pricked up and I looked around but couldn't make out where the sound came from. Probably someone far away was singing. But I had never heard such singing before.

Look who's here! Coming out of the drainpipe while I was listening to the strange sound.

This time I clearly recognized it—the ant I had saved from drowning. It was facing me and salaaming me by raising its two front legs and touching its head with them. What shall I call this black creature? Kali, Krishna? I must think about it. After all, one can't have a friend without a name. I put my hand on the window-sill, palm upwards. The ant brought his legs down from his head and crawled slowly towards my hand. Then it climbed up my little finger and started scurrying over the criss-cross lines on my palm.

Just then I started as I heard a sound from the door, and the ant clambered down and disappeared into the drainpipe.

Now Mother came into the room and gave me a glass of milk. Then she felt my forehead and said I had fever again.

Next morning the doctor came. Mother said, 'He has been restless the whole night, and kept saying "Kali" again and again.' Mother probably thought I was praying to the Goddess Kali, because I hadn't told her about my new friend.

The doctor had put the stethoscope on my back when I heard the song again. It was louder than yesterday and the tune was different. It seemed to come from the window, but since the doctor had asked me to keep still, I couldn't turn my head to see.

The doctor finished his examination, and I cast a quick glance towards the window. Hello there! It was a large black ant this time, and this one too was salaaming me. Are all ants my friends then?

And was it this ant which was singing?

But Mother said nothing about a song. Did it mean that she couldn't hear it?

I turned towards Mother to ask her, and found her staring at the ant with fear in her eyes. The next moment she picked up my arithmetic note-book from the table, leaned over me and with one slap of the book squashed the ant. The same moment the singing stopped.

'The whole house is crawling with ants!' said Mother. 'Just think what would happen if one crawled inside your ear.'

The doctor left after giving me an injection. I looked at the dead ant. He was killed while singing a beautiful song. Just like my great-uncle Indranath. He too used to sing classical songs, which I didn't understand very well. One day he was playing the tanpura and singing when he suddenly died. When he was taken to the crematorium in a procession, a group of keertan singers went along singing songs. I watched it and still remember it, although I was then very small.

And then a strange thing happened. I fell asleep after the injection and dreamed that, like the funeral of great-uncle Indranath, a dozen or so ants were bearing the dead ant on their shoulders while a line of ants followed singing a chorus.

I woke up in the afternoon when Mother put her cool hand on my forehead.

I glanced at the window and found that the dead ant was no longer there.

This time the fever kept on for several days. No wonder, because everyone in the house had started killing ants. How can the fever go if you have to listen to the screaming of ants all day long?

And there was another problem. While the ants were being killed in the pantry, hordes of ants turned up on my window-sill and wept. I could see that they wanted me to do something for them—either stop the killing or punish those who were doing the misdeed. But since I was laid up with fever, I could do nothing about it. Even if I were well, how could a small boy like me stop the elders from what they were doing?

But one day, I was forced to do something about it.

I don't exactly remember what day it was, but I do remember that I had woken up at the crack of dawn and right away heard Mother announcing that an ant had got into Phatik's ear and bitten him.

I was tickled by the news but just then I heard the slapping of brooms on the floor and knew that they were killing ants.

Then a very strange thing happened. I heard thin voices shouting, 'Help us! Help us, please!' I looked at the window and found that a large group of ants had gathered on the sill and were running around wildly.

Hearing them cry out I could no longer keep calm. I forgot about my fever, jumped out of bed and ran out of the room. At first I didn't know what to do. Then I took up a clay pot which was lying on the floor and smashed it. Then I started to smash all the things I could find which would break. It was a clever ruse because it certainly stopped the killing of ants. But it made my parents, my aunt, my cousin Sabi all come out of their rooms, grab hold of me, put me back on my bed and lock the door of my room.

I had a good laugh, though, and the ants on my window kept saying, 'Thank you! Thank you!' and went back into the drainpipe again.

Soon after this I had to leave home. The doctor examined me one day and said I should be sent to hospital for treatment.

Now I am in a hospital room. I've been here these last four days.

The first day I felt very sad because the room was so clean that I knew there couldn't be any ants in it. Being a new room, there were no cracks or holes in the walls. There wasn't even a cupboard for ants to hide under or behind it. But there was a mango tree just outside the window, and one of its branches was within reach.

I thought if there was a place to find ants it would be on that branch.

But the first day I couldn't get near the window. How could I, since I was never alone? Either the nurse, or the doctor, or someone from my house was always in the room. The second day too was just as bad.

I was so upset that I threw a medicine bottle on the floor and broke it. It made the doctor quite angry. He was not a nice doctor, this new one. I could tell that from his bristling moustache and from the thick glasses he wore.

On the third day, something happened. There was only a nurse in my room then, and she was reading a book. I was in bed wondering what to do. I heard a thud and saw that the book had slipped from the nurse's hand and fallen on the floor. The nurse had dozed off.

I got down from the bed and tiptoed to the window.

Leaning out of the window and stretching my body as far as it would go, I grabbed hold of the mango branch and began to pull it towards me.

This made a noise which woke up the nurse, and then the fireworks started.

The nurse gave a scream, came rushing towards me and, wrapping her arms around me, dragged me to the bed and dumped me on it. Others too came into the room just then, so I could do nothing more.

The doctor promptly gave me an injection.

I could make out from what they were saying that they thought I had meant to throw myself out of the window. Silly people! If I had thrown myself from such a height, all my bones would have been crushed and I would have died.

After the doctor left I felt sleepy. I thought of the window by my bed at home and felt very sorry. Who knew when I would be back home again?

I had nearly fallen asleep when I heard a thin voice saying, 'Sepoys at your service, sir—sepoys at your service!'

I opened my eyes and saw two large red ants standing with their chests out by the medicine bottle on the bedside table.

They must have climbed onto my hand from the mango branch without my knowing it.

I said, 'Sepoys?'

The answer came, 'Yes, sir—at your service.'

'What are your names?' I asked them.

One said, 'Lal Bahadur Singh.' And the other said, 'Lal Chand Pandey.'

I was very pleased. But I warned them to go into hiding when people came into the room, or they might be killed. Lal Chand and Lal Bahadur salaamed and said, 'Very well, sir.' Then the two of them sang a lovely duet which lulled me to sleep.

I must tell you right away what happened yesterday, because it's nearly five and the doctor will be here soon. In the afternoon I was watching Lal Chand and Lal Bahadur wrestling on the table while I lay in bed. I was supposed to be asleep, but the pills and the injection hadn't worked. Or, to be quite truthful, I wilfully kept myself awake. If I slept in the afternoon, when would I play with my new friends?

The two ants fought gamely and it was hard to say who would win when suddenly there was a sound of heavy footsteps. The doctor was coming!

I made a sign and Lal Bahadur promptly disappeared below the table. But Lal Chand had been thrown on his back and was thrashing his legs about, so he couldn't run away. And that was what caused the nasty incident.

The doctor came, saw the ant, and saying some rude words in English, swept it off the table with his hand.

I could tell from Lal Chand's scream that he was badly hurt, but what could I do? By that time the doctor had grabbed my wrist to feel my pulse. I tried to get up, but the nurse held me down.

After the examination, the doctor as usual made a glum face and scratched the edge of his moustache. He was about to turn towards the door when he suddenly screwed up his face, gave a leap and yelled 'Ouch!'

Then all hell broke loose. The stethoscope flew out of his hand, his spectacles jumped off his nose and crashed onto the floor. One of the buttons of his jacket came off as he struggled to take it off, his tie wound tighter around his neck and made him gasp and sputter before at last he managed to pull it free, the hole in his vest showed as he yanked off his shirt, jumping around and yelling all the time. I was speechless.

The nurse said, 'What is the matter, sir?'

The doctor continued to jump about and yelled, 'Ant! Red ant! It crawled up my arm—ouch!'

Well, well, well! I knew this would happen, and it serves you right! Lal Bahadur had taken revenge on his friend's behalf.

If they saw me now they would know how deliriously happy Sadananda could be.

(1962)   *Translated by Satyajit Ray*

THE PTERODACTYL'S EGG

Badan Babu had stopped going to Curzon Park after work. He used to enjoy his daily visits to the park. Every evening he would go straight from his office and spend about an hour, just resting quietly on a bench, beside the statue of Suren Banerjee. Then, when the crowds in the trams grew marginally thinner, he would catch one back to his house in Shibthakur Lane.

Now new tram lines had been laid inside the park. The noise of the traffic had ruined the atmosphere totally. There was no point in trying to catch a few quiet moments here. Yet, it was impossible to go back home straight after office, packed into a bus like sardines in a tin.

Besides, Badan Babu simply had to find some time every day to try and enjoy the little natural beauty that was left in the city. He might be no more than an ordinary clerk, but God had given him a lively imagination. He had thought of so many different stories sitting on that bench in Curzon Park. But there had never been the time to write them down. Had he, indeed, managed to find the time, no doubt he would have made quite a name for himself.

However, not all his efforts had been wasted.

His seven-year-old son, Biltu, was an invalid. Since he was incapable of moving around, most of his time was spent listening to stories. Both his parents told him stories of all kinds—fairy tales, folk tales, funny tales and spooky tales, tales they had heard and tales they had read. In the last three years, he had been told at least a thousand stories. Badan Babu had lately been making up stories himself for his son. He usually did this sitting in Curzon Park.

Over the last few weeks, however, Biltu had made it plain that he no longer enjoyed all his stories. One look at Biltu's face was enough to see that he had been disappointed.

This did not surprise Badan Babu very much. It was not possible to think up a good plot during the day; this time was spent doing his work in the office. And now that the peace of Curzon Park had been shattered, his only chance of sitting there in the evening and doing a bit of thinking was lost forever.

He tried going to Lal Deeghi a few times. Even that did not work. The huge, monstrous communications building next to the Deeghi blocked a large portion of the sky. Badan Babu felt suffocated there.

After that even the park near Lal Deeghi was invaded by tram lines and Badan Babu was forced to look for a different spot.

Today, he had come to the riverside.

After walking along the iron railings for about a quarter of a mile on the southern side of Outram Ghat, he found an empty bench.

There was Fort William, not far away. In fact, he could see the cannon. The cannonball stood fixed at the end of an iron rod, almost like a giant lollipop.

Badan Babu recalled his schooldays. The cannon went off every day at 1 p.m., the boys came rushing out for their lunch break and the headmaster, Harinath Babu, took out his pocket-watch religiously and checked the time.

The place was quiet, though not exactly deserted. A number of boats were tied nearby and one could see the boatmen talking among themselves. A grey, Japanese ship was anchored in the distance. Further down, towards Kidderpore, the skyline was crowded with masts of ships and pulleys.

This was a pleasant place.

Badan Babu sat down on the bench.

Through the smoke from the steamers he could see a bright spot in the sky. Could it be Venus?

It seemed to Badan Babu that he had not seen such a wide expanse of sky for a long time. Oh, how huge it was, how colossal! This was just what he needed for his imagination to soar.

Badan Babu took off his canvas shoes and sat cross-legged on the bench.

He was going to make up for lost time and find new plots for a number of stories today. He could see Biltu's face—happy and excited!

'Namaskar.'

Oh no! Was he going to be disturbed here too?

Badan Babu turned and found a stranger standing near the bench: a man, exceedingly thin, about fifty years old, wearing brown trousers and a jacket, a jute bag slung from one shoulder. His features were not clear in the twilight, but the look in his eyes seemed to be remarkably sharp.

A contraption hung from his chest. Two rubber tubes attached to it were plugged into the man's ears.

'Hope I'm not disturbing you,' said the newcomer with a slight smile. 'Please don't mind. I've never seen you before, so . . .'

Badan Babu felt considerably put out. Why did the man have to come and force himself on him? Now all his plans were upset. What was he going to tell poor Biltu?

'You've never seen me for the simple reason that I have never come here before,' he said. 'In a big city like this, isn't it natural that the number of people one has never seen should be more than the number of people one has?'

The newcomer ignored the sarcasm and said, 'I have been coming here every day for the last four years.'

'I see.'

'I sit here in this very spot every day. This is where I do my experiments, you know.'

Experiments? What kind of experiments could one do in this open space by the riverside? Was the man slightly mad?

But what if he was something else? He could be a hooligan, couldn't he? Or a pickpocket?

Good God—today had been pay day! Badan Babu's salary—two new, crisp hundred-rupee notes—was tied up in a handkerchief and thrust into his pocket. His wallet had fifty-five rupees and thirty-two paise.

Badan Babu rose. It was better to be safe than sorry.

'Are you leaving? So soon? Are you annoyed with me?'

'No, no.'

'Well, then? You got here just now only, didn't you? Why do you want to leave so soon?'

Perhaps Badan Babu was being over-cautious. There was no need to feel so scared. After all, there were all those people in the boats, not far away.

Still Badan Babu hesitated.

'No, I must go. It's getting late.'

'Late? It's only half-past five.'

'I have to go quite far.'

'How far?'

'Right up to Bagbazar.'

'Pooh—that's not very far! It's not as though you have to go to a suburb like Serampore or Chuchrah or even Dakshineshwar!'

'Even so, it will mean spending at least forty minutes in a

tram. And then it takes about ten minutes to get to my house from the tram stop.'

'Yes, there is that, of course.'

The newcomer suddenly became a little grave. Then he began muttering to himself, 'Forty plus ten. That makes fifty. I am not very used to calculating minutes and hours. My system is different . . . do sit down. Just for a bit. Please.'

Badan Babu sat down again. There was something in the man's eyes and his voice that compelled him to stay back. Was this what was known as hypnotism?

'I don't ask everyone to sit by me for a chat. But you strike me as a man different from others. You like to think. You're not bound only by monetary considerations like 99.9 per cent of people. Am I right?'

Badan Babu said hesitantly, 'Well, I don't know . . . I mean . . .'

'And you're modest! Good. I can't stand people who brag. If it was all just a question of bragging, no one would have the right to do so more than me.'

The newcomer stopped speaking. Then he took out the rubber tubes from his ears and said, 'I get worried sometimes. If I pressed the switch in the dark accidentally, all hell would break loose.'

At this point, Badan Babu could not help asking the question that was trembling on his lips.

'Is that a stethoscope? Or is it something else?'

The man ignored the question completely. How rude, thought Badan Babu. But, before he could say anything further, the other man threw a counter question at him, in an irrelevant manner.

'Do you write?'

'Write? You mean—fiction?'

'Fiction or non-fiction, it does not matter. You see, that is something I have never been able to do. And yet, so many adventures, such a lot of experience and research . . . all this should be written and recorded for posterity.'

Experience? Research? What was the man talking about? 'How many kinds of travellers have you seen?'

His questions were really quite meaningless. How many people were lucky enough to have seen even one traveller?

Badan Babu said, 'I didn't even know travellers could be of more than one kind!'

'Why, there are at least three kinds. Anyone could tell you that! Those who travel on water, those who travel on land and those who travel in the sky. Vasco-da-Gama, Captain Scott and Columbus fall into the first category; and in the second are Hiuen Tsang, Mungo Park, Livingstone and even our own globe-trotter, Umesh Bhattacharya.

'And in the sky—say, Professor Picquard, who climbed 50,000 feet in a balloon and that youngster, Gagarin. But all of these are ordinary travellers. The kind of traveller I am talking about doesn't move on water or land or even in the sky.'

'Where does he move then?'

'Time.'

'What?'

'He moves in time. A journey into the past. A sojourn in the future. Roaming around freely in both. I don't worry too much about the present.'

Badan Babu began to see the light. 'You're talking about H.G. Wells, aren't you? The time machine? Wasn't that a contraption like a cycle with two handles? One would take you to the past and the other to the future? Wasn't a film made on this story?'

The man laughed contemptuously.

'That? That was only a story. I am talking of real life. My own experiences. My own machine. It's a far cry from a fictitious story written by an Englishman.'

Somewhere a steamer blew its horn.

Badan Babu started and pulled his chadar closer. In just a few minutes from now, darkness would engulf everything. Only the little lights on those boats would stay visible.

In the quickly gathering dusk Badan Babu looked at the newcomer once more. The last rays of the sun shone in his eyes.

The man raised his face to the sky and, after a few moments of silence, said, 'It's all quite funny, really. Three hundred years ago, right here by this bench, a crocodile happened to be stretched in the sun. There was a crane perched on its head. A Dutch ship with huge sails stood where that small boat is now tied. A sailor came out on the deck and shot at the crocodile with a rifle. One shot was enough to kill it. The crane managed to fly away, but dropped a feather in my lap. Here it is.'

He produced a dazzling white feather from his shoulder bag and gave it to Badan Babu.

'What . . . are these reddish specks?'

Badan Babu's voice sounded hoarse.

'Drops of blood from the injured crocodile fell on the bird.'

Badan Babu returned the feather.

The light in the man's eyes had dimmed. Visibility was getting poorer by the second. There had been loose bunches of grass and leaves floating in the river. Now they were practically invisible. The water, the earth and the sky had all become hazy and indistinct.

'Can you tell what this is?'

Badan Babu took the little object in his hand—a small triangular piece, pointed at one end.

'Two thousand years ago . . . right in the middle of the river—near that floating buoy—a ship with a beautifully patterned sail was making its way to the sea. It was probably a commercial vessel, going to Bali or some such place, to look for business. Standing here with the west wind blowing, I could hear all its thirty-two oars splashing in the water.'

'You?'

'Yes, who else? I was hiding behind a banyan tree in this same spot.'

'Why were you hiding?'

'I had to. I didn't know the place was so full of unknown dangers. History books don't often tell you these things.'

'You mean wild animals? Tigers?'

'Worse than tigers. Men. There was a barbarian, about that high,' he pointed to his waist. 'Blunt-nosed, dark as darkness. Earrings hung from his ears, a ring from his nose, his body was covered with tattoo marks. He held a bow and an arrow in his hand. The arrow had a poisonous tip.'

'Really?'

'Yes, every word I utter is the truth.'

'You saw it all yourself?'

'Listen to the rest of the story. It was the month of April. A storm had been brewing for some time. Then it started. Oh, what a storm it was, the likes of which I have never seen again! That beautiful ship disappeared amidst the roaring waves before my eyes.'

'And then?'

'One solitary figure managed to make it to the shore, riding on a broken wooden plank, dodging the hungry sharks and alligators. But as soon as he got off that plank . . . oh, my God!'

'What?'

'You should have seen what that barbarian did to him . . . but then, I didn't stay till the end. An arrow had come and hit the trunk of the banyan tree. I picked it up and pressed the switch to return to the present.'

Badan Babu did not know whether to laugh or cry. How could that little machine have such magical powers? How was it possible?

The newcomer seemed to read his mind.

'This machine here,' he said, 'has these two rubber tubes. All you need to do is put these into your ears. This switch on the right will take you to the future and the one on the left will take you to the past. The little wheel with a needle has dates and years written on it. You can fix the exact date you wish to travel to. Of course, I must admit there *are* times when it misses the mark by about twenty years. But that doesn't make too much difference. It's a cheap model, you see. So it's not all that accurate.'

'Cheap?' This time Badan Babu was truly surprised.

'Yes, cheap only in a financial sense. Five thousand years of scientific knowledge and expertise went into its making. People think science has progressed only in the west. And that nothing has happened in this country. I tell you, a tremendous lot has indeed happened here, but how many know about it? We were never a nation to show off our knowledge, were we? The true artist has always stayed in the background, hasn't he? Look at our history. Does anyone know the names of the painters who drew on the walls of Ajanta? Who carved the temple of Ellora out of ancient hills? Who created the Bhairavi raga? Who wrote the Vedas? The *Mahabharata* is said to have been written by Vyasa and the *Ramayana* by Valmiki. But does anyone know of those hundreds of people who worked on the original texts? Or, for that matter, of those that actually contributed to their creation? The scientists in the west have often made a name for themselves by working on complex mathematical formulae. Do you know the starting point of mathematics?'

'Starting point? What starting point?' Badan Babu did not know.

'Zero,' said the man.

'Zero?'

'Yes, zero.'

Badan Babu was taken aback. The man went on.

'One, two, three, four, five, six, seven, eight, nine, zero. These are the only digits used, aren't they? Zero, by itself, means nothing. But the minute you put it next to one, it gives you ten: one more than nine. Magic! Makes the mind boggle, it does. Yet, we have accepted it as a matter of course. All mathematical formulae are based on these nine digits and zero. Addition, subtraction, multiplication, division, fractions, decimals, algebra, arithmetic—even atoms, rockets, relativity—nothing can work without these ten numbers. And do you know where this zero came from? From India. It went to West Asia first, then to Europe and from there to the whole world. See what I mean? Do you know how the system worked before?'

Badan Babu shook his head. How very limited his own knowledge was!

'They used the Roman system,' said the newcomer. 'There were no digits. All they had were letters. One was I, two was II, three was III, but four became a combination of two letters, IV. Five was again just one letter, V. There was no logic in that system. How would you write 1962? It would simply mean writing four different digits, right? Do you know how many letters you'd need in Roman?'

'How many?'

'Seven, MCMLXII. Does that make any sense at all? If you had to write 888, you would normally need only three digits. To write that in the Roman style, you'd need a dozen. DCCCLXXXVIII. Can you imagine how long it would have taken scientists to write their huge formulae? They would have all gone prematurely grey, or—worse—totally bald! And the whole business of going to the moon would have been delayed by at least a thousand years. Just think—some unknown, anonymous man from our own country changed the whole concept of mathematics!'

He stopped for breath.

The church clock in the distance struck six.

Why did it suddenly seem brighter?

Badan Babu looked at the eastern sky and saw that the moon had risen behind the roof of the Grand Hotel.

'Things haven't changed,' the man continued. 'There are still plenty of people in our country who are quite unknown and will probably always stay that way. But their knowledge of science is no less than that of the scientists of the west. They do not often work in laboratories or need papers and books or any other paraphernalia. All they do is think and work out solutions to problems—all in their mind.'

'Are you one of those people?' asked Badan Babu softly.

'No. But I was lucky enough to meet such a man. Not here, of course. I used to travel a lot on foot when I was younger. Went often to the mountains. That is where I met this man. A remarkable character. His name was Ganitananda. But he didn't just think. He wrote things down. All his mathematical calculations were done on the stones strewn about within a radius of thirty miles from where he lived. Every stone and boulder was scribbled on with a piece of chalk. He had learnt the art of travelling in time from his guru. It was from Ganitananda that I learnt that there had once been a peak higher than the Everest by about 5,000 feet. Forty-seven thousand years ago, a devastating earthquake had made half of it go deeper into the ground. The same earthquake caused a crack in a mountain, from which appeared a waterfall. The river that is now flowing before us began its course from this waterfall.'

Strange! Oh, how strange it all was!

Badan Babu wiped his forehead with a corner of his chadar and said, 'Did you get that machine from him?'

'Yes. Well, no, he didn't actually give it to me. But he did tell me of the components that went into making it. I collected them all and made the machine myself. These tubes here are not really made of rubber. It's the bark of a tree that's found only in the hills. I didn't have to go to a shop or an artisan to get even a single part made. The whole thing is made of natural stuff. I made the markings on the dial myself. But, possibly because it's hand-made, it goes out of order sometimes. The switch meant for the future hasn't been working for sometime.'

'Have you travelled to the future?'

'Yes, once I did. But not too far. Only up to the thirtieth century.'

'What did you see?'

'There wasn't much to see. I was the only person walking along a huge road. A weird-looking vehicle appeared from somewhere and nearly ran me over. I did not try going into the future again.'

'And how far into the past have you travelled?'

'That's another catch. This machine cannot take me to the very beginning of creation.'

'Indeed?'

'Yes. I tried very hard, but the farthest I could go back to was when the reptiles had already arrived.'

Badan Babu's throat felt a little dry.

'What reptiles?' he asked. 'Snakes?'

'Oh no, no. Snakes are pretty recent.'

'Then?'

'Well, you know . . . things like the brontosaurus, tyrannosaurus—dinosaurs.'

'You mean you've been to other countries as well?'

'Ah, you're making the same mistake. Why should I have had to go to other countries? Do you think our own did not have these things?'

'Did it?'

'Of course it did! Right here. By the side of this bench.'

A cold shiver ran down Badan Babu's spine.

'The Ganga did not exist then,' said the man. 'This place was full of uneven, stony mounds and a lot of wild plants and creepers. There was a dirty pond where you can now see that jetty. I saw a will-o'-the-wisp rise over it and burn brightly, swaying from side to side. In its light, suddenly, I could see a pair of brilliant red eyes. You've seen pictures of a Chinese dragon, haven't you? This was a bit like that. I had seen its picture in a book. So I knew this was what was called a stegosaurus. It was crossing the pond, chewing on some leaves. I knew it would not attack me for it was a herbivorous animal. But, even so, I nearly froze with fear and was about to press the switch to return to the present, when I heard the flutter of wings right over my head. I looked up and saw a pterodactyl—a cross between a bird, an animal and a bat—swoop upon the stegosaurus. My eyes then fell on a large rock lying nearby and the reason for such aggression became clear. Inside a big crack in the rock lay a shiny, round, white egg. The pterodactyl's egg. Even though I was scared stiff, I couldn't resist the temptation. The two animals began fighting and I pocketed the egg . . . ha, ha, ha, ha!'

Badan Babu did not join in the laughter. Could this kind of thing really happen outside the realm of fiction?

'I would have allowed you to test my machine, but . . .'

A nerve in Badan Babu's forehead began to throb. He swallowed hard. 'But what?'

'The chances of getting a satisfactory result are very remote.'

'Wh-why?'

'But you can try your luck. At least you don't stand to lose anything.'

Badan Babu bent forward. Dear God in heaven—please don't let me be disappointed!

The man tucked the tubes into Badan Babu's ears, pressed a

switch and grabbed his right wrist.

'I need to watch your pulse.'

Badan Babu whispered nervously, 'Past? Or the future?'

'The past. 6,000 BC. Shut your eyes as tightly as you can.' Badan Babu obeyed and sat in eager anticipation for nearly a whole minute with his eyes closed. Then he said, 'Why, nothing seems to be . . . happening!'

The man switched the machine off and took it back.

'The chances were one in a million.'

'Why?'

'It would have worked only if the number of hairs on your head was exactly the same as mine.'

Badan Babu felt like a deflated balloon. How sad. How very sad he had to lose such an opportunity!

The newcomer put his hand inside his bag again and brought out something else.

Everything was quite clearly visible now in the moonlight.

'May I hold it in my hand?' asked Badan Babu, unable to stop himself. The other man offered him the shiny, round object.

It was quite heavy, and its surface remarkably smooth.

'All right. Time to go now. It's getting late.'

Badan Babu returned the egg. Heaven knew what else this man had seen. 'Hope you're coming here again tomorrow,' said Badan Babu.

'Let's see. There's such an awful lot to be done. I am yet to test the validity of all that the history books talk about. First of all, I must examine how Calcutta came into being. What a hue and cry has been raised over Job Charnock . . .! Allow me to take my leave today. Goodbye!'

Badan Babu reached the tram stop and boarded a tram. Then he slipped his hand into his pocket.

His heart stood still.

The wallet had gone.

There was nothing he could do except make an excuse and get down from the tram immediately.

As he began walking towards his house he felt like kicking himself. 'Now I know what happened,' he thought. 'When I closed my eyes and he held my hand . . . what a fool I made of myself!'

It was past 8 p.m. by the time he reached home.

Biltu's face lit up at the sight of his father.

By then, Badan Babu had started to feel more relaxed.

'I'll tell you a good story today,' he said, unbuttoning his shirt.

'Really? You mean it? It won't be a flop like all those others . . .?'

'No, no. I really mean it.'

'What kind of story, Baba?'

'The Pterodactyl's Egg. And many more. It won't finish in a day.' If one considered carefully, the material he had collected today to make up stories for Biltu, to bring a few moments of joy into his life, was surely worth at least fifty-five rupees and thirty-two paise?

(1962)   *Translated by Gopa Majumdar*

SHIBU AND THE MONSTER

'Hey—Shibu! Come here!'

Shibu was often hailed thus by Phatik-da on his way to school. Phatik-da alias Loony Phatik.

He lived in a small house with a tin roof, just off the main crossing, where an old, rusted steamroller had been lying for the last ten years. Phatik-da tinkered with God knew how many different things throughout the day. All Shibu knew was that he was very poor and that people said he went mad because he worked far too hard when he was a student. However, some of Phatik-da's remarks made Shibu think that few people had his intelligence.

But it was indeed true that most of what he said sounded perfectly crazy.

'I say—did you notice the moon last night? The left side seemed sort of extended, as though it had grown a horn!' Or, 'All the crows seem to have caught a cold. Haven't you heard the odd way in which they're cawing?'

Shibu was mostly amused when he heard Phatik-da talk like this, but at times he did get annoyed. Getting involved in a totally meaningless and irrelevant conversation was a waste of time. So he did not always stop for a chat. 'Not today, Phatik-da, I shall come tomorrow,' he would say and skip along to school.

He did not really want to stop today, but Phatik-da seemed

more insistent than usual.

'You may come to harm if you do not listen to what I have to say.'

Shibu had heard that insane people, unlike normal people, could sometimes make accurate predictions. He certainly did not want to come to harm. So, feeling a little nervous, he began walking towards Phatik-da's house.

Phatik-da was pouring coconut water into a hookah. 'Have you noticed Janardan Babu?' he said.

Janardan Babu was the new maths teacher in Shibu's school. He had arrived about ten days ago.

'I see him every day,' said Shibu. 'Why—I have maths in the very first period today!'

Phatik-da clicked his tongue in annoyance, 'Tch, tch. Seeing and observing are two different things, do you understand? Look, can you tell me how many little holes your belt has got? And how many buttons are there on your shirt? Try telling me without looking!'

Shibu failed to come up with the correct answers.

Phatik-da said, 'See what I mean? You've obviously never noticed these things, although the shirt and the belt you're wearing are your own. Similarly, you have never noticed Janardan Babu.'

'What should I have noticed? Anything in particular?'

Phatik-da began smoking his hookah. 'Yes, say, his teeth. Have you noticed them?'

'Teeth?'

'Yes, teeth.'

'How could I have noticed them? He doesn't ever smile!'

This was true. Janardan Babu was not exactly cantankerous, but no other teacher was as grave and sombre as him.

Phatik-da said, 'All right. Try to notice his teeth if he does smile. And then come and tell me what you've seen.'

A strange thing happened that day. Janardan Babu laughed in Shibu's class. It happened when, referring to some geometrical designs, Janardan Babu asked what had four arms. 'Gods, sir,' Shankar cried, 'the gods in heaven have four arms!' At this Janardan Babu began chuckling noisily. Shibu's eyes went straight to his teeth.

Phatik-da was crushing some object with a heavy stone crusher when Shibu reached his house that evening. He looked at Shibu and said, 'If this medicine I'm making has the desired effect, I'll be able to change colours like a chameleon.'

Shibu said, 'Phatik-da, I've seen them.'

'What?'

'Teeth.'

'Oh. What did they look like?'

'They were all right, except that they were stained with paan and two of them were longer than the others.'

'Which two?'

'By the side. About here.' Shibu pointed to the sides of his mouth.

'I see. Do you know what those teeth are called?'

'What?'

'Canine teeth. Like dogs have.'

'Oh.'

'Have you ever seen any other man with such large canine teeth?'

'Perhaps not.'

'Who has such teeth?'

'Dogs?'

'Idiot! Why just dogs? All carnivorous animals have large canine teeth. They use them to tear through the flesh and bones of their prey. Especially the wild animals.'

'I see.'

'And who else has them?'

Shibu began racking his brains. Who else? Who had teeth anyway, except men and animals?

Phatik-da dropped a walnut and a pinch of pepper into the mixture he was making and said, 'You don't know, do you? Why, monsters have such teeth!'

Monsters? What had monsters to do with Janardan Babu? And why talk of monsters today? They were present only in fairy tales. They had large, strong teeth and their backs were bent . . .

Shibu started.

Janardan Babu's back was definitely not straight. He stooped. Someone had mentioned that this was so because he had lumbago.

Large teeth, bent backs . . . what else did monsters have?

Red eyes.

Shibu had not had the chance to notice Janardan Babu's eyes for he always wore glasses that seemed to be tinted. It was impossible to tell whether the eyes behind those were red or purple or green.

Shibu was good at maths. LCM, HCF, Algebra, Arithmetic—he sailed through them all. At least, he used to, until a few days ago. During the time of his old maths teacher, Pearicharan Babu, Shibu had often got full marks. But he now began to have problems, although he did try to pull himself together by constantly telling himself, 'It just cannot be. A man cannot be a monster. Not in these modern times. Janardan Babu is not a monster He is a man.'

He was repeating these words silently in class when a disastrous thing happened.

Janardan Babu was writing something on the blackboard. Suddenly he turned around, took off his glasses and began polishing them absent-mindedly with one end of the cotton shawl he was wearing. He raised his eyes after a while and they looked straight into Shibu's. Shibu went cold with fear. The whites of Janardan Babu's eyes were not white at all. Both eyes were red. As red as a tomato. After this, Shibu got as many as three sums wrong.

Shibu seldom went home straight after school. He would first go to the grounds owned by the Mitters and play with the mimosa plants. After gently tapping each one to sleep, he would go to Saraldeeghi—the large, deep pond. There he would try playing ducks and drakes with broken pieces of earthenware. If he could make a piece skip on the water more than seven times, he would break the record Haren had set. On the other side of Saraldeeghi was a brick kiln. Hundreds of bricks stood in huge piles. Shibu usually spent about ten minutes here, doing gymnastics, and then went diagonally across the field to reach his house.

Today, the mimosa plants seemed lifeless. Why? Had someone come walking here and stepped on them? But who could it be? Not many people came here.

Shibu did not feel like staying there any longer. There was something strange in the air. A kind of premonition. It seemed to be getting dark already. And did the crows always make such a racket—or had something frightened them today?

Shibu took himself to Saraldeeghi. But, as soon as he had put his books down by the side of the pond, he changed his mind about staying. Today was not the day for playing ducks and drakes. In fact, today was not the day for staying out at all. He must get back home quickly. Or else . . . something awful might happen.

A huge fish raised its head from the water and then disappeared again with a loud splash.

Shibu picked up his books. It was very dark under the peepal tree that stood at a distance. He could see the bats

hanging from it. Soon it would be time for them to start flying.
Phatik-da had offered to explain to him one day why bats' brains
did not haemorrhage despite their hanging upside down all the
time.

Shibu began walking towards his house.

He saw Janardan Babu near the brick kiln.

There was a mulberry tree about twenty yards from where
the bricks lay. A couple of lambs were playing near it and
Janardan Babu was watching them intently. He carried a book
and an umbrella in his hand. Shibu held his breath and quickly
hid behind a pile of bricks. He removed the top two in the pile
and peered through the gap.

He noticed Janardan Babu raise his right hand and wipe his
mouth with the back of it.

Clearly, the sight of the lambs had made his mouth water, or
he would not have made such a gesture.

Then, suddenly, Janardan Babu dropped the book and the
umbrella and, crouching low, picked up one of the lambs. Shibu
could hear the lamb bleat loudly. He also heard Janardan Babu
laugh. That was enough.

Shibu wanted to see no more. He slipped away but, in his
haste to climb over the next pile of bricks, tripped and fell flat on
the ground.

'Who's there?'

Shibu was going to pick himself up somehow when he
found Janardan Babu coming towards him, having put the lamb
back on the grass.

'Who is it? Shibram? Are you hurt? What are you doing
here?' Shibu could not speak. His mouth had gone dry. But he
certainly wanted to ask Janardan Babu what *he* was doing there.
Why did he carry a lamb in his arms? Why was his mouth
watering?

Janardan Babu stretched out a hand. 'Here, I'll help you up.'

But Shibu managed to get to his feet without help.

'You live nearby, don't you?'

'Yes, sir.'

'Is that red house yours?'

'Yes, sir.'

'I see.'

'Let me go, sir.'

'Goodness—is that blood?'

Shibu looked at his legs. His knee was slightly grazed and a few drops of blood was oozing from the wound. Janardan Babu was staring at the blood, his glasses glistening.

'Let me go, sir.'

Shibu picked up his books.

'Listen, Shibram.'

Janardan Babu laid a hand on Shibu's back. Shibu could hear his heart beat loudly—like a drum.

'I am glad I found you alone. There is something I wanted to ask you. Are you finding it difficult to follow the maths lessons? Why did you get all those simple sums wrong? If you have any problem, you can come to my house after school. I will give you special coaching. It's so easy to get full marks in maths. Will you come?'

Shibu had to step back to shake off Janardan Babu's hand from his back. 'No, sir,' he gulped, 'I'll manage on my own. I'll be all right tomorrow.'

'OK. But do tell me if there's a problem. And don't be frightened of me. What is there to be frightened of, anyway? Do you think I'm a monster that I'll eat you alive? Ha, ha, ha, ha . . .'

Shibu ran all the way to his house. He found Hiren Uncle in the living-room. Hiren Uncle lived in Calcutta. He was extremely fond of fishing. Very often he came over on weekends and went fishing at Saraldeeghi with Shibu's father.

They would probably go again this time, for he saw that

certain preparations had been made. But Hiren Uncle had also brought a gun. There was some talk of shooting ducks. Shibu's father could handle guns, although his aim was not as good as Hiren Uncle's.

Shibu went straight to bed after dinner. He had no doubt now that Janardan Babu was a monster. Thank God Phatik-da had already warned him. If he hadn't, who knows what might have happened at the brick kiln? Shibu shivered and stared out of the window.

Everything shone in the moonlight. He had gone to bed early because he had to wake up early the next morning to study for his exams. Normally, he could not sleep with the light on. But today, if the moonlight had not been so good, he would have left the light on. He felt too frightened today to sleep alone in the dark. The others had not yet finished having dinner.

Shibu was still looking out of the window, half asleep, when the sight of a man made him sit up in terror.

The man was heading straight for his window. He stooped slightly and wore glasses. The glasses gleamed in the moonlight.

Janardan Babu!

Shibu's throat felt parched once more.

Janardan Babu tiptoed his way to the open window; Shibu clutched his pillow tight.

Janardan Babu looked around for a bit and then said somewhat hesitantly, in a strange nasal tone, 'Shibram? Are you there?'

Good God—even his voice sounded different! Did the monster in him come out so openly at night?

He called again, 'Shibram!'

This time Shibu's mother heard him from the veranda and shouted, 'Shibu! There's someone outside calling for you. Have you gone to sleep already?'

Janardan Babu vanished from the window. A minute later,

Shibu heard his voice again, 'Shibram had left his geometry book among the bricks. Since it's Sunday tomorrow, I thought I'd come and return it right away. He may need it . . .'

Then he lowered his voice and Shibu failed to catch what he said. But, after a while, he heard his father say, 'Yes, if you say so. I'll send him over to your house. Yes, from tomorrow.'

Shibu did not utter a word, but he screamed silently, 'No, no, no! I won't go, I won't! You don't know anything! He's a monster! He'll gobble me up if I go to his house!'

The next morning Shibu went straight to Phatik-da's house. There was such a lot to tell.

Phatik-da greeted him warmly. 'Welcome! Isn't there a cactus near your house? Can you bring me a few bits and pieces of that plant? I've thought of a new recipe.'

Shibu whispered, 'Phatik-da!'

'What?'

'Remember you told me Janardan Babu was a monster . . .?'

'Who said that?'

'Why, you did!'

'Of course not. You did not notice my words, either.'

'How?'

'I said try to notice Janardan Babu's teeth. Then you came back and said he had large canine teeth. So I said I had heard monsters had similar teeth. That does not necessarily mean Janardan Babu is a monster.'

'Isn't he?'

'I did not say he was.'

'So what do I do now?'

Phatik-da got up, stretched lazily and yawned. Then he said, 'Saw your uncle yesterday. Has he come fishing again? Once a Scotsman called McCurdy killed a tiger with a fishing rod. Have you heard that story?'

Shibu grew desperate, 'Phatik-da, stop talking nonsense. Janardan Babu is really a monster. I know it. I have seen and heard such a lot!'

Then he told Phatik-da everything that had happened over the last two days. Phatik-da grew grave as he heard the tale. In the end he said, 'Hmm. So what have you decided to do?'

'You tell me what I should do. You know so much.'

Phatik-da bent his head deep in thought.

'We have got a gun in our house,' said Shibu suddenly. This annoyed Phatik-da.

'Don't be silly. You can't kill a monster with a gun. The bullet would make an about turn and hit the same person who pulled the trigger.'

'Really?'

'Yes, my dear boy.'

'So what do I do?' Shibu asked again. 'What's going to happen, Phatik-da? My father wants me to start from today . . .'

'Oh, shut up. You talk too much.'

After about two minutes of silence Phatik-da suddenly said, 'Have to go.'

'Where?'

'To Janardan Babu's house.'

'What?'

'I must look at his horoscope. I am not sure yet. But his horoscope is bound to tell me something. And I bet he has it hidden somewhere in his house.'

'But . . .'

'Wait a minute. Listen to the plan first. We will both go in the afternoon. It's Sunday today, so the man will be at home. You will go to the back of his house and call him. Tell him you've come for your maths lesson. Then keep him there for a few minutes. Say anything you like, but don't let him go back into the house. I will try to find the horoscope in the meantime.

And then you run away from one side and I from the other.'

'And then?' asked Shibu. He did not like the plan much, but Phatik-da was his only hope.

'Then you'll come to my house in the evening. By then I will have seen his horoscope. If he is indeed a monster, I know what to do about it. And if he's not, there is no cause for anxiety, is there?'

Shibu turned up again at Phatik-da's house soon after lunch. Phatik-da came out about five minutes later and said, 'My cat has started to take snuff. There are problems everywhere!'

Shibu noticed Phatik-da was carrying a pair of torn leather gloves and the bell of a bicycle. He handed the bell to Shibu and said, 'Ring this bell if you feel you're in danger. I will come and rescue you.'

Janardan Babu lived at the far end of town. He lived all alone, without even a servant. It was impossible to tell from the outside that a monster lived there.

Shibu and Phatik made their separate ways to the house. As he began to find his way to the back of the house, Shibu's throat started to go dry again. What if, when he was supposed to call out to Janardan Babu, his voice failed him?

There was a high wall behind the house, a door in the middle of the wall, and a guava tree near the door. Several wild plants and weeds grew around the tree.

Shibu went forward slowly. He must hurry or the whole plan would get upset.

He leant against the guava tree for a bit of moral support and was about to call out to Janardan Babu when he was startled by the sound of something shuffling near his feet. Looking down, he saw a chameleon glide across the ground and disappear behind a bush. There were some white objects lying near the bush. He picked up a fallen twig and parted the bush with it to take a closer look. Oh no! The white objects were bones! But whose bones were they?

Dogs? Cats? Or lambs?

'What are you looking at, Shibram?'

The same nasal voice.

A cold shiver went down Shibu's spine. He turned around quickly and saw Janardan Babu standing at his back door, watching him with a queer look in his eyes.

'Have you lost something?'

'No, sir I . . . I . . .'

'Were you coming to see me? Why did you come to the back door? Well, do come in.'

Shibu tried retracing his steps, but discovered that one of his feet was caught in a creeper.

'I have got a cold, I'm afraid,' said Janardan Babu. 'I've had it since yesterday. I went to your house. You were sleeping.'

Shibu knew he must not run away so soon. Phatik-da could not have finished his job. He might even get caught. Should he ring the bell?

No, he was not really in danger, was he? Phatik-da might get annoyed if he rang it unnecessarily.

'What were you looking at so keenly?'

Shibu could not think of a suitable answer. Janardan Babu came forward.

'This place is very dirty. It's better not to come from this side. My dog brings bones from somewhere and leaves them here. I have often thought of scolding him, but I can't. You see, I'm very fond of animals . . .'

Again, he wiped his mouth with the back of his hand.

'Come on in, Shibram. We must do something about your maths.'

Shibu could not wait any longer. 'Not today, sir. I'll come back tomorrow,' he said and ran away.

He did not stop running until he came to the old and

abandoned house of the Sahas, quite a long way away. Goodness—he would never forget what had happened today. He didn't know he had such a lot of courage!

But what had Phatik-da learnt from the horoscope? Shibu went to his house again in the evening. Phatik-da shook his head as soon as he saw Shibu.

'Problems,' he said, 'great problems.'

'Why, Phatik-da? Didn't you find the horoscope?'

'Yes, I did. Your maths teacher is undoubtedly a monster. And a Pirindi monster, at that. These were full-fledged monsters 350 generations ago. But their genes were so strong that even now it's possible to find a half-monster among them. No civilized country, of course, has full monsters nowadays. You can find some in the wild parts of Africa, Brazil and Borneo. But half-monsters are in existence elsewhere in very small numbers. Janardan Babu is one of them.'

'Then where is the problem?' Shibu's voice trembled a little. If Phatik-da could not help, who could?

'Didn't you tell me this morning you knew what to do?'

'There is nothing I do not know.'

'Well, then?'

Phatik-da grew a little grave. Then, suddenly, he asked, 'What's inside a fish?'

Oh no, he had started talking nonsense again. Shibu nearly started weeping, 'Phatik-da, we were talking about monsters. What's that got to do with fish?'

'Tell me!' Phatik-da yelled.

'Intestines?' Phatik-da's yell had frightened Shibu.

'No, no, you ass. With such retarded knowledge, you couldn't even put a buckle on a buck! Listen. I heard this rhyme when I was only two-and-a-half. I still remember it:

Man or animal whichever thou art
Thy life beats in thy own heart

A monster's life lies in the stomach of a fish
Cannot kill him easily, even if you wish.'

Of course! Shibu, too, had read about this in so many fairy
tales. A monster's life always lay hidden inside a fish. He should
have known.

'When you met him this afternoon, how did he seem?'
asked Phatik.

'He said he had a cold and a slight fever.'

'Yes, it all fits in,' Phatik's eyes began to sparkle with
enthusiasm. 'It has to. His life's in danger, you see. As soon as
the fish is out of water, he gets fever. Good!'

Then he came forward and clutched Shibu by the collar.
'Perhaps it's not too late. I saw your uncle go back to your house
with a huge fish. I thought Janardan Monster's life might be in it.
Now that you've told me about his illness I'm beginning to feel
more sure. We must cut open that fish.'

'But how can we do that?'

'We can, with your help. It won't be easy, but you've got to
do it. If you don't, I shudder to think what might happen to you!'

About an hour later Shibu arrived at Phatik-da's house
dragging the huge fish by the cord he had tied around it.

'Hope no one saw you?'

'No,' Shibu panted. 'Father was having a bath. Uncle was
getting a massage and Mother was inside. It took me some time
to find a cord. God—is it heavy!'

'Never mind, you'll grow muscles!'

Phatik-da took the fish inside. Shibu sat marvelling at
Phatik-da's knowledge of things. If anyone could rescue him
from the danger he was in, it was going to be Phatik-da. Dear
God—do let him find what he was looking for.

Ten minutes later, Phatik-da came out and stretched a hand
towards Shibu, 'Here. Take this. Keep it with you all the time.

Put it under your pillow at night. When you go to school, keep it
in your left pocket. If you hold it in your hand, the monster is
totally powerless and if you crush it into a powder he'll be dead.
In my view, you need not crush it because some Pirindi
monsters have been known to turn into normal men at the age of
fifty-four. The age of your Janardan Monster is fifty-three years,
eleven months and twenty-six days.'

Shibu finally found the courage to look down at what he
was holding. A small, slightly damp, white stone lay on his palm,
winking in the light of the moon that had just risen.

Shibu put it in his pocket and turned to go. Phatik-da called
him back, 'Your hands smell fishy, wash them carefully. And
pretend not to know anything about anything!'

The next day, Janardan Babu sneezed once just before entering
class and, almost immediately, knocked his foot against the
threshold and damaged his shoe. Shibu's left hand, at that
precise moment, was resting in his left pocket.

After a long time, Shibu got full marks in maths that day.

(1963)   *Translated by Gopa Majumdar*

MR ECCENTRIC

I never managed to find out Mr Eccentric's full name. All I did learn was that his surname was Mukherjee. His appearance was quite unforgettable. He was nearly six feet tall, his body was without the slightest trace of fat, his back arched like a bow; and his neck, arms, hands and forehead were covered by innumerable veins that appeared to be bulging out of his skin. What he wore almost every day was a white shirt with black flannel trousers, white socks and white tennis shoes. And he always carried a stout walking stick. Perhaps he needed it because he often walked on uneven, unpaved roads and amongst wild plants.

I met Mr Eccentric ten years ago, when I used to work for a bank. That year, I had taken ten days off in early May, and gone to Darjeeling—my favourite hill town—for a holiday. I saw Mr Eccentric on my very first day.

At about half past four, I had left my hotel for a walk, after a cup of tea. In the afternoon, there had been a short shower. Since there was every chance that it might rain again, I had put on my raincoat before stepping out. As I was walking down Jalapahar Road, the most picturesque and quiet road in Darjeeling, I suddenly spotted a man about fifty yards away. He was standing where the road curved. His body was bent forward, and he was leaning on his walking stick, gazing intently at the grass by the roadside. At first, none of this struck me as unusual. Perhaps he was interested in some wild flower or insect. Perhaps he had seen one of those in the grass. I cast a mildly curious glance in his direction, and kept on walking.

As I got closer, however, I realized that there was something odd about him. It was the intensity of the man's concentration. I was standing only a few feet away, staring at him, but he did not appear to have noticed me at all. He was still bent over the grass, his eyes fixed on it. Now I could not help asking a question: 'Have you lost something?'

There was no reply. Was he deaf?

My curiosity rose. I was determined to see what happened next. So I lit a cigarette, and waited. About three minutes later, life seemed to return to the man's limbs. He bent further forward, and stretched an arm out towards the grass. Then he pushed his fingers into the thick grass, and a second later, withdrew his hand. Between his thumb and index finger was held a small disc. I peered carefully at it. It was a button, nearly as large as a fifty-paise coin. Perhaps it had once been attached to a jacket.

The man brought the button closer to his eyes, scrutinized it thoroughly, turned it around several times, then said 'Tch, tch, tch!' regretfully, before placing it in his shirt pocket, and striding off in the direction of the Mall. He ignored me completely.

Later in the evening, on my way back to the hotel, I ran into an old resident of Darjeeling, Dr Bhowmik. He was standing by the fountain on the Mall. Dr Bhowmik was my father's classmate, and very fond of me. I couldn't help telling him about my encounter with the strange man. When I finished my tale, Dr Bhowmik said, 'Well, from your description, it appears that you met Mr Eccentric.'

'Mr who?'

'Eccentric. It's a sad case, really. I can't remember his first name, his surname is Mukherjee. He's been in Darjeeling for nearly five years. He rents a room in a cottage near Grindlays Bank. Before he came here, he used to teach physics in Ravenshaw College in Cuttack. I believe he was once a brilliant student, and has a German degree in physics. But he left his job, and came to live here. Perhaps he inherited some property, or has some private income, so he gets by.'

'Do you know him?'

'He came to me once, soon after he got here. He had stumbled and fallen somewhere, and cut his knee. It had turned septic. I treated him, and he recovered.'

'But why is he called Eccentric?'

Dr Bhowmik burst out laughing. 'He acquired that name because of his peculiar hobby. I couldn't tell you who was the first to think of that name!'

'What's his hobby?'

'You saw it yourself, didn't you? He picked up a button from the roadside and put it in his pocket. That's his hobby. He'll pick up any old thing and keep it safe in his room.'

'Any old thing? How do you mean?' For some reason, I began feeling increasingly curious about the man.

'Well,' said Dr Bhowmik, 'I call it that, but he claims that every object in his collection is most precious. Apparently, there is a story behind all of them.'

'How does *he* know that?'

Dr Bhowmik glanced at his watch. 'Why don't you ask him yourself?' he suggested. 'He's always pleased to have a visitor, for his stories are endless. All of it is pure nonsense, needless to say, but he's always glad to tell them. Mind you, whether *you* will be glad to hear them or not is a different matter!'

The following morning, I left my hotel soon after breakfast and went looking for Mr Eccentric's house. It proved quite easy to find it, since most people near Grindlays Bank seemed to know where he lived. I knocked on the door of house number seventeen. The man himself answered the door almost at once and, to my astonishment, recognized me immediately.

'You asked me something yesterday, didn't you? But I couldn't reply. Believe me, I just couldn't speak. At a time like that, if I let my attention wander, it can spell disaster. Do come in.'

The first thing I noticed on entering his room was a glass case. It covered a large portion of a wall. On each shelf was displayed a range of very ordinary objects, not one of which seemed to bear any relationship to the other. One shelf, for instance, had the root of some plant, a rusted padlock, an ancient tin of Gold Flake cigarettes, a knitting needle, a shoe-brush and old torch cells. The man caught me staring at these objects and said, 'None of those things will give you any joy, since only I know what they are worth.'

'I believe there is a story behind everything in your collection?'

'Yes, there certainly is.'

'But that is true of most things, isn't it? Say, if you consider that watch you are wearing . . .' I began, but the man raised a hand and stopped me.

'Yes, there may be a special incident related to many things,' he said. 'But how many of those things would *continue* to carry memories of the past? Of the scene they have witnessed? Only very rarely would you find anything like that. This button that I found yesterday, for example . . .!'

The button in question was placed on a writing desk on the opposite end of the room. Mr Eccentric picked it up and handed it to me. It was a brown button, clearly torn from a jacket. I could see nothing special in it.

'Can you see anything?' he asked.

I was obliged to admit that I could not. Mr Eccentric began speaking, 'That button came from the jacket of an Englishman.

He was riding down Jalapahar Road. The man was almost sixty, dressed in riding clothes, hale and hearty, a military man. When he reached the spot where I found that button, he had a stroke, and fell from his horse. Two passersby saw him and rushed to help, but he was already dead. That button came off his jacket as he fell from his horse.'

'Did you see this happen yesterday? I mean, all these past events?'

'Vividly. The more I concentrate, the better do I see.'

'When can you see such things?'

'Whenever I come across an object that has this special power to take me back to the past. It starts with a headache. Then my vision blurs, and I feel faint. Sometimes I feel as if I need support, or else I'd fall down. But almost immediately, various scenes start flashing before my eyes, and my legs become steady once more. When the whole thing's over, my temperature rises. Every time. Last night, until eight o'clock, it was nearly 102. But the fever does not last for more than a few hours. Today, I feel absolutely fine.'

Everything he said sounded far too exaggerated, but I felt quite amused. 'Can you give me a few more examples?' I asked.

'That glass case is packed with examples. See that notebook? It contains a detailed description of every incident. Which one would you like to hear?'

Before I could say anything, he strode over to the glass case and lifted two objects out of it. One was a very old leather glove, the other a spectacle lens. He placed them on a table.

'This glove,' he told me, 'is the first thing I found. It's the first item in my collection. Do you know where I found it? In a wood outside Lucerne, in Switzerland. By then I had finished my studies in Marburg, and was touring the continent before coming back to India. That day, I was out on a morning walk. A quiet and secluded path ran through the wood. After a while, I felt a little tired and sat down on a bench. Almost immediately, my eyes caught sight of only a portion of that glove, sticking out from the undergrowth near the trunk of a tree. At once, my head started throbbing. Then my vision blurred. And then . . . then I could see it all. It was like watching a film. A well-dressed gentleman, possibly an aristocrat, was walking down the same path. In his mouth was a Swiss pipe, on his hands were leather gloves, and he was carrying a walking stick. Suddenly, two men jumped out from behind a bush, and attacked him. The gentleman tried to fight them and, in the struggle, the glove on his right hand came off. Those criminals then grabbed him, killed him mercilessly and looted what money they could find in his pockets, and took his gold watch.'

'Did something like this really happen?'

'I had to spend three days in hospital. I had fever, and was delirious. There were other complications, too. The doctors there could not make a diagnosis. But, a few days later, I recovered as if by magic. After leaving the hospital, I started making enquiries. Eventually, I learnt that two years earlier, a wealthy man called Count Ferdinand was killed at that same spot, exactly as I had seen it. His son recognized the glove.'

The man told this story so easily and naturally that I found it hard not to believe him. 'Did you start building up your collection from that time?' I asked.

'Well, nothing happened for ten years after that first incident. By then I had returned home and was teaching in a college in Cuttack. Sometimes I went on holidays. Once I went to Waltair. That's when the second incident took place. I found this lens stuck between rocks on the beach. A South Indian gentleman had taken his glasses off to go and bathe in the sea. He never returned. He got cramps in his legs as he was swimming, and drowned. I can still see him raising his hands from the water and shouting, 'Help! Help!' It was heartbreaking.

This lens, which I found four years after the incident, came off his glasses. Yes, what I saw was true. It was a well-known case of drowning, as I learnt later. The dead man was called Shivaraman. He was from Coimbatore.'

Mr Eccentric replaced the two objects in the glass case and sat down. 'Do you know how many items I have got in my collection? One hundred and seventy-two. I've collected them over thirty years. Have you ever heard of anyone with such a collection?'

I shook my head. 'No, your hobby is unique. There's no doubt about that. But tell me, does each of those objects have something to do with death?'

The man looked grave. 'Yes, so it seems. It isn't just death, but sudden or unnatural death—murder, suicide, death by accident, heart failure, things like that.'

'Did you find all these things simply lying by the roadside, or on beaches, and in woods?'

'Yes, most of them. The rest I found in auctions or antique shops. See that wine jug made of cut glass? I found it in an auction house in Russell Street in Calcutta. Some time in the nineteenth century, wine served out of that jug was poisoned. An Englishman—oh, he was so tall and hefty—died in Calcutta after drinking that wine.'

By this time, I had stopped looking at the glass case, and was looking closely at the man. But I could find nothing in his expression to suggest that he was lying, or that he was a cheat. Was he perhaps insane? No, that did not seem to be the case, either. The look in his eyes did seem somewhat distant, but it was certainly not abnormal. Poets often had that look, or those who were deeply religious and spiritual.

I did not stay much longer. As I said goodbye and started to step out of the room, the man said, 'Please come again. My door is always open for people like you. Where are you staying?'

'The Alice Villa.'

'I see. That's only ten minutes from here. I enjoyed meeting you. There are some people I just cannot stand. You appear to be sympathetic and understanding.'

Dr Bhowmik had invited me to tea that evening. There were two other guests. Over a cup of tea and a plate of savouries, I couldn't help raising the subject of Mr Eccentric. Dr Bhowmik asked, 'How long did you stay there?'

'About an hour.'

'My God!' Dr Bhowmik's eyes widened with amazement. 'You spent nearly an hour listening to that fraud?'

I smiled. 'Well, it was raining so much that I could hardly go out and enjoy myself elsewhere. Hearing his stories was more entertaining than being cooped up in my hotel room.'

'Who are you talking about?'

This question came from a man of about forty. Dr Bhowmik had introduced him to me as Mr Khastagir. When Dr Bhowmik explained about Mr Eccentric, Khastagir gave a wry smile and said, 'Why have you allowed such people to come and live in Darjeeling, Dr Bhowmik? They do nothing but pollute the air!'

Dr Bhowmik gave a slight smile. 'Could the air of such a big place be polluted by just one man? I don't think so!' he remarked.

The third guest was called Mr Naskar. He proceeded to give a short lecture on the influence of frauds and cheats on our society. In the end, I was obliged to point out that Mr Eccentric lived in such isolation that the chances of the society in Darjeeling being influenced by him were extremely remote.

Dr Bhowmik had lived in Darjeeling for over thirty years. Khastagir was also an old resident. After a while, I just had to ask them a question. 'Did an Englishman ever suffer a heart attack while riding a horse on Jalapahar Road? Do you know of any such case?'

'Who, you mean Major Bradley?' Dr Bhowmik replied. 'That happened about eight years ago. He had a stroke—yes, I think it happened on Jalapahar Road. He was brought to the local hospital, but by then it was too late. Why do you ask?'

I told them about the button Mr Eccentric had found. Mr Khastagir seemed outraged. 'You mean that man told you this story, and claimed that he had some supernatural power? He appears to be a crook of the first order! Why, he's spent a few years in Darjeeling, hasn't he? He could easily have heard of Bradley's death. What's supernatural about that?'

To tell the truth, the same thought had already occurred to me. If Mr Eccentric had heard the story from someone in Darjeeling, that was hardly surprising. I changed the subject.

The next few minutes were spent discussing various other topics. When it was time for me to leave, Mr Naskar rose to his feet as well. He had to go past my hotel, he said, so he wanted to walk back with me. We said goodbye to Dr Bhowmik and left. It had started to get dark. For the first time since my arrival in Darjeeling, I noticed that the thick clouds had parted here and there. Through the gaps, the light from the setting sun broke through and fell, like a spotlight, on the city and its surrounding mountains.

Mr Naskar had struck me as a man in good health. But now, it became obvious that he was finding it hard to walk uphill. Nevertheless, between short gasps, he asked me, 'Where does this Eccentric live?'

'Why, do you want to meet him?'

'No, no. Just curious.'

I told him where Mr Eccentric lived. Then I added, 'The man goes out often for long walks. We might run into him, who knows?'

Amazingly, only two minutes later, just as we reached a bend, I saw Mr Eccentric coming from the opposite direction. In one hand, he was holding his heavy walking stick. In the other was a packet wrapped in newspaper. When he saw me, he did not smile; but then, nor did he seem displeased. 'There's something wrong with my electric supply,' he said. 'There's no power at home. So I came out to buy some candles.'

Courtesy made me turn to Mr Naskar. 'This is Mr Mukherjee. And this is Mr Naskar,' I said, making introductions.

Naskar turned out to be quite westernized. Instead of saying 'Namaskar', he offered his hand. Mr Eccentric shook it quietly, without saying a word. Then he appeared to turn into a statue, and just stood there, rooted to the spot. Naskar and I both began to feel uncomfortable. After nearly half a minute, Naskar broke the silence. 'Well, I had better be going,' he said. 'I had heard about you, Mr Mukherjee. Now, luckily, I've had the chance to meet you.'

I had to say something, too. 'Goodbye, Mr Mukherjee!' I said, feeling somewhat foolish. Mr Eccentric seemed truly insane. He was standing in the middle of the road, lost in thought. He did not appear to have heard us, nor did he see us leave. He might have taken a dislike to Naskar, but didn't he behave in a perfectly friendly fashion towards me, only that morning?

We left him behind and continued walking. After a few minutes, I turned my head and looked back. Mr Eccentric was still standing where we had left him. 'From what you told us, I thought the name "Eccentric" might be suitable,' said Naskar, 'but now I think it's a lot more than that!'

It was nine o'clock in the evening. I had just had my dinner, put a paan in my mouth and was toying with the idea of going to bed with a detective novel, when a bearer came and told me that someone was looking for me. I came out of my room and was most surprised to find Mr Eccentric waiting for me. What was he doing in my hotel at nine o'clock? He still looked a little dazed. 'Is there anywhere we can sit and talk privately?' he asked. 'I wouldn't mind talking to you outside, but it's raining again.'

I invited him into my room. He sat down, sighed with relief and said, 'Could you feel my pulse, please?'

I took his hand and gave a start. He was running a fairly high temperature. 'I have got Anacin with me. Would you like one?' I said, concerned.

The man smiled. 'No, no tablet is going to work now. This fever won't go down before tomorrow morning. Then I'll be all right. But I am not worried about my temperature. I have not come to you looking for medical treatment. What I need is that ring.'

Ring? What ring? The perplexed look on my face seemed to irritate Mr Eccentric. 'That man—Laskar or Tusker, whatever his name is!' he said a little impatiently. 'Didn't you see his ring? It's an ordinary, cheap old ring, not set with stones or anything. But I want it.'

Now I remembered. Yes, Naskar did wear a silver ring on his right hand. Mr Eccentric was still speaking. 'When I shook his hand, I could feel that ring brush against my palm. Immediately, I felt as if my whole body would explode. Then the same old thing happened. I went into a trance and began watching the scenes that rose before my eyes. But before the whole thing could finish, a jeep came from the opposite end and ruined everything!'

'So you didn't see the whole episode?'

'No. But what little I did see was bad enough, let me tell you. It was a murder. I did not see the murderer's face. I only saw his hand, moving forward to grasp his victim's neck. On his hand was that ring. The victim was wearing a Rajasthani cap, and glasses with a golden frame. His eyes were bulging, he had just opened his mouth to scream. One of his lower teeth had a gold filling. That's all I saw. I have got to have that ring!'

I stared at Mr Eccentric for a few seconds. Then I said, 'Look, Mr Mukherjee, if you want that ring, why don't you ask Mr Naskar yourself? I don't know him all that well. Besides, I don't think he views your hobby with any sympathy.'

'In that case, what good would it do if I asked him? It might be better if you . . .'

'Very sorry, Mr Mukherjee,' I interrupted him, speaking plainly, 'it wouldn't work even if I went and asked him. Some people are very attached to some of their possessions. Naskar may not wish to part with that ring. If it was something he was not actually using every day, he might have . . .' I broke off.

Mr Eccentric did not waste another second. He sighed, got to his feet and left, disappearing into the dark, damp night. His demand was really weird, I thought to myself. It was one thing to pick up objects from the roadside. But to ask for something someone else was using, just to add one more item to his collection, was certainly wrong. No one could have helped him in this respect. Besides, Naskar did not appear to be a man with any imagination. It was stupid to expect him to understand and just give away his ring.

The next morning, seeing that the clouds had dispersed and the day was bright, I left for a walk after a cup of tea. My aim was to go to Birch Hill. The Mall was full of people. I had to walk carefully to avoid colliding with people on horseback, and others walking on foot, like me. A few minutes later, I found myself in the relatively quiet road to the west of Observatory Hill.

Mr Eccentric's sad face kept coming back to me. If I ran into Naskar by chance, perhaps I would speak to him about that ring.

It might not mean a great deal to him, he might not mind giving it to me. I could well imagine the look on Mr Eccentric's face if I handed the ring over to him. When I was a child, I used to collect stamps; so I knew something about a collector's passion. Sometimes, one's passion could turn into an obsession.

Besides, Mr Eccentric did not meddle with anyone, he was happy living alone with his crazy hobby. He was not trying to harm anyone else, and this was probably the first time that he was coveting someone else's possession, although it was nothing valuable. To tell the truth, I had come to the conclusion the previous night that Mr Eccentric had no supernatural powers at all. His collection was based simply on his peculiar imagination. But if that brought him joy and contentment, why should anyone else object?

I spent almost two hours walking near Birch Hill, but did not see Naskar. On my return through the Mall, I had to pick my way through the crowd once again. However, this time many people in the crowd appeared agitated about something. Knots of people were scattered here and there, discussing something excitedly. As I got closer, I heard the words 'police', 'investigation' and 'murder'. I spotted an old gentleman in the crowd and decided to ask him what had happened. 'Oh, they say a suspected criminal fled from Calcutta and came here. The police followed his trail and are looking for him everywhere,' the man told me.

'Do you know his name?'

'I couldn't tell you his real name. I believe he calls himself Naskar.'

My heart jumped into my mouth. There was only one person who could give me more information: Dr Bhowmik!

As it happened, I did not have to go to his house. I ran into him and Khastagir near a rickshaw-stand. 'Just imagine!' Dr Bhowmik exclaimed. 'Only yesterday, the fellow came to my house and had tea. He had come to me some time ago, complaining of a pain in his stomach. Said he was new to the city. So I treated him, and thought I'd introduce him to some other people. That was only yesterday, for heaven's sake. And now this!'

'Has he been arrested?' I asked anxiously.

'No, not yet. The police are looking for him. He's still in Darjeeling, so they'll find him sooner or later, never fear.'

Dr Bhowmik left with Khastagir. My pulse started racing faster. It wasn't just that Naskar had turned out to be a criminal. That was amazing enough. But what about Mr Eccentric? He did say that ring was worn by a murderer. Could it really be that he had some supernatural power, after all?

I had to go and see him. Had he heard the news about Naskar? I must find out.

When I knocked on the door of house number seventeen, no one opened it. I tried again, with the same result. I couldn't really afford to wait outside, for the sky had become overcast again. So I left, and walked briskly back to my hotel. Within half an hour, it began raining very heavily. The bright, sunny morning had become a thing of the past. Where was Naskar hiding? Who had he killed? How had he killed?

At half past three, the manager of my hotel, Mr Sondhi, gave me the news. The police had found the house where Naskar was staying. Right behind it was a deep gorge. In that gorge, Naskar's dead body had been discovered. His head was crushed. Various theories were being put forward, including suicide, momentary insanity, and falling to his death while trying to escape. Apparently, there had been some disagreement with his business partner. Naskar had murdered him, hid his body and run away to Darjeeling. The police had eventually found the body in Calcutta and begun looking for Naskar.

Now I absolutely *had* to see Mr Eccentric. I could no longer dismiss his words. Events in Switzerland and Waltair might have been made up, he might have heard about Bradley's death in Darjeeling, but how did he know that Naskar was a murderer?

Around five o'clock, the heavy rain settled into a drizzle. I left my hotel and went to Mr Eccentric's house again. This time, the door opened immediately. Mr Eccentric greeted me with a smile, and said, 'Come in, my friend, come in. I was thinking of you.'

I stepped in. It was almost dark. A single candle flickered on the table.

'There's no electricity,' Mr Eccentric explained with a wan smile. 'They haven't yet reconnected the supply.' I took a cane chair, sat down and said, 'Have you heard?'

'About your Tusker? I don't need to hear anything, I already know the whole story. But I am grateful to him.'

'Grateful?' I felt most taken aback.

'He has given me the most important item in my collection.'

'Given you?' My throat suddenly felt dry.

'There it is, on that table. Look!'

I glanced at the table again. Next to the candle was the notebook and, placed on an open page, was Mr Naskar's ring.

'I was recording all the details. Item number 173,' Mr Eccentric said.

A question kept bothering me. 'What do you mean, he gave it to you? When did he do that?'

'Well, naturally he didn't give it to me voluntarily. I had to use force,' Mr Eccentric sighed.

This rendered me completely speechless. In the silence that followed, all I could hear was the clock ticking.

'I am glad you are here. I want to give you something. Keep it with you.'

Mr Eccentric rose and disappeared into a dark corner. I heard a faint clatter, and then his voice: 'This object is certainly worth keeping in my collection, but I cannot bear its effect on me. My temperature keeps shooting higher, and a most unpleasant scene rises before my eyes.'

He emerged from the dark and stood near the candle once more. His right hand was stretched towards me. His fingers were curled around the old, familiar, heavy walking stick.

Even in the faint light from the candle, I could tell that the red stains that covered the handle of that stick were nothing but marks left by dried blood.

(1972)   *Translated by Gopa Majumdar*

A STRANGE NIGHT FOR
MR SHASMAL

Mr Shasmal leant back in his easy chair and heaved a sigh of relief.

He had selected the most ideal spot indeed: this forest bungalow in northern Bihar. No other place could be more peaceful, quiet or safe. The room, too, was most satisfactory. It was furnished with old, sturdy and attractive furniture, all made during the Raj. The linen neatly spread on the large bed was spotless, and even the attached bathroom was spacious and clean. Through an open window came a cool breeze, and the steady drone of crickets. There was no electricity, but that did not matter. Frequent power cuts in Calcutta had taught him to read by the light of kerosene lamps. He was quite used to it. The lamps in this bungalow had plain glass shades. Possibly for this reason, the light that came from them seemed brighter than that from the lamps he had at home. He had brought plenty of detective novels, his favourite reading material, with him.

There was no one in the bungalow, except a chowkidar. This, too, suited him very well. It simply meant that he would not have to meet or talk to anyone. Good. About ten days ago, he had visited the tourist office in Calcutta and made a booking. Four days ago, he learnt from a letter from them that his booking was confirmed. He would stay here for at least three days before thinking of moving elsewhere. He had enough money with him to survive, quite easily, at least for a month. He had arrived in his own car which he himself had driven all the way from Calcutta, a distance of 550 kilometres.

True to his word, the chowkidar served him dinner by half past nine: chapatis, arahar dal, some vegetables and chicken curry. The dining room bore signs of the Raj as well. The table, the chairs, the china and a fancy sideboard, all appeared to belong to British times.

'Are there mosquitoes here?' Mr Shasmal asked over dinner. The area where he had his flat in Calcutta was devoid of mosquitoes. He had not had to use a mosquito net in the last ten years. If he did not have to use a net here, either, his happiness would be complete.

The chowkidar said they did get mosquitoes in winter, but it was now April, so there should not be a problem. However, he knew where a few nets were stored, and could put one up, if need be. At night, he added, it was best to sleep with the door closed. After all, they were in the middle of a forest. A fox or some other wild animal might get into the room if the door was left open. Mr Shasmal agreed. In fact, he had already decided to shut the door before going to bed.

He finished eating. Then he went out on the veranda outside the dining room, with a torch in his hand. He switched it on and directed it towards the forest. It fell on the trunk of a shaal tree. Mr Shasmal moved the beam around, to see if he could spot an animal. There was nothing. The whole forest was totally silent, except for the drone of the crickets. It went on, non-stop.

'I hope there are no ghosts in the bungalow?' asked Mr Shasmal lightly, returning to the dining room. The chowkidar was clearing the table. He stopped briefly on his way to the kitchen, smiled and told him that he had spent the last thirty-five years working here, plenty of people had stayed in the bungalow during that time, but no one had seen a ghost. This made Mr Shasmal's heart lighter.

His own room was the second one after the dining room. He had not bothered to shut the door before going in for his dinner. On his return, he realized that he should not have left it open. A stray dog had found its way there. A thin, scraggy creature, it had a white body with brown spots.

'Hey! Out, get out, shoo!' he cried. The dog did not move, but remained in one corner of the room, looking as if it had every intention of spending the night there.

'Get out, I said!'

This time, the dog bared its fangs. Mr Shasmal stepped back. When he was small, his neighbour's son had been bitten by a mad dog. He could not be saved from getting hydrophobia. Mr Shasmal remembered, in every horrific detail, how that boy had suffered. He did not have the courage to approach a snarling dog. He cast a sidelong glance at the animal, and went out on the veranda again.

'Chowkidar!'

'Yes, babu?'

'Can you come here for a minute?'

The chowkidar appeared, wiping his hands on a towel. 'There's a dog in my room. Can you get rid of it?'

'A dog?' The chowkidar sounded perfectly taken aback.

'Yes. Why, you mean there isn't a single dog in this area? What's there to be so surprised about? Come with me, I'll show you.'

The chowkidar cast a suspicious look at Mr Shasmal, and entered his room. 'Where is the dog, babu?' Mr Shasmal had followed him in. There was no sign of the dog. It had left in the few seconds it had taken him to call the chowkidar. Even so, the chowkidar looked under the bed, and checked in the bathroom, just to make sure.

'No, babu, there's no dog here.'

'Well, may be not now. But it was here, just a minute ago.'

Mr Shasmal could not help feeling a little foolish. He sent the chowkidar back and took the easy chair again. He had almost finished his cigarette. Now he flicked the stub out of the window. Then he raised his arms over his head and stretched lazily, and in doing so, noticed something. The dog had not gone. Or, if it had, it was back again, and was standing once more in the same corner.

How very annoying! If it was allowed to remain, no doubt his new slippers from Bata would be chewed to pieces during the night. Mr Shasmal was well aware of a dog's passion for unattended slippers. He picked them up from the floor and placed them on the table.

So now there was another occupant in the room. Never mind. Let it be there for the moment, he'd try to drive it out once again before he went to bed.

Mr Shasmal stretched an arm and took a novel out of the Indian Airlines bag he had kept on the table. He had folded the page where he had stopped reading. Just as he started to open the book, his glance fell on the corner opposite the dog. Quite unbeknown to him, another creature had slipped into the room.

It was a cat, with stripes all over its body, like a tiger. Curled into a ball, it was staring at him through dim, yellow eyes. Where had he seen a cat like that?

Oh yes. The Kundus, who lived in the house next door, had seven cats. One of them had looked just like this one. That night . . .The whole thing came back to Mr Shasmal quite vividly.

About six months ago, he had been woken one night by the sound of constant caterwauling. He was already in a foul mood. His business partner, Adheer, had had a violent argument with him just the day before, threatening to go to the police to expose him. It had nearly come to blows. As a result, Mr Shasmal was not finding it easy to sleep. And now this cat was screaming its head off. After half an hour of tolerating the noise, he ran out of patience. Picking up a **heavy** glass paperweight from his table, he hurled it out of the window, towards the source of the noise. It stopped instantly.

The next morning, the entire household of the Kundus was in an uproar. Someone had brutally murdered one of their cats—the striped tomcat, it was being said. This had amused Mr Shasmal. The murder of a cat? If this could be called a murder, why, people were committing murders every day, without even thinking about it! Memories of another incident came back to him. It had happened many years ago, when he was still in college. He used to stay in the college hostel. One day, he happened to notice a long row of little ants going up a wall in his room. Mr Shasmal had grabbed a newspaper, lit one end of it and run the burning flame down the column of ants. As he watched, each of the tiny insects shrivelled and died, before dropping to the floor. Could that be described as murder?

Mr Shasmal looked at his wristwatch. It was ten minutes to ten. For a whole month, he had had a constant throbbing in his head. That was now gone. He had also been feeling rather hot almost all the time, and had therefore started showering three times a day. That feeling had left him as well.

He opened his book and held it before him. He had read barely a couple of lines, when his eyes fell on the cat once again. Why was it staring so hard at him?

Obviously, there was no chance of being on his own tonight. The only good thing was that the other two occupants were not human. If the two animals behaved well and remained silent, there was no reason not to have a good night's sleep. Sleep was very important to him. He had not slept well over the past few days, for very good reasons. Mr Shasmal was not in favour of the modern practice of swallowing sleeping pills.

He picked up the lamp and put it on the smaller bedside table. Then he took off his shirt, hung it up on a clotheshorse, drank some water from his flask, and went to bed, the book still in his hand. The dog had been sitting at the foot of the bed. Now it rose to its feet. Its eyes were fixed on Mr Shasmal.

The murder of a dog?

Mr Shasmal's heart skipped a beat. Yes, it was murder, in a way. He could recall the incident quite clearly. It took place probably in 1973, soon after he had bought his car. As a driver, he had always been a bit rash. Since it was not possible to drive very fast in the crowded streets of Calcutta, every time he stepped out of the city, the needle of his speedometer shot up automatically. He did not feel satisfied unless he could do at least 70 m.p.h. That was approximately the speed he was at, when one day, he ran over a dog on the national highway, on his way to Kolaghat. It was an ordinary street dog, white with brown spots. Mr Shasmal realized what he had done, but sped on regardless. His conscience did bother him after a while, but he told himself it did not matter. It was only a stray dog. So thin that you could count all its ribs. What was the point in such a creature staying alive? What good would it have done anyone? Mr Shasmal now remembered his thinking these things then, to remove even the slightest trace of guilt from his mind.

He had succeeded at the time; but tonight, it was the sudden recollection of this incident that completely ruined his peace of mind.

How many animals had he killed in his life? Was each of them going to turn up here? What about that strange black bird he had killed with his first air gun, when he was a child? He did not even know the name of the bird. And then, during a visit to his uncle's house in Jhargram, didn't he use a heavy brick to . . .? Yes, it was here.

Mr Shasmal noticed the snake as his eyes moved towards the window. It was a cobra, about eight feet long. Its supple, smooth body had slipped in through the window, and was now climbing the table placed against the wall. Normally, snakes did not appear in April. But this one had. Two-thirds of its body remained on the table. The rest rose from it, the hood spreading out. Its unwavering, cruel eyes glittered in the light of the lamp.

In his uncle's house in Jhargram, Mr Shasmal had crushed a similar snake to death by throwing a brick at its head. The snake had been an old inmate of the house, well known to everyone. It had never done anyone any harm.

Mr Shasmal realized that his throat had gone totally dry. He could not even shout for the chowkidar.

The crickets outside had stopped their racket. A rather eerie silence engulfed everything. His wristwatch ran silently, or he would have heard it ticking. Just for a minute, Mr Shasmal thought he might be dreaming. That had happened to him in the recent past. Even as he lay in his own bed in his room, he had felt as if he was somewhere else, where there were strange people moving about, whispering among themselves. But that weird feeling had not lasted for more than a few moments. Perhaps one imagined such things just before drifting off to sleep. It was possible.

What he was seeing today, however, was certainly not a dream. He had pinched himself a minute ago, and realized that he was definitely awake. Whatever was happening was for real, and deliberate. It was all meant specifically for him.

Mr Shasmal lay still for nearly an hour. Quite a few mosquitoes had made their way into the room. He had not yet felt them bite, but had seen and heard them hovering around his bed. How many mosquitoes had he killed in his life? Who could tell?

An hour later, seeing that none of the animals were showing

signs of aggression, Mr Shasmal began to relax. Perhaps he could try to go to sleep now?

He heard the noise the instant he stretched out an arm to lower the wick of the lamp. The path that ran from the gate of the bungalow to the steps leading to the veranda outside was covered with gravel. Someone was walking along that path. It was no four-legged creature this time. This one had two legs.

Now Mr Shasmal could feel himself sweating profusely, and he could hear his heart pounding in his chest.

The dog and the cat were still staring at him. The mosquitoes had not stopped humming. The cobra's hood was still raised; it was swaying rhythmically from side to side, as if some invisible snake charmer was playing an inaudible flute.

The footsteps had reached the veranda. They were getting closer.

A small, jet-black bird fluttered in through the window and sat on the table: the same bird that he had shot with his air gun. It had fallen off the wall it was perched on, and dropped to the ground into the garden next door.

The footsteps stopped outside his room.

Mr Shasmal knew who it was. Adheer. Adheer Chakravarty, his partner. They were friends once, but of late, they had almost stopped speaking to each other. Adheer did not like the devious way in which Mr Shasmal ran their business. He had threatened to report him to the police. Mr Shasmal, in turn, had told him that it was foolish to be honest when running a business. Adheer could not accept this view. Had he known about Adheer's moral stance, Mr Shasmal would never have made him his partner. It had not taken him long to realize that Adheer had become his biggest enemy. An enemy had to be destroyed. And that was precisely what Mr Shasmal had done.

The previous night, he and Adheer had sat facing each other in Adheer's sitting room. Mr Shasmal had a revolver in his pocket. He had come with the intention of killing his partner. Adheer was sitting only a few feet away. They were arguing once more. When Adheer's voice had reached its highest pitch, Mr Shasmal had taken out his revolver and fired. Now, as he thought about the expression on the face of the man who had once been a close friend, Mr Shasmal could not help smiling. Adheer had clearly never expected to see him with a firearm in his hand.

Within ten minutes of the incident, he had set off in his car. He had spent the night in the waiting room at the railway station in Burdwan, and started on his journey this morning, to find this forest bungalow that he had booked ten days ago.

Someone knocked on the door. Once, twice, thrice.

Mr Shasmal could only stare at the door. His whole body was trembling. He felt breathless. 'Open the door, Jayant. It's Adheer. Open the door.'

It was the same Adheer he had shot the night before. When he left, Mr Shasmal was not entirely sure whether his partner was dead. Now, there could be no doubt. That dog, that cat, that snake, the bird—and now it was Adheer standing outside the door. If all the other creatures in the room had appeared here after death, it was only logical to assume that Adheer was dead, too.

Someone knocked again. And went on knocking.

Mr Shasmal's vision blurred, but even so, he could see that the dog was advancing towards him, the cat's eyes were only inches away from his own, the snake was gliding down a leg of the table with every intention of going straight for him; the bird flew down to sit on his bed, and on his chest had appeared countless little ants, his white vest was covered with them.

In the end, two constables had to break open the door.

Adheer Babu had brought the police from Calcutta. A letter

from the tourist department had been found among Mr Shasmal's papers. That was how they had learnt about his reservation at this bungalow.

When he found Mr Shasmal lying dead, Inspector Samant turned to Adheer Babu. 'Did your partner have a weak heart?' he asked.

'I don't know about his heart. But, recently, his behaviour had struck me as most peculiar. No sane person could possibly have played around with our joint funds, or tried to cheat me, the way he did. I felt convinced that he had actually gone mad when I saw a revolver in his hand. To tell you the truth, when he took it out of his pocket, I simply could not believe my eyes. It took me ten minutes to get over my shock after he fired the gun and ran away. That was when I decided this lunatic must be handed over to the police. If I am alive today, it is really purely by chance.'

Mr Samant frowned. 'But how did he miss, if he fired at close range?'

Adheer Babu smiled, 'How can anyone die, tell me, unless he is destined to do so? The bullet did not hit me. It hit a corner of my sofa. How many people can find their target when it's pitch dark? You see, there was a power cut in our area, and all the lights went off the minute he took out his revolver!'

(1979)   *Translated by Gopa Majumdar*

BHUTO

Naveen came back disappointed a second time. He had failed to get Akrur Babu's support.

It was at a function in Uttarpara that Naveen had first learnt about Akrur Babu's amazing talent—ventriloquism. Naveen did not even know the word. Dwijapada had told him. Diju's father was a professor and had a library of his own. Diju had even taught him the correct spelling of the word.

Akrur Chowdhury was the only person present on the stage but he was conversing with someone invisible, hidden somewhere near the ceiling in the middle of the auditorium. Akrur Babu would throw a question at him. He would answer from above the audience's heads.

'Haranath, how are you?'

'I am fine, thank you, sir.'

'Heard you have become interested in music. Is that true?'

'Yes, sir.'

'Classical music?'

'Yes, sir, classical music.'

'Do you sing yourself?'

'No, sir.'

'Do you play an instrument?'

'That's right, sir.'

'What kind of instrument? The sitar?'

'No, sir.'

'Sarod?'

'No, sir.'

'What do you play, then?'

'A gramophone, sir.'

The auditorium boomed with laughter and applause. Akrur Babu looked at the ceiling to ask a question and then bent his head slightly to catch the reply. But it was impossible to tell that he was answering his own questions.

His lips did not move at all.

Naveen was astounded. He had to learn this art. Life would not be worth living if he did not. Could Akrur Chowdhury not be persuaded to teach him? Naveen was not very interested in studies. He had finished school, but had been sitting at home for the last three years. He simply did not feel like going in for further studies.

Having lost his father in his childhood, he had been brought up by an uncle. His uncle wanted him to join his plywood business. But Naveen was interested in something quite different. His passion lay in learning magic. He had already mastered a few tricks at home. But after having seen a performance by Akrur Chowdhury, all that seemed totally insignificant.

Naveen learnt from the organizers of the show that Akrur Babu lived in Amherst Street in Calcutta. He took a train to Calcutta the very next day and made his way to the house of the man who, in his mind, had already become his guru. But the guru rejected his proposal outright.

'What do you do?' was the first question the ventriloquist asked him. The sight of the man at close quarters was making Naveen's heart beat faster. About forty-five years old, he sported a deep black bushy moustache and his jet black hair, parted in the middle, rippled down to his shoulders. His eyes were droopy, though Naveen had seen them sparkle on stage under the spotlights.

Naveen decided to be honest. 'I've always been interested in magic,' he said, 'but your performance the other day got me passionately interested in ventriloquism.'

Akrur Babu shook his head. 'This kind of art is not for all and sundry. You have to be extremely diligent. No one taught me this art. Go and try to learn it by yourself, if you can.'

Naveen left. But only a week later, he was back again, ready to fall at Akrur Babu's feet. During the last seven days he had dreamt of nothing but ventriloquism.

But this time things got worse. Akrur Babu practically threw him out of his house. 'You should have realized the first time I was not prepared to teach you at all,' he said. 'This clearly shows your lack of perception and intelligence. No one can learn magic without these basic qualities—and certainly not my kind of magic.'

After the first visit Naveen had returned feeling depressed. This time he got angry. Let Akrur Chowdhury go to hell. He would learn it all by himself.

He bought a book on ventriloquism from College Street and began to practice. Everyone—including he himself—was surprised at his patience and perseverance.

The basic rule was simple. There were only a few letters in the alphabet like 'b', 'f', 'm' and 'p' that required one to close and open one's lips. If these letters could be pronounced slightly differently, there was no need to move the lips at all. But there was one other thing. When answering one's own questions, the voice had to be changed. This required a lot of practice, but Naveen finally got it right. When his uncle and some close friends openly praised him after a performance at home, he realized he had more or less mastered the art.

But this was only the beginning.

The days of the invisible audience were over. Modern ventriloquists used a puppet specially designed so that it was possible to slip a hand under it and make its head turn and its lips move. When asked a question, it was the puppet who answered.

Pleased with the progress he had made, his uncle offered to pay for such a puppet for Naveen. Naveen spent about a couple of weeks trying to think what his puppet should look like. Then he hit upon the most marvellous idea.

His puppet would look exactly like Akrur Chowdhury. In other words, Akrur Babu would become a mere puppet in his hands! What a wonderful way to get his own back!

Naveen had kept a photograph of Akrur Babu that he had once found on a hand-poster. He now showed it to Adinath, the puppet maker.

'It must have moustaches like these, a middle parting, droopy eyes and round cheeks.'

What fun it would be to have a puppet like that! Naveen hoped fervently that Akrur Babu would come to his shows.

The puppet was ready in a week. Its clothes were also the same as Akrur Chowdhury's: a black high-necked coat and a white dhoti under it, tucked in at the waist.

Naveen happened to know Sasadhar Bose of the Netaji Club. It was not difficult to get himself included in one of their functions.

He was an instant hit. His puppet had been given a name—Bhutnath, Bhuto for short. The audience thoroughly enjoyed their conversation. Bhuto, Naveen told them, was a supporter of the East Bengal Football Club and he himself supported their opponents, Mohun Bagan. The verbal exchange was so chirpy that no one noticed Bhuto say 'East Gengal' and 'Ohan Agan'.

Naveen became famous practically overnight. Invitations from other clubs began pouring in. He even started to appear on television. There was now no need to worry about his future. He had found a way to earn his living.

At last, one day, Akrur Babu came to meet him.

Naveen had, in the meantime, left Uttarpara and moved into a flat in Mirzapur Street in Calcutta. His landlord, Suresh Mutsuddi, was a nice man. He knew of Naveen's success and treated him with due respect. Naveen had performed recently in Mahajati Sadan and received a lot of acclaim. The organizers of various functions were now vying with one another to get Naveen to perform for them. Naveen himself had changed over the last few months. Success had given him a new confidence and self-assurance.

Akrur Babu had probably got his address from the organizers of his show in Mahajati Sadan. Bhuto and he had talked about the underground railway that evening.

'You know about pataal rail in Calcutta, don't you, Bhuto?'

'No, I don't!'

'That is strange. Everyone in Calcutta knows about it.'

Bhuto shook his head. 'No. I haven't heard of that one. But I do know of hospital rail.'

'Hospital rail?'

'Of course. It's a huge operation, I hear, the whole city's being cut open under intensive care. What else would you call it but hospital rail?'

Today, Naveen was writing a new script on load shedding. He had realized that what the audience liked best were subjects that they could relate to—load shedding, crowded buses, rising prices. His script was coming along quite well when, suddenly, someone knocked on the door. Naveen got up to open it and was completely taken aback to find Akrur Babu standing outside.

'May I come in?'

'Of course.'

Naveen offered him his chair.

Akrur Babu did not sit down immediately. His eyes were fixed on Bhuto.

Bhuto was lying on the table, totally inert.

Akrur Babu went forward, picked him up and began examining his face closely.

There was nothing that Naveen could do. He had started to feel faintly uneasy, but the memory of his humiliation at Akrur Babu's house had not faded from his mind.

'So you have turned me into a puppet in your hands!'

Akrur Babu finally sat down.

'Why did you do this?'

Naveen said, 'That should not be too difficult to understand. I had come to you with great hope. You crushed it totally. But I must say this—this puppet, this image of yours, has brought me all my success. I am able to live decently only because of it.'

Akrur Babu was still staring at Bhuto. He said, 'I don't know if you've heard this already. I had a show in Barasat the other day. The minute I arrived on the stage, the cat-calls began—"Bhuto! Bhuto!" Surely you realize this was not a very pleasant experience for me? I may be responsible, in a way, for your success, but you are beginning to threaten my livelihood. Did you think I would accept a situation like this so easily?'

It was dark outside. There was no electricity. Two candles flickered in Naveen's room. Akrur Babu's eyes glowed in their light just as Naveen had seen them glow on the stage. The little man cast a huge shadow on the wall. Bhutnath lay on the table, as droopy-eyed as ever, silent and immobile.

'You may not be aware of this,' said Akrur Babu, 'but my knowledge of magic isn't limited only to ventriloquism. From the age of eighteen to thirty-eight I stayed with an unknown but amazingly gifted magician, learning his art. No, not here in Calcutta. He lived in a remote place at the foothills of the

Himalayas.'

'Have you ever shown on stage any of those other items you learnt?'

'No, I haven't because those are not meant for the stage. I had promised my guru never to use that knowledge simply to earn a living. I have kept my word.'

'But what are you trying to tell me now? I don't understand.'

'I have come only to warn you, although I must admit I have been impressed by your dedication. No one actually taught me the art of ventriloquism. I had to teach myself, just as you have done. Professional magicians do not teach anyone else the real tricks of the trade—they have never done so. But I am not prepared to tolerate the impertinence you have shown in designing your puppet. That is all I came to tell you.'

Akrur Babu rose from his chair. Then he glanced at Bhutnath and said, 'My hair and my moustaches have only recently started to grey. I can see that you have, in anticipation, already planted a few grey strands in your puppet's hair. All right, then. I'll take my leave now.'

Akrur Babu left.

Naveen closed the door and stood before Bhutnath. Grey hair? Yes, one or two were certainly visible. He had not noticed these before, which was surprising since he held the puppet in his hand and spoke to it so often. How could he have been so unobservant?

Anyway, there was no point in wasting time thinking about it. Anyone could make a mistake. He had obviously concentrated only on Bhutnath's face and not looked at his hair closely enough.

But it was impossible to rid himself of a sneaking suspicion.

The next day, he stuffed Bhuto into the leather case made specially for him and went straight to Adinath Pal. There he brought Bhuto out of the case, laid him flat on the ground and said, 'Look at these few strands of grey hair. Did you put these in?'

Adinath Pal seemed quite taken aback. 'Why, no! Why should I? You did not ask for a mixture of black and grey hair, did you?'

'Could you not have made a mistake?'

'Yes, of course. Those few strands might have been pasted purely by mistake. But would you not have noticed it immediately when you came to collect the puppet? You know what I think? I do believe someone has planted these deliberately without your knowledge.'

Perhaps he was right. The whole thing had happened without his knowledge.

A strange thing happened at the function organized by the Friends Club in Chetla.

A clear evidence of Bhuto's popularity was that the organizers had saved his item for the last. In the midst of a rather interesting dialogue on the subject of load shedding, Naveen noticed that Bhuto was uttering words that were not in the script. These included difficult words in English which Naveen himself never used—he hardly knew what they meant.

This was a totally new experience for Naveen, although it made no difference to the show for the words were being used quite appropriately and drawing frequent applause from the crowd. Thank goodness none of them knew Naveen had not ever been to college.

But this unexpected behaviour of his puppet upset Naveen. He kept feeling that some unseen force had assumed control, pushing him into the background.

Upon reaching home after the show, he closed the door of his room and placed Bhuto under a table lamp.

Did Bhuto have that little mole on his forehead before? No, he most certainly did not. Naveen had noticed a similar mole on Akrur Babu's forehead only the other day. It was really quite small, not easily noticeable unless one looked carefully. But now it had appeared on Bhuto's face.

And that was not all. There was something else.

At least ten more strands of grey hair. And deep dark rings under the eyes. These were definitely not there before.

Naveen began pacing up and down impatiently. He was beginning to feel decidedly uneasy. He believed in magic—but his kind of magic was something in which man was in full command. For Naveen, anything to do with the supernatural was not just unacceptable—it was evil. He could see signs of evil in the changes in Bhuto.

At the same time, however, it was impossible to think of Bhuto as anything other than an inert, lifeless object, a mere puppet in his hands despite his droopy eyes and the slight smile on his lips. And yet, his whole appearance was undergoing a change.

It was Naveen's belief that the same changes were taking place in Akrur Babu. He, too, must have started to go grey; his eyes, too, must have got dark circles under them.

Naveen had the habit of talking to Bhuto every now and then, simply to practise his technique. Their conversation went like this:

'It's rather hot today, isn't it, Bhuto?'

'Yes, it's very stuwy.'

'But you have an advantage, don't you? You don't sweat and perspire.'

'How can a ugget sweat and erswire? Ha, ha, ha, ha . . .'

Today, Naveen asked him quite involuntarily, 'What on earth is going on, Bhuto? Why is all this happening?'

Bhuto's reply startled him.

'Karwa, karwa!' he said.

Karma!

The word slipped out through Naveen's lips, just as it would have done on the stage. But he knew he had not said it consciously. Someone had made him utter that word and he felt he knew who that someone might be.

That night, he refused his dinner despite repeated requests from his cook.

Normally, he slept quite well. But tonight he took a pill to help him sleep. At around one in the morning, the pill began to work. Naveen put down the magazine he was reading, switched off the light and fell asleep.

Only a little while later, however, he opened his eyes.

Who had been coughing in the room?

Was it he himself? But he did not have a cough. And yet, it seemed as though someone at close quarters was coughing very softly.

He switched on the lamp.

Bhutnath was still sitting in the same spot, motionless. But he now appeared to be slouching a little with his right arm flung across his chest.

Naveen looked at the clock. It was half past three. The chowkidar outside was doing his rounds, beating his stick on the ground. A dog barked in the distance. An owl flew past his house, hooting raucously. Someone next door obviously had a cough. And a gust of wind must have made Bhuto bend forward slightly. There was no earthly reason to feel scared today, in the twentieth century, living in a busy street of a large city like Calcutta.

Naveen switched off the light and fell asleep once more.

The next day, for the first time in his career, he experienced failure.

The Finlay Recreation Club had invited him to their annual function. A large audience was packed into an enormous hall. As always, his item was the last. Songs, recitations, a Kathak recital and then ventriloquism by Naveen Munshi.

Before setting off from home, he had done all that he always did to take care of his voice. He knew how important it was for a ventriloquist to have a clear throat.

His voice sounded perfectly normal before he went on stage. In fact, he noticed nothing wrong when he asked Bhuto the first question. Disaster struck when it was Bhuto's turn to speak.

His voice sounded hoarse, like that of a man suffering from an acute attack of cough and cold. Naveen knew the audience could not hear a word Bhuto was saying. Strangely enough, it was only Bhuto's voice that seemed to be affected. His own still sounded normal.

'Louder, please!' yelled a few people from the back. Those sitting in the front rows were too polite to yell, but it was obvious that they could not hear anything either.

Naveen tried for another five minutes and then had to withdraw, defeated. Never had he felt so embarrassed.

He declined the organizers' offer to pay him his fee. He could not accept any money under the circumstances. But surely this horrible situation could not last for ever? In spite of his embarrassment, Naveen still believed that soon, things would return to normal.

It was a very hot and sultry night, and over and above there was this new and unpleasant experience. When Naveen returned home at about eleven-thirty, he was feeling positively sick. For the first time, he began to feel a little annoyed with Bhuto, although he knew Bhuto could not really be blamed for anything. His failure was his own fault.

He placed Bhuto on the table and opened one of the

windows. There was not much hope of getting a cool breeze, but whatever came in was a welcome relief for there was a power cut again. Today being Saturday, Naveen knew the power supply would not be restored before midnight.

He lit a candle and set it down on the table. Its light fell on Bhuto and Naveen went cold with fear.

There were beads of perspiration on Bhuto's forehead.

But was that all? No. His face had lost its freshness. The cheeks looked sunken. His eyes were red.

Even in a situation like this, Naveen could not help but take a few steps forward towards his puppet. It was as though he had to find out what further shocks and horrors were in store.

But something made him stop almost immediately.

There was a movement on Bhuto's chest, under the high-necked jacket. His chest rose and fell.

Bhuto was breathing!

Could his breathing be heard?

Yes, it could. In the totally silent night, two people breathed in Naveen's room instead of one.

It was perhaps both his fear and amazement that made Naveen exclaim softly, 'Bhuto!'

And, immediately, another voice spoke, the sound of which made Naveen reel back to his bed.

'This is not Bhuto. I am Akrur Chowdhury!'

Naveen knew he had not spoken the words. The voice was the puppet's own. Heaven knows through what magical powers Akrur Chowdhury could make it speak.

Naveen had wanted to turn Akrur Babu into a puppet in his hands. But never did he expect anything like this. It was impossible for him to stay in the same room with a puppet that had come to life. He must leave.

But what was that?

Was the sound of Bhuto's breathing growing faint?

Yes, so it was.

Bhuto had stopped breathing. The beads of perspiration on his forehead had gone. His eyes were no longer red and the dark rings had vanished.

Naveen rose from his bed and picked him up. Something queer had happened in this short time. It was no longer possible to move Bhuto's head or open his lips. The mechanical parts had got jammed. Perhaps a little more force would help.

Naveen tried to twist the head forcibly. It came apart and fell onto the table with a clatter.

In the morning, Naveen ran into his landlord, Suresh Mutsuddi, on the staircase.

'Why, Mr Munshi, you never showed me your magic with the puppet,' he complained, 'ventricollosium or whatever it is called!'

'I've given that up,' said Naveen. 'I'll try something new now. But why do you ask?'

'One of your fellow performers died yesterday. Saw it in the papers this morning. Akrur Chowdhury.'

'Really?'—Naveen had not yet looked at the newspaper— 'What happened to him?'

'Heart attack,' said Suresh Babu. 'Nearly 70 per cent of people seem to die of a heart attack nowadays.'

Naveen knew that if anyone bothered to enquire about the time of his death, they would discover that the man had died exactly ten minutes after midnight.

(1981)   *Translated by Gopa Majumdar*

PIKOO'S DIARY

I am writing my diary. In my new bloo notebook I am writing. Sitting on my bed. Dadu writes diary too but not now bcoz he is sick, so not now. I know the name of his sicknes and that name is coronani thombosi. Baba does not write diary. Not Ma or Dada. Only me and Dadu. My notebook is bigger than Dadu's. Onukul got it, he sed it cost one rupee and Ma paid him. I will write in diary evry day yes when there is no school.

Today I have no school but it is not Sunday. Just there was stryk so no school. Offen we have stryk and no school that is fun. Good this notebook has lines so my writing is strait. Dada can write strait without lines and Baba of corse but it is not holiday for Baba. Or Dada or Ma. Ma does not go to office, only works at home. Now Ma is out with Hiteskaku. She sed she will get me something from New Market. Thees days she gets me many things. A pencil-shapnar a wristwach but it only shows three oclock and a hockee stick and ball. Oh and a book. It is Grims Fairy Tails it has many picturs. God knows what she will get me today may be airgun so lets see.

Dhingra killed a maina with airgun so I will try that sparow. It comes and sits on the raeling evry day. I will aim and pull the triger bang bang it will definitly die. Last nite a bomb went off it made big bang. Baba sed bomb Ma sed no no may be police gun. Baba sed has to be bomb, thees days I hear bang bang offen thru my window. Hey thats a car horn. I know its Hiteskaku's standad heral so it must be Ma come back.

Yesturday Ma gave me airgun but Hiteskaku sed Pikoo babu it is from me not yore Mummy. Hiteskaku bot a band for his wristwach. I sed its name was Tissot but Hiteskaku sed oh no its Tisso bcoz the last t is not spoken. My airgun is very good and in a big box there are bulets lots of them. May be more than hundred. Hiteskaku taut me to fire so I fired in the sky and Onukul scared. That sparow never came yesturday and not today. It is very noughty but tomorow it must come so I will be reddy.

Baba came back from office he saw my airgun he sed

why did you get him a gun Ma sed so what. Baba sed we
already have bang bang all the time why bring a gun in the
house Ma sed it does not matter. But Baba sed you have no
sense then Ma sed why are you shoughting you have only
just come back from office. Baba sed something yes it was
in english and Ma also sed english very quickly like people
in the cinema. I saw Jery Louis and Clint Eestwud and a
Hindi cinema but it had no fiteing. I saw it with Milu didi oh
no I think the ink in my pen is go

I put Baba's green ink it is Quink with a droper in my
founten pen. It is Ma's droper she used it to put drops
when she had cold. Today I am writing my diary at Baba's
desk. Just now the phone went krring krring so I ran and
pickd it up and sed halo and guess what it was Baba he
sed is that you Pikoo so I sed yes and he sed isnt Ma
there I sed no. Baba sed were is she I sed she went out
with Hiteskaku. Baba sed oh I see and put the phone down
and I did hear it klick. Then I dialled one seven four they
told me the time sumtimes I do that to hear the time but
what they speak I just cant follow. Today that sparow
came. I was reddy with my airgun at the window and the

sparow came so I fired it hit a wall and then I saw a hole in Dhingra's wall. The sparow was very scared and flew away. Yesturday Dada has very good aim he put the smallest clay pot on the tank on our roof and fired from far away and the pot was broken. Some peeces fell down on the road I sed oh god if sumone is hurt we are in troubel. Dada is much biger he is biger by twelve years so his aim is so good. Dada goes to collage and I go to school. Dada goes out evry day but I am just at home only sumtimes I go to cinema and I saw one theatar. Dada came back very late last nite so Baba scolded him and Dada shoughted so laud I woke up so I didnt finish my luvly dream. I was rideing a horse and going so fast Dhingra cudnt catch me. Then Hiteskaku gave me a new gun it was a revolvur he sed its name is Fisso and Dadu he was a cowboy like Clint Eestwud he sed lets go to Viktoria Memorial and just then I woke up the dream broke. Now I will go to bathroom.

Yesturday we had a party. No it wasn't my birday or anything just a party. Only old people so I didn't go just wached a littel. Only Baba's frends and Ma's but not Dada's frends not one. Dada is not home he went day before

yesturday or may be before that I don't know whare. Dada
does politis it is hopeless Baba sed and also Ma. Ma told me
dont go whare the party is so I didnt but I ate three
sosseges and a cocacola. There was a sahib he was laffing
very lowdly ho ho ha ha ho ho and a mem too. And Mister
Menon and Mises Menon and one sardar I cud guess
immijetly bcoz he had a pugri. Evryone laffed and I cud
hear them from my room. Then Ma came in and went to
bathroom and then saw her face in the mirror. One more
ledy came in too and went to bathroom she was wareing
scent a new scent Ma hasnt got that one. Then Ma came in
again and sed why dear why are you still awake go to
sleep so I sed I was scared alone she sed dont be silly its
eleven just close yore eyes and you will sleep. I sed
whare is Dada she sed thats enuff just sleep and left.
But Baba did not come to my room now Baba and Ma were
fiteing they talk in english a lot only sumtimes in bangla.
But not in the party they did not fite in the party so the
party is good no fiteing only drinks one day sumone was sick
Ma sed he wasnt feeling well but Onukul sed he was
drinking thats why. We have bottels in our frij when they
are emty Ma fills them with water cold water. When they
smell Ma scolds Sukdeo she sez why dont you wash them

proparly. Sukdeo sez no memsab why does he call her memsab is Ma a mem or is she a sab no its really very funny. Then I fell asleep no one knows how sleep comes. Dadu sez if you die you go on very long sleep and you can dream what you want. only dream all the time.

I hide my diary in a plaice no one knows. It is our old gramofon no one plays it any more bcoz the new one is elktrik it is long playeing so no one touches the old one thats whare I hide my diary and so no one knows I write a diary. I write a lot so my finger pains a littel when Ma was cuting my nails I sed oooh so Ma sed why is it painful I sed no no its nuthing bcoz then she wud know I write my diary. Dadu sed show yore diary to no one only you will write and read it no one else. I have 22 bulets left I counted but that sparow is so noughty it didnt come again. I go to the roof and fire at the tank it makes a tong tong noize and then small round round marks so I think I will kill pidgeons. Pidgeons just sit and may be walk a littel but they dont fly that much. Dada has bin gone for five days his room is emty only there is a shart a white shart on the rack and a bloo pant and his books and stuff.

I was bloing bubbels yesturday then I herd a horn so I sed thats Hiteskaku and Ma sed darling why dont you go and play with Dhingra its his holiday. I sed Dhingra pulls my hair he hurts me I wont go then Ma sed well you can go to the roof with yore airgun so I sed then I will kill pidgeons. Ma sed oh no not that just fire it at the sky I sed thats no good how can I aim at the sky. Ma sed then go to Onukul I sed Onukul he only plays cards and durwan and Sukdeo and one more man they only play cards all day so I wont go anywhare. Then Ma slaped me hard and I nocked agenst the wood on my bed. So I cried a littel not much tho and Ma left so I cried sum more but not a lot and thot what can I now do. Then I thot lets see whats in the frij there was a creem role and two gulab jamuns I ate them then had water strait from a bottel no I didnt pore in a glass not at all. Then I saw one Illustated Weekly it was on Baba's desk but there was no nice pictur only a donald duk. Then I ran to the varanda and did hi-jump over a small stool that was easy but I tried a bigger stool I fell and got a cut. Only a littel blood but there was detol in the bathroom detol doesnt hurt but tincheridin does so I put detol. Then I ran out bcoz a jet plane went very lowdly I saw when Baba went in a jet I went to dum dum he braught a elektrik shaver from london that was for him and shoes for me and a astronot that was very big but Ronida spoylt it. Now I supose I shud go and do sums.

I am writing my diary agane today. All my bulets are gone why didnt one hit that pidgeon? That gun must be useles. I think I will thro it away. I saw a machbox in Dadas drawer it must mean Dada smokes cigrets or why shud he have machbox. But Dada did not cum back god knows whare he is or may be even god doesnt know. Now if Ma goese too there will be truble bcoz last nite Ma told Baba she will go I had slept in the afternoon so I cudnt sleep I was awake but my eyes were shut tight they thot Pikoo is sleeping so they did talk loudly. Now there is no one home just me and Dadu whare is Onukul he must be playing cards so only Dadu and me in the house. Dadu lives downstares bcoz Doctor Banarji sed Dadu can not climb stares bcoz he has coronani thombosi. So Dadu has a bell it makes a noize ting ting ting we can all hear it. Today I heard that noize once I was then spitting out of my window making it go far and just then I heard ting ting ting and I cud tell that was Dadu but I tried spitting four times againe one spit went over the wall outside

then I thot let me see what Dadu wants. I ran downstares
it made such a noize bcoz they are wood stares they make
thud thud noize. But Dadu was lying not talking but he wasnt
sleeping. So I sed whats the matter Dadu what is it but
Dadu sed nuthing he just stared at the fan. It is a Usha
only Dadu has Usha evry other fan is GEC. Then I heard the
fone ring so I ran and it rang so many times when I sed halo
sumone sed is mister shurma there I sed no shurma here
wrong number and put it down. It Klicked. I was huffing and
puffing bcoz I ran so fast so I lay down on the sofa and put
my legs up Ma wud scold me but shes not here I saw
immijetly my legs ware durty but Ma isnt here anyway. And
now I am again writing my diary sitting on my bed but no
pages left now and no one in the house only Dadu and me
and theres a fly it keeps coming again and again. A very
stoopid fly what a bothre and now this page is finished
notebook gone all over The End.

(1970)   *Translated by Gopa Majumdar*